BLOOD WILL TELL

Christine Pope

DARK VALENTINE PRESS

BLOOD WILL TELL

ISBN: 978-0615644639
Copyright © 2012 by Christine Pope
Published by Dark Valentine Press

Cover design and ebook formatting by Indie Author Services

To learn more about this author, go to
www.christinepope.com.

DEDICATION

To everyone who first took this journey with me...

PART ONE:
IRADIA

I

THEY HAD BEEN GONE FAR TOO LONG, that much she knew. Although there were no chronos in the compound's kitchens, Miala had trained herself to make a rough estimate of the passage of time without any visual aids. She knew that at least four, and possibly closer to five, hours had to have passed since Arlen Mast and his various lackeys and hangers-on had enthusiastically sallied forth en masse to watch the baiting and eventual deaths of his latest batch of prisoners. "Cheaper to kill 'em than to feed 'em!" he'd guffawed, and everyone had laughed at his wit, or at least pretended to.

Except Miala. Unlike the others, she had no stomach for that sort of thing. The compound had emptied down to the lowliest kitchen drudge—except for her. She had a knack for hiding in shadows, making herself easily overlooked, and so no one gone in search of her when she vanished into one of the larders as everyone else was hastening out the rear entrance of the building and into their various sand-skimmers and all-terrain transports. At the time she had only thanked God that she would have a few hours of uninterrupted time to resume her careful hacking into Mast's security system.

That fat bastard would probably have had a long-over-due heart attack if he knew how far she had already gotten, but she was careful to cover her tracks. Anyhow, she knew the basics of the system well enough; it was her father who had programmed it, after all, and he had trained Miala in the tricks of his trade. Good thing that Mast hadn't both-ered to investigate Lestan Fels closely enough to discover that Iradia's best hacker had a daughter, let alone one who rivaled her father in her ways with a security system. No, Mast had thought himself very clever to hire Fels and then have him killed once the security system was in place. He hadn't thought that there was anyone on this miserable rock who would even notice the hacker's death, let alone bother to avenge it.

She'd come here two months earlier, already aware of what had probably happened to her father, and she'd been careful to come disguised. Mast's lechery was legendary, and Miala, after carefully regarding her reflection before setting out, had come to the dispassionate conclusion that she was just pretty enough to attract attention if she didn't do something to alter her appearance. Nothing drastic, of course, but it was amazing what deliberately dirty hair pulled back in a severe knot, a few carefully applied blem-ishes, and exaggerated shadows under one's eyes could do to make a person look absolutely unappealing. Even so, she'd been on the receiving end of a few nastily significant glances from Barris Jax, Mast's self-styled majordomo and right-hand man. She counted herself lucky that it hadn't gone any further than that—and perhaps his unhealthy interest was what had led him to hire her in the first place.

But now—she settled back on her heels and sighed. She'd made good progress during the past few hours and felt confident that, given a little more time, she would finally be able to hack the codes that protected Mast's vaults and gain access to the treasures she knew he hoarded there. Of course she would never be able to bring her father back, but at least she could steal his murderer blind and finally get herself away from this forsaken planet once and for all. And while her main goal was to gain access to Mast's off-world accounts, she'd be a fool not to take as much cash from his vaults as she could. The amount she could carry would certainly not be enough for him to ever notice.

The silence around her was disturbing. She knew the compound as well as anyone, but it was an unsettling place even when fully occupied and somehow much worse when it was apparently deserted, as it seemed now. What could possibly have happened? There had been whispers that one of the other crime bosses had been planning to make a move on Mast, but treachery among the bosses was as expected on Iradia as its frequent sandstorms, and Mast had laughed off the rumors, claiming there was no one in the region who could possibly get the drop on him.

Still…

Miala pushed her chair away from the computer console in the security office. Like the rest of the compound, the room had been hewn out of the native Iradian sandstone, but the banks of machines were an incongruous note in the otherwise primitive surroundings. It was cool in here, though, air conditioners working overtime to ensure that the precious computers didn't overheat. Perhaps it was the temperature of the room that made her shiver.

Or perhaps it was something else. She suddenly felt she couldn't stand the silence a moment longer. The air seemed laden with ghosts; she wondered how many hapless prisoners had met a violent death in the building, and she shivered again, harder this time.

Anything would be better than sitting here and wondering until she slowly drove herself mad. She remembered how her father used to tease her for her endless questions. *Why are there three moons, Dad? Why do trees only grow in an oasis? Why doesn't it ever rain?*

Anything of course, but the questions she had really wanted to ask. *Why don't I have a mother like everyone else? Why did she hate me so much that she left?* But even at five Miala had known better than to ask some questions…

Shaking her head as if to rid herself of these unpleasant recollections, Miala made a sudden decision. She knew where the compound's sand skimmers were kept, and of course she would have no difficulty getting through the security system that sheltered them. Surely Mast's people had left one or two behind. If something really had gone wrong, wasn't it her responsibility to discover what had happened? She hadn't allowed herself to make any friends during her tenure at Mast's compound, but at the same time she didn't think she could leave people she had worked with to die out in the desert. Assuming that the worst had happened, of course. It was entirely possible that Mast had decided to be particularly creative with his executions this time, and they were taking longer than usual. Somehow, though, she guessed that was a false hope.

The parking garages were located at the rear of the compound, not far from the small landing pad kept for the private use of certain guests who didn't wish to fly into Aldis Nova. There were two sand skimmers left behind, both of them looking the worse for wear. Looks were deceiving, as she knew all too well; Mast's mechanics kept them well-tuned. On one wall of the garage was a gun locker, and she keyed in the code—stolen during one of her hacking sessions—and lifted out a heavy pulse rifle and a pair of smaller pistols. It was getting close to dusk, and although she knew from watching the sweeps made by the automated security systems that no hostiles seemed to be within a ten-kilometer range of the compound, she didn't want to be out any later than necessary. Anyone with two brain cells to rub together knew better than to wander the open deserts of Iradia after dark.

She selected the skimmer closest to the garage entrance, more for ease than because it looked better than the other one. Since it was an older model, it had a chip-matching system rather than a biometric starter, but the chips had been stored in the locker along with the guns, so it was easy enough to get the thing started and maneuver it out of the garage.

Even now, this close to dusk, the heat was intense, enervating. Miala knew she would never get used to it, even if she lived to be a hundred and died on this rock. But she had brought a few flasks of water with her, knowing that even without direct sun she could die of dehydration within a few hours if she wasn't careful. She took a few sips, then set the flask down on the passenger seat. The next stage of the journey was going to require both hands.

Mast's preferred spot for his executions was located roughly southeast of the compound, near a canyon that allowed him to pitch prisoners into the abyss when he tired of other amusements. Even going as quickly as the terrain would allow, it was a good hour's ride. Miala cast a nervous glance over her shoulder at the setting sun and prayed that she could make it there before the last bit of light disappeared. As good as Mast's security team might be, they couldn't drive away all of the planet's natural predators, and she didn't care to become yet another statistic. No one would come looking for her if she disappeared.

The smell of burning greeted her long before she reached the Malverdine Cliffs. Acrid, heavy, the scent of smoke hung in the hot desert air like the memory of a bad dream, impossible to ignore. Miala slowed the skimmer's headlong flight as she came onto the site of the disaster.

There was nothing left, except some scattered wreckage and a few unpleasant dark blotches on the sand. Whoever had hit Mast's party had obviously done so hard and fast. Black smoke still swirled heavily in the dead, hot air.

She brought the vehicle to a stop, then reached for one of her pistols. Just because she hadn't seen any movement didn't mean that predators couldn't be lurking nearby.

After making sure the safety on the pistol was off, she climbed out of the skimmer and moved toward the cliff's edge, stepping carefully between the pieces of shrapnel and other, less distinguishable bits of wreckage. The cloying smell of burning flesh rose to her nostrils, and she forced herself not to gag, making herself breathe through her mouth despite the painful dryness at the back of her throat.

There was nothing here, nothing to salvage, no one to save. It was stupid for her to have come; all she had done was risk her own safety when she could have holed up in the compound and worked at the security system until it yielded its remaining secrets. Obviously, no one would have come back to disturb her.

With a sigh, she turned and took a step back toward the skimmer. It was only then that she heard a faint moan from somewhere behind her.

Whirling, she held the gun out before her, one trembling finger hovering over the trigger. "Identify yourself!" she called into the gathering dusk, hoping her voice sounded more confident than she felt.

No reply except another faint groan, this one fainter than the last. Whoever or whatever it was, they didn't sound very threatening. However, she knew better than to lower the pistol as she retraced her steps toward the precipice, taking care to maintain a respectful distance from the cliff's edge. The whispered horror stories she'd heard from the other kitchen drudges—"You drop so far there isn't even a thud when you hit the bottom!"—were enough to convince her that she needed to give the jagged gash in the ground a wide berth.

As she inched closer, she finally saw the man who lay face down in the sand. From this angle he looked dead, his body armor scored and even smoking in a few places, the dark cloth he usually wore wrapped around his face and head torn away, lying like a ragged scarf against the ruddy sand. Even in the dimming light Miala could see blood gleaming in his short-cropped hair, black against black. But then she saw one of his hands move slightly, a futile clenching gesture that seemed as if he were trying to gain a purchase so as to pull himself farther away from edge of the cliff.

Although she'd never seen his face, she recognized him at once. Eryk Thorn, the notorious mercenary Mast hired for the times when he needed people disappeared instead of dropped off a cliff. Just one of the myriad scum the crime boss had infesting his compound. For one moment she was tempted to leave Thorn there to die—after all, the man made his living from human misery—but almost as soon as the thought crossed her mind, she knew she could not abandon him to the desert, no matter who he was or what he had done. Anyone who had the strength of will to survive an attack that had killed everyone around him deserved a second chance.

She squatted down in the sand next to him. "Thorn?" she asked softly. "Can you understand me?"

The smallest movement of his hand was his only reply.

Still, it was better than nothing. "I've come from the compound," she went on, thinking that perhaps her words would give him something to hold on to besides the pain. "I have a sand skimmer. I'll bring it closer so I can take you back."

This time there was no answering movement, and Miala could only hope he had heard and understood. As quickly as she could, she threaded her way through the wreckage back to the skimmer and then maneuvered it as close as possible to the wounded man. Once she had clambered back out again, she looked at Thorn and swore softly. He would be no help to her in his condition. How she was supposed to maneuver his approximately ninety kilos of dead weight into the skimmer was beyond her. She'd seen nothing in the immediate vicinity that would help her lift him up off the ground, and she was afraid to leave him to go look for something in the wreckage farther away.

In the end, she did it through brute strength and sheer force of will. She was young and healthy enough, and the last few months had hardened her muscles to the point that she found in herself the power to do what was necessary. Somehow she managed to half-lift, half-drag him to her vehicle and then push/pull him into the passenger seat. These operations did nothing to improve his condition—halfway through her maneuvering he finally fainted, for which she was grateful. She hated to think of even Eryk Thorn suffering the kind of pain her awkward handling must have caused.

Finally she was able to take the driver's seat and then push the accelerator to maximum, retracing her path back toward the compound. At some point during the time she'd been dragging Thorn into the skimmer, the sun had dropped even further, and now was only a bloody smear on the far horizon.

Speed was the only thing that could save them now, and she used it brutally, jouncing the skimmer with reckless determination over landscapes not meant for that sort of travel. She had thought Thorn still completely dead to the world, but after one particularly harsh drop-off she felt his hand tighten on her leg. Startled, she'd looked down for a second to see him shake his head slightly.

"Don't do that again," he whispered, before passing out once more.

"No problem," she muttered, but she did ease off the accelerator just a bit. He was right—it wouldn't help if she upended the skimmer in a ravine or particularly deep sand dune, or pulled the treads off their gears by hitting a rock outcropping at the wrong angle.

After what seemed like an eternity but was actually less than an hour, she saw the walls of Mast's compound appear on the horizon, glimmering faintly in the purple-hued hour after sunset. The security perimeter was still in place—she could see the faint bluish haze between each of the markers—but she had a remote with her that would deactivate it long enough to allow them inside. What she was going to do with Thorn after they reached the relative safety of the garage, she wasn't sure.

Whether it was just luck or the aura that still surrounded the compound even though its owner was now dead, they managed to slip inside the perimeter unremarked and unmolested. Miala pulled the skimmer into the garage, then leaned over to make sure that Thorn was still just uncon-scious and not actually dead. Yes, there was still a pulse in his throat, but it was thready and weak. She needed to get him into a med unit as quickly as possible.

Mast did have a fairly well-stocked med center in the compound, for whatever reason. Possibly to keep his victims alive between rounds of torture, or possibly because he had some valuable slaves and other hangers-on who were of more use to him alive than dead. Most likely, though, it was because he feared his own mortality but knew better than to avail himself of the official medical facilities in Aldis Nova. Although she had never been there, Miala knew where the med unit was located; she had made it her business to learn as much as she could about the compound and its inhabitants.

Again she spoke to Thorn, not knowing whether he could even hear her. "I'll be back soon. I have to get a stretcher for you." Thank God the med unit was equipped with a powered stretcher. She knew there was no way she could have dragged Thorn all the way from the parking garage to the med unit.

As it was, the trip nearly finished him. Just the act of dragging him out of the skimmer and onto the stretcher caused him to cough up a great gout of dark blood, staining what remained of his jacket, as well as half of the shapeless tunic she wore. After that his swarthy skin took on a strange, grayish pallor, and the black shadows beneath his eyes seemed to spread. All Miala could do was guide the stretcher along as quickly as possible, keeping one hand resting on his as she did so. Somehow she thought it was important that he know at some level someone was still with him, even if he had retreated so far into unconsciousness that it seemed almost like death.

Mast had spent a chunk of change on a mech for the med unit, probably because a mech could be trusted to keep its mouth shut. Its hum seemed to become steadily more disapproving as it moved its sensors over Thorn's motionless body, almost as if it thought she were somehow responsible for his current condition. After a moment, though, it began hooking him up to various life-support devices, even as it started to cut away his shredded clothing and the few bits of armor that still clung to it.

Embarrassed, Miala looked away, but not before she could see the extent of the lacerations that covered his torso, angry burns and something that looked like marks left by pulverized sand or bits of metal. She shuddered, then went to a cabinet off to one side of the bed on which Thorn now lay. Her back was beginning to throb, and she hoped she could find some sort of painkiller to keep the ache from getting any worse.

Sure enough, there was a row of analgesics and narcotics in the first cabinet she opened. She selected something low-level enough that it wouldn't make her drowsy but at least would take the edge off the pain. She had a feeling this was going to be a very long night.

Behind her the mech methodically worked away at Thorn, wrapping his body in some sort of healing pads until he was practically cocooned in them, with only his face visible. He had a few cuts and bruises across his forehead and on his chin, but that seemed to be the least damaged part of him; Miala supposed the fabric wrappings he normally wore had protected him somewhat before they were torn away.

"Will he live?" she asked finally, as the mech stepped away from the bed and began disposing of the bloodied pieces of clothing it had cut away from Thorn's body.

If a mech could shrug, Miala thought it might have.

Instead it said only, "A chance. Not much. He is strong. That helps."

Yes, it does, she thought. She supposed he would have to be, to survive for so long and so well in a profession as ruthless as his.

"The night will tell," the mech added cryptically.

For a moment she could only look at it, uncomprehending. Of course, she thought. If he lives through the night, he might survive after all.

"I want to stay with him," she said at length. "Stay here, of course, but you can shut down for now. I'll call you if I need you."

The mechanoid nodded its assent, then resumed its normal station in a far corner of the room, powering down against further need. The light in its eyes dimmed, and its head slumped forward.

Miala waved a hand to bring down the light level in the room; it was too harsh, too bright. She didn't know how Thorn could rest in that sort of light. Once it was a softer, more reasonable level, she went to one side of the room and rolled the chair she found there next to the bed. Then she took one of Thorn's hands in both of hers, but lightly, so the pressure of her fingers wouldn't do any more damage to the wounded flesh underneath.

"I'm here," she said again, wondering as she did so whether it made any difference. Really, why should she care if this man lived or died? She didn't know him. She was nothing to him. But irrational tears rose up in her throat and choked her as she thought of her father, dying alone and unregarded in this place, surrounded by strangers who had laughed and jeered at him. No one should have to die that way. Not even Eryk Thorn.

Was it her imagination, or did she feel a momentary pressure on her fingers from the hand she thought had lain so still beneath hers?

"I won't let you die," she whispered fiercely, and there it was again, a flutter so infinitesimal it could have merely been an involuntary reflex, just overtaxed nerves twitching beneath the flayed skin. But she refused to believe that.

The night will tell, she thought.

But what the next day would bring, she didn't dare think. All she could do now was sit here in the soft semi-darkness and pray that the shadows in Mast's compound wouldn't claim yet another uneasy ghost.

‖

AT ONE POINT DURING THE NIGHT she was certain Thorn had died. She had slipped into an uneasy sleep even as she sat in the chair next to the hospital bed, only to be awakened by the strident beeping of the equipment monitoring his vital signs. Before she could fully realize what was happening, the mechanoid was already at Thorn's side, making adjustments to the liquids that dripped into his arm and sliding an oxygen mask over his nose and mouth. When that didn't produce the desired result, the mech shocked him twice with the fibrillators built into its hands, and suddenly the alarm subsided into the low-level pulsing of a normal sinus wave. It was probably the soft murmur of the machine that had put her to sleep in the first place.

Through all of this Thorn hadn't moved. Miala reflected, as she tried to settle herself into a more comfortable position in the chair, that the only thing about him which seemed alive was the pulsing light of his heart-beat on the monitor.

"You shouldn't scare people like that," she said finally, after making sure the mech had settled back down into deceptive quiescence. Obviously it was on a hair trigger if anything in a patient's condition changed—she hadn't even awakened fully before the machine was working on Thorn.

She wondered whether he could hear her at all. Somewhere she thought she had read that people in comas could still sense when people were talking to them, but perhaps that only counted when the people involved actually knew one another. At any rate, talking to him made her feel better, and she hoped it would help keep her awake. Talking helped—if she kept talking, maybe she could shunt aside the worry that at any moment one of the other crime lords was going to figure out that Mast's compound was currently "guarded" by a young woman and a half-dead mercenary.

"You don't know me," she said, making her tone as soft and reassuring as she could. "My name is Miala, and I work here in the compound. That's where you are now, in the med unit. You're going to be fine."

Pausing, she glanced down at Thorn's slack features and thought he looked anything but fine. Still, a little misplaced optimism couldn't hurt. "Anyhow," she continued, "I'm hoping that you can help me out once you're on your feet again. I want to get off Iradia, and I know you've got a ship out back on one of Mast's private landing pads." Again she laid her hand on top of his bandaged one. "And if saving your life isn't enough, I'm willing to share Mast's treasure with you. I'm close to cracking the code. A day or so more, probably. That's what I'm doing here—I'm no more a kitchen drudge than you are, but it was a good disguise."

She stopped then, wondering if she had said too much. What was to stop him from killing her after she had broken the security system? Oh, she had saved his life, but was that enough? She knew next to nothing of him except his reputation as one of the most ruthless enforcers in the sector, but even mercenaries had to follow some sort of code, didn't they?

Well, there was no help for it now. Very likely he couldn't understand or even hear what she was saying, as far into unconsciousness as he had retreated. And if he had heard and understood, perhaps the lure of Mast's riches would be enough to give him the will to survive. It was what had sustained her over the past few months, ever since she realized that Mast had murdered her father after the final code for the security system was delivered.

The money...and revenge.

At first, of course, she had merely been unbelieving. Her father had been secretive about his latest job, but he had promised her that it was finally the big score, the one contract that would earn them enough to get off Iradia forever. His skills with computers had never translated to any sort of talent with finances, and they had always led a precarious existence, never sure if they were going to make the rent or have enough to eat—at least until Miala was old enough to take matters into her own hands. From the time she was fourteen she had managed the household, and things had run a bit more smoothly as a result, but they had never been able to scrape together enough units for passage off Iradia.

Lestan Fels was a Gaian native. It was a freelance assignment with a mining company that had brought him to Iradia, where he fell in love with the beautiful red-haired daughter of a silk weaver from Aldis Nova. That much Miala knew, but what exactly had transpired when she was barely six months old, her father would never say. All she knew was that her mother had left, apparently with the remainder of his earnings from the mining contract. Lestan ended up trapped on Iradia with an infant daughter to raise and no immediate prospects of returning to his home world. It was not in his nature to complain, but Miala knew he hated Iradia almost as much as she did.

When he had been missing for two days, she'd known that the worst must have happened. Although of course Lestan hadn't told her for whom he was working, it didn't take a differential equation to figure out that there were only one or two potential clients in the area who had both the need for that high-level a security system as well as the means to pay for it.

Not knowing what else to do, she'd gone to the local Gaian garrison to make a report. Unlike most of the other inhabitants of Aldis Nova, who maintained that Iradia was a sovereign world and should not have to submit to any sort of Gaian presence, she was on good enough terms with the troops stationed there. Perhaps the rumors of Gaian oppression were true, perhaps not. All she knew was that the presence of the squad of soldiers and the officers who led them kept at least a semblance of order in the rough desert town. Certainly she would not have been able to walk the streets so freely if it weren't for Captain Malick and his men.

It was Captain Malick who saw her, and for that she was grateful; he was young for the post and had always been friendly. Too much so, her father had grumbled—he didn't like the idea of his daughter flirting with the leader of the local garrison. Miala hadn't seen what the problem was. Captain Malick was charming and only seven or eight years older than she, and certainly of a far higher caliber than the local boys, who talked incessantly of target practice with the local fauna or tricking out their skimmers and not much else. At least Gerald Malick was educated and well-spoken, which was more than she could say of the boys her own age.

But when she sat down in his office and poured out her troubles to him, at first he had looked away, his pleasant features clouded.

"We can file a missing-persons report, of course," he said formally, and she could see his blue eyes shift past her to the two soldiers standing on either side of his open door.

"How can he be missing if I'm pretty sure I know where he is?" she demanded, and after that he stood and palmed the door shut, then returned to his desk.

"I wish I could help you, Mia," he said, and even the sound of her father's nickname on his lips had brought the tears she had been suppressing for too long to her eyes.

"Why can't you, Captain Malick?" She had been deliberately formal, using his title, although she had spoken his given name before in private.

Even though the door was shut, he had lowered his voice. "The GDF has a policy of not getting involved in Mast's affairs. We leave him alone, and he leaves us alone to do as we wish. The arrangement has worked thus far."

"Even if innocent people are involved?"

"Unfortunately, yes."

She'd wanted to hate him then, but couldn't; the dismay in his face was all too obvious. He wasn't responsible for the Gaian government's edicts and was only trying to make the best of a difficult situation. An officer who asked too many questions would soon find himself on the fast track to nowhere—although she couldn't think of many posts worse than Iradia. It was, as she'd heard one of the soldiers comment once, the "ass-end of space."

"So what am I supposed to do?" she'd asked at length. "Just pretend that nothing's happened?"

"That would be the wisest course, yes." Unexpectedly, he had reached out and taken one of her hands in his. "I know this is improper of me, but—"

She'd narrowed her eyes then, wondering what was going to come next. Unwanted advances were certainly the last thing she needed right now.

But he had surprised her. "I have enough saved to get you off-world. You could be in danger, if your father has let Mast know that he has family here. Let me get you away from here—my tour is over in three months, and I could come see you before I'm sent on to my next post."

The unexpected generosity almost undid her. It would have been so easy to let Captain Malick take care of her, hustle her off-world to someplace safe. Perhaps he had convinced himself that he was in love with her, or perhaps it was merely some sense of old-fashioned honor that spurred him to attempt her rescue.

She hadn't known what to say. She'd made a few inarticulate attempts, had begun to really cry, then let him fold her into his arms and hold her while she wept. If nothing else, it had felt good to have his strong arms around her, to feel the reassuring roughness of his uniform jacket against her cheek.

In the end she had been able to leave without really promising anything, knowing even then that she would never forgive herself if she didn't do something to avenge her father's death. What poor Captain Malick thought of her disappearance, she didn't want to contemplate. Probably that Mast's goons had spirited her away, finishing the job once and for all.

But now Mast was dead, along with all the rest of his hangers-on. It wouldn't be too long before the next piece of scum rushed in to fill the vacuum his death had caused, but Miala thought she had a few days before the news spread. She only hoped that a few days would be enough.

The compound was empty of all but a few maintenance mechs, for which she was thankful. She never thought she'd be grateful for Mast's raging ego, but obviously he had wanted the largest audience possible for his latest—and last—round of executions.

There was the slightest shift of the hand that lay beneath hers, and she glanced down, startled. Thorn did look better after all; the shadows under his eyes seemed a little less black, and that frightening grayish tint had disappeared from his face. And now she could actually see his chest rising and falling as he breathed, sending the healing oxygen through his body.

"You're too mean to die, aren't you?" she asked, but softened the words by reaching up to touch the dark wavy hair at his temple, now matted with blood. Once he had recovered enough, he was definitely going to need a good cleaning-up.

Miala wasn't sure, but she thought she saw the smallest quirk at the corner of his mouth. Then again, it could have just been a trick of the lighting.

Speaking of cleaning up, she thought, looking down at herself as if for the first time. The right side of her tunic was splattered with blood, and she was streaked with grime everywhere. Thorn looked as if he were holding on, and now she could think of nothing else but an extended spell in a shower. And clean clothes. There had to be something fit for use somewhere in the compound.

After rousing the mech and instructing it to keep a close watch on Thorn, Miala went down the hall and up to the third story, where she knew the slave girls' dormitory was located. That is, everyone referred to them as "bond servants" to pay lip service to Gaian laws, but "slave" was a lot closer to the mark, and as long as the whole sordid business was kept more or less quiet, no one interfered too much. Miala had always felt sorry for the girls and wished she could do something to help them, but they were far beyond help now. However, the rooms they once occupied were probably her best chance at finding the toiletries she needed, along with a change of clothes.

Sure enough, the bath chamber was stocked with all sorts of little luxuries; apparently Mast liked his slave girls sweet-smelling and moisturized before he loaned them out as "favors" to the scumbags who came to visit from time to time. Miala stood in the shower for at least a half-hour, reveling in the warm water that cascaded through her filthy hair and washed the grime from her body. In her own meager house the shower had a five-minute timer, to save water, but obviously Mast did not care to participate in Iradia's mandatory water rationing. She had to wash her hair three times before she felt it was clean enough, and it was utter bliss to finally cleanse her face of the dirt and false blemishes she had adopted as part of her disguise.

After that she dried off and then wrapped the towel around herself, going in search of something to wear. Although Miala didn't doubt Eryk Thorn would enjoy waking up to see her in one of the slave girls' scantier ensembles, she had something a little more substantial in mind. She had seen several of the girls when they arrived at the compound, and they had worn ordinary enough clothing. It had to be around here someplace.

As it was, shoved into the farthest corner of the wardrobe that all of the girls had apparently shared. Miala thought she even recognized the fitted tunic and loose pants the Eridani girl Genna had first worn when she came to Mast's compound. That was good, because Genna was closer to Miala's size than any of the other slave girls, and the outfit fit very well.

It felt odd, to be wearing a dead girl's clothing, but Genna certainly didn't need it anymore, and Miala did. Besides, the feel of something besides rough synthetics against her skin was pure heaven. The low-necked dark tunic and pants were obviously made of the local moon-moth silk, sleek and elegantly draped. And the clothing wasn't any of the endless variations on off-white, ivory, and beige that were ubiquitous on Iradia as a defense against the heat and the blistering sun. Miala thought she could go her entire life without wearing a single one of those non-colors again.

But she had spent enough time here. She ran a comb one last time through her damp tresses, then slid on a pair of sandals she had found on the floor of the wardrobe. Finally she left the room and headed down, past the second floor where Thorn slept, all the way to the cellar where the kitchens were located. Although she felt considerably better than she had before she showered, she knew she wouldn't be able to keep going without a cup of coffee...or several, she thought. It wasn't the first time she had pulled an all-nighter, but a healthy dose of caffeine would be just what she needed.

It was somewhat unpleasant to be returning to the kitchens, where she had labored in ugly anonymity for several months, but at least now she felt like herself again. She made short work of brewing the coffee and decided to bring the whole jug of it with her back to the med unit, along with half a loaf of only slightly stale bread. Miala couldn't remember the last time she had eaten anything.

When she returned, all was as she had left it: the mech hovering by Thorn's bedside, the mercenary lying still under his covering of bandages.

"How is he?" she asked, as she set the jug of coffee and the bread on a counter.

"Better," the mech replied, and pointed at the monitor as if it thought she could translate its readings. "He comes out of the coma soon."

"Good." She busied herself with pouring a cup of coffee. Behind her, the mech seemed to hesitate for a moment, then moved off to its corner.

The rush of the stimulant along her nerve endings was almost as heavenly as the shower had been; she hadn't realized how groggy she was until she let the caffeine wake her up. It was good, too—only the best off-world brew for Mast. The bitter-chocolate taste awoke her stomach as well, and she pulled off a chunk of bread and took several healthy bites. It was only after she had satisfied her appetite somewhat that she picked up her cup of coffee and resumed her watch over Thorn.

She didn't think him particularly handsome, although there was something about his mouth that suggested he might have a nice smile—not that he probably had much use for it. Certainly he seemed swarthy and exotic when compared with someone who more closely fit her masculine ideals, such as Captain Malick.

Not for the first time since coming to Mast's compound, she found herself thinking of the young captain and his offer to her. Was he even still on Iradia at all? He'd said his tour was up in three months, and she had been here more than two. It was entirely possible that he would be gone by the time she finally cracked the security system. No, her only real hope of leaving remained with the man who lay so still before her. At least now she was certain he was going to make it, although she couldn't imagine at the cost of what pain. Right now the mech had a heady cocktail of narcotics coursing through his system so he could rest, but he couldn't function that way indefinitely. Sooner or later he would have to heal on his own.

Despite the coffee, she could feel her head beginning to droop. Perhaps it would be best if she went back up to the slave girls' dormitory and caught a few hours of sleep on one of the narrow beds there. Thorn didn't seem to be in any immediate danger, and right now her eyelids were beginning to feel like lead.

So she rose, and turned to set her empty cup down on the counter, but not before a hoarse whisper from the bed behind her halted her movement.

Miala whirled to see Thorn staring up at her, eyes very black beneath the heavy brows.

"Did you," he asked, in so soft an undertone she could barely understand him, "say something about Mast's treasure?"

III

For a moment all she could do was stare at him, not believing he could have actually spoken. A few drops of coffee spilled from the mug that dangled from her suddenly heedless fingers before she recovered herself enough to place it on the counter.

"You heard that?" she managed at last.

His eyes shut briefly, lashes black against his bloodless cheeks. "I heard a voice. Gave me something to concentrate on."

"Does it—does it hurt very much?"

There was no mistaking the ironic glance he gave her as he opened his eyes once more. "Probably not as much as falling off that cliff would have."

Well, she deserved that. Obviously he was lucid, if still very weak. And since he had heard her comments about Mast's treasure, there was no going back now. She said, "Arlen Mast hired my father to rebuild his security system. Then he had him killed." She paused, but Thorn made no comment. "So I came here to crack the security system and steal whatever Mast might have hidden in his vaults. Now he's dead, so my job is a lot easier."

"But you need a way out of here," Thorn whispered, his voice cracking on the last syllable.

Concerned, Miala looked over at the mech. "Should he have some water or something?"

The machine drifted over, looked at Thorn's vital signs, then laid a temp strip across his forehead. After that it flashed a light into each of his eyes. Through all of these dubious ministrations the mercenary remained stoic, unmoving.

"Water, okay," the mech finally decreed, pulling a perma-sealed moisture pack from one of the cupboards and attaching it to a long flexible tube. It pushed one end of the tube through Thorn's cracked lips and hung the pack from another arm of the rack holding the various fluids that were slowly seeping into him.

Thorn took a few careful sips, then nodded at the mech, which removed the tube from his mouth. "Better," he said. "So you'd give me half Mast's treasure just to get you off-planet?"

"That's right."

He was silent for a moment, apparently considering. "You don't need me to get off Iradia."

Miala tried to remind herself that he was in a lot of pain. "Well, yes, I do, actually, because you've got a ship right here. I don't know how much is in those vaults, but I'm pretty sure it's more than I could load onto a skimmer, and those are the only vehicles left in the garages now. And in case you weren't aware of the fact, the chances of a single unarmed skimmer making it all the way from here to Aldis Nova are pretty slim. So you and your ship are my best bet."

Before answering, he gestured with one bandaged hand to the mech to give him another few sips of water. Then he said, "Better half than nothing?"

"Exactly."

Another, longer silence this time, one in which she could only imagine what he must be thinking. Probably that she was unbelievably naïve and would be easy enough to take advantage of later on, after the treasure was actually secured. There were hundreds of places to stash a body in the compound, after all…

"All right," he said finally. "I owe you one."

That was the second time this evening he had managed to render Miala speechless. She had expected much more of an argument over her request, but she should have known that whatever else he might be, any mercenary who'd survived this long in the business would have to be a realist.

However, she was able to recover herself enough to nod coolly and say, "Good." Inwardly, though, she was cheering. Now all she had to do was crack that damned code.

He nodded, but his eyes were sliding shut already. Even that brief exchange seemed to have exhausted him.

"Sleep now," she said, "but I'll be just upstairs. Have the mech message me if you need anything."

The barest movement of his head was the only reply she received, but Miala was satisfied. He seemed willing to help her. The best thing now was for him to get plenty of rest so he could heal as quickly as possible. In the meantime, she needed her sleep as well, if only for a few hours. Then it was time to really review the defenses of the Mast's compound and hope that she and Thorn could retrieve the treasure and take off before any of Iradia's teeming underworld showed up with the same idea.

Miala had planned to sleep for only a few hours, but almost seven passed before she awoke with a start, fumbling for a few moments at the unfamiliar covers before she remembered she'd put herself to bed in the slave girls' dormitory, and not on the lumpy pallet which had been her sleeping accommodations for the past few months. A few narrow bars of sunlight made it past the heavy metal shutters on the window, bright and sharp as laser beams in the otherwise dim chamber.

She had been so tired the night before she hadn't even tried to find some sort of garment to sleep in and instead had collapsed onto one of the narrow cots fully clothed. Now the garments she had chosen so carefully the day before were crushed and stale, but she couldn't worry about that now. She had work to do.

The computers in the security station were as she had left them, of course, still humming quietly to themselves in the unnaturally chill air. Miala briefly detoured to check on Thorn as she made her way downstairs, but he slept soundly, with the mech a watchful shadow in one corner. She thought there were one or two fewer bags of medication attached to him than there had been the night before, and once again she had uttered a silent prayer of thanksgiving for his apparent resilience. Maybe they could get out of here even more quickly than she had hoped.

Her father, like most hackers, made a habit of building back doors into his code. Although clients disliked the practice and usually hired other hackers to come in and disable the back doors, the truth of it was, if you were hiring the best, there wasn't much you could do but pay your experts enough to keep them happy so they would have no reason to use the back doors. Or you could just have them killed, as Mast had done with her father and no doubt many others. Miala had so far been able to access the standard security protocols, the automatic systems that kept the perimeter activated and restricted entry in and out of the compound—except to those who knew the access keys. So far, however, she had been unable to pick her way through the forest of code that protected Mast's vaults and the databases that contained his personal financial information.

She could not allow herself to become frustrated. Unraveling code was as delicate and time-consuming an affair as picking apart a skein of moon-moth silk, and once false move could be just as deadly. The standard bits of data her father usually embedded so he could access all areas of a system without having to go through the regular protocols were suspiciously absent in Mast's security systems. Either Arlen Mast had been wise to him from the beginning, or her father had worked scared, burying the back doors so deeply that even his own daughter could not begin to guess at the keys that could unlock them.

The hours passed, uncounted and unnoticed. It wasn't until the pain behind her eyes grew too sharp to ignore any longer that Miala finally sat up from the console, leaning back against a chair intended for a far larger occupant. As she did so, the base of her spine added its protest to her already outraged brain cells.

"Okay," she said softly, easing herself out of the chair. Dimly, she realized she was hungry as well. What time was it, anyway?

She glanced up at the chrono on the wall, saw that more than six hours had passed, and swore. No wonder her head was killing her. And what of Thorn?

When she arrived in the med unit after a guilty dash upstairs, Miala saw that her concern was unfounded. The mercenary was sitting propped up against the cushions, sipping some kind of broth through a tube.

"Nice of you to drop in," he commented.

"I figured you weren't going to die any time soon," she said, giving him a sour look.

"Right. 'Too mean to die' is what you said, I think."

"Feel free to correct me if I'm wrong." What was it about him that just rubbed her the wrong way? He was far too self-assured for someone who had come within inches of being squashed to a jelly.

Her stray thought of the evening before had been correct—he did have a nice smile, even with the chapped lips and abrasions marring his chin and left cheek. "I'd say that assessment was correct."

"Hmm." She made a show of scanning the life-support machines at his bedside, although she could make very little sense of most of the readings, except the heart-rate monitor. "So you're eating already?"

"The mech seemed to think it was okay."

"Well, that's more than I've gotten today," she said, aware all over again of how empty her stomach felt.

If it was sympathy she was looking for, she had definitely come to the wrong place. He just watched her, face expressionless, and she was suddenly all too aware of her rumpled clothing, the hair she had knotted back into a careless braid hours ago when she tired of it continually falling into her eyes. Of course, what the hell did it matter what she looked like, anyway?

Annoyed, she said, "Since you're obviously not going to drop dead any time soon, I'm going to go fix myself something to eat. Then I'll get back to work."

"Sounds like a good idea." Thorn's tone was carefully neutral, but she got the impression he was laughing at her.

Son of a—she thought, but she only gave him an irritated nod before stalking out. Who knew she could come so close to throttling a man she had just saved the day before?

Several days passed in much the same fashion. Thorn continued to gain strength, although the mech insisted that he stay in bed and not risk disturbing the bandages that protected his healing flesh. Miala knew he must be in considerable pain. She could see it in the sudden tightening of his jaw sometimes when he spoke, or in a subtle deepening of the lines around his eyes, but he uttered not one word of his discomfort. If she hadn't known better, she would have thought he was pulling the stoic act for her benefit, but as far as she could tell, Eryk Thorn didn't do things for anyone's benefit but his own.

The forced inactivity must have been driving him mad—Miala knew she would have been climbing the walls in similar circumstances—but he never let on that his convalescence was anything more than a minor inconvenience. His only request was that she retrieve a tablet computer he had secreted in his rooms. She had done so, and after that he had sat up for hours in bed, making notations, scribbling away at who knows what.

For her own part, Miala felt no closer to breaking her father's code than she had when she first arrived in the compound. She knew intellectually that was not exactly true, but still the hours of careful tinkering with very little to show for them were beginning to wear on her. Thorn's silence on the subject didn't help, either. After one inquiry—to which he received a reply that even she had to admit was snappish—he had refrained from mentioning the subject again.

Failure was not something she could begin to contemplate. Hadn't her father trained her in code since she was old enough to understand what it was? Couldn't she, even before she was out of what passed in Aldis Nova for a secondary school, hack programs people twice her age couldn't crack? So what was it about this one that seemed so uniquely unbreakable? Miala had to give her father grudging credit for what was undeniably his masterwork, but at the same time she found herself wishing he had been just a little less thorough.

It was after one of these brain-bending sessions that she found herself distractedly wondering what was going on in the world outside. They had been so isolated here, so hidden away, that she'd forgotten time was passing for the rest of the Iradia as well. So far there had been no challenges to the security of Mast's fortress, no interlopers seeking to seize the apparently unguarded compound, but Miala knew that could change in an instant.

She had to go to Mast's chambers for a comm station that connected into the planet-wide communications net—probably he hadn't wanted his underlings to be informed of current events. Previously she had avoided the crime lord's noisome personal suite, having no reason to go there, but a scan of the communications system for the palace showed that his were the only rooms with a properly connected console.

Even after standing empty for days, the chambers emitted a foul reek, as if something had crawled in there and died—which it might very well have, she reflected. But the rooms seemed empty enough, although she tried to avert her eyes from the walls, which were covered in erotic art so garish it would have made an Eridani blush.

The comm station, in direct contrast to the barbaric decorations of the rest of the room, was sleek and new, a very late model. Nevertheless, she had a difficult time finding a clear channel at first—many of the images that came through were fuzzy and filled with static. Most disturbing of all, the channels that usually carried the official Gaian-generated newscasts and other Consortium-based programming were completely blank.

"What the hell…?" she murmured, hands moving over the keyboard. Had the entire planet erupted while she and Thorn were secreted away here in the abandoned compound?

Apparently it had. Finally she was able to locate a relatively clear station, one that was filled for a moment with an unfamiliar symbol, one that appeared to depict two crossed lightning bolts against a dark blue background. Then a dark-haired woman's face filled the screen. She wore the typical Iradian garments of ivory and beige, but her head scarf had been pushed back down over her shoulders.

"Although isolated fighting still continues, largely it appears that the local Gaian garrisons have collapsed. Leaders of the insurgency are now convening in Aldis Nova, where they are in the process of setting up an interim government. During this period of transition, we encourage residents to remain in their homes whenever possible—"

Hand shaking, Miala turned off the comm. What the hell? Oh, there had always been unrest, isolated flare-ups here and there as the Iradians tried to establish their own sovereignty, to tell the Gaians the world was a colony no longer and that it should have its own voice in the Consortium. But that's all they had been—flare-ups, tiny spot fires that the Gaian Defense Forces quickly quashed. Had that simmering unease finally come to a boil during the months she had been isolated here at Mast's compound?

What this might mean for her, she wasn't sure. The Gaians kept a tight rein on Iradia, but at least their presence had maintained some semblance of order. With the local garrisons apparently crushed for now, she could only think anarchy would soon follow, no matter what that announcer had said about an interim government being set up.

Miala found herself hoping that Captain Malec had made it off-world before the insurgency struck. Perhaps he had been off-duty, enjoying the brief leave he had mentioned to her during that long-ago meeting in his office, and so was safe. For a member of the GDF, the only security lay in being far away from Iradia.

Her mouth was dry, and it wasn't just because of the parched air. Perhaps she and Thorn were safe here for now—or perhaps the collapse of the Gaian forces would be the final impetus to send all the scum of Iradia running in their direction. Even as she hurried down the deserted corridors of the compound, she found herself mentally reviewing all its defenses, hoping they would be enough, worried that they were woefully inadequate. Maybe it would be better if they just ran for Thorn's ship now and got out while they still could.

Not that Thorn would have any reason for taking her with him now, before the treasure had been secured. There was also the very good chance that he was still far too unwell to drive a skimmer, let alone pilot a spacecraft.

Miala hadn't even realized she was running to the med unit until she found herself pausing at the open door. She waited there for a moment, looking in; Thorn seemed to be asleep, the tablet lying on his chest, his bandaged hands folded across its surface.

"You've been running," he said then, even though his eyes were still shut.

Had she really been breathing that loudly? She supposed she was; she knew her heart was beating so heavily she was surprised he hadn't mentioned that, too. "I just—" she began, then realized she didn't know exactly what to say. Again, the gravity of their situation hit her, and she gripped the skirt of her tunic with both hands, hoping that would be enough to quiet their shaking.

At that point Thorn did open his eyes and look over at her. She thought she saw the faintest flicker of concern cross his shadowed features, but his voice was expressionless enough as he asked, "Is there a problem?"

"You might call it that," she said, and gave a short laugh, which she clamped down even as it escaped her lips. If she started in with that there was no telling where she might end up. "I just monitored the comm station in Mast's chambers. Thorn, the Iradians have risen up against the garrisons…sounds like the locals are in charge. Which means it's all going to fall apart."

If she had been expecting any sort of outward response, she would have been disappointed, but by now she had come to realize that Thorn revealed very little of his emotions. Still, with news as astounding as that, she would have thought he'd look at least even slightly shocked.

He didn't, of course. The dark eyes narrowed a little, but that was all. "Interesting," he said, after a lengthy pause.

"'Interesting'?" she demanded. "That's all you have to say?"

With that he did give her a quick glance, and there was the faintest quirk at the corner of his mouth. "All that's changed for me is who might be paying the bills," he replied.

Outraged, she glared at him, wanting to say something witty and cutting in response, but she knew that was impossible in her current state. "So what are we going to do?" she managed at last.

"What we have been doing. I'm not fit to get out of here yet, and you haven't broken the security code. So I don't see much changing." Almost as an afterthought, he added, "Although if you could work a little faster, it might be a good idea."

All the epithets her father had hurled at recalcitrant computers and Gaian tax collectors came bubbling up to her lips, but Miala knew better than to say anything out loud. She couldn't risk antagonizing Thorn now, not when things were even more unstable than she had thought. "If you think I haven't been working myself to death over that code—" she spluttered finally, knowing even as she said them how weak the words sounded.

"I know you have," he said, and although she should have been reassured, somehow she wasn't. There was something very cold and measured in the glance he gave her. "Believe me, if I thought you weren't doing everything in your power to break that security system, I'd have been standing down in the security station with you, holding a gun to your head."

He meant it, Miala knew. For the first time she realized how dangerous he really was—and how very little she meant to him. She was a tool, nothing more. And if that tool should prove to be useless…

"I'd better get back to work, then," she said at last, when she thought she could speak without completely breaking down. She had no idea how she could possibly concentrate at such a time, but she also knew she had to get out of Thorn's presence as soon as possible.

"You do that."

And taking that as a dismissal, she turned and fled in the direction of the security station. It was only once she was there in its relative safety that she collapsed in her usual chair, shaking in the overly air-conditioned air, forcing her palms against her eyes in a futile attempt to hold back the tears that had already begun to stream down her cheeks. If someone had asked, she probably couldn't have even explained why she was crying, whether it was for her father, or the collapse of the only system she had ever known, or simply because she was so very, very tired.

Once the fit of weeping had passed, though, a deeper chill took hold of her. All this time she had feared the outsiders who might converge on Mast's compound at any moment—and all the while she had been harboring a man who could prove to be a greater danger than any of them.

IV

IN HER DREAMS MIALA HEARD an insistent shrilling that went on and on, a sound that could not be ignored, even though she only wanted to sleep for at least a hundred years. With a gasp she sat up in bed, clasping the side of the cot on which she lay in an attempt to orient herself. The room was dark, except for a light fixture she had left burning at quarter-power in the dressing area, but it took only a few seconds for her eyes to adjust to the dim light. Nothing seemed any different from the time she had put herself to bed—had it been hours or only minutes ago? Then she realized the screaming sound had not originated in her dreams but had actually interrupted them—it was the siren for Mast's perimeter security system. That could mean only one thing.

Cursing, she pushed the covers away and bolted for the door, tripping over the sandals she had left on the floor next to her bed. She paused just long enough to gather them up and half-skip, half-run as she slid her feet into first one, then the other, even as she pounded down the hallway to the staircase that led to the ground floor of the compound. As Miala passed the landing to the second floor, she heard a loud crash from the vicinity of the med unit and looked back, startled, only to see Eryk Thorn stagger out into the hallway, pulling at the bandages on his hands even as he headed toward her with grim determination.

"What the hell do you think you're doing?" she demanded, stopping to let him catch up to her.

"Is that the perimeter alert?" he asked.

She scowled at him, provoked that he was out of bed at all, and even more irritated that he had so obviously brushed off her first question. "Yes," she said shortly. "I can handle it."

"You?" he asked, and raised an eyebrow. Before she could reply, he went on, "Are the main defensive controls in the security station?"

"Yes, but—"

He didn't bother to wait. Limping a little, he hurried down the stairs as Miala trailed in his wake, desperately racking her brains for any argument that would be effective at getting him back into bed and finding none. Not for the first time she mentally cursed the monks who had built the place—they had deemed elevators a worldly indulgence, instead building stairs everywhere. Mast had a private lift that went to his suite, but it was locked down, and she'd had better things to do than break the code just to avoid a little exercise.

At this hour the compound was dark; no one was around, after all, to see that proper illumination was

provided. Thorn seemed to have very good night vision—
he must have eyes like a Stacian, she thought—but even he
accidentally collided with some low-hanging chimes in
one doorway, the sound a sweet discordance against the
continued shrilling of the siren.

She wondered how he was able to find his way to the
security station so easily. It was not as if he had been a regular
inhabitant of the compound, after all, but perhaps it was his
practice to familiarize himself with his surroundings wher-
ever he went. Again she thought of his murderous career, and
of all the survival skills he would have been forced to develop
along the way.

Light flooded out of the security station into the dark
hallway. Miala wasn't sure whether she had forgotten
to shut it down when she had retired for the evening or
whether the overhead lighting came on automatically once
the perimeter security system was activated.

Thorn pushed on ahead of her into the room, heading automatically for the main security console. The viewscreens revealed only dark desert, broken here and there by
the bluish glow of the perimeter wards—all screens except
the one that showed the rear approach to the compound.

"What is that?" she asked, pointing at the dark bulk that
seemed to fill the screen. In shape it recalled vaguely the
ore processors that moved over Iradia's surface, harvesting
any trace minerals they happened to come across, but otherwise it resembled those slow, lumbering vehicles about
as much as the local boys' hopped-up skimmers resembled
a GDF attack cruiser. The unknown vehicle had an oily,
gunmetal finish that shimmered oddly in the glare of the

activated defense field; its outline seemed to be spiked with a number of strategically placed cannons.

"Get me into the system," Thorn commanded, once again ignoring her question, but Miala knew better than to argue. She hastened to the console, tapped in the code, then stepped aside.

Thorn lifted his bandaged hands to the controls and paused. Then he seemed to shake his head slightly, and pulled at the wrappings that covered his fingers. One by one they came away, revealing mottled, half-healed skin still marked by livid bruises, angry red abrasions, and burns.

Swallowing slightly, Miala forced herself not to look away. If his hands were still that bad after healing for almost a week, she hated to think what his wounds must have looked like when the mech first treated him.

Now unencumbered, Thorn's hands flew over the controls. Miala watched as he poured extra power into the shields that protected the rear of the compound and activated the pulse cannons mounted to either side of the massive front gates.

"But why—" she began. She couldn't understand why he was bothering with the cannons if the attackers were coming from the rear. As she spoke, however, the forward perimeter defenses flared as small dark figures came out of the night, guns firing.

"Take the controls," Thorn said, and she hurried to take his place at the keyboard even as he moved to the right, grasping the heavy console-mounted cannon grips.

The compound's defenses were good against most types of gunfire, whether pulse or projectile, but no defense field could keep out biological attackers, which was why Thorn had increased power to the shields guarding the rear of the facility. Somehow he had known ground forces would be attacking the main gates, and that increasing the force field there would have been of no use.

He had pushed as much power as he could to the rear shields, but he didn't know the system the way she did. Miala had spent hours working through its subroutines and codes and knew where she could steal the power they needed—from the back-up generators, the underutilized environmental controls, even the power-cell chargers in the garage. She was but dimly aware of Thorn working beside her as she hacked away at the computer system, shunting power to the rear defense fields. The only systems she considered sacrosanct were the weapons controls, of course, and the environmental support systems for the ground floor of the compound. The last thing she needed was for either her or Thorn to overheat and collapse in the thick of battle.

No sooner had she completed the first pass through the system than the pulse cannons on the massive vehicle threatening the rear of the compound let loose, bombarding the shields with a barrage of coruscating energy. The ground shook beneath them, but the shields held.

"Take that," she muttered, but she didn't have time to enjoy her victory for very long. Again the cannons opened up, and this time they knocked the shields back by a good twenty percent.

"Can you hold them?" Thorn asked, not taking his eyes off the viewscreen in front of him. His fingers seemed to move on their own, working the cannon controls. She could see from a quick glance at the screen that the ground in front of the compound's gates was already thick with bodies.

"You hold yours, I'll hold mine," she replied, fingers pounding away at the keyboard. She could steal some power from the environmental systems on the upper floors of the building, as no one was up there to care how hot it got. And of course—the refrigeration units in the kitchens. Several days ago Miala had transferred all the remaining edible food to one unit instead of having it scattered amongst four, but she hadn't bothered to shut down the power to the three that were now empty. That would do nicely.

The attacking vehicle fired again, and again, but once more the shields held. Beside her Thorn paused, and the endless firing of the defensive cannons ceased.

"What—" she began, lifting her gaze once again to the screen that showed the front gates. Whoever the attackers were, she couldn't think there were very many of them left. Mast had probably lost more people at the Malverdine Cliffs, but not that many more, and she guessed there weren't a lot of crime lords in the area who could afford to sacrifice so many men.

"Watch out," Thorn said, and sure enough the vehicle fired again. This time there seemed something almost petulant in its attack, as if those manning the controls knew all too well that their ground forces had just been decimated.

Miala pushed the back-up power she had just located into the shields, and although they lost a few percentage points, they were still holding just fine. "Why don't we fire back?" she asked. "There are gun emplacements to the rear of the compound as well!"

"No point," he said. "We'd have to drop the shields, and right now the shields are doing better for us than the guns would. I'm not sure they'd even be enough to punch through the shielding on that thing."

He was probably right, but part of her was still annoyed that they couldn't fire at the invaders, blow a hole in the huge unwieldy machine that continued to fire at them. Now that Thorn had stopped firing the forward guns, she did steal a little power from the cannons to bolster the shields. That seemed to have done it, for after one last shot the firing abruptly ceased, and the bulky vehicle slowly lumbered back into the inky blackness of the Iradian night.

For a moment she watched the viewscreen, unbelieving, certain that reinforcements were just around the next dune. But all she could see was the restored bluish glow of the perimeter wards, as the security system reestablished itself now that the interlopers were gone. "We did it?" she asked finally.

"Looks like it," Thorn replied, easing himself down into one of the oversized chairs. Unlike her, he almost fit. Then he turned his hands over, looking down at the newly bloodied palms with mild interest.

Despite herself, Miala let out a sound of shocked dismay. "Your hands!"

"It's nothing," he said, closing his fists. "Guess I should have kept the bandages on."

Miala stared at him for a moment. His face was calm enough, but she could see from the tightness of his jaw that he was probably in considerable pain. Then, a little amazed by her own boldness, she went to him and reached out, forcing one of his hands open with both of hers. His skin felt rough and warm under her cold fingers.

"You'll be lucky if that doesn't get infected," she said. "I'm surprised the mech let you get up at all."

He kept his fingers outstretched under hers even as the dark eyes crinkled a bit at the corners. Was he laughing at her, at her feeble attempts to play nursemaid?

"Let's just say that the mech and I had a difference of opinion."

She recalled suddenly the crash she had heard as Thorn left the med unit. "You didn't—"

"I'm sure it can be repaired." Again that swift, dark look from beneath the level black brows. "Are you any good with mechs?"

Miala dropped his hand, wishing she had the courage to tell him to go to hell then and there. "We couldn't afford any," she snapped. "But I guess you'd better hope I am, since I doubt I'd be any better at fixing you if that gets infected because I couldn't get the mech back together."

"You might surprise yourself."

And you might get stuffed, she thought, but said only, "Do you think they'll come back?"

He looked over at the viewscreens, head cocked slightly. "Probably. But we've earned some breathing room. I don't think they were expecting to meet quite this much resistance. So now they'll go back and plan and regroup."

Hopefully we'll be out of here before they get to that stage, was Miala's next thought, but she only nodded. "Then we'd better get some rest—and we'd better do what we can with your hands."

Thorn seemed to be in agreement, for he stood and left the security station after a final quick glance at the perimeter. She followed him back up to the med unit, where indeed the hapless mech had been knocked into a corner, its head askew and one arm completely broken off.

Miala wondered where she would ever find the time to fix the machine and continue hacking the security on Mast's vault. *Oh, well, sleep is highly overrated, I hear,* she thought wryly, moving to the cupboards and pulling out a disinfectant wash and several unopened bandage packs.

"Get back into bed," she instructed, and to her surprise Thorn did as he was told, climbing under the covers and laying his head back down on the pillow. Perhaps even he had had enough by this point. She couldn't begin to imagine how painful it must have been for him to continue firing those cannons as the skin on his hands broke and bled.

So it was with more gentleness than she had first intended that she swabbed at his abraded palms, feeling herself tense as the antiseptic surely stung on the open wounds. Of course Thorn made no sound throughout these operations, but she thought he looked a little pale, and once or twice he shut his eyes as if to better cope with the pain.

Finally she was done, Thorn's hands newly covered in clean bandages. Miala hoped that she'd gotten the wounds clean enough, since she shuddered to think what kind of microbes could have been left behind by the last person to grip the handles of the cannons' firing mechanisms. Mast's personal security contingent weren't generally known for their hygiene. Still, without the assistance of the mech, she was left with only the rough first aid she had learned growing up, tending her father's occasional cuts and bruises as well as her own. Until her father's heart attack, neither one of them had ever been ill enough to require the services of the local clinic.

She gathered up the empty packaging and was dropping it into the waste receptacle when Thorn spoke.

"You did well down there."

She looked over at him, startled. Was that actually a compliment? "Excuse me?"

He looked at her steadily, expressionless as usual. "You do well in a crisis. Better than I had thought."

Trust Thorn to neatly undercut any words of praise in such a fashion. Miala felt the color flood to her cheeks. "Well, I know I'm just a girl," she replied, her tone mocking. Better than he had thought? Nice to know that his expectations had been so low!

"Precisely," he said, completely ignoring her jab. "How old are you?"

"Twenty standard," she said. "As if that should make any difference!"

Thorn moved his head on the pillow so he looked directly up at the ceiling and then shut his eyes before replying. "I don't know many twenty-year-olds who could have handled themselves as well. So don't argue with me, Miala," he added.

It was the first time he had ever called her by her given name. There was something oddly intimate about hearing "Miala" on his lips—as if this were the first time he had actually thought of her as a real person with feelings and thoughts of her own and not simply an unwelcome and unnecessary intrusion, or at best a tool to be used and discarded.

"Thank you, Thorn," she said at last, when she thought she could trust her own voice. She told herself she was just tired and overcome by the aftermath of the adrenaline rush of the battle. The warning sirens had pulled her out of deep sleep, after all—who wouldn't be shaky after something like that?

"You're welcome," he said, and again she could see the little quirk at the corner of his mouth that bespoke a secret amusement.

After an awkward pause, she said quickly, hoping he hadn't noticed the uncomfortable silence, "Well, I'd better be off to sleep, too. I'll try to come back and check on you in a few hours."

"That's not necessary. I'll be fine."

She supposed he probably would be—how long did it take for an infection to develop, anyway? More than just a few hours at least, and she knew she needed to get some sleep or she wouldn't be of any use to anyone. Without the mech to alert her if Thorn's condition took a sudden turn for the worse, she knew she didn't have many options.

"Good night, then," she replied, and turned and left the chamber.

It seemed as if there were far more stairs going back up to the slave girls' dormitory than there had been when she had hurried down them only a few hours ago. Miala pulled herself up the long, weary climb step by step, fumbling her way in the darkness. Only when she finally returned to the narrow cot she had claimed as her own and laid her head down on the lumpy pillow did she feel herself begin to tremble with reaction.

It hadn't been enough to be attacked by unknown enemies. That had been frightening, of course, but she had mentally prepared for it as best she could. Also, somehow, she couldn't feel as frightened as she knew she should have been, not when she had gone into battle with Eryk Thorn at her side. There was something strangely reassuring having someone next to her who had probably faced down much worse throughout his life. He had lived to fight another day, and so she'd been confident she would survive as well.

No, that wasn't it. What made Miala shiver now was the sudden wave of emotion that had passed over her when Thorn had spoken kind words to her—when he had said her name and looked at her with a new respect. She didn't know exactly what that emotion was. All she knew was that when she finally wished him a good night, she'd had to fight a sudden urge to reach out and run her fingers through his wavy dark hair, to gently touch the bandaged hands that lay crossed on his chest.

It was impossible. She didn't even like Thorn very much. Was she so pathetic, so starved for human contact, that only a few kind words from him were enough to turn her into the sort of girl she had always despised, the ones who trailed after the boys in Aldis Nova, giggling and flirting and trading stolen kisses behind old Nala's coffee house?

You're just tired, she told herself. *It will all be better in the morning.*

But when she shut her eyes, all she could see was that tiny smile at the corner of Eryk Thorn's mouth, and all her traitor mind seemed capable of was wondering what that mouth would feel like pressed against hers.

Biology was a crazy thing. She much preferred the cool logic of computers, but logic seemed to have deserted her for the moment.

Sleep was a long time coming.

V

THE HOSPITAL BED WAS EMPTY when Miala finally returned to check on Thorn late the next morning. Again she had overslept, although it was difficult to say whether her reluctance to get up that morning could be attributed to the disruptions of the previous night or a natural disinclination to avoid seeing the mercenary after such unwelcome feelings about him had surfaced.

Still, having once steeled herself to face him—after a protracted grooming session in the dressing area of the slave girls' quarters, when it seemed no matter what she did her hair would not behave itself—she was nonplussed to see that he was gone. The pieces of the broken mech had been gathered up and stacked neatly in a corner, and the bed itself was likewise made up, with the sheets pulled taut over the pillow and the coarse, dark blanket tucked in with military precision.

Well, at least he's not a slob, she thought, but still she felt a stab of irritation. Who did he think he was, anyway, getting up and roaming around the compound when he was barely healed? She would have thought he'd sleep until early afternoon after the excitement of the previous night, but once again he'd proven her wrong.

She found him in the security station, of course. He sat in front of the main viewscreen, fast-forwarding through a series of images that looked as if they'd been taken from the cameras that watched the front palace gates.

He looked up as she approached. The bulky bandages were gone. The skin that had been hidden underneath was still mottled and red in patches, but the healing process was obviously further along than she had thought. Somewhere he'd found a loose-fitting shirt and pants in standard-issue Iradian beige to cover himself. In the mundane garments he should have looked less exotic, less alien, but somehow their very ordinariness only served to contrast with the swarthy skin, the unusual cast to his features. Miala found herself wondering where exactly on Gaia his forebears had come from.

She opened her lips to speak and found her mouth oddly dry. She swallowed, then said, "You should be in bed."

"No time for that." He turned back to the images that scrolled in front of him.

"What are you doing, anyway?" she asked, moving farther into the room. Somehow it was easier to approach him when he wasn't looking directly at her.

"Going through the old security logs. I'm trying to see if our friends from last night ever paid Mast a visit while he was still alive."

"Know thy enemy?" she asked, and was rewarded with a quick approving glance.

"Right. But I've gone through eight standard months of these logs, and so far nothing. Doesn't mean much, of course. People in Mast's circle can hold grudges for a long time. Could be a crony of Mendel Bronson's."

"Who's that?"

"The boss who thought it would be a good idea to attack Mast as he was dropping prisoners off the Malverdine Cliffs. All that accomplished was killing everyone on both sides. Well, present company excepted." He leaned forward once more, dark eyes flickering as he scanned the images on the screen.

Typical that Thorn wouldn't find anything unusual about being the sole survivor of probably the worst crime lord face-off in the last twenty years. She opened her mouth to ask how he had accomplished that particular feat, then decided he probably wouldn't tell her. Fine. Instead, she forced her gaze away from his profile, which was actually very fine, with the firm chin and long, strong nose, and made herself look at the viewscreen as well.

It was amazing what a collection of scum had come to call on Mast. Most of them seemed to have come to pay him sort of tribute. The great majority of the visitors revealed on the security cameras brought various boxes of loot— hard currency, precious metals, drugs, skeins of moon-moth silk—all of which were handed over to the security guards and secreted away somewhere in the vaults. The display brought home to her just how much treasure they were probably sitting on, as well as her continuing failure to recover it.

"I'm going for some breakfast," she said at last, when it grew obvious he didn't care to indulge her in any more conversation. "You want any?"

Still he did not look up. "Sure. And some coffee, if you've got it."

Back to kitchen drudge, she thought, but, after all, she *had* offered. They had to eat, and he was showing remarkable signs of improvement. Probably he was relieved that at least now he could be an active member of the team; she couldn't begin to comprehend how the forced inactivity had probably chafed at him. If the mech were still functioning, she was sure it would have had a few choice words about Thorn getting up so soon, let alone removing the bandages, but in the final analysis it was the mercenary's body, and he should have the power to decide what he was or wasn't capable of. He didn't seem be in a great deal of discomfort—not that that meant anything. Thorn had to be in the sort of pain that would have brought screams from lesser men before he'd allow even a grimace.

Considering the erstwhile crime lord's bulk, it wasn't too surprising that Mast had hoarded off-world delicacies the same way he'd hoarded cash and narcotics. In the kitchen's refrigeration units she'd found rare aged cheeses from Gaia itself, some kind of creamy sweet dessert topped by swirled nuts, and filets of the tenderest herd animals from Archeron, known for its vast grasslands.

None of that seemed appropriate for breakfast, but there was still the bread she had made a few days earlier, as well as the makings of *leth*, a common grain-based hot dish common on Iradia. For protein she added several wedges of creamy cheese to the tray she had set aside to take back to Thorn in the guard chamber. During all these preparations, the coffee brewed away, sending its rich bitter-chocolate aroma into the air. In the process it woke up Miala's stomach, which strenuously protested the lean rations she'd been feeding herself lately. She ate her own bowl of leth standing up as she waited for the coffee to finish brewing. It was enough to keep her going until noontime, and she wanted to get back to work as soon as she took Thorn's food to him.

That thought brought to her the uncomfortable realization that the computer console where she did all her hacking was located in the same chamber where the mercenary was even now viewing the security recordings. True, the two workstations were situated on opposite sides of the room. However, up until now she had always had complete solitude in which to work, and she wasn't sure how well she'd do knowing that Thorn would be less than ten feet away from her as she pounded away at the elusive code. Still, there wasn't much she could do about it, save order Thorn out of the security station, and she wasn't sure she had the courage to do that.

Once the coffee had finished brewing, she poured it into two large mugs, one for her and one for Thorn, and set them both on the tray. The route from the kitchens to the security station was somewhat long and circuitous, but Miala had no doubt she could follow it in her sleep. She had gone that way far too many times already.

At least the mercenary did her the courtesy of looking up and nodding when she came in with his breakfast.

"That smells good," he said.

"Well, it's nothing fancy, but it should be better than whatever liquids the mech was pumping into you," she replied, relieved that she sounded relatively normal. Paradoxically, she found it easier to be with him now. There was certainly nothing in his voice or manner to suggest he had any idea that her feelings for him had undergone a significant alteration the night before. Maybe she would be able to get out of this without making a complete fool of herself after all.

Thorn turned away from her, attention consumed by his breakfast and the ever-changing images that flickered across the viewscreen. Miala hesitated for a moment, then realized he would not bother to say anything else to her because right now he had better things to do with his time.

Biting back a caustic remark about leaving a tip for the waitress, she clutched her own mug of coffee somewhat grimly as she crossed the room to take her usual position at the main computer console. After logging in, she sat staring at the screen for a few moments, frowning. Even though fewer than ten hours had passed since the last time she sat in front of this screen, it felt as if it had been ten days. How could she concentrate? How could she follow the unending streams of numbers and symbols, picking each one apart until she found the missing bits of data she could finally reassemble into the code that would unlock Mast's vaults?

Thorn was silent as always, but still she could hear each creak of the chair as he shifted his weight, the light tapping of his fingers on the keyboard—even, Miala fancied, an occasional sigh as yet another sequence of images revealed nothing. She typed in a few lines of code, then another, feeling she had to do something. He wasn't holding a gun to her head, she thought, but he might as well have been. There was no way she could think with him in the room.

"Excuse me," she said at last.

He looked around, one eyebrow lifted slightly.

"Look, I know you're trying to help, but I just can't concentrate with you in here. Sorry," she added lamely, although his impassive features certainly had not invited any apology.

To her dismay, Thorn rose from his seat and came toward her. Then he paused a few steps away, arms crossed over his chest. He was not particularly tall, although he topped her by more than a few inches, but she hadn't realized before now how well-built he was, how much strength was in the heavily muscled arms and chest. Of course, up until now most of his physique had been concealed by layers of bandages.

He regarded her narrowly for a moment, the dark eyes unreadable. Then he looked from her to the streams of data that flowed over the computer screen, and back again. "Right," he said finally, and turned and left without another word, pausing only to gather up the empty breakfast dishes and pile them on the tray. Then he was gone.

Miala hadn't realized she'd been holding her breath until the door whooshed shut behind him. Once she realized she truly was alone again, she let the breath out and shut her eyes, trembling slightly. The man definitely had a knack for intimidation, whether he intended it or not.

"Okay, then," she said softly. "Let's do this."

After all, Thorn had granted her the gift of solitude. Now it was up to her to use it wisely.

"Miala."

She pushed at the rough hand that clasped her shoulder, not really comprehending at first whose it was. "I'm almost ready," she muttered, then realized she was face down on the keyboard, her left arm the only thing protecting her cheek from myriad square indentations from the individual keys. She sat up, pushing the chair straight back into Thorn's midsection.

"Easy now," he admonished. He must have been standing behind her, reaching down to nudge her awake.

"What—what time is it?" Her brain still felt fuzzy. After Thorn had gone she had buried herself in the code, working at it, teasing it, all to no avail. Every pathway she had gone down seemed to be a dead end.

The hours had passed, and at one point she had begun to feel hungry again, but the pangs disappeared after a while as she continued to work. Some time later her eyelids had started to droop, and she had fought the weariness, forcing herself on, sure that the answer was almost within her grasp. At some point, she supposed, she must have simply passed out from exhaustion.

"Past midnight," he said. "I thought I'd leave you to work, but when I came back in from going over my ship, I saw the light still on, so—" He frowned at her. "Making yourself sick isn't going to get us out of here any sooner."

"I'm okay," she countered, even though she felt anything but all right. Now that she was awake, she felt ravenously hungry, and so dizzy she was afraid she'd have a hard time standing up.

He didn't bother to reply, instead handing her some kind of rough sandwich he had apparently cobbled together for her from the supplies in the kitchen.

"Thanks," she said, and took a bite. Surprisingly, it was good. She took another bite, accepted a cup of water he produced from a tray he had brought in with him, and drank deeply. After a few minutes she began to feel a little more human. "I guess that wasn't very smart of me," she added, even as her cheeks flushed with the admission.

"No," he agreed.

Miala noticed that he had discarded the baggy Iradian-style clothing he had worn earlier and was clad instead in a close-fitting dark jumpsuit. Well, he had mentioned going out to check on his ship. Apparently he'd been able to scare up a change of clothes while he was out there. "Is your ship all right?" she asked. The last thing they needed was for their only off-world transport to have been damaged in the attack.

He nodded. "The landing pad's inside the security perimeter, so it's okay." To her surprise, he touched her shoulder briefly, then said, "Come on. You need to get to sleep."

The touch had been fleeting, but she could still feel the weight of his hand of her shoulder. Miala stood, a little surprised at how shaky her knees felt, how stiff her back was. It would feel good to lie down on a proper bed.

She stumbled a bit as she tried to maneuver past Thorn and the chair in which she had been sitting, and he reached out to put a steadying hand on her elbow.

"I'm all right," she protested. As tired as she was, she

couldn't trust her reactions right now. Better to keep contact with him to a minimum.

He withdrew his hand, but remained close behind her as she made her way to the main staircase and began the climb to her room on the third floor. Perhaps he was worried she would trip and fall on the stairs—a distinct possibility in her current condition, she thought.

All the way up she clung grimly to the handrail, as much pulling herself along as actually walking up the steps. The part of her mind she'd begun to despise wondered idly whether he would catch her if she tripped and fell, and what it would feel like to have those strong arms close around her and hold her securely. Good thing she hadn't taken complete leave of her senses yet, because she knew deep down she would never allow herself to do anything so foolish.

Finally—after she felt as if she'd climbed twenty flights of stairs instead of just two—they paused outside the doorway to the slave girls' dormitory. Thorn eyed the portal with some curiosity, then asked, "Why up here? The guest chambers on the second floor are easier to get to."

There was nothing in his face save a mild interest, but Miala still hesitated a moment before replying. "I—I didn't have much in the way of clothes, and there's a good deal here in the closets that I can use. So I just decided to stay up here." Of course she'd never admit that she would have felt odd sleeping on the same floor of the compound as he, even though they would have been separated by at least ten rooms.

"Mmm," was all he said, and again she got the feeling he was secretly amused by her. Perhaps he was imagining some of Genna's more creative outfits and wondering whether he'd ever see her in one of those.

Not a chance in hell, she thought, *so keep dreaming, Thorn!*

"Good night," she said then, making sure her voice sounded firm and in control. No sense in giving him any further ideas.

Once again she thought of how alone the two of them were here. It had been much easier when he was an invalid. Then at least she had known what the boundaries were between them. Now he was suddenly an active part of her life, and although part of her craved his company, she couldn't help but be a little afraid of him as well. It had only been a few evenings ago that he'd threatened to hold a gun to her head, after all, although of course he hadn't done anything remotely that sinister. Still, she began to wonder what would happen if he ever started to look at her as a woman and not just as the means to Mast's treasure.

"'Night," he said, and again his face was impassive, giving no hint of what he was thinking. Without another word he turned and headed back down the stairs, leaving Miala to stare after him in the darkness.

After a moment she stepped inside the dormitory, then pressed the controls to shut the door. For the first time she realized the door had no lock. It made sense, of course; in Mast's mind, his slaves were property, with no more right to privacy than a mech or a pack animal. But the lack of security bothered her more than she cared to admit, even though she realized that a simple door lock was certainly not enough to deter a man like Eryk Thorn. If he wanted to get inside, he would, and that was that.

Perversely, the thought did not comfort her. She would have preferred a lock, ineffectual as it might prove to be. Perhaps she should move to one of the guest quarters on the floor below. Then she noted that she couldn't possibly move her room now, or Thorn would be sure to comment.

"Damn him, anyway," she muttered, as she moved into the room and pulled out the simple long shirt she had been using to sleep in. Even though she knew the door was shut and the windows securely shuttered and latched, Miala still felt exposed. She changed as quickly as she could and resisted the impulse to pull the covers up to her chin. It was way too hot for that, especially since the vents to the slave girls' quarters had been partially blocked so they wouldn't use up too much of the precious air conditioning.

Tired as she was, sleep seemed to elude her. Every time she shut her eyelids, she'd suddenly hear a sound from the corridor outside, and then she would startle, eyes flying open, straining to see something—anything—in the darkened room. Of course nothing was there, so she'd slide back down against the coarse sheets, heart pounding irrationally in her chest.

She shut her eyes and told herself she was being ridiculous; Thorn was probably dead asleep in his own room, and she should be sleeping as well. Sure, she was a little afraid of him, even as she felt some attraction to him, but he certainly did not seem to share her feelings. She needed to realize he had no reason to come here to her room. No, she was just exhausted and not thinking rationally. She would wake up in the morning and feel like a complete idiot.

And it was with these no-nonsense words echoing in her mind that she was finally able to fall into an uneasy sleep, one in which no specter of Eryk Thorn haunted her dreams. Instead, she dreamed that she wandered the halls of Mast's compound, certain each doorway led to freedom, only to find all of them barred against her. In her dream she finally collapsed in some dim and forgotten corridor, weeping, certain she would be trapped here forever in a nightmare of her own making.

Miala awoke in the dim reaches of the night, tears still wet on her cheeks. Never before had she felt so alone. At that moment she would have welcomed Eryk Thorn's presence—anything to keep the darkness at bay. But of course he slept somewhere in his own room below her, and she knew she would never go in search of him. To do so would be a display of weakness, and she could never allow that. So far she had earned at best a grudging respect from the mercenary. She was not about to jeopardize that because of a silly nightmare.

Hugging the lumpy pillow to her, Miala turned over in bed, willing herself to breathe deeply. *You only need him for one thing,* she thought, *and that's to get off-world. And he only needs you to get Mast's treasure. Beyond that, you mean nothing to one another.*

But even as she slipped back into the shadowy edges of dreams once again, she knew she was lying to herself. Perhaps she might mean nothing to him, but she feared he had begun to mean more to her than she wanted to admit.

VI

"RAFE DARLESTER," ERYK THORN SAID, not bothering to turn from the viewscreen.

"What?" Miala hesitated at the entrance to the chamber, caught off-guard by Thorn's cryptic comment.

With that he swiveled halfway toward her. Then he gave a slight inclination of his head in the direction of an image frozen on the screen behind him. "Our friendly visitors from the other evening. Think I finally got a lock on 'em."

Again, his simple, matter-of-fact attitude was immediately reassuring. Although she had spent a considerable length of time in front of the dressing-room mirror this morning berating herself for her foolish thoughts of the night before, Miala had still been anxious at the thought of confronting Thorn once more. What if he could read some of her internal turmoil in her face? But she saw nothing in his own features save a slight satisfaction at finally solving the mystery of their attackers.

"So who's Rafe Darlester?" she asked, hoping that she hadn't paused too long before replying.

"Typical Mast wannabe," he replied. "Maybe not completely typical. He's pretty well-backed. Let's call him the number-two or -three fish in this small pond."

For a second she stared at him blankly, not comprehending the reference. Then she recalled a few of the things she'd read about Gaian biology, including the creatures that actually lived in water. Trying to assume a sage expression, she said, "Got it."

His response was the same slightly lifted eyebrow, as if he knew all too well that she didn't have any idea what he was talking about. "He was in a lot of the same stuff as Mast—smuggling, racketeering, slaving. Looks like Mast got the better of him once or twice, which would have given him a reason to come sniffing around—as if just picking at the leavings in the compound wasn't enough reason."

Despite herself, she moved farther into the room, pausing only a few feet away from the screen that showed the aforementioned paragon. The image from the security camera was grainy and small, but she made out a human male of about her father's age, only built on a far grander scale. Lestan Fels had been a slim man of middle height. This Rafe Darlester would have topped her father by almost a head and was proportionately broad, though not fat. He wore dark, elaborate robes that were ridiculously inappropriate for the Iradian climate and was surrounded by a group of thugs only marginally larger than he.

"Nice," she commented. Then she noticed the empty pot of coffee sitting on the desktop next to a stained mug and a plate decorated with a few scattered crumbs. "Have you been in here all night?"

He shrugged. "You need to be alone to work, and I wanted to finish this up. Seemed like a reasonable allocation of resources."

She tried to estimate how many hours he'd been up straight without rest. At least thirty-six, as far as she could guess, which was far too long for a man who should have still been convalescing in bed. She knew better than to remonstrate with him, however, and said only, "Well, I'm up now, so if you want to catch a few hours' sleep, go ahead." At his brief hesitation, she added, "Don't worry—I promise I'll come get you if any other wandering thugs come by."

The dark eyes watched her carefully, and Miala felt a small flush start to her cheeks. She could only hope that her desert tan would hide most of it. What he saw in her face she couldn't begin to guess, but he gave a small nod and stood. Positioned so, he was very close to her—closer than he had ever been, and Miala remained frozen in place, wondering what he would do next and trying not to notice his peculiarly male scent of soap and clean sweat.

Then, without another word, he left the room.

Miala hadn't realized she'd been holding her breath until he was gone. Then she let it out slowly, wondering if she would ever be able to completely control her reactions around him. That brief second when he stood—when he had been so close to her—had been enough to start her heart pounding. Again he had given her no encouragement, no reason to think he had meant to do anything but rise and exit the chamber. But still—

Stop being a girl and get to work, she thought, grimly pulling out the chair that faced the main computer console. *You don't have time for this romance-vid bullshit!*

To her relief, however, this time she was able to concentrate well enough. Whatever the reason—whether it was the fact that Thorn had absented himself before she began to work, or whether he had at least put a name and a face to the threat which had confronted them two nights ago—she could feel that familiar sensation of sliding into the endless numbers, feeling them almost like a living force as she picked through one data stream after another, searching for the anomalies, looking for the one microscopic piece of data that seemed out of place.

To her surprise, after a few hours of this Miala actually found something. It was tiny, only one letter, but it was not where it should have been. She pushed herself back in her chair, staring at the screen, then leaned forward and tapped a few keys. The data flowed past, again with that tiny blip in the center of the complicated stream of numbers and symbols.

"What were you up to, Father?" she murmured. It had to mean something, of course. This was often how her father programmed in his back doors, by putting in random word associations known only to him and his daughter. These combinations had ranged from arrangements as simple as the letters of her own name to the name of her favorite vid-star, spelled backward. All she had to go on now was one letter, which she had to admit wasn't much. Still, it was more than she'd had a few hours ago.

"B," she said aloud. She did that occasionally, usually

while trying to solve a particularly difficult puzzle. Her father had teased her for the practice, but somehow the sound of her own voice was reassuring. Besides, it wasn't as if anyone could hear her now anyway. "Well, you put that in every possible combination with every other letter in the alphabet and get, what? A few hundred million possibilities?"

Still, she refused to be deterred. Of course, it wouldn't be something random out of those hundred million possibilities. It had to be something of importance to Lestan Fels...or possibly his daughter.

She tried to think of things that started with "b," hoping all the while that her father hadn't reversed the order of the letters or turned the entire word inside out. Otherwise, she'd be here forever. "Box, bacteria, Bethany—" Miala smiled briefly, thinking of the kind-faced older woman who had run Aldis Nova's one reputable dining establishment. The smile faded, however, as she remembered how Bethany Larsen had been pushed out of business by several of the seedier cafés, probably with the backing of Mast's thugs or people connected with them. At any rate, she somehow doubted her father would have used a woman they barely knew as the code word for the back door into Mast's security system. "—Box Canyon, Barris Jax—"

Now that was even more unlikely, although the irony of having Mast's right-hand man as the key was not lost on her. She scrolled through more data, looking for an *i* or an *e* on the simple assumption that the word had to have a vowel in it somewhere. It didn't take long for her to locate the *e*.

Big deal, she thought, *only the most used letter in English.* But she could tell she was getting closer.

It had to be something important. So who or what had been so significant to Lestan Fels that he had used the letters of their name as the code-breaker for the toughest piece of security he had ever written?

The answer came to her suddenly, in a piece of insight as blazing as the first rays of Iradia's sun when it broke over the horizon each morning.

"Belissa," she breathed. Of course, who better—what better—to be the hidden piece of code than the name of the woman who had betrayed him and left him here on this barren piece of rock twenty years ago?

With fingers that shook only a little, Miala brought up the login screen for Mast's private security system. At the prompt, she typed in Belissa, and watched the login screen fade away, to be replaced with a graphical interface that allowed her access to the vaults, Mast's personal files, his off-world accounts—everything she'd pursued relentlessly for the past few months and had begun to think she would never find.

She wasn't sure where to start, but the vaults seemed the best bet. After all, even with the codes that allowed her access to Mast's off-world accounts, it would take some work to do anything with the funds—she would have to set up her own accounts, come up with plausible reasons for the transfer of large sums of money from one account to another, and who knew what else. But the vaults were here, and they held tangible goods. And it was really a half share of the contents of those vaults that she had pledged to Eryk Thorn.

Thorn, she thought, and glanced up at the chrono on the wall. A little more than three hours had passed since she had begun her work, which meant it would be scorching high noon outside and far too soon to comfortably rouse the mercenary. She doubted, though, that he would appreciate her solicitude in letting him sleep while she went to inspect the contents of the vaults. The last thing she needed was for him to suspect her of hiding any goods from him.

She unlocked the vaults remotely from her workstation and then rose, leaving the security station and heading upstairs for the guest room on the second floor of the compound where Eryk Thorn slept. Of course the door was locked, but it had a courtesy page system, and she pressed the button and waited.

He was at the door sooner than she would have thought possible. "What's the matter?"

He must sleep in that jumpsuit, Miala thought irrelevantly, and then wondered whether she was disappointed that he hadn't been a little less…clothed.

She cleared her throat. "I did it."

"Did what?"

"Broke the code. The vaults are open."

For a long moment he only stared at her, almost as if he wasn't quite sure he could believe her words. Then he said, "Show me."

So she led him down the stairs, past the security station, past the kitchens, and then down another flight of steps, this one narrower and more dimly lit. They were now in a sub-level of the palace, not far from where Mast had once kept his prisoners. The air still stank slightly of stale sweat and another darker, more subtle smell—the scent of fear.

At the end of a short corridor was a set of three heavy doors composed of overlapping metal plates. Next to each of the doors was a control pad where one could type in the access code if necessary. Since Miala had already unlocked the doors from her workstation in the security chamber, the light on each control pad glowed green.

She stepped forward and palmed the lock to the center door. It slid open, and the contents of the vault were revealed to them.

Secretly, Miala had harbored visions of some glistening golden cave filled with treasure uncounted—visions inspired no doubt by some of the more lurid vids she had watched as a child, of space pirates and interstellar buccaneers. The truth was much more drab, yet no less rewarding. Inside the vault were neatly stacked storage containers and crates. Thorn walked up to one and opened the lid, revealing glistening silver-gilt units. Miala had never seen so much money in her life.

Eryk Thorn turned toward her, and the look of approval on his face seemed at that moment just as priceless to her as the riches contained in Mast's vaults. "Good work," he said.

"Thanks," she replied carelessly, but inside she was rejoicing. Was he actually smiling at her?

"We'll need to get some powered carts down here," he went on, surveying the contents of the vault with a practiced eye. "Have you seen any?"

Miala didn't hesitate. After all, she'd spent enough time

here that the compound was as familiar to her as her own home. "There are two in the garages, and another one down near the back gates."

"Good," he said. "Why don't you get the cart by the back gate, and I'll bring in the two from the garage. It'll take a few trips, but we should be able to get everything into the *Fury*."

Nice, friendly name for a ship, she thought, although she knew better than to say anything aloud. At least she was reassured that he had said "we" and didn't appear to be planning to kill her any time soon.

Of course, she thought wryly a while later, as they both returned with the carts and began loading the contents of the vaults onto them, *there's no point in him doing away with me now. He'd just have to do all this work by himself.*

It was soon evident that it would take far more than one trip with the carts to load everything. Thorn had seemed sanguine about being able to haul away the contents of all three vaults, but Miala found herself wondering just how much the cargo hold of his one smallish ship—a highly modified Eridani Vector-class—could really carry. But once they had deposited one load in the *Fury*'s hold, it appeared there was still plenty of room left, and she trudged back down to the vaults with him, even as she wondered whether he was going to work her until she dropped from hunger or exhaustion.

Miala tried to remember how many hours it had been since her meager breakfast. At least six or seven, which normally wouldn't have been so bad, but moving the various crates and caskets was backbreaking work.

"Thorn," she said finally, after they were midway through the third load. "I have to stop for a while."

He deposited another crate on the cart closest to him. "Why?"

She reached back to rub the part that ached the worst, right at the base of her spine. "Because, unlike you, I'm not some sort of machine! I'm starving, and my back is killing me!"

"Your back," he repeated, eyes narrowing slightly. He considered her for a moment, and Miala felt herself grow tense. Was this it, then? Would it be now, when she revealed her weakness, that he would decide she was of no further use to him and would rid himself of her once and for all?

Still, she refused to let him see her fear. "Yes, my back!" she snapped. "I appreciate the need to get all this loaded on your ship, but we do need to take a break every once in a while. Besides, you wouldn't have had any of this if it weren't for me!"

She had expected some sort of argument. Instead, he nodded and said, "True." Then he took a step toward her. Then another.

Not knowing what else to do, Miala stood her ground. He was close—so close she could practically sense the heat radiating off his body from his exertions. Slowly he reached out, his hand descending until he touched the small of her back. Then she could feel his strong fingers begin to knead at the aching muscles, as if he could dispel her exhaustion merely with his touch.

Of all the ways she had dreamed of him touching her, this was one she had never considered. Still, she was afraid to protest, afraid to try to move away—and it did feel good, she had to admit to herself, especially when he brought down his other hand and began to rub her back in earnest, powerful fingers digging into her flesh.

A small moan escaped Miala's lips. Once she had let it out, she wished beyond anything that she could take it back, but the sensations rushing over her now were too strong, too unlike anything she had ever felt before.

"Better?" Thorn asked, again with that quirk at the corner of his mouth. He paused, but kept his hands placed firmly against the small of her back.

A wave of fury rushed over her then, and she opened her mouth to fling back some sarcastic retort, some insult, *anything*—but he was too fast for her. Before a word could escape her lips, his mouth was on hers, and he pulled her against him, holding her so tightly there was no hope of escape. There was nothing except the feel of his mouth touching her mouth, the sensation of his body pressed up against hers, the strange roaring in her ears as she realized what was happening.

It wasn't her first kiss. No, she had given that up years ago, as so many other girls in Aldis Nova had—out near the lean-to behind Alt the mechanic's shop in a place that afforded shelter both from prying eyes and the glare of Iradia's sun. The boy had been in her class and had been called Drix, and that was all she remembered of him. At any rate, that kiss compared to this one roughly the same way Thorn's small ship compared to a Quasar-class troop ship. Drix, she recalled, hadn't seem to know what he was doing at all, whereas Eryk Thorn obviously did. He seemed to fill her universe, the taste of him, the clean smell of his sweat, the slight rasp of his unshaven cheek against her skin, and she knew she was lost. She could no more tear herself from his grasp than a starship could free itself from the gravitational pull of a black hole.

Finally, though, he lifted his mouth from hers, although he still held her closely, as if he were afraid she would turn and bolt if he let her go completely. He watched her, even as she stared back up at him, into those dark eyes that seemed black as the depths of space, the thin-lipped mouth that just seconds ago had been pressed so firmly against hers.

Miala took a breath, then another. It required a conscious effort, as if somehow the autonomous systems regulating her heartbeat and breathing had somehow been disrupted by that kiss.

"I've been wanting to do that for a while," Thorn said at last.

Again she could feel her face flush, but Miala also was strangely triumphant. Eryk Thorn had wanted to kiss *her*, of all people. She wondered what sort of exotic women he had known across the galaxy, then clamped down on that thought. His past didn't matter. What mattered was that he had wanted her, here and now.

"So have I," she whispered, and he smiled.

"I could tell," he replied.

So much for all her feeble attempts at trying to conceal her feelings. Still, what did it matter now? He had wanted the same thing, after all.

She held herself in the encircling strength of his arms, feeling the slow rise and fall of his chest against hers. How odd that he should seem so calm, while her own heart pounded against her ribcage and each breath felt shaky and jagged.

He watched her for a few seconds, and then she could see him bending down to kiss her once again. She raised her lips to his, waiting for that electric moment when they touched.

It never came. Instead Miala heard the familiar shrilling of the perimeter alarm, and Thorn stepped away from her immediately.

"Darlester," he said, "has impeccable timing..."

VII

THORN TURNED IMMEDIATELY and began moving toward the steps while Miala hurried after him, still not completely comprehending. "How do you know it's Darlester?"

"I don't. But it seems like his style. Probably took him a few days to gather all the necessary reinforcements."

They both ran up the stairs, Miala trailing in Eryk Thorn's purposeful wake. She knew where he was heading, of course—back to the security station. How unfair that Rafe Darlester—or whoever the new intruders turned out to be—should show up when she and Thorn were so close to loading all the treasure and getting off Iradia forever.

And when you were so close to getting kissed again, she thought, but she refused to dwell on that. There was a time and a place for everything, after all, and this definitely was not the time to be thinking of anything quite so frivolous— even though she fancied she could still feel the touch of his lips against hers, the pressure of his hands against her back.

But once they entered the security station, the main view-screen did show the same ore-processor-on-steroids vehicle

Miala had seen the other night, although it looked odd in the harsh sunlight, its dark sides gleaming with a peculiar oily shine. The light on the comm station was blinking, indicating an incoming transmission.

Thorn went straight to the comm, although Miala noticed he was careful to toggle the switch that changed the outgoing signal to audio only before he allowed the message to come up on-screen.

Immediately the viewscreen filled with the not-alto-gether-pleasant image of Rafe Darlester, who sat in a large command chair that was flanked by a pair of well-mus-cled goons, both human, although the one on the right had the broadest shoulders she had ever seen, and she guessed he had been dipping into some black-market ste-roids. Darlester had fixed what he apparently thought was a pleasant smile on his face, although the impression was spoiled somewhat by a pair of platinum-capped incisors. He leaned toward the viewer slightly and said, "Greetings, defenders of Mast's holdings! I feel that perhaps we got off on the wrong foot the other evening—may I know whom I have the honor of addressing?"

Miala raised her eyebrows at Thorn, who shook his head slightly even as he gave her a brief, tight grin. Did this Darlester person think he was speaking to members of the Consortium Council or something?

"That information is not necessary for our conversa-tion," Eryk Thorn said, after a pause. "What do you want, Darlester?"

The smuggler's pouchy eyes tightened briefly before he replied, "I fear you have me at a disadvantage, sir. You have my name, but I don't have yours. In addition, you keep your face from me. I would not call this a promising prelude to negotiations."

Smoothly, Thorn said, "Call me a lieutenant to Mast, if you must."

"Then perhaps you should consider giving yourself a battlefield promotion, considering that your master is now scattered in a thousand pieces across the Arkellian wastes." Again Darlester leaned toward the viewer. He did not improve on close-up. "And judging by the amount of other body parts we found near the Malverdine Cliffs, it appears that most, if not all, of Mast's coterie perished with him. Were you planning on defending the compound alone… indefinitely?"

"Only until I got rid of you," Thorn returned, and Miala couldn't help but smile. She got the feeling that Eryk Thorn ate guys like Rafe Darlester for breakfast.

Darlester's platinum-accented smile grew a little tight around the edges. Still, his voice was smooth enough as he replied, "You may find that a little more difficult this time around. And after all, I'm only trying to reclaim what's mine."

"What's yours?" Thorn echoed.

"A rather large shipment of silk, which Mast stole from my warehouses. You understand—I'm just a legitimate businessman trying to make my way in the galaxy. It's difficult when the competition steals your product."

"So you came in here, guns blazing, all to recover a stolen silk shipment." Thorn's tone was neutral, but somehow he managed to convey a wealth of skepticism in that very blandness.

"One can never be too careful," Darlester replied, settling back into his oversized chair. The goons to either side of him crossed their arms, and Miala watched, fascinated, at the display of rippling muscle this action precipitated.

"So if I return this missing silk, we can call it even?"

Darlester smiled then, a smile as oily and unpleasant as the finish on his oversized ore processor. "Not quite. You see, I incurred significant damages the other evening—loss of personnel, repairs to my vehicle, that sort of thing. I expect to be compensated."

"I would call those justifiable damages, considering you attacked the compound first."

The smuggler didn't even blink. "Not at all. We were forced to open fire after your perimeter defenses launched the first salvo."

Despite her distaste for the man, Miala had to respect his sheer audacity. She knew for a fact that the defense system was just that—once the security wards were set off, the compound's shields were immediately raised. She and Thorn hadn't gone on the offensive until Darlester's ground troops had begun to assault the front gates. After that— well, Darlester was right about one thing. Thorn had decimated a significant number of personnel that night.

"Interesting," Thorn replied, "since my records show that I didn't begin firing until your troops attacked the place."

Darlester waved a hand. "Semantics. At any rate, I calculate that approximately sixty percent of the contents of Mast's vaults should take care of your debt."

"That a fact?"

The smuggler allowed himself a smile. "Yes."

Miala had been watching Eryk Thorn carefully during this exchange, and his expression had never changed throughout. Now, however, he frowned slightly, then rubbed one finger over his chin, as if considering some possible action. He glanced away from the viewscreen, gave Miala a thoughtful look, then nodded to himself even as he hit the "mute" button on the comm.

"Think you can handle this guy for a few minutes?" he asked.

Appalled, Miala looked over at the viewscreen, at the smugly complacent features of Rafe Darlester. It was definitely the face of a man who was used to getting what he wanted. Did Thorn really think she could deal with Darlester without getting the two of them into even more trouble? Still, she knew she couldn't let her companion down. Obviously he had thought of something, but he needed her to keep Darlester occupied while he slipped away.

"What do you need me to do?" she asked.

"Just keep him talking. Pretend you're my assistant. Act like we're going along with his demands." Thorn gave her a quick glance. "Take your hair out of that braid."

"What?" Miala looked up at him, wondering whether he had finally begun to lose his stranglehold on sanity. "What the hell difference does that make?"

"Rafe Darlester likes a pretty girl. As soon as I'm out of this room, I want you to put the comm on visual. But you should let your hair down."

She glared at him even as she reached up to pull away

the bit of string that bound the end of her braid. Typical that he would think to distract Rafe Darlester that way, instead of employing her to man the cannons or perform some other infinitely more exciting task. Instead he wanted her to play secretary! She decided it wasn't worth arguing over, however, and shook the loose ends of her long red hair over her shoulders.

"All right?" she demanded.

"Much better," he agreed, and for a second she could see his gaze moving over the unbound lengths of her hair. Then he fixed her eyes with his, all business once more. "Just keep him talking. Agree to anything—act as if you're looking up information on the computer. Flirt if you have to."

"You've got to be kidding," she said flatly, looking over her shoulder toward the impatient visage of Rafe Darlester on the viewscreen.

Thorn didn't bother to reply, instead giving her a small handheld. "When I give the signal, drop the rear shields."

"What are you going to do?"

"You'll see." And with that cryptic remark he left the room.

Miala sighed and approached the comm, then toggled the switch to activate the video feed on her end. "Um... Mister Darlester?"

The smuggler, who had been clearing his throat in an ostentatious manner and was obviously annoyed at being left hanging for so long, straightened up in his chair. His expression of petulant irritation slowly transformed into a small leer as he focused on her features. "And who might you be?"

"My name is Miala." The second after she said the words she realized that perhaps handing him her real name hadn't been the wisest thing to do. Still, there was nothing she could do about it now. "I'm told I need to assist you with reparations?"

He watched her for a moment, apparently thinking over her sudden appearance. "Where's your boss?"

Damn, Miala thought. *How do I keep getting into these messes?* But she managed to arrange what she hoped was a pleasant smile on her face and replied, "Checking your inventory, sir."

He lifted a bushy eyebrow, then nodded slowly.

Not allowing herself to give a relieved sigh, Miala turned to the computer and began pulling up the inventory lists of the vault contents. It seemed a better idea for her to appear as legitimate as possible, and at any rate she was sure that Darlester couldn't see the contents of the screen before her. Surely Mast had to have been storing silk down there along with everything else, although she and Eryk Thorn had not found any in the first two vaults they emptied.

Hoping she had the appropriate expression of helpful concern fixed on her features, Miala ticked her way through the inventory lists. She even went so far as to slide a finger over the computer screen as she went along, so Rafe Darlester could see how industrious she was being in restoring his stolen goods.

After a few moments, she thought she had located the items in question. "Aha!" she exclaimed, and then smiled winningly at the smuggler. "I think I've found it, sir. Forty-five cases of moon-moth silk?"

"Forty—" Darlester began to splutter, then cleared his throat and smiled...a fat, greedy smile. "That sounds about right."

Miala was fairly certain what had been stolen from him wasn't even half that number—just one case constituted a fortune, let alone forty-five—but if it kept him happy and unaware of whatever Eryk Thorn might be up to...

"And then, sir," she went on, trying to recall the brisk yet formal way Captain Malick's underlings had reported to him, and hoping that sort of delivery made her sound more efficient, "there is the matter of the damage to your vehicle?"

"Well, yes," Darlester said, clearing his throat and squinting, as if he were trying to return his focus back to her. Apparently the mere mention of forty-five cases of silk had unsettled him somewhat. "I had to replace the plating all along one side, and then there was the damage to the guns..."

"I assume you kept the bill?" she asked, then wondered whether batting her eyelashes would be too much. She decided it would, and instead gave Darlester another sticky-sweet smile.

He cleared his throat again. "I'm sure I could lay my hands on it if I had to," he muttered, for a second looking flustered.

"Well, we can do with an estimate for now," Miala said, straining to keep her false smile from turning into a grin. This was beginning to be downright fun.

She could almost hear the coins jingling in Darlester's head as he calculated how much he could plausibly claim. "Thirty thousand," he said finally.

You could have bought a whole new vehicle for that much, she thought, but of course said no such thing, instead pretending to make a notation in the computer. "Anything else?"

"Of course," Darlester responded immediately. "The little matter of twenty-two of my men, dead! And most of them with families—I'm a generous man, my dear, but even I can't hope to support that many dependents."

It took every effort of will Miala had not to burst out laughing at that remark. She was certain Darlester would rather send all those hungry mouths to the grave along with their fathers before he'd stoop to support a single one of them, but she had to admit the man's overweening self-delusion was somewhat amusing.

"Well, sir," she said after a moment, when she was sure she could maintain a reasonably sober tone of voice, "of course no one can put a price on a human life, but—"

"I'll take ten thousand for each of them," he said promptly.

None of which would make it to any surviving dependents, Miala was sure—if they even existed, which she was beginning to doubt. She gave a dubious glance at the two henchmen who flanked Rafe Darlester and thought that if they were a representative sample of the smuggler's staff, then any one of them would have had a difficult time finding someone with whom he could procreate.

"So I believe," she said, tapping away at the computer keys, although in actuality she was doing nothing but scrolling between two inventory lists, "that would make it a grand total of a quarter-million units, plus the forty-five cases of silk?"

He frowned, and paused for a moment. Miala fancied she could see his lips moving slightly as he did the sums in his head. Then an expression of lazy greed moved over his fleshy features. "That sounds about right."

Damn. She'd been halfway hoping he'd put up more of a fight—it was beginning to look as if they'd settle this more or less peacefully, and yet there was still no sign of Eryk Thorn. Thinking quickly, she asked, "Would you like that in cash or in kind?"

Darlester sat up straighter in his chair. "What did you have in mind?"

"Only that we could offer you more silk, or some other sort of goods that perhaps you could get a better price for, exchange rates being what they are. You could make back your damages and still profit."

The smuggler scratched his chin, watching her carefully. Then he smiled, and the glare of Iradia's sun glinted off his platinum-capped incisors. "You've got a good head on your shoulders, girl," he said, in what Miala supposed he thought were ingratiating tones. "Now Mast's gone, maybe you should think about jumping ship and coming to work for me."

Okay, now would be a good time, Thorn! she thought, even as she hurriedly fixed another manufactured smile on her lips. "That's um, very flattering, sir, but I still have work to do here—"

"I could make it worth your while," he interjected, and there was no mistaking the leer he gave her along with those words.

Miala thought she'd rather jump off the Malverdine Cliffs than go to work for a man like Rafe Darlester, but she was saved from a reply by the squawk of the handheld and Eryk Thorn's command, "Now, Miala!"

Without thinking she pulled up the screen that controlled the rear defenses and shut them down. From somewhere behind Rafe Darlester she heard someone call out, "They're dropping the rear defense shields, sir!"

The smuggler pinned her down with a furious stare. "What the hell are you playing at?"

In all honesty Miala was able to reply, "I don't know what you're talking about, sir!"

With a curse Darlester heaved himself up out of his seat, but by then Miala knew it was too late. She had caught a glimpse from the secondary viewscreens, the ones that surveyed the rear of the compound, and now she saw what Eryk Thorn had planned.

His arrowhead-shaped ship came out of the late afternoon blaze of the sun, apparently hurtling headlong toward Darlester's modified ore processor. The cannons of the land vehicle had already begun to fire, but the first bolts bounced harmlessly off the ship's shielding even as Thorn banked at the last moment—just as two torpedoes dropped from the underside of the *Fury* and plowed directly into the ore processor.

The explosions were immediate, and oddly satisfying. Two huge gouts of orange-red flames blew out from either side of the smuggler's vehicle, even as the image on the viewscreen faded to a wall of static. Miala quickly shut off the comm and turned her attention to the feed from the primary security camera, the one fixed on the front gate.

Not pausing to enjoy the success of his first pass, Thorn came back around again and dropped another pair of projectiles. They, too, connected, and the sporadic firing that had continued after the first torpedoes hit abruptly ceased. Explosion after explosion shook the vehicle, followed by waves of black smoke. By the time it had cleared, Miala could see that the ore processor had been completely flattened.

Miala slowly let out a breath, and then shook her head. There was something very odd about being in the middle of a conversation with a person and then having that person suddenly snuffed out of existence. Not that the universe would miss Rafe Darlester, she thought, but it was still a peculiar sensation. One minute he had been there, and the next—

And the next there had been nothing but static. Static and smoke. But at least he was gone, and that meant one less thing for her and Eryk Thorn to worry about.

She looked up and he was suddenly there, pausing in the doorway to the guard chamber.

"Nice shooting," she commented.

He shrugged. "They were an easy target. Hadn't even bothered with particle shielding."

"How did you know?"

"I analyzed the data from the first attack. Sloppy. Then again, most land-based attackers don't use torpedoes, so I suppose they weren't out of line in thinking they were safe." The black eyes glinted at her, his amusement showing in the slight crinkles at the outer corners. "You did a good job of keeping Darlester talking."

"Well, it's easy when you've got someone who likes the sound of his own voice." She stood, feeling suddenly awkward, and pushed her loose hair back over her shoulders. "Of course, he also liked what I was promising him."

"Which was?"

"Forty-five cases of silk and about a quarter-million in loose change."

"No wonder he wanted to go on talking."

Miala crossed her arms, and fixed Eryk Thorn with what she hoped was a no-nonsense stare. "Well, I had to keep feeding him what he wanted to hear, considering how long it took you to finally get it together."

He lifted an eyebrow. "Ever been on a spaceship?"

"No—so what?"

"Even the fastest ship takes a few minutes to power up. You can't force some things."

Once again, he was right. Whenever she was around Thorn, Miala seemed to be constantly reminded of how little she actually knew about how the galaxy worked, of how sheltered her life had really been. It was not a feeling she enjoyed. For the first time she realized she had always thought of herself as—how had Thorn put it?—a big fish in a little pond. She'd always considered herself superior to the denizens of Aldis Nova, people whom she'd considered to be narrow-minded at best and positively backward at worst. It humbled her to realize how insignificant she really was.

"Miala."

She lifted her head to look at him. Someone who hadn't spent the last week watching his face would have thought there was no expression on those dark features, but she knew better. There was approval in his eyes, approval and growing respect. Once again he had set a task for her, and she had not been found wanting. She had a feeling that it was no easy thing to earn Eryk Thorn's respect.

"I suppose we'd better get back to work," she said, and at that he actually smiled.

"I had something a little different in mind," he replied, and held out his hand.

She took it, wondering what was going to come next. She should have known.

"I hate being interrupted," he said, pulling her toward him.

Once again his mouth met hers, and she let herself fall into the embrace, letting him surround her, become her universe, until nothing else mattered. She had only an intellectual understanding of what drowning was, but she thought dimly that this must be what it felt like—to swirl down into darkness, to feel nothing but the pounding of your heart in your breast, the pulse of blood in your ears and throat.

Finally he let her go, and she stepped back, gasping a little.

He smiled a bit, just that small lift at the corner of his mouth, then said, "Now we get back to work." And with that he turned and headed back out into the corridor, obviously expecting Miala to follow him.

Which of course she did, her pulse still racing and breath coming to her with difficulty. As she trailed after Thorn, she wondered if she would ever begin to understand him—whether he was just toying with her, or whether he felt for her even a little.

What frightened her was that she found she didn't care. As long as she could be with him, nothing else mattered.

VIII

THE FORTY-FIVE CRATES OF SILK turned out to be hidden in the third and final vault, just as Miala had suspected. She paused in her exertions for a moment as Thorn stood and looked at the neatly stacked crates, his eyebrows creasing slightly. Probably he was trying to decide whether it would all fit in the already overloaded cargo hold of the *Fury*.

"We're leaving it," he said finally, and Miala stared up at him in shock.

"Leaving it?" she demanded. "Do you have any idea how much that stuff is worth?"

"Probably more than you," he replied, fixing her with a quelling dark gaze. "But I'm not a smuggler or a silk dealer. I've got no use for it."

Miala opened her mouth again, took a closer look at Thorn, then decided it was better not to argue. He was right—of course she had no idea what the street value of that much silk could be. However, she was fairly sure it was quite a bit, probably as much as the treasure they'd already loaded.

Still, he must know what he was doing. She thought for a moment of the difficulties involved in trying to move that much silk around, realizing that without connections they'd have a very tough time unloading the stuff. While she didn't know all the ins and outs of the silk trade, she did know that if you weren't on file with the silk merchants' guild, you could be in big trouble if you tried to sell it as an indie.

"Besides," he added, pushing the button to close the doors to the vault, "if the bones aren't picked completely clean when the next scavengers show up, there's less of a chance they'll start wondering where the rest of the treasure went."

It took a few seconds for the full import of his words to sink in, but once it did, Miala cast a worried look up at Thorn. "So you think there'll be more?"

"Of course. The universe has an unending supply of scum." He must have noticed the concern on her face, for he went on, "But don't worry—we'll be long gone before the next one shows up."

That did reassure her, as well as the fact that he had said "we." The fear had still been there, buried but not forgotten, the worry that he would just go off and leave her here once the treasure was loaded. Even as she watched Eryk swoop down on Darlester's ore processor, one small part of her mind had wondered whether he would just keep going once he finished his attack run. After all, he was on board a ship already loaded with the bulk of Mast's treasure. There had been nothing to stop him from heading on out into space.

Nothing, except…except what? He had kissed her, but even Miala knew she wasn't naïve enough to think that necessarily meant anything. People left all the time. Her mother had run off, and she'd abandoned a husband and baby. All Eryk Thorn would have left behind was a silly girl who'd been foolish enough to think he owed her some kind of debt.

But he didn't leave, she thought fiercely. *He came back, and he's still here now. That's got to count for something.*

"When are we going?" she asked. Best to confront the source of her worry at once—not that she would necessarily know whether he was lying to her or not.

His reply was immediate. "Tomorrow morning. I've been monitoring the local transmissions and just hearing the usual chatter, nothing to indicate anyone is planning on coming here any time soon. We've bought some breathing room. And the ship's ready to go if any more trouble crops up sooner than that."

"Good," she said, perhaps with a bit more depth of emotion than she had intended. Thorn gave her a searching look, and she added, "I could do with some rest first. And a decent meal."

He nodded, but didn't look particularly enthusiastic.

"Steaks straight from Gaia," Miala offered, and he raised an eyebrow.

"Where'd you get those?"

"Lost treasures of Mast's refrigeration units," she replied.

"Appropriate."

"Dinner at nineteen hundred, then," Miala said, and was gratified to see him nod. After all, they deserved a little celebration for their last night on Iradia…

She tried to make everything as perfect as she could. Cooking for her father all those years had certainly given

Miala a certain level of skill, for of course they'd never been able to afford a mech to take on those sorts of tasks. But they'd also never had the funds to buy the sort of foodstuffs she was making now for Eryk Thorn, and she fretted over their preparation much more than she ever had over a meal for her father.

Of course there were the gorgeous pink beef filets, but along with the steaks she concocted a rich side dish of delicate rosy-veined tubers with cream, accompanied by fresh-baked bread and a salad of various off-world fruits that she'd found in a back corner of one of the freezers. The wine cellars located just below the kitchens yielded all kinds of riches, but Miala had no real idea of what she was looking at or what would work best with the meal she had prepared. After scanning the various labels (those that she could read; several were in alien scripts), she stood there for a moment, irresolute, and finally grabbed two bottles: one red wine and one pale straw-colored one. Thorn could decide which kind he wanted—if he drank at all, she realized suddenly. Still, from what she had read and what she had seen on the various 'net programs, wine was usually expected with dinner, and she did not want to appear ignorant.

Mast of course had had no real use for a dining hall, but the compound had first been built by a group of Buddhist monks…before they figured out that the frontier world had very little use for such a peaceful philosophy…and so the old dining room was still there, more or less intact. The other kitchen drudges had mentioned that it was used every once in a while, if Mast had important enough visitors, but that had never happened during Miala's tenure at the compound.

She wiped down the old polished travertine dining table and dusted off the rustic wooden chairs, then found an ancient pair of carved stone candlesticks and a box of candles in one of the kitchen cupboards, along with some faded but clean table linens. The candles intrigued her; she'd seen lighted candles once years before at a friend's home as part of their holiday celebrations, but they were a rarity in Aldis Nova, an archaic tradition that even then Miala had found strangely charming. Now she thought they would add an elegant touch to the table.

Allowing herself once last quick glance around the kitchen to make sure everything was in hand, Miala then ducked out and hastened up the steps to the slave girls' dormitory. It was almost 19:00, and she'd told Thorn she would call him on the handheld when dinner was ready, but she had one last thing to take care of. Off went the serviceable but now stained tunic and pants she had been wearing, and she drew out of the wardrobe an outfit she'd spied several days ago but hadn't thought she ever have a reason to wear. Like Genna's other pre-slave cast-offs, it consisted of a fitted tunic over narrowly cut pants, but this one was of shimmering copper-colored fabric, embroidered in black and gold around the deeply cut neckline and side-slit hem. It was sleeveless, and in the trinket box the slave girls had shared Miala found a stack of gold-colored bangles, five for each wrist, and a pair of dangling earrings to finish off the look. The flat sandals she had been wearing all along would have to do.

Once she was done, Miala paused in front of the mirror

in the dressing area and surveyed herself carefully. Thorn had obviously liked seeing her hair down, and she had to admit the effect was good, especially the way the long coppery-red strands blended into the silky fabric of the tunic. There were pots of cosmetics stacked neatly along the counter, but Miala didn't really know what to do with them, and now was not the time to for experimentation. Instead she settled for giving her hair a few quick brush strokes before she turned away from the mirror and hurried back downstairs, all the while telling herself she was making a fuss over nothing. Thorn did not seem like the sort of man to be impressed by fancy clothes—far from it—but Miala told herself that it would be disrespectful to the meal she had prepared to sit down at table in the same disheveled garments she had been wearing. Let Eryk Thorn make of her appearance what he would.

The sun was low on the horizon when she returned to the dining room. Miala lifted the mechanized lighter she'd found in the kitchen to first one, then the other of the two candles she had set out on the table, and watched as the flickering light combined with the ruddy glow of the sunset to turn the chamber into a swirl of red and copper that reflected off the polished stone of the table and the faded frescoes on the walls. The color found an echo in her hair and the clothes she wore, and for a second she felt as if she were suspended in light, floating on the edge of another world. Then she blinked, and the impression was gone, though the room was still awash in copper-tinted hues.

She lifted the handheld. "Any time you're ready," she said.

Thorn's voice came through immediately. "Got it."

Miala set the handheld down on a sideboard and returned to the kitchen, where she transferred the food to its serving pieces and began moving it to the table. She'd already unstoppered the wine and set the red bottle in front of Eryk Thorn's place setting and the pale yellow one in front of hers. The plates she had set out were old, old metal, probably left over from the monastery days as well. The monks had been ascetic to the extreme, but even they had had to eat—well, at least before one of Iradia's crime lords decided their compound was the perfect place for his base of operations and came in and exterminated the lot. The oversized wine goblets were newer and bore all the signs of Mast's trademark ostentation—glass bowls set into dark metal bases that looked like writhing serpents—but she hadn't been able to find anything more appropriate and so had set them down on the table with a sigh.

"Expecting company?" Thorn asked, pausing at the entry to the dining chamber and eyeing the elaborate spread.

"Just you," she replied, hoping the ruddy light that spilled in through the arched windows hid the flush in her cheeks.

He made no reply, instead taking in her elaborate costume with a slightly arched eyebrow. Then he gave an almost imperceptible shake of his head before moving to the chair at the head of the table and sitting down in it.

Miala gritted her teeth and told herself, *Count to ten...*

If that was how he was going to be, fine. She pulled out her own chair with a rough scrape of wood across stone and settled a napkin in her lap. "I thought it would be nice to celebrate my last night on Iradia," she said evenly. "I'm sure planet-hopping is old news to you, but I've never been anywhere but here."

After a quick survey of the table, Thorn nodded. "This looks about as good as anything I've had off-world."

"Well—thank you." Once again he had caught her off-guard with a compliment. To cover her confusion, Miala lifted the ruddy-hued bottle and asked, "Wine?"

"Normally, no, but—" He lifted his shoulders. "I suppose it couldn't hurt."

She poured him a glass, filling it only halfway. Those goblets were enormous, scaled apparently to Mast's prodigious appetites; it would be far too easy to overindulge if one didn't pay attention. After she did the same with her own goblet, she set the wine bottle back down, then noticed with some surprise that Thorn had lifted his glass and apparently was waiting for her to do the same.

"To Arlen Mast," he said, a sly glint in his eyes, "without whom this feast would not be possible."

"To Mast," she echoed, unable to repress a smile.

Really, Thorn had the oddest sense of humor. She lifted the glass to her lips and drank, feeling the warmth of the heavy wine work its way down her throat. The sensation made her feel very adult and somewhat wicked. She's only tasted wine once before, at an engagement reception for a school friend of hers, and it had been nothing like this. At the time she had thought wine rather sour and nasty, and certainly not worth the fuss. But this deep red vintage tasted of fruit and earth and an alien sun that made things grow instead of burning them into dust, and Miala thought she could definitely get used to it.

After that they were silent for a few moments as she loaded Thorn's and her own plates with all the various foods she had spent the afternoon preparing, and they began to eat. It seemed years since she'd had a proper meal besides hastily scrounged bites. The drudges had never gotten that much to eat, and she had been careless about meals once she was on her own. Now the tender meat and carefully seasoned side dishes tasted like a little piece of heaven.

Thorn appreciated the meal as well, she could tell. She'd spent too many years feeding her father not to know when a man was enjoying his food. He ate efficiently and quickly, but not so rapidly that she couldn't see him pause every once in a while to savor a bite.

"Computers and cooking," he said at length, after taking a small sip of wine. "Any other hidden skills I should know about?"

"Not that I'm aware of," Miala said, pleased that he seemed to be enjoying himself. "Although I should warn you that I play a mean hand of poker."

"I don't gamble," he said flatly. "Waste of time."

Lifting an eyebrow, Miala replied, "My father preferred to think of it as a game of skill. He found it an interesting way to teach me probability."

"Mmm." Thorn applied himself to another piece of filet.

"My father didn't gamble," she said, suddenly irritated by what she saw as a silent condemnation. "We liked to play cards together."

He looked up from his food and gave her a slow, measuring stare. "Did I say anything?"

She had to admit that he hadn't, really. What was it about him that always made her feel on the defensive? There was no way, after all, that Eryk Thorn could have known her father's fascination with poker was one of the chief reasons they never had enough money to get off-planet. In silence she poured herself another half-glass of wine, trying to ignore Thorn's pointed stare as she did so.

"So what about your father?" she asked finally.

"My father didn't play poker, either."

"Funny. I mean, what did he do?"

Was it her imagination, or did his jaw muscles tighten involuntarily, just for a second? It was hard to tell in the flickering light, but she noticed he lifted his own glass and took another drink before replying. "I have no idea. Besides spend money on whores, that is."

Oh. She knew she'd hit a sore subject, but Miala couldn't think of a good way to backpedal without sounding even more tone-deaf. "So you didn't know your father?"

"No. I was born in a brothel on Mykiel V. Anything else you want to know?"

She shook her head, wishing she had just kept her mouth shut after all, and watched as he refilled his plate. The man definitely could eat when the opportunity presented itself, but she supposed that was just another survival tactic. *Might as well eat when the eating's good*, she thought. She wondered who Eryk Thorn's father had been, and from there tried to imagine what the mercenary must have looked like as a little boy and failed miserably. He was one of those people who seemed to have sprung full-grown into the universe.

The silence between them had grown tense with that one brittle sentence of his. Miala, at a loss but sensing she should say something, commented, "My mother took off when I was six months old, so I only knew one of my parents, too."

She hadn't expected sympathy, and she got none. Thorn speared another piece of filet, then chewed it carefully before saying, "That's not always a bad thing."

How in the world was she supposed to reply to that? Casually she lifted her wine goblet and made an off-hand gesture before taking a sip. "You never went looking for him?"

He lifted his shoulders, but the dark eyes watching her were careful, measuring, almost as if he had told her these things just to see how she reacted. "I didn't see the point. Anyway, it turns out he died before I was even born."

Miala considered his words. She'd always thought if she did get the chance to get off Iradia, then she would do what she could to find out what had happened to her mother. Whether she'd have the courage to confront the woman who had abandoned her so many years ago, she didn't know, but somehow the notion of at least knowing whether her mother was alive or dead appealed to her.

For the first time she contemplated the notion of just letting it go, of getting on with her life. What difference would it make, after all? Even seeing her mother wouldn't return all those years Miala had spent without her.

"I guess I can see why you'd feel that way," she said, after a long pause.

He lifted his glass toward her, as if in salute. "Now you're getting it."

Was he mocking her, ever so slightly? Sometimes it was impossible to tell. However, she chose to believe he wasn't, mostly because she had grown weary of feeling that she was a source of private amusement to him.

"Anyhow," she went on, wondering whether it was between the ninth and tenth or fourteenth and fifteenth sips of wine that she had begun to feel a little dizzy, "what's the plan after we leave Iradia?"

"I was going to ask you the same thing. You're the one who wanted off-planet."

I knew that, Miala thought. "Right, then." Frowning slightly, she gazed at Thorn, realized she was staring at his mouth, and shifted her glance so it appeared she was looking past his shoulder to the age-smudged fresco on the wall behind him. "So how much is my take, anyway?"

"Don't know for sure. Probably five, six million."

Blinking, Miala studied his face carefully to see if he was joking, then decided that he probably wasn't. With a hand that shook just a little, she tore off a piece of bread and put it in her mouth, chewing thoughtfully. Five million units. With that she could go anywhere in the galaxy, do pretty much anything she wanted. But she knew what she should do, what her father would have wanted her to do.

"I need to go to a university. A good one," she said finally.

He appeared nonplussed. "What for?"

Surprised, she looked at him for a moment, studying his features in the uncertain candlelight as she considered her reply. Going to a university—or maybe one of the GDF's training academies—was the only ambition of anyone Miala had known who had the slightest bit of gumption. It was the only way to get off Iradia and earn some respectability at the same time. And her father had certainly drummed into her the necessity for a formal education. Her thoughts had run in that path for so long she had never considered any alternative, never believed there could be anything else for her. But obviously Thorn thought differently.

"I'm guessing you never went to college," she said.

At that he really did give what sounded like a genuine laugh. "You're guessing right." He lifted his glass and drank, black eyes watching her closely over the rim of the gaudy cup. "Can't say I missed it."

Miala lifted her shoulders. "It's just what I always thought I'd do. Go to a good university, then work as an analyst somewhere."

"Sounds safe."

Those words made her want to cringe. Safe, was that how he thought of her? "Or not," she said boldly. "I guess with five million units I can do whatever I want, right?"

He was silent for a moment, then replied, "I think your first plan's a good one."

Oh, he was impossible. At that moment, Miala thought if someone showed up on the spot and offered her a full scholarship at the university on Eridani, she'd turn it down just to spite Thorn. "I don't even know whether I can get into a decent school, anyway," she remarked. "My education here was pretty irregular, and most universities are sort of picky about that kind of thing. Who knows how long it will take to get someone to even look at my transcripts?"

"Shouldn't be a problem, if you flash enough units around," he said.

She wanted to retort that that wouldn't make any difference, but Miala knew better than to start another argument. This dinner wasn't going at all how she had planned. What had happened to the feeling of romance, of possibilities, that she had sensed when she first lit the candles and thought of the man who would soon be joining her in the copper-washed dining chamber?

He's being Eryk Thorn again, she thought, and rolled her eyes. Really, she would be better off rid of him. He could just drop her off on some nice planet, say Monteverde or even Eridani itself, and she could get her degree and bank her half of Mast's treasure—thank you very much for your assistance, Master Thorn, have a nice life. If only it were that easy.

"What are you going to do with your half?" Miala challenged, feeling reckless.

"Bank it," he said, imperturbable.

Again it was impossible to know whether he was joking or not. In desperation she said, "Thorn, if you don't shut up right now and kiss me, I think I'm going to throw this wine goblet at your head."

He smiled then, a slow, easy smile. "If that's what's bothering you—" And he pushed his chair back and stood, going over to her and raising her up out of her own chair.

Much better, Miala thought. *When he's kissing me, I don't think about how much I'd like to kill him.*

And as he continued to kiss her, she realized she didn't have to think about anything else at all. The universe seemed to compact itself down to the feel of his mouth on hers, the warmth of his body, the taste of the wine on his tongue.

And everything else, she decided, could wait.

IX

THEY WALKED IN SILENCE for a time along a sweeping terrace that hugged the circular main tower of Mast's compound. Probably it had been constructed by the monks as a platform for stargazing, though Miala doubted that any of the denizens of Mast's household had wasted much time watching the stars. Hot as the desert was during daylight hours, it was equally chill at night, although the warm sandstone of the building still radiated the heat it had stored up during the day.

Ixtal, the largest of Iradia's three moons, hung low in the eastern sky, a huge golden orb that cast a glittering track across the desert sands. Miala paused at the curved stone balustrade that edged the terrace, gazing down at the desolate landscape beneath her. She'd had the fancy that perhaps one last look at the world which had been her only home would arouse some feelings of nostalgia, but now she felt nothing but relief that after tomorrow she would never have to see these sand-scoured wastes again.

Thorn was quiet, watching her from the shadows. He had held her for some time in the candlelit dining hall, in a prolonged embrace from which she had emerged gasping once again and not quite sure what to do with herself. Luckily, the prosaic interruption of cleaning up after dinner had leveled her head somewhat, although at the time she had wondered why she was even bothering with the dishes or the mess in the kitchen. Certainly it was not out of respect for whichever crime lord or bandit might take over the compound next. Something in her had simply rebelled at leaving the place out of order. She'd spent too many years straightening up after her father, and keeping things tidy was ingrained in her by now.

At least Thorn made no protest when she pulled herself from his embrace, and he had even carried dishes into the kitchen in stoic silence. Once she was finished with the remnants of dinner, he had accompanied her here without protest, although even she wasn't sure at the time why she had come.

"What do you think's going on out there?" she asked finally, waving one hand in a general westerly direction, as if to indicate Iradia as a whole.

He turned his head in that direction. The warm golden light of the moon seemed to smooth out the scars and lingering redness that were constant reminders of the injuries he had sustained during the battle at the Malverdine Cliffs. "Fighting. Confusion. People dying."

"So how does that make it different from any other day?" she retorted.

Thorn allowed himself a small smile. "You sound like me."

"It's all this time I've been spending in your charming company."

Her words did not seem to anger him. Instead, he shook his head and stepped toward the balustrade to stand next to her. A chill tendril of desert wind caught in the dark close-cropped strands at his hairline, ruffling them slightly. "They've gotten farther this time than they have in the past, but they've got to know it can't last. Maybe not today, maybe not tomorrow, but sooner than they like, the Gaian Central Council is going to send a whole lot of ships and troops over here to make sure everything gets back to normal. Gaia pulls too much money out of this planet to just let it go."

"So is it safe to leave? Will they try to stop us?"

"Right now I'm guessing that whatever Gaian forces are still alive probably have more important things to worry about than us."

Miala shivered slightly, and Thorn dropped a casual arm around her, pulling her closer to him. Stupid of her to have come up here anyway without grabbing a cloak or shawl first, although she had to admit there were worse ways of staying warm than to have Eryk Thorn holding you close. The cold didn't seem to bother him at all, although his long-sleeved jumpsuit of course was warmer than the thin sleeveless tunic she wore.

"Eridani, or even Monteverde or Nova Angeles," he went on. "Someplace civilized. That's the sort of planet you need."

You need. Not *we* need. The words grated on her, though Miala tried to tell herself that the mercenary was simply giving her predicament precedence. He'd agreed to help her, and so his concern now was solely for her. She had no doubt that, if left to his own devices, he could fly right through a battle between Gaian and Iradian forces and come out the other side completely unscathed.

"I don't know anything about any of those planets," she said flatly, staring out into the empty moonlit desert. It must have been the wind that brought the stinging tears to her eyes.

"Planets are planets," he replied. "They all have good and bad. Some have more of one than the other." For a second his eyes narrowed, although whether it was a reaction to a sudden gust of wind or some internal reflection, she wasn't sure. "This one's pretty much a dump, though."

It wasn't even in her to defend her home world, for she knew he was right. Perhaps someone else could have seen something admirable in the tenacity of the silk harvesters and the other inhabitants who tried to scratch an honest living from this rock, but all Miala could do was wonder why anyone would live here when they had the rest of the galaxy to choose from.

"We'll have to see how far we can even get," he went on, and he, too, stared out into the desert night, as if unable to meet her eyes. "All those planets are several sectors away, and I'm guessing the Council will be sending as big a peacekeeping force as it can muster. We'll be dodging GDF ships no matter which direction we go."

"You'll figure out something," Miala replied, and tried to take comfort in the strength of his arm around her, the warmth radiating out from his body like the banked heat of Iradia's now-absent sun. "I trust you."

At those words he became still, almost rigid in his silence. She suddenly wondered how long it had been since anyone had said anything like that to Eryk Thorn—or whether anyone ever had. Possibly it had been imprudent of her, but she couldn't take the words back now, and for some reason she believed them. He could have betrayed her earlier today, and had not. Besides, she'd just spent the larger part of two months looking over her shoulder, not confiding in anyone, always afraid she would be caught before her work here in Mast's compound was done, and it felt better than she had thought possible to lay some of her burden on Thorn's very capable shoulders.

Miala wondered if he would protest or demur, but he remained silent, although he did finally turn to look at her. What he saw in her face she couldn't know, although she was relieved her eyes were now relatively dry. In the uncertain light of the one moon his own face was even more unreadable than ever, but she stared back up at him steadily, willing him to hold her gaze. *I believe in you*, she prayed that gaze told him. *I trust you to get me safely away from here, even if this world is tearing itself apart.*

They stood that way for a long moment, until at last he said, "It's too cold for you out here." Then he dropped his arm from around her and instead took her hand, leading her back inside the building.

Not sure at first where Thorn was taking her, Miala followed him down the winding staircase. The light was dim in here. A few battery-powered sconces at strategic points gave enough illumination to keep a person from tripping over themselves on the steps, but they did nothing to dispel the shadows that lurked in the corners. Once again she had that sensation of ghostly presences hidden in the darkness, whispers at the very edge of hearing. Miala shivered, glad she would be quit of this place in a few short hours.

It was only when they paused on the landing to the second level that she realized what Thorn intended. Just a few doors down from where they stood was the chamber where he had slept for the past few nights. Miala looked up at him, mouth suddenly dry.

He returned her gaze, his face expressionless as always. "If you don't want to—"

Oh, but she did, and that was what both frightened and thrilled her at the same time. Somehow she knew that once she followed Eryk Thorn into that chamber, she would have left her old life behind forever, that she would finally have stepped over the shadowy threshold between adolescence and adulthood. Her life had already undergone wrenching changes, but this was different. From this there would be no going back.

"I do," she replied, marveling at how steady her voice sounded.

One eyebrow lifted, and she thought he looked a little amused, but he said only, "Good." And then he palmed the lock and led her into his sleeping quarters.

He had left one lamp illuminated in the far corner of the room so it lent a soft wash of light to the chamber, just enough to reveal off-world furnishings that no doubt had been expensive but were the height of bad taste—carved stone touched with silver and gilt paint, window hangings in a particularly excruciating shade of mauve, a gruesome piece of art depicting a group of dancing girls. In short, it was a suite that Mast had probably preserved for his favorites.

"Nice," Miala commented. "I'm glad I decided to sleep upstairs in the slave girls' dormitory."

"Bed's comfortable at least."

She was tempted to reply, Prove it, but knew she'd probably find out for herself soon enough. And he gave her no time to think of an alternative retort, for once again he pulled her against him, his mouth on hers, his hands moving through the free-falling masses of her hair, finding the pressure clasps that closed up the back of her tunic. It fell from her with shocking ease, and suddenly she could feel his fingers moving against her bare skin, sending little shivers all over her body.

At the same time she reached up to pull at the tab to the locking fastener that closed the front of his jumpsuit. It separated to reveal a well-muscled torso, albeit one that showed skin still reddened and scarred by the firefight at the Malverdine Cliffs. But Miala found she didn't care, instead running her hands over his bare flesh, feeling the hardness of his muscles under the roughened skin.

Then his mouth moved down her neck, brushing over the collarbones, down to her breast, even as his tongue flickered out and made contact with the sensitive skin there. She gasped, shocked that such a delicate touch could bring such waves of pleasure coursing over her body.

Somehow they were then on the bed, his lips still brushing against her breast, as his hand dropped between her legs, stroking. She could no more stifle the cry that escaped her lips at his touch than she could have stopped him at this point, but she had no desire to. Instead she reached out to touch him as well, finding the hardness of him, taking him into her hand as if she had done this a hundred times before. He gasped—maybe he hadn't been expecting that from her.

After a few moments thus entwined—or perhaps it was a few hours…time seemed to have no meaning as they held one another—he moved on top of her, his mouth finding hers even as she relinquished her hold on him and instead wrapped her arms around his body, feeling the hardened muscles shift under her hands. As Miala shivered from the pleasure his touch had brought her, a tiny frisson of fear trailed its way down her spine. They were so close—so very close. She knew there was no stopping him now, no way to prevent him from taking the next step.

It hurt, but not as much as she had been afraid it would. She'd read enough about relations between men and women to have heard that it was not always pleasurable for a woman the first time, and so she had feared this moment almost as much as she had looked forward to it. But after the first few seconds she relaxed into his embrace, instead reveling in the sensation of finally being at one with the man who had done so much to keep his true self hidden from her. There could be no barriers between them now, she thought, not when they had shared the ultimate intimacy. And finally, when he cried out and then collapsed against her, his lips brushing against her jaw line as he smoothed the tousled hair away from her forehead, she almost wept at his close-ness, the sensation of his body pressed against hers, the taste of his sweat on her tongue.

They lay there for a time, listening to one another's

heartbeats, until finally he rose from the bed and went to the restroom. She could hear the water running as she remained lying there, stretched across the sweat-dampened sheets, feeling as if every nerve ending in her body had suddenly been given a charge from a power generator.

I feel different, Miala thought suddenly, although if challenged she probably would have been unable to say how. All she knew was that until this moment she had felt only half alive.

A few moments later he returned to the bed and lay down beside her. She could see the water glistening in the wavy dark hair around his forehead before he settled himself against one of the pillows.

"I didn't know I was your first," he said finally.

"Well, I haven't had a lot of opportunity," she replied, thinking at the same time how glad she was of that fact. He was silent, and she added, "Does that bother you?"

"No." He moved his head on the pillow so he was looking directly at her and then said, "But I could have been more careful—"

"It was perfect," she said firmly, and meant it. She was sure that Thorn would not have avoided taking her to bed if he'd known she was a virgin, but it would have changed the dynamic between them. As it was, he had approached her solely as a woman he wanted, and Miala preferred it that way. Things were complicated enough as it was.

He did not reply, but instead rolled over and kissed her almost harshly on the mouth, as if to make up for any perceived weakness in his earlier diffidence. "'Night, then," he said, and with that he returned to his former supine position. His eyes closed, and almost immediately his breathing slowed into the regular rhythms of sleep.

Must be another survival trait, Miala thought. Still, she was a little shocked at how quickly he had slipped away from her. It seemed odd to have experienced such intimacy and then, just as suddenly, become two separate beings again.

She supposed it was sensible to make the most of this last night's sleep in Mast's compound—who knew what they would encounter as they left Iradia the next day—but no matter what she did, she could not seem to make herself at ease. The mattress was, as Thorn had claimed, extremely comfortable, but she could not find a restful position. Luckily her tossings and turnings did nothing to disturb the sleeping mercenary; probably he had already logged her presence as a non-threat and so was immune to her restive behavior.

Finally she rolled over on her back and stared up at the ceiling, at the faint whorls and scrape marks in the rough-hewn sandstone as revealed by the uncertain light of the small nightlight he'd left burning in the bathroom. Beside her Eryk Thorn slept, his chest rising and falling slowly under the thin sheet. She could feel the warmth of his body next to hers and recalled with a rush of heat the sensation of that body against her, inside her.

Her whole being seemed to ache as she thought of him, and she said aloud, in a soft, wondering voice, "I love you."

He did not stir, of course, and she had not wanted him to. Those were words she would never have the courage to say to him, not unless he had given her overt encouragement to do so beforehand, and she could not imagine that happening for a long time—if ever. No, she let those three words float on the night air, merely an acknowledgment to the universe of her feelings for him. She had never been in love before, had never known before what it meant or how it would feel.

At least she assumed she was in love with him. That must be what made this strange ache in her breast as she looked down at him while he slept, this overwhelming rush of emotion that made her want to lean over and kiss him awake so she could feel him as one with her once more. She held herself still, however, trying to content herself merely with the sight of him, the heavy dark crescents his lashes made against his cheeks, the wide thin mouth, the scar that creased one eyebrow. No, he was not handsome, as she had thought dispassionately days ago—a lifetime ago—when she had first looked down at him as he lay unconscious on the powered stretcher. But there was not one thing she would change about that face, now so familiar to her, so beloved.

"I love you," she said again, this time in barely a whisper. *No matter what happens*, she thought, *no matter if the only world I've ever known is tearing itself apart. I've had this time with you, and no one can take that away from me.*

She thought of what they might be facing once they left Iradia, of all the strange worlds that up until now had only been words and images on a computer screen. She knew she should have been frightened, but somehow she wasn't. Somehow she knew that Thorn would keep her safe, and the rest of the galaxy be damned.

It was then, finally, that she was able to relax into slumber, to let the deep, calm breaths of her lover be her final guide into sleep. She closed her eyes, secure in the knowledge that he would be there beside her when she awoke.

Miala opened her eyes. The ceiling above her was unfamiliar, stenciled around the edges in a vaguely unpleasant scroll design in purple and gold. For a brief second she couldn't remember where she was, and then memory returned, along with a subtle soreness in her body that had not been there before last night. She reached out to where Eryk Thorn had lain, but the bed was empty.

"Time to go," he said, looking down at her from the foot of the bed. He was dressed already, of course, in the familiar black jumpsuit, and in one hand he held a wad of dark fabric—presumably the wrappings he customarily wore around his head and face whenever he went out in public.

Relief made her silent for a moment. For just one second she had been sure he had left after all, abandoning her and her foolish dreams. She should have known better. He hadn't let her down so far.

"Let me just go gather my things," she replied, then began to slide out of bed, pausing for a second once she realized her clothing was still in a heap on the floor. Cheeks flaming, she looked away from him as she bent over to pick up her discarded tunic and pants, then quickly pulled the tunic on over her head. Damn it, this sort of thing was so much easier to handle when it was dark...

Still not meeting Thorn's eyes, she hurried out of the guest chamber and up the stairs to the slave girls' dormitory, where she allowed herself a brisk five minutes in the shower before collecting the few odds and ends she considered worth taking off-planet: her scarred old tablet computer, a few changes of clothing, the one pair of sturdy boots she owned. All of these items she stashed in a wilted duffel that she'd found tucked into a far corner of the wardrobe, and at the last minute she added a random sampling of the toiletries from the dressing area. All in all, it was a meager collection, but she didn't mind. With her half of Mast's treasure, she'd be able to buy herself anything she wanted once she and Thorn were safely away from Iradia.

Miala had to go all the way down to the guard chamber to find the mercenary, as he had not bothered to wait for her in his borrowed guest suite.

"Everything looks clear," he said. "Just thought I'd do one more sweep of the perimeter before we drop the shields."

"Well, I'm ready," she replied. ...*barely*, she added mentally, thinking of her still-dripping hair and rumpled clothing. But she'd known better than to make Thorn wait any longer than was strictly necessary.

"Right, then." He stepped away from the console. "You can take it from here."

Of course. She'd cracked the security system, but she'd never given him the access codes—and he'd never asked her for them. If she'd bothered to think about it earlier, she should have known that was one indication of his intention to do right by her. Otherwise, he would have forced the codes from her and then disposed of her as he pleased.

She moved past him to enter the password to log in to the main security screen, then tapped in the command to lower the shields. After she had done so she looked up at Thorn, surprised by how vulnerable she suddenly felt, although there had been no indication that any enemies were within a hundred kilometers of the compound. "We're ready."

He nodded. "Come on, then."

And it was with that unceremonious command that she trailed after him out of the guard chamber, through the dim corridors of the building that had been her home for the past few months, and out into the blinding heat and light of an Iradian morning. The ramp to the entrance of his ship had already been lowered, the doors standing open; clearly he had been prepared for a fast getaway.

The metal of the ramp clanged hollowly under her feet as she climbed up behind Eryk Thorn into the cramped cockpit. The ship had clearly been engineered for speed and not much in the way of creature comforts, and she had the uneasy thought that it would get uncomfortable in here pretty damn fast. Then again, she should just be glad that Thorn even had a ship of his own, as most people had to rely on the much slower passenger liners that plied their trade among the galaxy's various inhabited systems.

But in the meantime the setup was both awkward and unexpected, and she had to clamber into her seat even as Thorn slid into his with practiced ease. She fumbled with the safety harness, and after he flicked a switch to close the rear hatch he reached over to assist her, his hand carelessly grazing across one of her breasts.

"Sure we have time for that?" she snapped, and he grinned.

He didn't bother to protest his innocence, instead saying only, "Later."

It wasn't worth arguing over, she decided, especially since the memory of his touch had sent pleasant chills racing across her body. Miala knew she would only be a hypocrite if she protested, so instead she allowed herself a small shake of the head and then turned to watch the vista of dusty desert and hard blue sky visible directly through the viewport ahead of her.

Eryk Thorn toggled a few more switches, and she could feel the engines come to life, the subtle vibrations seeming to penetrate to her very bones. Once, a few years ago, her schoolmate Drix had taken her for a ride in his Zephyr, a small plane designed only for atmospheric flight—no doubt in a failed attempt to impress her—but that fragile little vehicle could not begin to compare to Thorn's scarred but powerful ship.

Despite herself Miala felt her fingers clench on the worn synthetic leather of her armrests, even as the *Fury* reached full power and began to rise majestically from the sandy landing pad on which it had rested. *It's all right*, she told herself. *Millions of people go into space every day. It's perfectly safe.* But she was unable to release the death grip on her seat as she felt her home world's gravity begin to claw at her, forcing her to breathe consciously, making her feel as if all of her limbs had suddenly turned to lead.

But then the great sandy-orange disk of Iradia was before her, filling the viewport. To one side the sun erupted over the planet's terminus in a spectacular wave of searing yellow-white light.

"Any final words?" Thorn asked.

Miala glanced over at him. He looked serious, but she knew better, since she'd grown adept at reading the subtle nuances of a barely lifted eyebrow, the faintest shadow at the corner of his mouth. Then she turned and stared for a long moment at the ochre-hued planet before her, the only home she had ever known. Her father had died somewhere down there; in a shabby corner of Aldis Nova, a small house where she had once lived was no doubt already overrun with sand borers and rock beetles. After a long pause she gave a grim smile and said, "Good riddance."

He gave an approving nod but made no other reply. Instead he reached over to the controls at his left and made a few adjustments, and the *Fury* turned away from Iradia, picking up speed as it moved deeper out into space.

If Thorn had been expecting any opposition as they left the system, he must have been disappointed, Miala thought. As they rounded the smallest of Iradia's three moons, she thought she saw the tiny winking lights of another vessel at far range, but that was all. And then there wasn't time to focus on anything else, for Eryk Thorn pulled down a handle to engage the subspace drive, and the universe exploded around her.

"So where are we going, anyway?" Miala asked at length, once she was sure she'd grown accustomed enough to the stomach-churning spectacle of subspace to speak in a reasonably normal tone of voice.

"A place named Callia," he replied.

She frowned. "Never heard of it." Which, she had to admit, didn't mean much. Galactic cartography had never been her strong suit.

"It's about fourteen standard hours from Iradia. It's in Eridani space, basically a resort world." He gave her a sideways glance. "Lots of tourists, lots of strangers. And since it's in an Eridani-controlled sector, we run a lower risk of bumping into any GDF ships. It should be safe enough. No one will look twice at us there."

That sounded fairly reassuring, except for the part about it being a journey that would last at least fourteen hours. The seat she currently occupied was actually quite comfortable, despite its battered appearance, but Miala wasn't sure she could sit in one place for that long.

Some betraying expression must have crossed her face, for he continued, "There's a small cabin and a bathroom through that door to your left if you need to get up."

It made sense. This ship was his home, after all—he couldn't possibly spend his entire life in this cockpit, although she had the feeling he had slept in the captain's chair more often than not. The three steps from the door he had indicated to the cockpit were just enough to make the difference between life and death in a risky situation. Still, she was glad to know she could get up and move around a bit if necessary.

Which she did after a while, as Thorn seemed indisposed to conversation and there was only so long she could sit in her own chair and stare out at the odd, twisting shards of space that flashed past the viewport at speeds beyond comprehension. The cabin was mean and small, even to Miala's eyes. But now it served well enough for her to lie down and rest her head on the somewhat lumpy pillow. At least this bed was far too narrow for Thorn to have ever shared it with another woman.

That thought led her to wonder what he had felt, if anything, about last night's encounter. Certainly today he had been all business—except for that brief touch just before they took off from Iradia—but what else, really, had she expected from him? For him to go down on one knee and proclaim his undying love for her? He'd be more likely to sprout wings, and even if he had done something so completely out of character, Miala had the uneasy feeling she would have burst out laughing at such behavior. No, frustrating as his complete unresponsiveness could be at times, that was the man she had fallen in love with, not some soppy hero from a romance vid.

And she was here after all, lying on his distinctly uncomfortable bed, breathing in the recycled air that seemed faintly scented with his sweat—she supposed it was ingrained in the ship's air-circulation system after so many years of housing the same inhabitant—and not left on Iradia with a knife in her back or, worse, abandoned to the tender mercies of bandits and crime lords such as Rafe Darlester. Eryk Thorn was taking her someplace he felt was reasonably safe, and they still had a lot to do.

Once they had acquired secure lodgings, she would need to procure a computer much more high-powered than her outmoded old tablet and then go about the tricky business of setting up new accounts for both herself and Thorn so she could begin to transfer the funds from Mast's off-world accounts. There wasn't necessarily that much true hacking involved, since she already had the access codes for Mast's accounts, but it would take work and delicate handling just to keep the money transfers from attracting any unwanted attention. At least the current unsettled conditions on Iradia should work in their favor. Miala doubted very much that anyone would be paying too much attention to accounts suddenly being depleted when the legitimate owner wasn't around to protest their sudden diminished state…

She must have dozed off at some point in her ruminations, for Miala awoke suddenly, feeling as if some invisible hand had tried to push her off the bed. After a few seconds spent reorienting herself, she realized what she had most likely sensed was the ship's transition back into normal space. It didn't seem as if she could have been asleep that long, but then again, her slumber of the previous evening had not been particularly restful.

Staggering a bit—the lumpy pillow and flat mattress seemed to have kinked her spine—she stood and made her way back into the cockpit. Thorn seemed not to have moved at all since she left, although it was possible he had slept briefly at some point. He gave her a brief nod as she resumed her place in the seat next to his.

"Rested?"

She thought about making a snide comment regarding the mattress, then decided against it. "Sure."

"We're coming up on Callia now," he said. "Looks all right."

It was only the second planet she had seen from space, but it was as different from Iradia as two planets could be. Even from orbit her home world was dry, dusty, and dead; this Callia shimmered both blue and green, banded with lacy white clouds. One tiny moon peeped out past the planet's terminus, and Miala could see the tiny flickering lights that bordered the continents in the darkened edges of a crescent shadow as it turned its face from its star.

"It's beautiful," she breathed. Of course she had seen images of other planets, even ones as lush and lovely as this one, but they didn't convey the sense that these water worlds somehow appeared in real space as delicate jewels that could be cupped in the palm of one's hand.

He made a noncommittal sound.

Trust Thorn to ignore the aesthetics of the situation, Miala thought, but she was amused rather than annoyed. Quite possibly he had seen planets much more impressive, but she was still enchanted by the promise those glowing colors represented. Were there real oceans down there, mile upon mile of water completely uncontained by any sort of storage facility?

She did not have time for further contemplation of the

planet's beauties, however, as a hostile female voice suddenly sounded over the comm.

"Unidentified ship, this is Callia Spaceport Authority. State your name and business."

Thorn leaned in toward the comm. "Callia Spaceport Authority, this is the light cargo vessel *Endeavor II*, inbound from Lathvin IV. Transmitting ship I.D. and cargo manifest now." He tapped away at the modified keyboard to his right, no doubt sending the promised information to ground control.

Miala raised an eyebrow, and he gave her a small, tight smile before saying, "Always have a cover story prepared. We could have made planetfall in stealth mode and maybe none the wiser, but we're trying to look legitimate—and I'm not here on business, anyway."

She nodded, and then the comm beeped again.

"*Endeavor II*, you are cleared to land on pad 127 in the port in Chistan Major—or what's left of it. Transmitting coordinates."

Thorn lifted an eyebrow. "Callia Spaceport Authority? Clarify 'what's left of it'?"

Something that sounded suspiciously like a sigh came over the comm. "Full details aren't available at this time. However, a large portion of our coastal resorts have been decimated by a series of tidal waves. Chistan Major is partially located on high ground, so the spaceport there is still intact. Mostly."

Miala wondered what a tidal wave was, then decided this was probably not the best time to ask. It didn't sound good, however.

Thorn appeared to hesitate for a moment, and then said, "Coordinates accepted, Callia Spaceport Authority. Preparing for our descent into Chistan Major." He toggled the comm, then glanced over at Miala. "Better strap yourself in. I'm not sure what's going to meet us down there."

"Wouldn't it be better to just turn around and leave?" But even as she asked the question, Miala slid into the co-pilot's seat and began struggling with the elaborate safety harness.

His response was immediate. "No. That would look suspicious, and since this is my first time here, I don't have a lot of intel as to what kind of a system force they have and how zealous they are. Sounds like they were hit with some kind of natural disaster, anyway, and not an enemy attack. It may be kind of a mess, but that may work to our advantage. If they're busy with cleaning up the place, they're not going to be paying much attention to us."

As he spoke his hands were busy on the controls, and the blue-green disk of the planet expanded in the forward viewport until Miala had the sensation that they were falling into it, captured by its gravity, certain to disappear into its vast oceans. Suddenly the concept of that much water wasn't all that appealing.

But of course they weren't falling, but sweeping in a smooth, controlled dive that took them through the upper levels of the atmosphere and then down into billows of grayish-white material that Miala at first couldn't place and then realized must be clouds. On Iradia the only clouds one ever saw were high, thin strips of cirrus formations against the metallic blue sky, but she had read that clouds were composed of water vapor and could be quite developed on some planets.

As they were here, obviously—so much so that as the *Fury* dropped lower into the atmosphere, their misty consistency turned into discrete water droplets and then, as the ship finally emerged from the cloud cover, outright rain. They were flying low over a silvery gray landscape partially obscured by the heavily falling precipitation, and so all Miala could make out was the low jagged edge of a continent moving up toward them through the drifting veils of moisture. She wondered how anyone could fly in such conditions, thought that perhaps Iradia's unending blue skies had their positives. But Eryk Thorn seemed unfazed by the torrents of water, slowing the *Fury* to get it into position to land on its designated pad, and suddenly her only view was of a square patch of gray sky and a frightening quantity of loose water streaming off the forward viewport.

Once again the comm beeped. "Endeavor II, you will refrain from disembarking until a spaceport official has confirmed your paperwork and cargo. Someone will be with you shortly."

"Understood," Thorn replied. He reached down to undo his own safety harness and stood.

Miala began to slowly unbuckle her own seatbelts, but that last request from Callia Spaceport Authority had her more than a little concerned. Sure, it was one thing to beam a bunch of false information down to some bored officer who didn't know any better, but how on earth was Thorn going to get a hold full of cash and other obviously ill-gotten loot past a customs official?

"Um, Thorn," she began, after she had disentangled herself from the last bits of harness and eased herself out of the seat. "I'm assuming that what we've got in the cargo hold doesn't exactly match whatever manifest you sent down to the spaceport authority when you requested permission to land."

"Yeah, so?"

"So what are you going to do about it?"

One eyebrow lifted. "I remember you saying you trusted me."

"Well, yes, but—"

He stepped closer to her, then bent down and gave her a swift, hard kiss, smothering her protests. "So trust me."

She wondered exactly what trick it was he had up his sleeve, but she knew better than to question him further. All right, she would trust him. After all, he'd had a great deal more experience racketing around the galaxy than she had, and he didn't look at all worried. In fact, that eyebrow of his was still quirked, indicating some private amusement. All she could do was sit back and wait to see what happened next.

XI

THE FIRST THING MIALA NOTICED when Thorn opened the hatch was the scent of moisture and of damp vegetation, both overlaid with a wild salty smell that she couldn't place at all. The air was cool and wet, and a strong breeze blew stray droplets of rain into her face. Even when standing in a shower she'd never quite experienced the sensation of an atmosphere so heavily laden with water, and for a few seconds she felt as if she couldn't breathe, that the air was too thick and she would drown in it.

Standing outside in the rain, and looking none too happy for it, was apparently the port official who had come to inspect the *Fury*. He was a slender Eridani male of indeterminate age, and his face, under the plastic-wrapped cap he wore, was pale lavender. He held a tablet and scowled at Miala as she descended the boarding ramp a few feet behind the mercenary.

"Who's that?" he asked. "I didn't see her name on the manifest."

"Just took her on at my last port," Thorn replied smoothly. "I haven't had time to update my records."

"Name?" the official inquired, after darting a quick glance at Miala's low-cut neckline.

"Sheri Napoli," Miala replied promptly. Sheri was an old classmate of hers, and Miala figured she wouldn't mind if her name were borrowed in a good cause. Besides, the chances of Sheri ever being on Callia were virtually nil.

"Occupation?" The official's derisive look made it quite obvious what he thought her primary function was on board the *Fury*.

"First mate." It was all Miala could do to keep from laughing. She supposed at some other time she would have been offended by the spaceport official's assumptions regarding her status, but he wasn't really that far off from the truth in this particular instance.

The man's eyes narrowed, although he went ahead and made a notation on his tablet anyway. "All right, Captain Marr, let's take a look at what's in your hold."

Marr? Miala mouthed at Thorn as they moved toward the cargo bay. He gave her a barely perceptible shake of the head, from which she inferred that she should follow his lead and keep her mouth shut. Apparently "Captain Marr" was an alias he used occasionally. She assumed that the false identity matched whatever doctored manifest he had beamed down to the port authority in the first place.

The cargo hold looked the same as when they had left it: neatly stacked containers of various sizes secured by webbing. Miala couldn't help giving Thorn an anxious glance. It didn't appear as if anything had been touched, and so she couldn't imagine what he might have done to conceal the fact that they were carrying a load of contraband Gaian units.

Face impassive as always, Thorn paused by one of the containers.

The spaceport official pointed at the crate. "Open it."

Hardly daring to breathe, Miala looked on as Thorn unlatched the container and lifted the lid. Inside were... what? Certainly not Gaian units. The crate appeared to be full of cushioned foam into which had been carefully laid pieces of some sort of machinery—possibly mining equipment, since she thought she recognized the fluted metal bits that were sometimes used to bore through rock. Rusted pieces similar to the ones in the crate were a familiar sight around Aldis Nova, home of more failed mining projects than the officials there cared to admit.

The official pulled off his dripping cap, revealing thinning dark purple hair. "That one, too."

Eryk Thorn unlatched the container the official had indicated and stepped back. This one looked as if it held a medium-sized generator, the sort that would be used on-site to power the types of drill the other crate had contained. He raised an eyebrow at the official. "Any more?" His tone indicated nothing except boredom and, perhaps, the mildest irritation at having to go through the motions of an inspection he'd had to suffer a thousand times before.

But the spaceport official wasn't about to let it go that easily. "That one in the back," he said, pointing to a container in the far corner of the cargo hold.

The sigh Eryk Thorn gave was scarcely audible, although Miala was fairly certain it was mostly for show. She supposed even someone who didn't have anything to hide would be irritated by the request—was this annoying little man going to make the mercenary open every container in the cargo hold?

The final container's contents were as innocuous as the other two, as this time the items revealed proved to be no more incriminating that spare sand skimmer parts.

Still, the official held up his tablet one last time, obviously rereading the manifest Thorn had sent to the spaceport authority. "Resupply for the mining colony on Nylos, huh?"

"Right."

The spaceport official made a few final notations, then tucked the data pad under his arm. "Logged and noted, Captain Marr. Callia Spaceport Authority welcomes you to Chistan Major. Information for off-world visitors can be found on the local net, channel 185."

Thorn inclined his head. "Thanks."

And finally the troublesome official took himself off, replacing the cap on his head before he stepped out into the persistent rain showers.

Miala turned to Thorn. "What—"

"Not now. Gather up your things—we're getting out of here."

So even though she was full of questions—the most important being, *where the hell are all our units?*—she remained silent while she retrieved the shabby duffel that was her only luggage and followed Eryk Thorn out into the rain.

It was cold, and the raindrops felt like fine needles on her bare arms. She shivered, thinking it would have been nice if Thorn could have warned her about the climate on this world. Still, she supposed he'd had more important things on his mind.

The spaceport itself was a mess. One-half of the complex seemed to have slid down a hillside and was now closed off by bands of glowing green tape. Everywhere she looked she saw crowds of annoyed tourists, some human, some Eridani, and even several hooded and cloaked Zhore, most of them standing in queues and looking as if they wanted to be anywhere but here.

Great vacation spot, Thorn, she thought, but decided it was better to save her arguments until they were somewhere private.

They had no trouble getting a mech-operated taxi. Most people seemed to be leaving Chistan Major, not arriving, and there were fleets of the compact little aircars circling the spaceport.

"The Eridani Majesty," Thorn said to the mechanoid cabbie, and Miala raised an eyebrow.

"Sounds posh," she commented.

He gave her a very small smile. "You'll see."

Up in the taxi's driver's compartment the mech cabbie began burbling away cheerfully. "Eridani Majesty, sure… you're lucky, the Majesty survived the waves, high ground, you know. Just ten minutes, and they'll be glad to see you… tourists running away like *boojins* off a sinking ship… who'd've thought a series of underwater earthquakes could have made so much trouble…"

"Earthquakes?" Thorn interrupted. Until then he'd been leaning back against the seat, lids half-closed as if to block out some of the mech's babbling, but he sat up suddenly, black eyes narrowing.

"That's what they're saying," the mech responded cheerfully. It was a model Miala didn't recognize, a spindly little thing with four arms and a narrow, flattened head. "Whole series of them…fault line they didn't even know was there…totally wiped out the Unis Islands. Tidal waves everywhere. Chistan Major's still here just because it's mostly on high ground."

"Any aftershocks?" Thorn's eyes were still narrowed; Miala could almost see the tension in his body.

"Oh, sure. Not that you'll feel 'em in the Majesty, as long as the floor doesn't collapse." The mech's jolly tones never altered during the relaying of this information—probably it had been programmed to be artificially cheerful at all times.

"That's reassuring," Miala muttered.

"Are we almost there?" Thorn grated.

Although he seemed to have relaxed slightly once he began to realize that the worst of the natural disaster was already over, it was clear he would have liked nothing better than to blow the head off the garrulous mech. Maybe Eridanis—who had colonized Callia—liked their mechs talkative, unlike the quiet, unobtrusive models Miala had seen on Iradia.

"Just 'round this corner."

And sure enough, the mech took the bend at a speed Miala wasn't sure was entirely safe, and the Eridani Majesty stood before them.

Up until that time, the largest structure she had ever seen was Mast's compound. The Majesty would have dwarfed the former monastery with just one wing. It was a huge edifice of white stone—or possibly white concrete made to look like stone—that had been built on a bluff overlooking the ocean. Three domes that appeared to be

made of multicolored glass topped the mammoth structure, although Miala couldn't be certain of the materials,
since the dimming light and still pouring rain made it difficult to see details clearly.

The taxi whooshed to a stop under a portico whose
underside had been decorated in a complex mosaic depicting some sort of alien marine life. Apparently the Eridani
Majesty eschewed mech labor, for it was a young Eridani
man who opened the car door for Miala and offered her a
gloved hand, helping her out onto an elaborate runner of
intricately worked design.

"Welcome to the Eridani Majesty!" he announced.

"Uh...thank you," she replied, allowing him to retrieve
her battered duffel from the floor of the back seat, feeling
even more acutely aware of the rumpled garments she wore
and the sad state of her hair. She brushed at the wrinkles on
her tunic, then added in what she hoped were space-weary
traveler tones, "Such a dreadful flight! I thought we'd never
get here."

From the back seat she heard something that sounded
suspiciously like a snort. The porter leaned down as if to
help Thorn out of the taxi, then backed up quickly after
receiving a freezing stare from the mercenary. Thorn
unfolded himself from the back of the cab, still glaring at
the nervous young man.

"Thanks," Eryk Thorn said finally, and tossed a five-unit
chip at the porter, who caught it and looked relieved that
Thorn hadn't thrown anything incendiary at him.

"Great people skills, Thorn," Miala said, once they were
safely out of earshot.

"That's 'Captain Marr,'" he replied, not bothering to look back at her. "Don't forget it."

Yes, sir! she thought, but remained silent as she trailed after him across the enormous marble-paved lobby of the hotel. In here the walls seemed to be made entirely of glass, encasing tanks of what she assumed were the more colorful examples of local marine life, while overhead huge glass globes cast a warm light across the enormous room.

It seemed to take forever to get to the main desk. There was a lot of real estate to cover, although the lobby was conspicuously empty, with staff obviously outnumbering guests at least three to one. Again, the clerk who waited for them was Eridani, this time a young woman probably not too many years older than Miala herself, although impossibly more elegant, with her dark purple hair in an intricate knot high on her head and a sparkling white suit that Miala knew would have been stained in about five minutes if she'd been the one wearing it.

"Reservations?" she asked.

For a second Miala wasn't sure what Thorn was doing, exactly, and then she realized he was smiling. It was such a rare expression that she gave him a startled look. Then she realized exactly what he was up to.

"Well, I don't exactly have any, but I was hoping you could help me out—" And he slid a credit chip across the counter.

Apparently Miala wasn't the only one to be affected by that smile. The clerk looked at Thorn and returned the smile with one of her own. "Well, sir, we do have some rooms available—"

"Excellent."

The clerk swiped the credit chip, and her eyes widened slightly. Then she tapped away at her keyboard. "In fact, given the present situation—that is, the Eridani Majesty values your patronage, sir. We'd like to offer you a free upgrade to one of our governor's suites by way of thanks."

"Well, thank you—" and here Thorn leaned in a little closer, as if to take a better look at the glowing letters on her name tag, "—Selchen. I do appreciate it."

She blushed, her pale lavender skin turning a darker purple high on her cheekbones. "Oh, it's no problem, sir." Then she handed a coded security card and the credit chip back to him. "Please let us know if there's anything we can do to make your stay here more comfortable."

"Will do." He pocketed the card and the chip, then gestured for Miala to follow him toward the bank of elevators that stood at the far end of the lobby.

Once they were safely inside, Miala turned to her companion. "All right, where is Eryk Thorn, and what have you done with him?"

Again that flash of teeth. "That's 'Captain Marr,' Miala. And I didn't deviate from my standard procedures—I merely analyzed the situation and then used the approach I had determined would work best."

"Whatever you say," she replied. Maybe that was true, but she'd gotten the feeling Thorn had positively enjoyed cranking up the old charm to get what he wanted from that clerk.

Once she saw the suite, however, she was not inclined to argue with Thorn's methods. The main bedroom alone could have swallowed up her old house in Aldis Nova, and the bathroom was so large she wondered whether they were supposed to sleep in there as well, especially since there was an elegant little lounging couch placed against one wall of the dressing area. Best of all, though, the suite's far wall was made entirely of glass and overlooked the ocean, now dark as blood in the last light of the setting sun.

"All right, I forgive you," she said finally, after returning to the sleeping area.

"For what?"

"For flirting with that clerk." Miala took another look around the sumptuously decorated chamber, from the blue-green hangings of some foreign, shimmering fabric on the walls to the vases of flowers that stood on the bed-side tables. Their blue and purple blooms gave the room a delicate, spicy scent, at once alien and enticing. "Actually, considering how nice this suite is, I forgive you for any-thing you might ever have done wrong."

"That's a lot of forgiving."

He was most certainly correct in that, she thought, but at the moment she didn't care. "But I really have to know," she continued. "Where the hell are all our units?"

"Still safely in the cargo hold."

"Excuse me?" What load of moth droppings was he try-ing to sell her now? "I don't remember seeing any units—just a bunch of mining equipment."

"Don't forget the sand skimmer parts," he said, setting the synth-hide bag he had brought with him on the foot of the bed.

"Whatever. So what did you do with the units?"

"I didn't do anything with them."

Miala gave him an unbelieving stare.

Finally, he appeared to relent and said, "I told you I'm prepared. I always carry a few cases of what looks like legitimate cargo around with me, something to match whatever fake cargo manifest I'm currently using."

"But he picked those cases at random!" she protested.

"Did he?" Thorn returned, with a lift of the eyebrow.

"What, did you use some sort of hypnosis on him or something?"

"No. Most customs officials are lazy and invariably choose cases toward the front of the cargo hold."

Miala took a breath. "Fine, but he also had you open up one in the very back. What about that one?"

"Finest hologram projectors money can buy."

She raised an eyebrow.

"It's true. Since they're projecting a fixed image, the fidelity is very high. And they fit right under the lid of just about any crate or container you're trying to disguise. Can't tell it from the real thing, unless you try to stick your hand in it."

"And what happens if someone sticks their hand in it?"

"Their hand gets shot off."

Well, that was more like the Thorn she knew and loved. "Subtle."

"Whatever works."

There wasn't much arguing with that, she knew. Frowning, she gazed up at him, at the expression of complete unconcern on his face. "You seem pretty casual about walking around where everyone can see you," she commented.

He shrugged. "It's hard for people to recognize you when no one knows what you look like."

Again, she couldn't really dispute that statement. It was true, after all. She hadn't seen Eryk Thorn's face until she had removed the dark wrappings he'd worn since the moment she first laid eyes on him in Mast's compound. For all she knew, he'd spent his entire adult life hidden that way. If that were the case, then who would know what he looked like once he set the disguise aside? Besides, she was fairly certain that the well-starched staff of the Eridani Majesty would have been less than thrilled if one of the galaxy's most notorious mercenaries suddenly appeared in the lobby and demanded a room. Odd that in this case Thorn's true face was his best disguise.

"So what about the earthquakes?" she inquired, sitting down on the foot of the bed and pulling off her sandals. The carpet felt indescribably soft under her feet.

"I haven't felt any aftershocks since we got here. Have you?"

"That's not very reassuring, Thorn," she said, her tone a gentle rebuke.

"Just making a comment." Even as he replied, he stepped toward the enormous suite-spanning windows and touched a small control pad in the wall. The glass gradually darkened to black, blotting out the dim view of the night-shrouded harbor beyond. "Better," he said.

"I liked the view," she protested.

"You can't see anything at night anyway. It was too exposed for my taste."

Miala wondered whether she would ever win an argument with Thorn and decided probably not. Still, she was determined to enjoy herself. She was off Iradia, after all, and right now she was living in luxury she had never imagined, let alone seen with her own eyes. "So what now?" she asked.

Was that a swift glance he gave toward her, toward the bed? Miala couldn't be sure, and in any case he actually moved away from her, toward the communications console embedded in the elegant little carved table across the room. "I thought I'd introduce you to an interesting off-world custom. It's called room service."

Later—much later, actually, after a divine meal of which Miala recognized nothing but enjoyed everything, too many glasses of some glorious fizzing wine Thorn said was imported all the way from Gaia itself, a leisurely soak in the bathtub (which did fit two very comfortably, as Eryk Thorn had pointed out), followed by a prolonged session in a bed that was even more comfortable than the one in Mast's compound, Miala lay back against the pillows, certain that she had never felt so contented in her life. She tried to think if there was anything that could have made the evening better and decided that was impossible.

Thorn lay in bed next to her, idly playing with a strand of her unbound hair. His expression was almost sleepy, but she knew better. If any threat had presented itself, he would gave been on the alert faster than she could blink.

"Thank you," she said at last.

He paused, one coil of shining copper hair still wrapped around his forefinger. "For what?"

"For getting me away from Iradia. For bringing me here. For everything." She wanted to say, *For letting me love you*, but she knew that would be going too far. Even though they had shared all the intimacies a man and woman could share, she knew as well that was the one boundary she dared not cross. Oh, he had caressed her, held her, brought her to the heights of pleasure as she dug her fingers into his barely healed back and cried out his name over and over again—but even as she had fallen back against the pillows, sated by pleasure, she had known that she could say nothing more, could only whisper his name one last time as she collapsed from the aftermath of the waves of pleasure he had wrung her body. "*Thorn…*"

The dark eyes watching her in the muted glow of the overhead lamps seemed amused. "I told you I owed you one."

"Then you repay your debts very well." And she leaned over and kissed him on the corner of his mouth, in that one spot where he usually betrayed his amusement with her.

"In this case, that's easy enough," he murmured, and shifted slightly, allowing her to pull close to him once again. His free arm dropped around her, and then his eyes closed, his body relaxing against hers.

Did I wear you out, old man? she wondered with some amusement. Miala wasn't exactly sure how old he really was, but she knew he had to be at least fifteen years or so her senior. Not that it really mattered, she supposed, and she was weary as well, her body finally succumbing to the night's over-indulgences. Her eyes closed slowly, and she relaxed, feeling the warmth of his body and the rise and fall of his chest against her back. *Every day is a victory*, she thought, in those last few seconds before sleep claimed her. *Every night a reprieve. Every moment longer he stays with me, I've won that much more.*

Even then she knew better than to ask herself how long it might last.

XII

THE DAYS SLIPPED BY. Although Thorn disappeared from time to time on business he would not discuss with Miala, she still had plenty to keep herself occupied during the hours she was left alone. Her second day on Callia she purchased a computer and set about moving a good portion of Mast's off-world funds into several accounts she set up for herself. For some reason Eryk Thorn would not allow her to establish an account for him, and neither would he give her any information on where to send his share of the fortune.

"Keep it safe for me," he said, in answer to her slightly irritated queries. "I can get it from you when I need it."

"You're joking," she replied.

"I don't joke about money," he said. Then he got that sardonic glint in his eye and added, "I trust you."

Miala wasn't sure whether to be offended or amused...was he mocking her? In the end she had only shaken her head and continued with her work. It wouldn't have been wise to drain the former crime lord's accounts completely, anyway. Instead, she siphoned off amounts of money that seemed somewhat obscene to her but, if noticed as missing, might only lead one to conjecture that perhaps Mast hadn't been doing quite as well as he had wanted everyone to believe.

At the same time she hacked into the admissions system at the University of New Caledonia and retrieved the transcripts she had sent there a little over a year ago. She had been accepted, but the tuition proved out of reach, and nothing had come of it. Extracting her transcripts from their system was the easiest way she could think of to apply to the other universities on her list. First among them was the university on Nova Angeles—previously Miala had thought she would never be able to afford the tuition, but of course that wasn't a concern any longer. Epsilon Eridani was another option, and she submitted an application there and to a few other places as well.

As she waited for word, she amused herself by exploring Chistan Major and its environs. On a few occasions Thorn accompanied her, usually when the outing involved something physical in nature—climbing the low ridges that encircled the city to the north and east, riding a glass-bottomed hoverboat out into the shallow green waters beyond Chistan Bay, or even attending the local version of horse-racing, although here on Callia the "horses" were nimble six-legged beasts that Thorn told her had originally been bred on Eridani. But during all of these diversions she noticed a restlessness in him, saw the way his gaze would sometimes turn westward to where the spaceport was located, and it troubled her.

He was marking time, she realized finally. Their pact had originally involved only his getting her away from Iradia, but whether from a sense of misplaced chivalry or concern that she still couldn't make it on her own, he was staying with her until she had her future settled and knew where she was going. This was not how he lived his life normally—trapped in an over-civilized city, sleeping on fine sheets, searching for ways to fill the empty hours.

Of course it was not a lifestyle to which she was accustomed, either, but the novelty of living on Callia was enough to keep her entertained. What a refreshing change it was never to worry about how much anything cost or whether there would be enough to eat, to wander into the shopping districts and buy whatever she wanted, to have a team of hotel staff that catered to her every whim, whether it was bringing up another meal or sending a stylist to her suite to make sure every hair was in place before she went out to dinner. No, there were definitely worse ways of spending one's time.

But she knew the idyll couldn't last. The fear had been there, ever since she had admitted to herself how much she cared for Thorn, but she'd been able to push it aside. Now that grew more difficult with every passing day.

It came to her one morning as she stood in front of the mirror. Her hair still fell in complicated ringlets from the style of the night before, and her eyes were smudged with leftover cosmetics and lack of sleep. *He's bored. There's a whole galaxy going about its business out there, fighting and scheming, and he's stuck here with you.*

It hadn't been much of a surprise when she heard on the news reports that the Gaian Defense Force had swarmed Iradia, quelling the uprising within a few weeks of its birth. Military rule was established, and some of her home world's lawlessness had retreated, at least so it wasn't quite so blatantly obvious. Although Miala worried about the few friends she had left behind there, she knew better than to try to contact any of them. She couldn't risk giving away her whereabouts, not when she had done such a good job of disappearing from Iradia. Perhaps it was wrong to leave them to think she was dead, but she'd taken that risk the day she went to work at Mast's compound. Even then it was as if she had known she would never return to the shabby little house she had shared with her father on one of Aldis Nova's back streets.

So she waited to hear back from any of the universities to which she had transmitted applications, tried not to ask Thorn where he went during the day—she had a sneaking suspicion that he was in the midst of stockpiling supplies, or planning his next job—and attempted to quell the fear that seemed to rise in her a little higher every day.

It didn't help that on several occasions she felt quite ill and remained in bed longer than she normally would have. She wanted to attribute her queasiness to the rich seafood-based Callian cuisine, but she knew better than that. On her eighteenth birthday she'd gone and gotten the contraceptive implants custom expected, even though at the time she hadn't thought she'd have much use for them. But she'd heard horror stories of how the techs at the clinics sometimes switched out the implants with placebos so they could sell the valuable pharmaceuticals on the black market. She'd always assumed the stories were just that, urban legends with no real basis in fact, but her body seemed to be telling her something quite different.

And she was damned if she knew what the hell she was going to do about it.

The message looked innocuous enough. *From the Registrar's Office*, it said, and Miala assumed it was merely an acknowledgment that her transcripts had been received. Still, she clicked on it, if only to clear it out of her incoming messages folder. Her eyes scanned the few paragraphs the message contained, and then she sat quite still.

"Close message," she said at length, and Thorn stuck his head out from the dressing area.

"Did you say something?"

Miala stared at him for a moment, as if trying to memorize every line of his face, every detail, from the sheen of his still damp hair to the dark stubble on his unshaven chin. "I got in," she replied finally, marveling that her voice sounded so calm.

He didn't bother to ask what she meant. "Where?"

"Nova Angeles. My first choice. I didn't think they'd get back to me so fast." *No*, she thought, *I thought I'd have a few more weeks at least. A few more weeks with you.*

Nothing in his face, no response, not even the slightest hint of disappointment or surprise. He asked, "When do you start?"

She picked up the cup of now-lukewarm coffee that sat on the table next to her computer, took a careful sip, and forced herself to swallow, even though the liquid tasted like gall. "Winter term starts in five standard days. I have to look into transport, but it's probably going to take me at least three days to get there, so—"

"So—" he repeated, and looked down at the sonic razor he held in his hand as if wondering how it had gotten there.

Say something, she thought. *Say anything. Say you'll go with me—say that you don't want me to go—say that you want me to stay.*

A long pause, one in which Miala was certain Thorn could hear her heart pounding within her ribcage. Then he said, "You'd better start packing, then. I told you that you bought too many clothes."

And with that he disappeared back into the dressing area. A few seconds later she heard the sound of the razor being switched on.

The computer screen before her seemed to blur. Angrily, she blinked back the tears. *Don't give him the satisfaction*, she told herself. *What did you expect, anyway?*

The message from the University of Nova Angeles had a biometric acceptance system. Her thumbprints and retinal scans had been included with the transcripts she had transmitted and were already on file. With a savage gesture she lifted her hand and pressed her thumb against the screen, indicating she had accepted their offer.

The hell with you, Thorn, she thought, and went to retrieve her suitcases from the wardrobe.

The taxi that carried them to the spaceport was larger than the one they had first used after their arrival on Callia. It had to be, to accommodate Miala's luggage.

Through it all, the last-minute travel arrangements, the conversion of her share of Mast's units into vouchers or deposits in the accounts she had established, she managed to avoid any confrontations with the mercenary. She'd even allowed him to make love to her one last time, although for once she took no real pleasure from the act. She watched everything she did as if standing to one side and observing, as if it were all happening to someone else.

Now and then she reflected on how strange it was that one person could change her priorities so greatly. Six weeks ago she couldn't have imagined a better future than attending a prestigious university, especially without having to beg for scholarships or grants. Now, when she thought about school at all, it was with a feeling of gray indifference.

Still, she had made her decision, the only logical one she could have made. She was proud of herself for never having wept in front of Thorn, not even the one dim morning when she had crept from bed and gotten sick in the bathroom. She had stayed there much longer than necessary as she clung to the edges of the commode and tried to calm the wracking sobs that shook her body. Thank God he'd slept through it all. She couldn't have found the words to explain to him exactly why she was feeling so wretched.

He sat beside her now, face unmoving, as the sights of Chistan Major streaked past. Today of course was beautiful, the sky a delicate blue-green traced with slender clouds. It seemed to mock her dark mood.

At least this time she set out looking like a lady. No one would have guessed her dubious origins by looking at her, she thought. The Zeta Sector, where Nova Angeles was located, had a reputation for snobbery. But between her expensive clothes and the trace of Gaian accent that was her only inheritance from her father, no one could possibly guess that fewer than two standard months earlier she had been scrubbing pots in Mast's compound.

The taxi came to a slow stop outside the spaceport's main entrance—the only one functioning after the disaster of a month ago—and the door lifted open. At least this time their trip hadn't been interrupted by an overly talkative mech. This one seemed to have had its voice circuits permanently disabled...probably by a disgruntled off-world tourist.

Thorn got out and extended a hand to her. For a second she hesitated, then took it. After all, she told herself, she couldn't exactly make a grand exit if she ended up tripping over the heavy skirts of her traveling suit.

Handler mechs appeared to extract her luggage from the cargo compartment of the aircar. She handed the thin plastic ticket to one of them. It passed a reader over the ticket, nodded, and directed the other mechs to take the luggage to the complex of landing pads controlled by Eridani Royal Spacelines.

Still without speaking, she handed the mech cabbie a credit voucher, waited while it scanned the voucher and collected its fare, then turned to go inside the spaceport. At least it looked as if they'd done some cleaning up in the intervening weeks. The green caution tape was gone, and new glass gleamed along the entrances.

"I can go from here," Miala said at last. "Thanks for coming with me this far."

Thorn gave her the familiar narrow look from under

his dark brows, and shook his head. "I'll see you over to the boarding area."

She knew there was no point in arguing with him, and so she merely lifted her shoulders and walked into the spaceport, pausing briefly to study the glowing holographic map just inside the door. The ERS lounge was at the far end of the spaceport—*naturally*, she thought wryly—and it appeared the moving walkways were still broken. At least she had had the sense to wear flat shoes.

The corridors of the spaceport were considerably more crowded than they had been when she and Eryk Thorn first arrived on Callia. Tourism seemed to be picking back up, for which she was glad. The local economy had been in a freefall since the series of tidal waves that had obliterated most of the coastline. Of course, as Thorn had dryly pointed out after she returned from yet another shopping expedition, that didn't mean Miala had to single-handedly shoulder the responsibility of reviving it.

As they walked, neither speaking, she wondered what stubbornness or final sense of duty led him to come with her. She knew better than to hope for a final impassioned outburst. *He probably just wants to make sure I really do get on the ship*, she thought. *I've complicated his life enough as it is. If he only knew just how much more complicated I could have made it...*

The ERS lounge held a few travelers, mainly humans. It had survived most of the damage that had touched the rest of the spaceport. Dull gold hangings softened the huge windows, and alien flowers bloomed in tastefully grouped planters.

Thorn paused only a few steps into the lounge area, far enough away from the other travelers so he and Miala wouldn't attract any attention. At least, she assumed that was his intention, although she reflected that spaceport lounges such as this one had probably been the stage for countless teary goodbyes and other not quite socially acceptable scenes.

At least her eyes were dry—for now. She glanced up at Thorn, and tried to look at him with the eyes of a stranger. Then he became just another swarthy, stony-faced man of slightly greater than average height, with nothing in particular to recommend him.

I can do this. If nothing else, Thorn has certainly taught me a good poker face.

If her own lack of expression discomfited him, he didn't show it. "So you're sure you have everything set?"

She nodded. "The housing agent at school already has an apartment secured for me. I'll get the rest of what I need once I arrive on Nova Angeles."

Was it her imagination, or was he beginning to a look a little uncomfortable? He frowned slightly, and she stifled a sudden absurd impulse to laugh. Who would have thought that the galaxy's greatest mercenary would be laid low by a simple goodbye at a spaceport?

"It's been fun, Thorn," she said, making sure her voice sounded brittle and light. "I'd promise to write, but since I have no idea where you'll even be—"

"Miala." His voice was quiet, but something about his tone quelled her, stopped the flow of deliberately sarcastic words. "You know I'll always be able to find you."

"Right," she replied. "How could I forget? The great Eryk Thorn always gets his man."

He didn't bother to correct her with any nonsense about a Captain Marr.

"The question is," she continued, forcing a twisted smile to her lips, "whether you'll want to find me."

"Do you undervalue yourself that much?"

"Why not?" From the speaker system she heard the announcement for her flight. It had an odd, tinny quality, as if she were hearing it with ears not her own. Then, knowing a good exit line when she heard one, she added, "You did."

And with that final shot she turned away from him and forced herself to follow the other passengers down the corridor that led to the ship. Even as she did so, she wondered whether he would try to stop her.

Of course, he did not.

Her passage was for first class, naturally. Since Miala's only experience of space flight had been her trip to Callia in the *Fury*, she was pleasantly surprised by the luxury that greeted her as she entered the main compartment. No cramped grav seats here; the first-class lounge looked more like the lobby bar of the Eridani Majesty than the interior of a spaceship, and her sleeping quarters, although small, had been designed with every convenience in mind.

The handler mechs had done their jobs. Her luggage was already there, stowed under the bed and in the small wardrobe. A comfortable chair stood near the small square viewport, and she sat down on the well-padded seat to watch her departure from Callia.

In a gentle, majestic movement, the liner lifted straight up from the landing pad. Miala watched the ground slowly recede until all of Chistan Major lay spread out below her. Immediately ahead of her the sea glinted blue and green, glowing one last time in her vision before the ship moved up through the cloud layer. Then the curve of the planet transformed into a disk, even as the luxury liner turned away from Callia and pointed toward the black of deep space.

The shift into subspace was barely perceptible on a ship of this size. But Miala watched the starfield distort into streaks of pale fire and realized she was already on her way to Nova Angeles. Suddenly she felt very tired.

So he was gone. She realized she had never even said goodbye.

Everybody leaves, she thought. One by one, they had all abandoned her in their way. Her mother. Her father. Why had she thought Eryk Thorn would be any different?

The hurt came then, a deep cramping ache that felt like the accumulation of every unshed tear she had ever held back, every word of love she had never spoken to him. Suddenly it seemed as if she were being suffocated, and she pulled in a deep gasping breath. At last the tears followed, and she leaned her head against the viewport and wept. She wept not because she expected any comfort from it, but because she knew if she held the tears in any longer, she would surely die.

Time passed, and gradually her sobbing eased. She raised her aching eyes to the viewport and watched the subspace-distorted heavens streak by. His absence from the pretty little stateroom felt like a gaping hole in the fabric of her universe, but she knew no amount of tears would change that.

Her mouth was dry, filled with the taste of dust and ashes, like the dryness of an Iradian summer. She stood and went to the little refrigeration unit. It, too, had been stocked with all manner of conveniences, and she pulled out a small pouch of mineral water.

The water revived her somewhat, but it did little to dispel the bitterness she could still taste. It came from somewhere deep inside her, and no amount of water could change that.

Everybody leaves, she thought again, and she brought her hand to rest against the still flat contours of her abdomen. *But I won't. I'll always be here for you, little one.*

Thorn might be gone, but she had this one last legacy from him, something he could never take away from her. Something to remember him by.

Where Thorn was now, she had no idea. Away from Callia already, no doubt. Quite possibly he went straight to his own ship after she was safely gone. There would always be the next job, the next score. It was what drove him, and she knew she could no more change that than change the color of his eyes.

You may think you're alone in the galaxy, she thought. *But there will always be this other part of you, this one good that came from my love for you.*

She wished she could stop loving him. It would be easier that way. The best she could hope to do was transfer that love to his child—and hope that, one day, it would be enough.

PART TWO:
NOVA ANGELES

XIII

THE DESERTS OF IRADIA swirled past the viewport, gold and ochre and mottled brown. They did not seem to have changed much over the past eight years.

Miala shifted in her seat and frowned. *After all the times I swore I would never come back here*, she thought, then turned away from the window and began to busy herself with gathering up her belongings—her computer tablet, a half-drunk pouch of water—and placing them in the sleek leather satchel that was the only piece of luggage she had brought with her into the passenger compartment. The rest of her clothing and other personal effects were still safely stowed in the small cabin that had been her home for the past two days.

"Mistress Felaris?"

She looked up to see Master Dizhan, the Eridani who had hired her, hovering near the door to the passenger compartment. Besides herself, the only occupants were a pair of slightly shabby humans. The man and woman were dressed in the same rumpled, loose-fitting clothing that Miala herself had grown up wearing. Now, however, in her tailored synth-linen suit and tight brown boots, she looked no more like them than a Bathshevan water dancer did a cowherd.

At least no one would ever guess that this was my home world, she thought.

She'd given herself the last name of "Felaris" when she settled on Nova Angeles, hoping to leave shabby little Miala Fels and her past far behind. Most of her friends there called her Mia as well; she'd taken her father's pet name for her and given that to everyone she met on Nova Angeles. In her mind, however, she was still Miala and always would be.

"The captain informs me that we are about to land," Master Dizhan went on. "A transport is already waiting to take us to Mungar's home."

"Thank you, Master Dizhan," she replied, then stood. "I'll go and ready the rest of my things."

He nodded, then stepped aside to allow her to move past him and down the corridor toward her cabin, one of only eight the small passenger liner contained. These days she was used to flying in much higher style, but Iradia was far enough off the beaten path that the first-class passenger ships generally did not travel there.

As she tidied up the cabin and set her two suitcases near the doorway for the handler mechs, she wondered again at herself. So much for resolutions. Then again, even Felaris Security Systems didn't get a 1.5-million-unit contract every day.

At first she had refused. But that was before she had known what they were offering…

"I'm afraid I'm not interested." Miala had pushed the pale blue sheet of synth-paper and its accompanying credit voucher toward the lavender-skinned Eridani who faced her. "This really doesn't sound like the sort of project that requires the services of FSS."

The alien man blinked his dark blue eyes. "Mistress Felaris, it is imperative that my employer secure the services of a reputable security agency. Your company's reputation has spread far beyond this sector, all the way to Iradia. He insists that no one else will do."

Iradia, of all places. Just the mention of the planet that had been her home for the first twenty years of her life brought a dry, bitter taste to her mouth. She'd vowed when she left that she would never return, and this unappealing offer certainly wasn't enough to make her change her mind.

Still, she'd felt a little sorry for the poor man who had come all this way on a fruitless errand. She said, "My apologies, Master Dizhan, but I'm afraid you've made a long journey for nothing. I'm sure that you can find someone a little closer to home to take on your project."

The Eridani's face remained expressionless—at least, the alien male revealed no visible emotion. "I've been authorized to bid up to 1.5 million units, if that is what it requires."

One point five million? she thought. That put a different spin on things entirely. Why anyone would think a standard software security installation required that sort of cash outlay boggled her for a second. If she'd learned anything over the past few years, however, it was never to underesti-mate the lower limits of human or alien intelligence. If the Eridani's mysterious employer really felt it necessary to pay her almost double what the job required, far be it from her to dissuade him.

She'd allowed herself a small smile, and extended a manicured hand to the alien. "Master Dizhan, I believe we have a deal."

The Eridani took her hand briefly, then inquired, "And how soon will you be able to fulfill the contract?"

"Some space appears to have just opened up on my schedule," she replied. "Within a standard week, if not sooner. As soon as I have everything set here, I'll be en route."

He nodded. "Excellent."

Mia pushed a button on her intercom, opening a direct line to her assistant. "Risa, Master Dizhan is ready to sign a contract. Standard security setup, expedited fulfillment. I'll be on this one right away."

"Of course, Mia," came her assistant's reply, with the slightest lift of a question at the end. Normally things didn't move quite that quickly around Felaris Security Services.

Dizhan bowed his head once more, and rose as he saw her assistant appear at the door. Risa ushered him out with practiced ease, leaving Miala alone in her office.

Once she had committed herself to the project, she experienced a slight twinge of unease. She had gone away on business trips before, but never so far—merely to New Chicago, Nova Angeles' neighboring planet, and then only for a few days. This trip to Iradia would require at least ten standard days. Then again, her son Jerem was almost eight now. Perhaps it was time to be a little less protective of the boy.

But Iradia—she closed her eyes for a moment, recalling the heat and the dust, the odd smell of baked rock and gritty sand. Were even a million and a half credits worth it? Felaris Security Systems had thrived over the mere four years of its existence, and she already had a waiting list of clients. Of course, she'd had plenty of seed money to get the business started—her half of the units she and Eryk Thorn had taken from the unguarded treasure chambers of Mast's compound.

Mia shook her head. No need to start thinking of that now...thinking of him. He was gone, buried in the past, as had been the name with which she was born. No one here on Nova Angeles knew that her last name had once been Fels, or that the long absent father of her son was none other than the notorious Eryk Thorn.

And she'd been reminded of that fact once again when she'd broken the news to her son that she would be traveling to Iradia and would be gone for at least a week and a half.

The level dark brows had pulled down in a scowl while he contemplated her words. "I want to come with you," Jerem said finally.

She buried a smile. How typical of him. Most children would have wondered why she had to be gone so long or why she had to leave at all. Jerem didn't bother to question her on these minor points—he had merely wanted to make sure he wouldn't miss out on anything interesting.

"That's impossible, sweetie," Miala said. "This is a business trip. Besides," she added, as she saw his frown deepen, "You know how dull it is when I'm working on the computer. Imagine a whole week of that."

A sideways glance from beneath the heavy black lashes. "But aren't you from Iradia?"

"Yes," she replied promptly. "And that's how I know you'd hate it there. It's hot and dry and dusty. Sand everywhere with no beaches."

He remained silent for a moment as he contemplated her words. The only world he knew was Nova Angeles, and it was everything Iradia was not: lush, covered in oceans, civilized. From the time he could barely walk he had played in the water; he'd learned to swim long before Miala did. In fact, it was Jerem's love of the water that had finally forced her to put her fear of the waves aside and join him in the ocean. She'd told herself that it was necessary so she could keep a closer eye on him, but she'd known better. Even at four the boy could swim rings around her. It was more likely that he would have to come to her rescue, rather than the other way around.

In the end she'd gotten him to reluctantly agree that Iradia sounded like a very dry, dull place, and with promises of a special trip to the Marinis Islands, which were a popular resort not very far from their home in the the large city of Rilsport, Miala was able to get herself away without too much more argument. The guilt she was feeling now was just a normal mother's separation anxiety, she told herself. She could get past that.

They landed at the spaceport at San Drea, which was marginally larger and of better repute than the 'port at

Aldis Nova. Besides, apparently this Mungar's home sat only an hour or so outside the city limits, making San Drea the logical destination.

Miala had never been there before, but as she stepped outside, she reflected that San Drea didn't look much different from Aldis Nova. The city around her boasted the same squatty structures of sun-bleached stone or adobe painted in shades of ochre and rust, the same motley mixture of humans and a few aliens, all of whom seemed to have a rather furtive look—although that, she thought, might simply have come from squinting against the brutal glare of the planet's sun.

She lifted her own pair of photo-reactive glasses out of her satchel and planted them firmly on her nose before moving all the way out into the sun. Several men went to retrieve the rest of her baggage, since mechs were too valuable on Iradia to be used for such menial duties. Master Dizhan waved her toward a sleek, dark enclosed aircar that looked somewhat out of place in the shabby surroundings.

The car's climate controls were working at full blast, and a welcome wave of cold air surrounded her as she maneuvered her way inside. The Eridani followed her and settled himself across from her on the expensive lizard-skin upholstery of the passenger compartment. Whoever this Mungar was, apparently at least he had the means to back up his inflated offer for her services.

Miala felt the car begin to move, and the shabby surroundings of San Drea flashed past outside the heavily tinted windows until at last the vehicle moved out over the open desert.

"About an hour outside of town, you said?" she inquired, wondering whether she should pull out her computer and do a little more preliminary work.

"A little farther," Master Dizhan replied.

Something in his voice made her hesitate, and she looked back over at him. But his face, as always, held no expression that she could interpret. Shaking her head at herself—*barely less than ten minutes back on Iradia, and already jumping at shadows*, she thought—she leaned down to retrieve the tablet from her satchel.

Much more quickly than she would have thought possible, the Eridani man grasped her shoulder with one hand and then slapped something against the side of her neck. Miala couldn't even cry out—the soft hiss of a hypodermic was the last thing she heard before the world swirled crazily into darkness.

Her head felt as if it had been dropped from a very great height and then split open. Wincing, Miala put her fingers up against her forehead, but everything seemed to be intact as far as she could tell. Then she opened her eyes.

She sat in a small cell whose walls seemed to be carved from the native Iradian sandstone. Dark metal rods like teeth barred the opposite side of the cell, which opened out onto a walkway with a sand floor. The whole place looked very primitive, but also oddly familiar. But somehow Miala couldn't get past the pain in her head to make the connection, so instead she carefully stood, glad that at least she was able to do so without too much difficulty. Her satchel sat on the ground near the rough bench where she had lain. It didn't appear that anything had been taken from it, including her tablet.

What the hell? she thought. The whole situation was so surreal that she couldn't even summon up the fear she thought she should be experiencing at finding herself in such a place. Instead, absurdly, she felt more angry than anything else. What exactly was going on, anyway? Did they think they could coerce her into working for them for free, now that they held her captive?

"Awake, I see," Master Dizhan's voice came from down the hallway, and Miala immediately approached the bars and glared at him.

"Just what the hell do you think you're doing?" she demanded. At least her voice sounded reasonably steady, although she wished that her once-pristine synth-linen suit wasn't quite so rumpled and stained. "Do you realize I'm a prominent citizen of Nova Angeles? Once they find out what you've done—"

"And how precisely are 'they' going to discover that, Ms. Fels?"

Miala opened her mouth to snap a retort back at him, then realized suddenly that he had addressed her by her real name, not the one she had adopted after settling on Nova Angeles. The words seemed to die in her throat, and she stared at the impassive alien face, feeling the first stirring of fear somewhere down low along her spine.

He nodded. "You begin to perceive something of your situation. Very good. Now you are awake, Lord Mungar will want to see you. Immediately."

The Eridani tapped some sort of code into the lock, and

the bars retracted into the floor and ceiling. Miala moved toward him, wondering if she dared tackle him—he wasn't that much taller than she, and between her home gymnasium and chasing after a boy who was Eryk Thorn's son in more than just looks, she'd kept herself in shape over the years. But then she saw the small but deadly-looking pistol he held pointed toward her heart, and realized it was useless.

With a meekness she certainly didn't feel, she waited as Dizhan closed the cell behind her and then indicated that she follow him down the walkway and up a set of narrow, poorly lit steps. As they emerged onto the main floor, Miala cast a few quick, surreptitious glances around her. She saw curved ceilings, also of the same native reddish sandstone, dark metal wall sconces, a large circular staircase at the end of the hall they now traversed.

Eight years had passed since she last walked through this corridor, but it still haunted her dreams. Mast's compound. The place where she had toiled in anonymity, seeking to break the security system her father had built for Mast and for which he had subsequently died. The former monastery where she had brought a mortally wounded Eryk Thorn and kept him from death, only to lose her own heart to him.

She could have been out for many hours. The compound was located on the opposite side of the planet from San Drea, but of course she had no way of knowing whether they had driven all the way here in the aircar, or whether they had simply transferred her into an orbital skimmer or other short-range craft once she was safely unconscious. She supposed that it really didn't matter.

This Lord Mungar must have taken up residence in the empty compound once it became known that Mast was truly dead. Or perhaps he was just the last in a long line of petty warlords who had quarrelled over ownership of the dead crime lord's quarters. Miala had never paid attention to Iradia after she had escaped it so many years ago. That part of her life she had put as resolutely behind her as she had her old name. She'd never thought it would return to haunt her in such a spectactular fashion.

The compound seemed cleaner now than it had in Mast's heyday. The guards she passed in the corridor were all human. And the odd smell that had seemed to linger in the hallways of the building and which she had never been able to place was gone at last. However, these refinements didn't do much to improve Miala's opinion of this Lord Murgan, whoever he was.

Then they entered what used to be Mast's audience chamber. When she had last seen it, the vast space had been empty and still; neither she nor Thorn had any real reason to spend any time there during the short week they spent in the compound together.

Now roughly twenty people occupied the audience chamber, a far cry from the motley horde with which Mast had surrounded himself. The current group consisted mostly of humans and Eridanis, but the creature who occupied the throne was neither of these. He was a large male, his golden skin and the mass of metal-studded braids down his back proclaiming his Stacian origins. His robes were well-made, but not overly elaborate; then again, a Stacian male generally made his impression through his sheer mass.

His copper-eyed gaze fell on Miala and Dizhan as they entered the chamber, and he smiled—but Miala found no comfort in that smile. It seemed too practiced, an expression he had put on because he thought it might be useful, not because the sight of her pleased him.

"Lord Murgan," Dizhan said. "This is Miala Fels."

She didn't bother to contradict him. If they knew who she had been, it was possible they knew far more than that. So she merely stood her ground and waited, trying to ignore the unfriendly, speculative stares of the other occupants of the chamber.

"The famous Ms. Fels," commented Murgan, and his eyes narrowed a bit as he looked down at her. Then he stood, stepping off the dais and approaching her. Up close he was even more overwhelming. Miala had never been in such close proximity to a Stacian before, as the Stacian Federation and the Gaian Consortium were always on the edge of war, and the two races did not often mingle. But she managed to hold herself still, lifting her chin as she gazed up at him.

"You're quite young to have such a reputation," he continued, after a pause. If he was disappointed by her lack of reaction, he didn't show it. "But even with that reputation, it took me some time to finally ascertain that the successful Mia Felaris of Nova Angeles was one and the same as Miala Fels, formerly of Aldis Nova on Iradia."

Miala didn't blink. "Nice detective work," she said. "So what is this all about? Blackmail?"

To her surprise, he threw back his head and laughed. "No, dear girl, nothing that crude."

"Then what?"

He did not immediately reply. Instead he made an expansive gesture that indicated the audience chamber and, by extension, the compound which surrounded it. "Many pretenders sought to control this place, to become another Mast. And they all lost. I have called this place home for the past three years, and my network has grown at the same time." He stepped closer to Miala, so close that she could feel the heavy rolled collar of his over-robe brush against her hip. "But I inherited a compound that had been plundered of its treasures. All my predecessors claimed the treasure was long gone by the time they took control, save for some crates of silk left down in the vaults. But what of Mast's vaunted storehouses of hard currency, precious metals, and gems? Apparently they had all vanished into thin air."

Miala knew where this was going. The fear that had lain coiled at the base of her spine seemed suddenly to spread, to move upward and out, strangling the breath in her throat. But she still said nothing.

The Stacian reached out and ran a finger down the side of her face, following the curve of her cheekbone. "You're lucky I don't have Mast's tastes, my dear," he said. "I'm sure he would have found you delectable. I, on the other hand, am interested in only one thing." With fingers that felt like iron he grasped her chin, forcing her to meet those inhuman copper-hued eyes. When he spoke again, the words were colder still. "I'm only going to ask this once, Mistress Fels.

"Where is Mast's treasure?"

XIV

JEREM FELARIS WAS BORED. The most probable cause of his current ennui was his mother's continuing absence from Nova Angeles, but he would rather have died than admit that to anyone. In fact, a few months ago when Petyr Varlsen had accused Jerem of being a "momma's boy," Jerem had pounded the hapless Petyr so hard the other boy had run screaming home to his own mother. That particular incident had earned Jerem a week's worth of solitary in his room, but the results were worth the hard time. None of the other boys at school had even dared look sideways at Jerem after that.

No, it just seemed as if his mother's absence had somehow left a huge gaping hole in the house, a hole that couldn't be filled by Els-E, their overworked and now somewhat obsolete nanny-mech, or even the presence of Risa, his mother's assistant and friend, who had bravely volunteered to help watch over Jerem while Mia was off on

Iradia. Jerem liked Risa well enough; she was friendly and pretty, and unlike most adults she didn't have the need to butt in every five minutes and interrupt anything interesting he might be doing. But she wasn't his mother, and for the short eight years of his life his mother had been pretty much the whole world.

This wasn't her first business trip, but in the past she'd only traveled as far as the next continent over on Nova Angeles, and once or twice to New Chicago, Nova Angeles' twin planet. The travel time involved was negligible, and she'd only been gone two nights at the most. It had been almost exciting to see that she trusted him to more or less behave himself while she was gone, even though she'd apparently felt compelled to fix him with a stern eye and make him promise not to blow anything up.

At the time he'd just dug his toe in the ground and heaved an exaggerated sigh. She was never going to let him live that down. Just because he and his friend Mikhal had gotten a hold of some rescue flares from Mikhal's stepdad's boat and shot them off inside the garbage compactor behind the house didn't mean he'd actually blown it up. True, the outer wall of the compactor had become positively convex, but it wasn't as if they'd exploded it or anything. But his mother had reacted as if he'd set off the flares inside the house instead of safely outside.

Adults tended to overreact about the strangest things, he and Mikhal had agreed, but their parents had gotten together and made them consent to a mutual non-explosion pact, so that particular avenue of recreation had been cut off. He could probably have gotten Risa or Els-E to take him to the park or over to Mikhal's or Alic's house, but none of those ordinary amusements seemed particularly appealing to him right now.

He sat on top of the fort he and the other two boys had built in his mother's expansive backyard—the biggest yard in the neighborhood, a neighborhood unusual for Rilsport because it had real houses with real yards, instead of apartments or townhouses stacked on top of each other. From his perch he could just see past the lacy blue-green trees that edged the property and all the way down to the harbor. The sky was a pale delicate turquoise, streaked with feathery clouds, and the air smelled sweet and warm. He should have been off exploring with Mikhal and Alic, or riding his bike, or…something. Instead he sat here, kicking his heels against the synth-wood of the fort and thinking, which wasn't something he normally did a lot of. He'd always been more the action type.

His mother had been gone for three days now, which according to her was only enough time to get to Iradia and start on the security project. She hadn't gone into any details, not that Jerem had expected she would. Computers bored him, and he could never understand her fascination with them, or the way she could spend hours staring into a screen, her silences punctuated by staccato bursts of rapid-fire typing. He'd once complained of how dull the machines were, to which she'd only replied, "Why does that not surprise me?" and given him a rueful grin.

But because he knew very little about what her job entailed, it was hard for him to visualize exactly what could keep her busy for so long on Iradia. The very fact that she'd gone there at all puzzled him a bit. She'd been born there, but she didn't like to discuss the fact, and she'd always admonished him not to talk about it with anyone else. Jerem never could figure out what the big deal was, but because it was obviously important to her he had kept the secret. Iradia wasn't really a place to be proud of, he guessed; he'd read about it on the 'net and the UEG (Unabridged Encyclopedia Galactica), and it sounded like a hot, dry, dusty slagheap populated by crime lords and lots of other unsavory types. No wonder she didn't want to talk about it.

The other thing she simply wouldn't talk about was his father. Oh, she'd given Jerem one or two tiny details, mostly to get him to stop pestering her, so he knew his father had been a pilot with the GDF and had died in the fighting in the siege of Arlinais against the Stacians. Mia called Jerem's father a hero, but she said very little else about him. The lack of a father had never bothered Jerem particularly. His father had died before he was born, after all, and it was difficult to miss someone you'd never known. What did bother him was the complete lack of any evidence of his father's existence. Some of the other boys' fathers were also dead, or just gone—Mikhal's real father had died on Nylos in a mine collapse, and Petyr's father just decided one day he'd had enough and had moved away to New Chicago. Mia said that was half of Petyr's problem right there, not having a dad, but why it should be a problem for Petyr and not for Jerem, when he didn't have a father, either, she'd never satisfactorily explained. But at least the other boys had pictures of their fathers, and Petyr even went to stay with his dad once or twice a year.

Jerem had nothing. He could only guess at his own missing parent's appearance because he had decided early on that his dead father must have looked like him. Certainly Jerem, with his wavy dark hair, deep olive skin, and brown eyes, looked nothing like his mother. She had warm red hair that fell straight down her back when she didn't wear it up, and her eyes were an unusual mixture of gray and green and amber—definitely not brown.

When he'd asked Risa why his mother would travel so far to take on a commission, Risa had laughed and said, "Because they're paying her a lot of money, that's why. You like your nice big house with your nice big yard? Well, none of that's free, you know."

Jerem had wanted to retort that of course he knew that, he wasn't a *baby*, but since he liked Risa most of the time he didn't feel like arguing with her. There was a big hole in her argument, anyway—Jerem and Mia had always lived in this house, even while she was still going to the university, and obviously that was before she had started Felaris Security Systems and began making all this money off commissions. How a college student, especially one from as poor a planet as Iradia, could have afforded a place like this had also never been explained to his satisfaction.

His life was like that, full of little inconsistencies and questions that weren't supposed to be asked. Jerem knew he didn't have much cause for complaint, because it was certainly a pretty nice life as far as he could tell, except for school maybe. And even that wasn't so bad, because all his friends had to go, too, so at least they were all stuck there together.

In an odd way it was sort of reassuring to know that his father had been a pilot, even though Jerem had thought to himself once or twice that he couldn't have been that great a pilot, or he wouldn't have gotten shot down over Arlinais. Of course he knew better than to mention these traitorous thoughts to his mother. Still, maybe his father's flying skills could explain why Jerem was able to hit the plastic targets Mikhal set up on top of the fort ten times out of ten (he missed only every once in a great while, and then usually because Mikhal had done something to distract him), or the way Jerem could eyeball the distance between himself and any other object and guess it down to the tenth of a meter, or—well, there were lots of things like that. If nothing else, his uncanny motor skills guaranteed that he was always chosen first for the pulseball games at school.

Jerem knew he hadn't inherited any of that from his mother—she was still slender and trim, but probably because she worked out for an hour in the home gym five days a week and spent the rest of the time she wasn't at work chasing after him. She certainly didn't care much for sports or other physical activities, things that seemed to come to Jerem as easily as breathing.

Scowling at the glittering harbor, Jerem hefted a rock—left on the fort's roof from one of his previous target-practice sessions—and threw it at the border of mothlace trees at the edge of the property. As he had predicted, the rock cleanly sliced through the slender branch at which he had been aiming, and the whole piece fell off and onto the grass below. Once he had thrown the rock, he felt a little guilty about the damage he had caused, but he tried to excuse it by telling himself the gardeners would have trimmed it back soon anyway.

With a sigh, he launched himself off the roof of the fort in a perfect arc, hitting the ground rolling and then bouncing straight up into a standing position. His mother probably would have given him what-for if she'd seen him pull that particular stunt. But he'd done it dozens of times before, and since she wasn't here to scold him, he just brushed off the knees of his pants and wandered back inside. Maybe he might as well go over to Mikhal's house after all.

As he switched on the comm and punched in Mik's number, Jerem wondered idly whether his mother was as bored as he was.

Miala swallowed, then thought despairingly, *I'm going to die here...and my son will never know what happened to me. He'll think I abandoned him.*

The Stacian continued to glare at her, even as his fingers ground into her jaw. She knew her face would be bruised later...if there even were a "later."

She knew that any answer she gave him would be the wrong one, and she certainly wasn't about to tell him the truth. That money was hers, rightfully taken in payment for her father's blood, for the man who hadn't lived to see his grandson because of Mast's perfidy. Some of it had been spent while she went to school, but she had earned a great deal back over the past few years, and a majority of the funds were still intact. That didn't even count Thorn's share, of course. His portion of the money she had deposited in a bank on New Chicago, where it had steadily gathered interest over the intervening eight years.

So she glanced up at the Stacian with as guileless a look as she could manage and said, "I don't know where the money is."

"Wrong answer," he replied immediately, and his fingers moved from her jaw down to her throat, pressing on the delicate skin there, squeezing down on her windpipe.

"I swear I don't know!" she gasped, desperately trying to draw enough air into her lungs to choke out a protest. "I don't know why you think I have it!"

The pressure on her throat eased the tiniest fraction. "Because," Murgan said softly, bending his braid-crowned head toward hers, "it was your father who installed Mast's security system. Because the last trace of you in Aldis Nova was a report submitted to the local garrison regarding your missing father. Because rumor states that you were nearly as good a hacker as he. Who else could have taken it?"

"Anyone," Miala wheezed. "The place was wide open after Mast was killed. Anyone could have come in here and gotten the treasure."

"'Anyone'? Does that include Rast Darlester, whose transport was mysteriously destroyed by unknown defenders in this very compound, days after Mast was killed?"

Well, no matter what else she could say about him, Murgan obviously had damn good intelligence. She'd almost forgotten about Darlester. But his destruction was his own fault. If he hadn't come poking and prying, then she and Thorn wouldn't have been forced to defend themselves.

But obviously she couldn't admit to any of that, so

instead she only said, in a choked whisper, "I don't know what you're talking about."

"Quite a few protestations of ignorance from a woman who's supposed to be a genius," commented Murgan. "Here's an easy one, then. If you didn't take the treasure, how did you get off Iradia in the first place? Everyone in Aldis Nova said you and your father were dirt-poor."

"It's not that hard to hitch a ride if you're friendly enough," she replied, and gave a small hiccupping laugh, all she could manage with Murgan's hand on her throat. The lie wasn't that far from the truth anyway. She and Thorn certainly had had a much closer relationship than merely as business partners.

The Stacian's eyes narrowed, but whether in scorn or simply disgust, Miala couldn't be sure. Not that she cared what he thought of her.

But then the pressure on her throat intensified once more, even as Murgan said, "I think you're lying. The truth, before you die."

A reddish mist swam up before Miala's eyes, even as the room seemed to grow steadily dimmer. Desperately she brought her hands up to claw at Murgan's ever-tightening fingers, but the Stacian might have been made out of steel for all the difference her feeble attempts made.

"She can't tell you anything if she's dead."

That voice. She knew it—and had never thought to hear it again. It had the slightest rough edge, contrasted with a faint singsong intonation that she hadn't heard from any-one else. Eryk Thorn's voice.

Miala knew better than to turn and look for him in the

crowd that had stood watching as Murgan throttled her, but her hands dropped suddenly to her side as she felt the Stacian release his hold ever so slightly.

"No one asked for your opinion, mercenary," Murgan rasped.

"I'm giving it anyway."

Apparently nonplussed, Murgan scowled, then suddenly let go of Miala's throat. She gasped, feeling the welcome air rush back into her lungs. It was all she could do to keep from collapsing at the alien's feet.

The crowd shifted slightly, and for the first time she saw Eryk Thorn. His face was mostly hidden behind wrappings of dark fabric, and instead of the jumpsuit he had worn the last time she'd seen him, he wore robes that seemed to echo the local garb, albeit in shades of dark gray and black. But it was indisputably him.

With an almost physical ache Miala remembered how his arms had felt around her, the slight rasp of his shaven cheek against hers, the strength of his mouth on her lips. All the sensations she thought she had locked away forever seemed to flood her at once, and she quickly glanced down at the floor, afraid that the longing she felt would be plain to all those who looked on her.

"Who's running things around here, scum?" Murgan demanded. "You, or me?"

"You," said Thorn, his tone casual. "But she's no good to you dead, is she?"

The Stacian made a sound like a low growl in his throat. With a sudden, vicious movement he backhanded Miala against the side of her cheek, and she stumbled and fell onto the stone floor. The pain was immediate and shocking, like a white-hot explosion in her flesh. She ground her teeth together, shutting her eyes for a moment.

Don't cry. Whatever you do, don't let him see you cry...

It was hard for her to focus past the throbbing in her cheek. Through slitted eyes she saw Thorn shift his weight, almost as if he wanted to come forward to help her but knew better than to show her any particular solicitude.

Then Murgan squatted down next to Miala, pushing her disheveled hair out of the way so he could see her face more clearly. "That hurt, didn't it?" he asked. "I can make you hurt a lot more before I kill you. Perhaps you should think on that for a while." Moving with ponderous majesty, he stood, hauling Miala upright as he did so.

The room seemed to swim around her, but she blinked vigorously against the pain. After a few seconds she thought that at least she wasn't going to pass out.

All the while she found herself wishing she could think of some clever retort, but her cheek hurt too much. Instead, she stood there silently, praying that he was tired of her for now and would toss her back in her cell for some much-needed rest.

As it turned out, that appeared to be his plan. The Stacian gestured toward the two tall humans who had stood behind him all this time, and they stepped forward and each grasped one of Miala's arms.

"Perhaps a few hours of contemplation will persuade you to tell me more about Mast's treasure," Murgan said. He reached out and touched her bruised cheek. Even that light contact was enough to make her wince. "You have a pretty face, my dear. Think about whether it's worth preserving or not." And with that he nodded toward the two guards, who pulled her through the watching ranks of Murgan's henchmen and back down the corridor, pushing her roughly when she stumbled. Her boots slipped on the steps once or twice, and she was certain she would fall, but their bruising grasp on her arms kept her upright.

Once they were back on the prison level, they shoved her back inside her cell and watched with satisfaction as the bars clanged shut. Miala stumbled to the bench and sat down, thankful for even the harsh comfort it provided.

One of the guards, the taller of the two, whose face was marked by a wicked burn on one cheek, gave her a leering smile. "Better tell him what he wants," he said. "He's promised us that we'll be able to borrow you for a while before he kills you. You might want to think about that." Then he blew her a kiss and laughed, with the other guard joining in and grinning.

In answer Miala only huddled herself closer to the wall, turning her burning cheek away from them and up against the cool sandstone. After a moment, apparently disgusted by her lack of response, they left, but not before making a few more choice remarks that made the blood rush to her face.

It's all right, she told herself. *Thorn is here. He'll come down here and break me out as soon as he gets a chance. He won't let Murgan do anything else to me.*

All she could do now was wait for him to save her.

XV

SHE MUST HAVE DOZED OFF, so Miala had no clear idea of how much time had passed before she heard the barred cell doors open with a sudden whoosh. Instantly she sat upright, heart beating a sharp staccato in her chest. Had they come for her already?

"Quiet," came Thorn's voice.

Straining her eyes against the darkness, she thought she saw him enter, moving slowly. His form looked oddly misshapen, almost hunch-backed.

"Off the bench," he instructed, and she immediately stood, pulling her satchel out of the way as well.

As soon as she had moved, Thorn stepped forward and then dropped some sort of unwieldy object on the bench.

"What is that?" she whispered.

"That," he replied, his voice also pitched low, "is a 'friend' of one of the guards. She's not a perfect match for height and build, but her hair's about the same color as yours."

Mystified, Miala inquired, "Am I missing something?"

Thorn seemed to do something with the girl's limp form—Miala thought he was turning her toward the wall in roughly the same position Miala had just occupied. "Security's on a four-minute loop. When the cameras track back on this cell, they'll think you never moved. So let's get going."

He grasped Miala by the arm, and she winced slightly— the guards had left bruises on her bicep. But Thorn appeared not to notice. Or perhaps he just didn't care.

Then he pulled her out of the cell and closed the doors once again. To the casual observer, such as a guard watching a remote video feed, it would appear all was normal— at least until someone noticed that Miala's hapless replacement was missing from her normal haunts.

Nor was the comatose girl the only casualty of Thorn's rescue effort, apparently. Once they were a few steps down the hallway, which was only dimly lit by a few fading sconces, Miala saw the guard who had taunted her earlier. At first she thought he stood at attention outside a cell at the end of the hall, and she couldn't help giving a frightened little gasp. But then she noticed he looked oddly stiff and suddenly realized that the man was either unconscious or dead and had been neatly attached to the bars of the cell with very fine cord.

"Nice work," she commented in an undertone.

Thorn swiveled his dark-swathed head toward her. "I try to cover my tracks."

Miala was silent for a few seconds, then said, "Thank you, Thorn."

"Thank me later. We're not out of here yet."

The hallway branched into two more corridors. Thorn chose the left one, which appeared to be a service passageway of some sort. At any rate, there were no more cells here, just a series of closed doors, most of which had electronic "lock" buttons glowing red in the darkness.

Here Thorn paused for a moment. Miala stood quietly and waited as he typed what looked like a series of complicated commands into some sort of device mounted on his forearm.

"How did you know I would be here?" she asked quietly.

He didn't look up. "I didn't. I heard Murgan was having some sort of security consultant come in. Then I saw it was you."

It was impossible to tell from his inflection whether he had been at all surprised to see her—or whether encountering her again after so many years had affected him in the slightest. Well, what had she expected, anyway? For him to fling his arms around her and declare his undying love right there in the passageway?

"You probably should have done a background check on Murgan before you took the gig," he went on. "Careless."

Scowling, Miala snapped, "Of course I did a check! My assistant looked into Murgan's history before I left Nova Angeles, and it didn't show anything out of the ordinary or that he was anything more than Dizhan had said he was— the owner of a shipping company who was expanding into mining here on Iradia."

"Believe everything you read?"

Obviously the intervening years hadn't made Thorn any

less impossible. What really irritated her was that she had been kicking herself over the same issue. Risa had checked out Murgan, however, and as tidy little bits of data on a computer screen, he had seemed perfectly respectable. If someone was bound and determined to cook their files and hide anything unsavory, it would require a lot more effort to dig up that information than the simple investigation Miala always performed before she took on a contract. Up until now it had never been an issue—but, as was usually the case, this one exception had turned out to be a doozy.

She wanted to argue with Thorn and knew that it was pointless. So instead she just crossed her arms and glared at him, waiting for him to make the next move.

Perhaps he smiled behind the layers of dark fabric. Perhaps not. She would never know.

Instead he gestured upward, as if to indicate the bulk of the compound, located somewhere above their heads. "Funny thing is, Murgan really could use a new security system. Thing hasn't been replaced since we were here eight years ago. And his guards are a joke. This passage comes out about ten meters in front of the garage, and my ship is on a landing pad about another twenty meters past there. I figure we have a good ten minutes or so before anyone figures out Sleeping Beauty in there isn't you—"

From his words Miala guessed that the unfortunate young woman was only unconscious. She hadn't had the courage to ask Thorn whether the victim was alive or dead. "So—she'll be all right?"

"She'll wake up with a hell of a headache, and possibly questioning her taste in men." His head cocked to one side.

"That's immaterial. What concerns us is how many hostiles are between us and my ship."

"How many?"

He shrugged. "Between five and eight, if they stick to their usual patterns. No reason not to."

"I suppose you'd know all about it." Miala lifted an eyebrow. "How long have you been here?"

"About two years, off and on. Just contract work."

It was on her lips to make a sharp comment about Thorn not being overly picky when it came to his own employers, but she knew better. After all, the mercenary had worked for Mast and God knows how many other unsavory types with deep pockets over the years. Why he'd felt the need to take on that kind of work when he could have come and claimed his half of Mast's treasure at any time boggled her. Was working for slimebags like Murgan so much more preferable to seeing her?

Trust Thorn, she thought, *to tick me off so much that I almost forgot he just got me out of Murgan's jail cell!*

Maybe he got a kick out of working for the dregs of the galaxy. Maybe being at the beck and call of scum such as Murgan held more appeal than having to look her up on Nova Angeles and politely request his half of the treasure. Hell, it had been his idea for her to hang on to it in the first place. At the time she hadn't argued, but of course she'd hoped, deep down, that he would come back for it one day. Then a year had passed, and another, and his son had gone from infant to toddler to a boy who held in his face and his actions the promise of being almost a carbon copy of his father. And somewhere along the way she'd given up hope of ever seeing Eryk Thorn again. If he never claimed the money, she'd leave it to his son. But never, ever would she touch one unit of it. Not that she'd had any need to.

If Thorn noticed her hesitation, he gave no sign of it. "The way things are set up, Murgan's not expecting any trouble from within. He's got most of his security focused on the perimeter and the gates, not on interior surveillance. This corridor doesn't have a video feed at all. That's why we came this way."

No wonder Thorn had chosen this particular spot to stop and discuss the situation with her. Miala nodded, then asked, "But what happens if they do see us?"

"Leave that to me."

Meaning hit the deck and ask questions later. Still, one thing hadn't changed. She couldn't think of a better person to be with in a tight situation, even if there were times she could have cheerfully throttled him.

Then he held up a hand in front of his face, as if to forestall any further questions, and gestured for her to follow him.

The corridor began to slope upward and Miala moved quietly behind him, wishing she'd worn something a little more practical. Her suit had been chosen to create an impression of authority and style, not for ease of movement, and her boots had only been worn once before and had now begun to rub on the back of her heels. After all, she'd thought she'd be sitting behind a computer terminal, not running around in the bowels of Mast's compound. Still, it couldn't be helped now, and she knew better than to ask Thorn to slow down. If her feet started to bother her too much, she'd just kick off the damn boots and go barefoot.

They emerged from the underground passageway into the open space behind the speeder garage under the warm golden light of Ixtal, the largest of Iradia's three moons. All seemed still; Miala could sense no movement in their immediate surroundings. She and Thorn might have been alone in the compound as they once had been.

It was on a night like this, she thought. Once they had stood on the terrace that edged Mast's tower in the warm moonlight, and they had spoken of the future until Thorn drew her inside, to the chamber where he had made love to her for the first time. Back then she had thought she could never be closer to another living being, and now the mercenary might as well be a complete stranger for all the regard he had shown her.

But she remained silent as she moved quickly in Thorn's wake. Perhaps there would be time for recriminations and accusations once they were safely away from here—not that she would probably have the courage to confront him directly about his prolonged absence.

His object appeared to be the wall of the garage. Once there, he flattened himself against the sun-warmed sandstone, and Miala followed suit. His head moved as he appeared to survey their surroundings.

He must have judged it to be safe enough, for he crept cautiously around the corner of the building, still hugging the wall. Miala did the same, wincing once when the heel of her boot knocked against a stone that lay half-buried in the sand. The sound seemed thunderous in the silence, but Thorn appeared not to notice.

Beyond the garage was another open space, and

beyond that, half-buried in the sand, lay a series of rough landing pads for those privileged enough to be able to fly directly onto the compound's grounds. Miala could not see the *Fury*, but directly in front of them was the oval-shaped bulk of an old York-class freighter. Possibly it blocked the *Fury*, which was a much smaller vessel.

"Looks clear," Thorn murmured. If she hadn't been standing a scant few centimeters away from him, she wouldn't have heard him at all.

"So why are we still standing here?"

"I don't like it." Shifting slightly, he looked back the way they had just come, then turned his head once more toward the landing pads. "Too empty. There should be at least a few guards patrolling this area."

Miala wanted to quip, *Maybe they're all on a break*, but guessed that sort of comment probably would not be very well-received. Besides, Thorn knew his business, and if it felt wrong, then it probably was wrong.

No sooner had she formulated that thought than she heard a hated voice from somewhere behind them, back toward the entrance to the underground corridor they had just left.

"Going somewhere?" asked Murgan.

She whirled, but Thorn was even faster. He spun around and dropped to one knee, pistol out and trained on the Stacian.

Murgan, surrounded by what looked like the entire complement of his household guard, stood behind them, gazing over at Miala and Thorn. An unpleasant smile twisted his features.

He looks even uglier by moonlight, Miala thought irrelevantly, but she stood frozen, waiting to see what Thorn would do.

"Not a very good idea, mercenary," continued Murgan. "I have no doubt that you could take me down, but you are grossly outnumbered here."

The snout of Thorn's gun didn't waver. "Too bad you won't be around to care."

The Stacian lifted his hands, his oily smile only spreading a little further. "And neither would you—or your little friend there." He focused on Miala for a moment, and his eyes thinned a bit as he scowled at her. "Who could have known that you'd be so soft-hearted as to rescue a lady in distress?"

"Maybe she just made me a better deal," rasped Thorn. Still he didn't move, his black eyes, barely visible behind their wrappings, fixing Murgan with an unwavering stare.

"Possible, but doubtful." It might have been just the two of them talking. Both men stared at one another as if Miala and the henchmen didn't exist. "More likely the two of you were previously acquainted. She is from this slag heap, after all, and you yourself are no stranger to Iradia, Master Thorn."

The mercenary made no reply. He only stood there, watching Murgan as if he had all the time in the world. Miala could feel the tension radiating off his body, however; he was strung wire-taut, just waiting for the trigger that would send him into action. She began to wonder how quickly she really could drop to the ground and out of the line of fire.

"Stalemate, then?" Murgan inquired, his tones almost silky. But Miala saw the almost infinitesimal gesture he made with his left hand—and she knew that if she had seen it, then Thorn must have spotted the movement as well.

Several things happened at once. The guards flanking the crime lord raised their guns even as the muzzle of Thorn's weapon exploded with greenish fire. Miala heard a horrible high-pitched scream and realized it must have come from Murgan, but she couldn't spare the time to make sure because she'd just discovered that she could drop to the ground very quickly indeed, so quickly that she almost knocked the breath out of herself as she hugged the cool sand.

More screams, and Miala lifted her head just far enough to see Murgan writhing on the ground, possibly mortally wounded but not yet dead. The guards to either side of him dropped as well, laid flat by Thorn's unerring gunfire. But the rest of the henchmen seemed to have recovered from their shock well enough to start returning fire, and she had no idea how Thorn would ever manage to dodge that many pulse blasts.

Somehow he did—at least at first. Then a stray shot glanced off his shoulder, and he winced slightly even as Miala gave out a little scream. Her cry was not enough to distract him, apparently, for he pivoted slightly and flattened the guard who had just shot him.

Suddenly the night—already streaked with pulse fire— lit up with a glare almost as bright as day. A roaring sound filled Miala's ears, and she raised her hands to her head as a huge gout of pulse fire raced down from the sky, cutting down the henchmen who still stood the way a thresher machine mowed *leth*-grain at harvest time. For a second she could not understand what had happened—it was as if some god from antiquity had rained down fire and wrath from the heavens. Then the humming sound from overhead resolved itself into the familiar noise of a plasma engine, and she realized what must have just occurred. Somehow Thorn had called his ship to him, and the pulse cannon on board the *Fury* had done the rest.

Sure enough, the ship came to ground a few seconds later, crushing a few of the hapless guards beneath its weight. Miala sat up carefully, giving her surroundings a wary glance, but she soon saw there was little need for her caution. The sprawled bodies everywhere showed that the crime lord's forces had obviously already departed this plane of existence.

Thorn typed something into the control unit mounted on his forearm, and the hatchway to the *Fury* opened, revealing a square of pale yellow light.

"Nice toy you've got there," she said, and then was surprised by how shaky she sounded.

"It can be useful," he admitted. He reached a gloved hand down to her, and she pulled herself upright. His head shifted slightly to look downward, and Miala followed his gaze to see that her precipitous fall to the ground had somehow split her narrow skirt to mid-thigh.

Well, at least he still wants to look, if nothing else, she thought. "I'm fine," she added. "Thanks for asking."

Something that sounded almost like a chuckle came from inside the fabric wrapped around his face. Then she heard a slight groan off to her left, and Thorn turned away from her, alert, even as he moved to the pile of bodies that had once been Murgan and his henchmen.

She followed Thorn, and then stood next to him as he looked down at the Stacian's prone form. The alien's eyes opened briefly, although they were slitted with pain.

"Felled by the mighty Thorn," he gasped, and a trickle of dark blood began to show at the corner of his mouth.

The dark-robed figure looked down at Murgan. Gazing at the two of them, Miala suddenly thought that Eryk Thorn looked hardly less alien than the Stacian.

"Not the first," said the mercenary. Then he raised his gun and shot Murgan directly between the eyes. The greenish pulse fire illuminated the night for a split-second once more, and then the unpleasant smell of charred flesh rose to Miala's nostrils.

"And not the last," Thorn added, then deliberately placed his weapon back in its holster. He extended the same hand to Miala, and she took it, not knowing what else to do. "Let's get out of here."

And he drew her away from the carnage, away from the acrid scent of smoke and death, up the walkway into the *Fury*. Then the hatch closed behind them, and she was alone with him once more.

XVI

"JUST YOU WAIT UNTIL YOUR MOTHER GETS HOME!" snapped Risa, her arms crossed over her chest.

Jerem's wary gaze slid from Risa's frowning face to the equally irritated features of Dr. Chand, the school principal. No help there, either. Not that Jerem had really expected it. He and Dr. Chand were old friends.

"What were you thinking?" Risa went on. Her toe began an ominous tapping that did not bode well for Jerem. Not that he expected her to actually spank him or anything—but he foresaw a long period of house arrest, probably without access to the entertainment system or anything good. Usually Risa maintained an aspect of placid good nature, but Jerem got the feeling he really had gone too far this time.

Well, it had seemed like a good idea, anyway...

The school was a private institution that catered to the more elite citizens of Rilsport, Nova Angeles' largest city. Most of the time Jerem scraped along tolerably well, although the endless rules did tend to chafe. But he had good friends, and he even did pretty well in most of his studies, more to please his mother than because he really cared one way or another whether he got nines and tens or fives and sixes on his report cards. Still, after a while the inevitable boredom would begin to creep in, and he'd start looking for ways to indulge his passion for thrill-seeking.

A few months earlier the school had invested in a fairly expensive holographic sign-projector that was intended to display information about events such as plays, sporting events, and important dates on the school calendar. His mother had made a few pointed comments about the tackiness of said sign when it went up, so Jerem had figured— maybe wrongly—that she wouldn't care too much if someone explored some of its more unorthodox possibilities.

Jerem didn't possess the programming skills required to alter the sign—but his friend Alic was a whiz with computers of all kinds. And with Founder's Day coming up, Jerem figured that offered the perfect opportunity to have some fun.

Wisely, the school officials kept the controls for the sign well-locked inside the main office. But there was a secondary control unit mounted directly behind the sign—which just happened to be located about twenty meters off the ground on the roof of the main administration building.

Even Jerem might have balked at climbing so far unaided, but there just happened to be a small access ladder at the rear of the building, probably so maintenance staff could get up to the roof to work on the refrigeration units and that sort of thing. The school had anticipated that adventurous students might want to climb the ladder, and so the first three meters had been securely chained off. But that proved to be no problem for Jerem, who had shinnied himself up past the chained-off portion and then climbed the rest of the way on the ladder.

Once he was on the roof, it was easy enough for him to locate the sign's control unit, pop open the box that protected it from the elements, and go to work. Alic had sent a preprogrammed tablet along with Jerem, who hooked it up to the control unit and let the two computers start talking to one another.

All this activity had taken place in the middle of the night. Alic sent the tablet home with Jerem the day before, and Jerem simply sneaked out of his room after Risa put him to bed. If his mother ever discovered that the tree outside his window had branches that were far too obliging in the matter of midnight excursions, she probably would have cut it down or at least trimmed it back, but Jerem had always been careful about being seen. Something about the dark, quiet hours spoke to him, and he'd been regularly escaping the confines of his bedroom and wandering about the streets of Rilsport at night for almost two years now. It had been simple for him to cut across his backyard and through the neighbors' properties, evading their security cameras with the ease of long practice. From there he slipped down the quiet streets and onto the school property. Rilsport Academy had fairly sophisticated security protecting the building, but not the grounds, and no one noticed the small dark figure that carefully made its way to the roof.

Although he knew that once his task was complete he should have immediately collected the tablet and run, Jerem lingered for a moment on the rooftop, watching the lights of Rilsport shimmer out across the waters of the harbor. The city had risen up around a huge crescent-shaped bay, and the glitter of the myriad beams cast by air-cars, skyscrapers, and street lamps was dazzling even at this late hour. Of course, with Rilsport being as huge as it was, the metropolis never really slept.

Sometimes Jerem would wonder what all those people were doing all night, and he'd get dizzy just thinking about all the different lives, each with their own problems and worries and loves and hates. He'd get a weird ache inside him, similar to the way he felt when he watched a particularly involving vid. Maybe it was just the sensation of wanting something more, of beginning to realize just how big the galaxy was and how much it offered, far beyond his safe life on Nova Angeles.

He'd tried to say as much to his mother once, and she'd gotten an odd look in her eyes, then smiled and gave him a quick hug. "The galaxy will still be there when you're older," she'd promised. "I was kind of hoping you might stick around a little while longer."

"Well, I'd want you to come with me," he'd said promptly, and she'd given him another quick hug and sent him out to play.

Thinking back on the scene, Jerem wondered if those had been the beginning of tears he'd seen in her eyes. He hadn't stopped to consider it at the time, because he'd followed his mother's advice and gone off to Mikhal's house, but that strange expression she'd quickly covered up had almost looked like fear. What she could have been afraid of, he didn't know, and he'd forgotten about the incident until now.

But there wasn't time to worry about it anymore—it was time he got home. Risa had been staying at the house while his mother was gone, and she did have an annoying habit of getting up in the middle of the night and raiding the refrigeration unit in the kitchen. Getting caught now definitely was not part of the plan.

So he'd slid down the ladder, jumped down once he got to the chained-off portion, and rolled easily into the soft dirt at the bottom. Once he reached the front of the building, he looked up at the results of his handiwork, grinned, then sped off into the night.

They probably would have gotten away with it—if it weren't for the fact that by now Dr. Chand and the rest of the administration invariably looked to Jerem whenever a prank like this occurred. Once or twice he'd even been wrongly accused, but luckily those times he'd had alibis, and they couldn't prove anything.

This time, however, they'd put pressure on Alic, and he'd confessed everything. Jerem liked Alic, but he did have a tendency to be too much of a goodie-guts. Mikhal was made of sturdier stuff, but since Alic had already squealed, there hadn't been much point for him to continue protesting his involvement. Anyway, Mikhal had been a co-conspirator, but he hadn't actually done that much this time around.

Whereas Jerem—

"Perhaps your youth can explain some of your ignorance," Dr. Chand said sternly, his heavy black brows drawing together over his high-bridged nose. Dr. Chand's frowns could be fearsome—and he used them mercilessly on Jerem. "But did you even stop to think what an effect your little prank might have on some people whose ancestors were survivors of the war?"

Jerem looked from Dr. Chand to Risa, who frowned at him as well. However, the expression wasn't nearly as impressive on Risa, since she had wide blue eyes and the sort of mouth that always looked as if it were smiling.

"Um…" hedged Jerem. Truthfully, he really hadn't thought about it. He'd just thought it would be funny. Besides, the patriotic fervor on Nova Angeles about Founder's Day always seemed a little silly to Jerem, considering that Nova Angeles had been forcibly annexed by the GDF. Or at least that's what he had gleaned from the history texts they made him study, even though said texts tried to make it sound as if the transfer of power had been welcomed by the planet's original settlers. But he knew he'd better try to look contrite, or they'd keep talking at him for hours. "Um, no, sir," he continued. "I guess we didn't."

"I thought so," said Dr. Chand, looking pleased with himself. "Consider this a valuable lesson, Jerem—just because you might think something is amusing doesn't mean that other people necessarily share your opinion."

"Yes, sir," Jerem said, looking down at his boots and wondering how much longer this would go on. He'd rather just go home and get started on his punishment right away. Maybe they could get it over with before his mother even got back.

Dr. Chand watched him carefully for a moment, eyes narrowed. Jerem tried to stare back as guilelessly as possible. If the principal sniffed out the slightest hint of insincerity, he'd keep at Jerem without mercy.

But apparently he was satisfied with Jerem's air of contrition, for after a moment Dr. Chand looked over at Risa and said, "You can take him home now. But he has early detention the rest of this week. And I will need to speak to his mother when she returns."

"Yes, Dr. Chand," Risa said wearily. Jerem knew that his mother hated morning detention because it meant she had to get Jerem ready and out of the house that much earlier, and he imagined Risa didn't like the idea any better.

She hustled him out of the principal's office and down to the waiting aircar, scolding him the whole time. Jerem tuned out most of her complaints, and then paused for a second while she opened the door to the car. As he stared up at the gleaming white façade of the administration building, he got a sudden image of it the way it had looked the night before, with the words "Free Nova Angeles!" shimmering in a bright acid green that could be seen for miles. Jerem and Mikhal had argued over whether it should say "Nova Angeles for the Natives" or "Free Nova Angeles!" but decided on the latter simply because it was shorter and so, as Alic had pointed out, they could use a bigger font. They hadn't actually believed it, after all.

Grown-ups get bent about the weirdest things, he thought, as Risa whipped the car up into the traffic lanes above the school and merged with the other vehicles at a not entirely safe speed. Her smiling mouth was pressed to a thin line. But at least the stream of reprimands had stopped—for now. Jerem had no doubt they would start up again once they were home.

Well, even if it meant no vids for a week and early detention, it still had been worth it. He grinned suddenly, although he made sure to keep his gaze studiously in his lap as he did so. After all, no matter what Risa might think, he was still getting off a lot easier than he would have if his mother had been home.

"You don't have to do this," Miala protested, watching helplessly as the huge sandy-yellow disk of Iradia fell away somewhere off to starboard.

Thorn didn't turn to look at her. His hands moved expertly over the controls of the *Fury*, maneuvering them with ever-increasing speed away from her home world.

"I think I do," he replied. "Only way to make sure you get home safe."

She wanted to snap back at him, but realized that not only would he ignore her anyway, but it was somewhat rude to be abusing the man who just saved her from certain death—or worse. Lips clamped shut, she stared out the viewport, watching the starry pinpoints outside blur into washes of non-color as they entered subspace.

"Besides," he added, reaching up to unwrap the fabric from around his head, "I'll need to collect some of that cash you've been holding for me all these years, since I doubt Murgan's going to pay off my commission any time soon."

In silence Miala watched as he finally revealed the face she had dreamed about, wondered about, for the past eight years. He did not look much different. The lines were cut more deeply into the skin around his eyes and mouth, and she thought she could see the first faint traces of gray brushing the dark hair at his temples, but otherwise he was very much the same man she remembered from all those years ago.

Something inside her seemed to turn over. She held her breath, willing the hurt away. *It was so much easier when I couldn't see his face.*

"You still have it, don't you?" he asked.

What? Miala thought. *Oh, of course. The money.*

"As a matter of fact, I do," she retorted, forcing herself to look at him. "All of it, plus interest. Which is quite a lot after eight years."

A look of amusement came and went in those dark eyes. "So I'm rich now?"

"Something like that." Indeed, it had surprised her how quickly money could accumulate when it kept earning interest and the principal remained untouched. She had had to dip into her own part of the treasure when she was first starting out, but over the years she had gradually replaced what had been spent, and built on it as her business grew. Even by Nova Angeles standards she was considered a rich woman. Never again for her the gnawing worry of whether there would be enough money to buy food or pay off the landlord for yet another month.

"How much?"

"A little over ten million units," she replied. At least, that had been the balance as of the last statement she'd received. It might have compounded again since then.

She'd known he wouldn't react much, even to such a huge sum, but he did lift an eyebrow slightly. "Guess I am rich."

And now he seemed bound and determined to return her to Nova Angeles. Miala had known this day might come, but now, confronted as she was with the reality of

Thorn soon landing on her adopted home world, she could feel panic begin to well up inside her. *Not now—it's too soon*, she thought. Even though she had at times longed for Thorn to know his son, she knew she was a fool if she didn't fear his anger…at least a little.

But perhaps she could delay him a bit. "Your money's not even on Nova Angeles," she pointed out. "It's in a numbered account on New Chicago. I thought that might be safer. It would make more sense to go there first."

"Do you have to be there in person to withdraw it?"

Well, he had her there. She'd set up the account so she could access it remotely if need be. Miala had tried to plan for every contingency, and she hadn't wanted to risk his wrath by making the money too inaccessible. She wondered if she should mention the waiting period to withdraw the funds if she did it remotely, caught a glimpse of the grim set of Thorn's mouth, and decided he probably didn't want to hear any more excuses.

Her silence seemed to be the only answer he required. "Right," he said after a slight pause. "We'll be at Nova Angeles in about ten standard hours."

So fast? she thought miserably. Of course, that second-rate passenger liner she had taken to Iradia would be much slower than Thorn's hyper-modified private ship.

"Lie down for a while," Thorn added, not unkindly. "You look like you could use it."

As much as she hated to admit it, Miala knew he was right. Even now her legs felt shaky with fatigue, and one of her knees was throbbing where she had skinned it when she fell to the ground in the courtyard of Mast's compound.

Besides, the less time she spent in his presence, the less chance she had of betraying herself somehow.

So she nodded and took herself back to the small, cramped bathroom, where she cleaned up her dirt-smudged face as best she could, then pulled a hairbrush from her satchel and pulled her hair back into a sleek, tight braid. The satchel only contained a few necessary items such as the brush and an extra tooth scrubber, both of which made her feel a little better but couldn't do much to help with her torn and stained clothing. After ineffectually brushing at the worst of the dirt, Miala gave up in disgust and went off to the ship's one small passenger compartment.

That, too didn't seem to have changed much over the past eight years, although she thought the dingy blanket on the narrow bed used to be blue, and this one was dark green. No matter; she arranged the lumpy pillow under her head as comfortably as she could and lay back, trying to ignore the familiar scent of Thorn that seemed to permeate the pillow and the bedclothes. It wasn't a bad smell, just a peculiarly masculine scent of clean sweat and some other indefinable aroma that reminded her partly of leather and partly the crisp taste of metal.

How she'd tried to forget that over the years, that and the way his mouth had felt on hers, and the way his freshly shaved cheeks had rubbed against her smooth skin. Why was it that every other man's touch had felt wrong after his?

Oh, she'd tried. Even with a child whose father she wouldn't name, Miala had been the object of more than one pursuit. They'd been handsome young men, much closer to her own age and far more suitable, and she'd been completely bored by every last one of them. Even so she'd kissed several of them, and once or twice let things progress even further than that, but she'd never been able to bring herself to consummate the relationships. Each time she'd abruptly broken things off, and Miala supposed she had gotten quite a reputation as a tease through a certain segment of the young male population in Rilsport. It certainly hadn't been intentional—each time she'd thought things would be different, and each time she'd proven herself wrong. And so, by the time Jerem was five, she'd given up on men completely. If it was her fate to be alone the rest of her life, so be it. Better that than the continued awkwardness of trying to pretend a relationship was something it wasn't.

Once she'd even looked up Captain Malick, the young officer who had commanded the garrison at Aldis Nova. He had shown her kindness, and she had been dealing with a troublesome two-year-old and fighting a loneliness that threatened to overwhelm her at times. It had been more difficult than she thought to make friends on Nova Angeles, whose populace had a tendency toward coolness for outsiders. And she, aching for someone, especially someone who could provide a connection—however tenuous—to her old life on Iradia, had seized on the thought of finding Captain Malick.

It hadn't been as difficult as she had thought. Money bought all sorts of things, including skilled investigators. Miala soon had a comm address, and discovered that, after serving a second four-year stint, he had resigned his commission and returned to a quiet civilian life. It hadn't taken too much persuasion for him to come visit her on Nova Angeles.

Oh, how she'd wanted to love him. He'd been so happy to hear from her, even though at first he was wary, wondering why she would be seeking to contact him after so much time had passed. He hadn't asked awkward questions about Jerem, and the little boy clearly grew attached to him quickly. They had all spent several idyllic weeks together on Nova Angeles over the summer break from school, and Miala had almost convinced herself that she was making the right choice—Gerald clearly adored her and had dropped a few hints that he would be more than happy to join her here on Nova Angeles permanently.

But even as she had been on the brink of taking the next step in their relationship, she realized she just couldn't do it. The specter of Eryk Thorn seemed to haunt her, and she acknowledged finally that poor Gerald Malick couldn't replace the mercenary any more than any of the other young men she'd seen on Nova Angeles. And then he left, still not understanding exactly what had happened. Miala wept for the pain she caused him, but she could no more have made a life with him than she could have given her son to another woman to raise.

And now Eryk Thorn had unexpectedly dropped back into her life. Not in a way she would have wanted—if nothing else, she felt slightly ridiculous for being taken in by Murgan and worried that Thorn thought her still foolish and not entirely grown up. Even though she had spent the last eight years planning what she would say to him if she ever saw him again, still she wanted more time.

But time was not on her side. She slept some, fitfully, but the exhaustion that settled in after she lay herself down on Thorn's uncomfortable bed soon claimed her. Before she knew it, Miala felt the ship drop out of subspace and knew they had arrived at Nova Angeles.

Like so many others, it was a blue jewel of a planet, overlaid with wisps of pale clouds, its many continents strewn like semiprecious stones against a sapphire sea.

"Where to?" asked Thorn, as he looked up to see her standing in the doorway to the cabin.

"Rilsport. It's the main city on the continent of North Cape."

Miala watched as he contacted the spaceport and received permission to land at one of the public platforms. As before when they had gone off-planet, he gave the authorities the false name of Captain Marr, and no doubt the ship's I.D. he transmitted was just as false. Not that it mattered. Nova Angeles was probably about the last place anyone like Eryk Thorn would usually frequent—certainly no one would be looking for him here.

The landing was smooth, and when they left the ship the familiar breezes of late spring caught at her hair. The air smelled faintly of salt from the nearby harbor.

Without protest Miala let Thorn call them a taxi. She knew there was nothing she could do now to head him off—although she was relieved to find that they had landed at midday. At least Jerem would still be at school. Perhaps she could deal with Thorn before her son even came home. Anything, she thought, to keep him from discovering the truth.

The house looked just as she had left it—not that she had expected anything different. She had two household mechs to keep things tidy, and Jerem knew better than to leave his tablet or his toys lying about. He could have as messy a room as he liked, as long as there was still space to walk on the floor, but the rest of the house was sacrosanct. At least there would be no betraying little-boy clutter for Thorn's sharp eyes to catch.

"Nice place," he said at length, after she led him through the foyer and into the ground-floor office she maintained for working at home.

"Well, they say you can't go wrong with real estate," Miala replied, tension adding to the brittle sarcasm of her tone.

He looked around at the expensive blond-wood furniture, the exotic plants, the delicate light sculpture that glistened at one corner of her desk. Some time while she slept Thorn had changed out of the conspicuous dark robes and into a plain gray jumpsuit, but he still looked dangerous and out of place in the elegant room. "You've done well for yourself," he said.

Miala could feel herself blush slightly. Was his approval really still that important? "I can access the accounts from here," she said quickly. "There's a waiting period, though."

"No problem."

Still he continued to glance around the room, and she was grateful she'd just recently taken down the portrait of Jerem that usually sat on her desk. He'd complained that he looked stupid in it, since he'd been missing a tooth at the time, and since the school was about to issue new portraits anyway, Miala hadn't argued the point.

She'd just booted up her computer and was waiting to establish a connection with the bank on New Chicago when the door to her office flew open and Jerem came bounding in.

"You're back!" he exclaimed. "I thought you wouldn't

be home until the end of—" And he came to a sudden halt as he stared at Eryk Thorn, who had turned from his study of one of the light sculptures to see who the intruder was.

For the longest moment no one spoke. Miala could feel Thorn's gaze travel from Jerem to her and back to Jerem, where it lingered.

"I got back early," she managed at last, willing herself to keep her voice calm. "It didn't take as long as I had thought on Iradia. Speaking of early, why aren't you in school?"

"Short day," Jerem replied promptly. "Teacher training or something."

How could he not see it? To her the resemblance between father and son was almost overwhelming. But although Jerem looked somewhat puzzled to see a strange man standing in her office, that seemed to be the extent of his confusion.

"Jerem, I have a—a client with me right now," she went on. "Can you give me a few minutes?"

Her son nodded, looking over at Eryk Thorn with a slight frown. "Um, sure. Can I go over to Mikhal's?"

Her voice a little strangled, Miala replied, "That sounds like a great idea. I'll call you when it's time for dinner."

"Okay." Jerem gave a quick glance at Thorn, then said, "Bye, sir."

Thorn inclined his head slightly, but didn't reply. Then Jerem ran out, the slap of his rubber-soled boots loud on the tiled hallway.

Silence then, as Thorn gazed out the door through which Jerem had just disappeared. Then he turned slowly and fixed Miala with a hard stare. "Is there," he asked softly, "anything you want to tell me?"

XVII

MIALA'S HANDS FOUND THE BACK of her office chair. Somehow the feel of the expensive leather under her fingers was oddly reassuring. Or perhaps she felt a little safer because both the chair and the bulk of her desk provided some sort of barrier between her and Eryk Thorn.

He waited, watching her carefully. As always, she could not tell what he might be thinking.

How often had she gone over this scene in her mind? How many times had she tried to decide what would be the best way of telling him about Jerem? She'd always thought she would have more time to prepare, more time to soften the news. There was no way to deny the boy's parentage—Thorn's legacy revealed itself in every line and curve of Jerem's face.

"He's yours," she said simply, forcing herself to keep her gaze level and steady, fixed on the mercenary.

The dark eyes seemed to bore back into hers. "Were you ever going to tell me?"

At that remark she gave a small, bitter laugh. "And how was I supposed to do that? You didn't exactly make yourself available."

One eyebrow lifted slightly. "I can be found—if you know where to look."

"Well, you knew exactly where I was, and you never came calling," Miala snapped. Then she looked down at her hands, white-knuckled as they clenched the soft leather of the seat back. Damn it—she had sworn that she wouldn't take him to task for his absence. She'd known she had no hold on a man such as Eryk Thorn. Taking a breath, she replied, in as reasonable a tone as she could manage, "I made the decision to have him. So it was my responsibility to raise him."

Finally Thorn looked away from her and glanced around the room, at every detail, from the softly pulsing light sculpture on her desk to the expensive antique lithographs on the textured walls.

Perhaps he thought she had raised the boy in too soft an environment. Miala had always tried to make sure that Jerem never lacked for anything—not in his home, not in his school—not even in the friends she'd made sure he cultivated. Outsiders they were and always would be, but Miala's continuing successes and the unremarkable life she and her son led had eventually won over most of their acquaintances in the upscale neighborhood. Not for Jerem a life on the margins, where he never fit in or felt comfortable in his surroundings. Too often in her own childhood she'd considered herself ignored, superfluous—she was the reason her father got stuck on Iradia in the first place, after all, and between her half off-worlder status and their continuing poverty, Miala had always felt on the outside, even in as marginal a place as Aldis Nova.

But in making sure everything was safe for Jerem, perhaps she had denied his heritage. Maybe the continuing scrapes he got into at school were simply the expression of a restlessness he had inherited from his father. Miala knew nothing about Thorn's background, except his admission during that one half-drunken dinner they'd shared at Mast's compound that he'd been born in a brothel, begotten by a man he'd never seen or met. But who that father was, or which world he called home, she had never known.

Thorn spoke then, in that same flat voice which revealed nothing of his true thoughts. "And you never thought it was your responsibility to let me know he existed?"

He had her there, and she knew it. So many times over the years she'd thought of hiring an agent to track down Thorn and inform him that she wanted to meet, but over and over again she'd rejected the idea. Miala could never think of a way to approach Thorn that somehow didn't seem like the cry of a desperate woman, and so she'd maintained her silence, telling herself that Jerem was doing just fine without a father. The unfairness of it struck her now, as she looked on Eryk Thorn's hard face. She could see nothing there of the passion they had once shared. He might have been a stranger.

It hurt. Of course she'd known he wouldn't sweep her into his arms and murmur soft words of forgiveness into her ear, but at the same time she'd hoped that perhaps he would soften once he had seen Jerem, once he realized what a fine son he truly had.

"I wanted to tell you," Miala said at length, and to her horror her voice sounded thick, choked with tears she only just now realized had sprung to her eyes. Blinking, she tried to force them away. The last thing a man like Thorn wanted to deal with was some weeping female. "I just didn't know—know how," she ended and, to her dismay, began to sob. *Idiot!* she berated herself. *He'll definitely walk out on you now...*

To her surprise, he did exactly the opposite. Almost before she realized what was happening, his arms were around her, and she found herself held once more by the only man who had ever felt so strong, so real. All the others over the years had been but ghosts.

Miala leaned her head against his firm chest, felt the wonder of his hand stroking her loosened hair. And what was that? Had his lips just brushed against the top of her head?

Some of his strength seemed to flow from him into her own body, and, almost as immediately as they had begun, the tears dried on her flushed face. It was enough for now just to feel his chest rise and fall against her cheek, to feel the heavy warmth of his hand against her hair.

After what seemed like several eternities, Miala lifted her face to his. "Sorry about that," she said, and raised a hand to wipe at her eyes. "I always swore I wouldn't fall apart, but—"

"It doesn't matter." He watched her closely, eyes narrowing a bit. "Does he know about me?"

Biting her lip, Miala shook her head. "I couldn't tell him. Not when I didn't know if I would ever see you again." She managed a shaky laugh, then added, "Besides, he's enough of a handful without trying to be the next Eryk Thorn."

That remark brought the quirk she remembered to the corner of his mouth. Seeing it, Miala experienced a sudden rush of relief. Perhaps there would be additional recriminations later, but she realized he would not make a scene over this. She'd forgotten that, above all things, Thorn was a realist—and a cold one at that. Accusations and threats would not change the fact that he had a son. Best to deal with the situation calmly and logically.

That's probably why he held me just now, she thought, with an odd mixture of wryness and sorrow. *What's the fastest way to get a crying woman to shut up, anyway? Take her in your arms and tell her everything is going to be all right.*

Of course, Thorn hadn't really said any such a thing, but his actions had been enough. Just the sensation of his heart beating against hers had calmed her.

Looking up, she caught his gaze and tried to convey some of her regret to him as his eyes locked with hers. "I'm sorry, Thorn," she said. "I didn't do it to—to hurt you, or to have something to hold over you later. You have to believe me about that."

"I believe you," he replied quietly. "So why? You were going to a new planet, a new life. Why tie yourself down like that?"

Why, indeed. Did she dare explain to him that Jerem was the living expression of the love she had felt for Eryk Thorn, that the mercenary's child had given her the devotion she could never have expected from his father? But confessing that would reveal how much Miala had loved him—still loved him, she realized suddenly. It didn't matter that eight years had separated them, that he had never tried to see her during all that lonely time, even that he was probably angrier with her now than he chose to reveal. She had never dared to tell him how much she really cared. Perhaps he knew, perhaps not. Strange that telling Eryk Thorn how she felt suddenly seemed so much more difficult than admitting Jerem was his son.

All sorts of flip answers bubbled their way to her lips, but she knew that uttering any of them would be worse than useless. "He was a part of you I could keep," Miala said at last.

The silence between them seemed to lengthen painfully as Thorn stared down at her. For the first time she noticed how taut the muscles in his jaw looked and thought of how difficult this must be for him, a man who had spent almost his entire life alone, who had made sure he had no personal entanglements to tie him down.

"This doesn't have to change anything if you don't want it to," she went on, wishing that just this once she could read those impassive dark eyes. "If you decide to go back to your ship and fly out of here, I won't blame you. And Jerem would never have to know."

For the first time she saw a brush of anger pass over his features. "What kind of man would I be if I did that?"

"I don't know," she admitted. "But I suppose some might say it was the way they'd expect a mercenary such as you to react."

"All the more reason not to," he said immediately, and she could finally hear the edge to his voice that indicated a deeply buried rage. "I honor my debts."

"There's no debt here," Miala replied, and she could sense the anger begin to build in her as well, as she recalled all the times over the years when she had despaired of ever seeing Thorn again, all the sleepless nights she had spent worrying over their son and wondering if he were somehow going to turn out irreparably damaged because he had never known his father. "No one knows he's yours. And I've already told you I don't expect anything from you for him."

"Who does he think his father is?"

Desperately, she said, "I told him his father died in the siege of Arlinais."

An eyebrow went up. "A brave Gaian defending his home world's honor?"

"Well, of course," she snapped.

"Of course," Thorn echoed, and again his mouth twitched.

Did he think it was funny? God, if he only knew how long she'd agonized over what story to tell Jerem about his father—this fictional parent had to be dead, so there was no hope of Jerem ever trying to find him, but at the same time she wanted the father Jerem had never known to be someone he at least could be proud of. Time after time she had reproached herself. *I am going to burn for the lies I've told my son.* Desperate and alone, she could think of nothing else to do.

"I had to tell him something," Miala said at length. "What was I supposed to do?"

Another long pause. Finally Thorn replied, "I don't know." To her surprise, he reached out and smoothed the hair away from her brow, then traced his fingers along the curve of her cheek. His gaze was intent, as if he were refamiliarizing himself with the contours of her face.

His touch was almost too much for her shaky composure. Miala took a deep breath, then another. *What can one more revelation do?* she asked herself, then said, "I never meant to fall in love with you."

"I know," Thorn replied. He hesitated, a slight frown pulling at the level dark brows. Miala could only guess that he was wrestling with thoughts and feelings he'd never thought he would have to articulate. "That's why I thought it would be better if I left."

"Because you didn't have the same feelings for me," Miala said flatly. Even though she'd known he might say something like this, still the pain of it seemed to cut through her the way she imagined a pulse rifle wound must feel—intense, white-hot, searing agony.

"No," he replied, his voice quiet. "Because I did."

A cautious joy began to spread through her. Had he really just said—

"Connections kill," Thorn continued. "That's what I thought. I'd let you get too close. I couldn't take the risk of caring for someone. You'd be a target."

"So you let me go off to the university here—"

"—where you'd be safe," he finished. "And no one the wiser. If I'd known—if you'd said anything—"

"What could I have said?" Miala asked. "I was so sure you were tired of me, that you wanted to see me off so you could get on with your life—"

His response was to bring his mouth down on hers, smothering her useless explanations. For a shocked second

Miala remained absolutely still, and then she returned the kiss, her own mouth opening to his, remembering the familiar taste of him as if he had last done this only hours ago instead of years. A rush of desire washed over her, so strong that for a moment it made her dizzy. No wonder everyone else had seemed pallid and insipid compared to him, her lost mercenary. Somehow, insane as it seemed, she had always known he was the only man in the galaxy for her.

Eventually Thorn pulled away from her. His dark eyes had a warmth she remembered from their time together in Mast's compound. "So who's going to tell him?" he asked.

"Tell who what?" she responded, feeling a little dazed. Miala had the sudden thought that she should pinch herself to make sure this wasn't yet another of the feverish dreams of Eryk Thorn that had haunted her over the years.

"Tell Jerem his father isn't quite as dead as he'd been led to believe."

The import of his words slowly sank in as she stared up at Thorn. If he wanted Jerem to know the truth, that could mean only one thing. "You'll stay?" she whispered. Somehow it seemed tempting fate to say the words out loud.

"As long as I can," he replied.

It wasn't everything she wanted, but it would do for now. "I'll talk to him," Miala said.

Thorn watched her carefully for a moment, then shook his head. "I'll do it. Better he should hear it from me. It's time we got acquainted anyway."

Slowly, Miala nodded. "I'll go call him at Mikhal's—" she began.

"No need." Thorn glanced past her to the large windows that opened on the backyard. "He's still here."

Puzzled, Miala followed his gaze to see a small flash of blue at the far end of the yard, out by the fort Jerem had built with several of his friends. Not even her usually hypersensitive maternal radar had picked him out, but leave it to Eryk Thorn to have every living asset in an area marked and noted.

"All right," she said slowly. "Be—be kind."

"He's mine, too," Thorn replied. And with that he turned and left her as he went out into the bright day to meet his son.

Apparently he had forgotten the cardinal rule of Mikhal's house, which was Always Call Before Coming Over. Or so Mikhal's mother had told him, her dark eyes shaded with a frown when she'd seen Jerem on her doorstep.

"Mikhal's doing his homework," she'd said crisply, the frown deepening as she looked down at Jerem. "I'm surprised you're not grounded, after what the three of you pulled. And don't bother coming over tomorrow, either. I know how to punish my boy, even if your mother doesn't."

Jerem had mumbled an apology, then beat a hasty retreat. In his surprise at seeing his mother back so soon, he'd completely forgotten the prank that had pulled him into Dr. Chand's office for the latest go-round, but she would certainly find out when she called Risa to check in. He was not looking forward to that interview.

But his dismissal from Mikhal's house left him at loose ends in his backyard as he waited for his mother to be finished with her "client." Weird, because she hardly ever had customers come to her home office. She'd always said she thought that sort of thing should be taken care of at the main office in downtown Rilsport. And something about the man bothered him—he looked sort of familiar, as if Jerem had seen him someplace before, but try as he might he couldn't remember where. Also, you'd think that his own mother would be excited to see him, even after being away just a few days, but she'd appeared worried and preoccupied, and had rushed Jerem out of the office so quickly it seemed almost rude.

Nothing in the backyard called to him—not the half-constructed "laser barrier" he and Mikhal had started building along the perimeter of the fort's roof, not the repulsor-hoop game his mother had bought him for his last birthday, not even the miniature aircar that wouldn't go more than about five kilometers per hour but had still become the bane of the gardener mechs. Everything seemed stale and flat, dull.

So he sat on the low step that bordered the flameflower hedge, looked out into the sunny day, and sighed, feeling very put upon. Then Jerem scowled. *What the heck is he doing out here?* he wondered, as he suddenly spied the stranger from his mother's office coming toward him with purposeful steps.

The man paused a few feet away and gazed down at him for a minute. Then he looked past Jerem, staring at the fort. "Nice fort."

"Yeah," Jerem said. No doubt his mother would have given him a warning glare over his sullen tone, but he didn't care. Why was this guy out here, anyway?

The stranger seemed not to notice Jerem's state of the sulks. "I told your mother I'd come out and talk to you."

At that statement Jerem squinted up at the strange man. Again a nagging sense of recognition caught at him, but now he knew he'd never seen this person before. He was swarthier than most of the inhabitants of Nova Angeles, and not overly tall, but there was something about the way he stood that suddenly reminded Jerem of Clynn Rogeson, one of his favorite vid stars. As if he were ready to go into action at any moment or something. He definitely didn't look like any of the other men his mother had brought home.

"Talk about what?" Jerem asked. Despite himself, he felt almost curious.

"Your father," the stranger said.

"What about him?" Although his tone was casual, for some reason Jerem could feel his heart beginning to pound. "He's dead."

"Not exactly." The man stared down at him with dark eyes that all of a sudden began to seem oddly familiar. "Jerem, I'm your father."

Jerem wanted to laugh, but the stranger looked deadly in earnest, and his words seemed to unlock the puzzle in his mind. Of course the man looked familiar—in his face was the promise of what Jerem's would be when he was grown. Still, he figured it was better to be cautious. "My mother told me you were dead," he said, the words flat, a challenge.

"It's complicated."

"That's what adults always say when they don't want to explain things to you," Jerem shot back, and the man actually grinned.

"You're right." The stranger gestured toward the low wall on which Jerem sat. "Mind if I take a seat?"

Jerem shrugged, and the man settled himself down a few feet away from him. Despite himself, Jerem couldn't help staring. This stranger who called himself his father was obviously a good deal older than his mother; he had deep lines around his eyes and a series of odd scars across one cheek. But the shape of his eyes, the color of his skin, even the wave of his hair, were all the same as Jerem's.

"So who are you?" Jerem asked. He was having a hard time trying to comprehend that this person might actually be his father, but that wasn't about to stop him from gathering some facts.

"My name is Eryk Thorn."

Jerem could feel his eyes widening as he stared at the stranger. Eryk Thorn? *The* Eryk Thorn? Even here on Nova Angeles Jerem had heard of the famous mercenary—he was rumored to be the inspiration for some of Jerem's and Mikhal's favorite comics. He was merciless and never lost a fight. He had a thousand disguises and had evaded the authorities on a hundred worlds. Eryk Thorn was wicked cool.

Somehow Jerem found his voice. "You don't look like Eryk Thorn."

"How would you know what I look like if I always have my face covered?"

That sounded reasonable enough, and Jerem had to concede him the point. "So where's your mask and hood?"

"I don't need them here on Nova Angeles."

Again, Jerem couldn't argue with that. Nova Angeles

had to be the safest, dullest place in the galaxy. No seedy spaceports or underworld hideouts around here, that was for sure. He frowned, gazing back at the man, trying to wrap his brain around the idea that somehow his mother—his respectable, elegant mother, the one who went to parents' night and rode him about sticky fingerprints on the refrigeration unit—had known Eryk Thorn. And not only known him, but had been with him in that weird manner which resulted in children. They'd gone over basic biology in school, but his main response so far had been to think it was kind of squicky.

But still—Jerem's head reeled. Eryk Thorn was his father. Not some long-dead, faceless pilot with the GDF, a fact which had elicited some sympathy for Jerem but had never seemed all that special, but Eryk Thorn, the mercenary.

"So how did you know my mother?" he demanded. He still couldn't figure out how the two of them could have ever gotten together.

"We met on Iradia," Thorn replied. "She rescued me after I barely survived a firefight with some of Mast the crime lord's friends."

"Whoah," Jerem breathed. "And she saved you?"

"I was pretty banged up. She patched me together, and then she gave me half of Mast's treasure to get her off Iradia."

"Mast's *what*?"

A corner of the man's mouth twitched. "His treasure. Mast died, and your mother hacked his computer system to get at the money he left behind."

Jerem was beginning to feel the way he once did after he stepped off the high-velocity spinner wheel at the local fair. Head whirling, he said, "My mother. Mia Felaris."

"Well, her real name is Miala, but yes."

That tidbit required another few seconds for Jerem to digest. "I didn't know she was that cool," he said after a moment.

"Yeah." The man—Eryk Thorn—got that little lift at the corner of his mouth again. "She's a remarkable woman."

Maybe he wouldn't have put it that way, but Jerem thought that Thorn probably was right. Anyway, this information about Mast's treasure sure did explain a lot. "So were there mob bosses and hitmen after you? Is that why you couldn't come here to Nova Angeles?"

His father raised an eyebrow. "I think you must watch too many cop shows."

But it wasn't a straight-out denial, and Jerem sighed happily. Who knew so much excitement and adventure lurked in his mother's past? He couldn't even be angry at Eryk Thorn for never being around—his intrinsic coolness completely outweighed his lengthy absence...at least for now. "So are you going to stay here for a while? On Nova Angeles, I mean."

"For a while."

Jerem got to his feet. "Man, just wait until Mikhal and Alic hear about this! They're going to blow a gasket!"

Eryk Thorn stood as well. "You should keep this quiet, Jerem."

Uncomprehending, Jerem stared up at his father's impassive face. Then understanding slowly sank in. "Oh, right. 'Cause you're here incog—incog—"

"Incognito," the mercenary finished. "Something like that."

Of course. If Eryk Thorn's enemies found him here on Nova Angeles, all heck could break loose—and of course his father wouldn't want Jerem and Miala caught up in it. "Okay, I won't tell," Jerem said. It was a little disappointing, but still, at least he knew Eryk Thorn was his father, and no one could take that away from him.

"Want to go in?" his father asked, and jerked a thumb back toward the house. "I think your mother might want to see the two of us."

Jerem liked the sound of that. *The two of us*, he thought. *Me and my dad.*

"Yeah, let's go inside," he replied. Then it would be the three of them, all together for the first time since he was born. He would actually have a real family, just like he'd seen on the vids. Except his would be even better, because Eryk Thorn was his father.

Grinning at the prospect, he raced toward the house, not looking to see if the mercenary was following him. Somehow Jerem knew that, from now on, he would be there.

XVIII

THROUGH AN ENORMOUS EFFORT of will, Miala stayed behind in the house, even though she longed to walk beside Eryk Thorn as he went off to meet their son. But she also knew that it was important for Jerem to meet his father without her hovering in the background, so instead she took refuge in the kitchen, where she tried to occupy herself with preparing food worthy of such a momentous occasion.

The house provided labor-saving devices that took all the drudgery out of such a task, and over the years Miala had come to enjoy the time she spent in the kitchen. Back on Iradia she had cooked for her father because they couldn't afford to do otherwise, but once she realized she could expend her efforts on combining ingredients with care and imagination, preparing meals became an outlet for her creativity instead of a daily chore to be dreaded.

So she took stock of the components available in the refrigeration unit, steaks and the lovely delicate shellfish that were caught locally, and set to work, trying to keep her mind away from what Jerem and Thorn might be saying to one another. Miala was very proud of her son, recognizing in him much of the resourcefulness and careful wit she had seen in his father. But even in one who had a maturity beyond his years—the occasional prank notwithstanding—such news could very well be world-shattering.

Troubled, she was just reaching into the cupboards for her large tempered-glass salad bowl when the wall-mounted comm beeped. With a sigh, Miala turned and hit the switch. Risa's familiar face immediately appeared on the flat video monitor.

Risa's eyes widened in surprise. "Back already?"

"It's a long story." *And I hope you never ask me for all the details, either,* Miala thought, but she merely looked back at Risa and waited.

"Well, okay—you just surprised me. I thought I was going to get Jerem. And I'm sorry—I just completely forgot it was a short day at school, or I would have been there already. Then that damn decorator dropped in the office out of the blue with those new blinds you ordered—"

Miala held up a hand, stopping Risa's headlong rush of words. If nothing else, the explanations and excuses brought her back to the normal round of her life. Even a few days away from Nova Angeles had made Miala forget that here she had so many little commonplaces to attend to—school schedules, meal planning, even that annoying decorator, the one who felt that keeping appointments was beneath him because he was so in demand. She wondered suddenly what in the world Risa would think of Eryk Thorn.

"It's all right, Risa," Miala said. "I'm home now, and Jerem hadn't managed to get into any trouble, so it's no problem you not being here."

Risa bit her lip. "Well, about that whole 'not getting into trouble' thing—"

I should have known. But she said only, "What now?"

"I guess Jerem and his friends thought it would be funny to reprogram the holo-sign at the school—" And Risa launched into an entire recounting of Jerem's latest exploit, along with the dressing-down he'd gotten from Dr. Chand.

Throughout the story Miala could only feel a sort of tired thankfulness that it hadn't been anything worse. For a moment she had the thought that perhaps she should just let this one slide, in light of Eryk Thorn's reappearance, but then she decided Jerem shouldn't get away with the prank without facing some sort of consequences. Besides, it would probably do Thorn good to know exactly what he was getting into with his son.

After Risa had wound down, Miala said, "I'm sorry you had to deal with that while I was gone. I'll definitely have a talk with Jerem."

"No problem," Risa replied, and then she gave Miala a closer look. "Are you all right? You seem a little…distracted."

Considering everything that's going on right now, I think "a little distracted" is doing pretty well. She merely lifted her shoulders and said, "Probably just a little space-lagged. Nothing that a good night's sleep couldn't fix."

"Okay—see you in the office tomorrow?"

Oh, hell, she hadn't even thought about that. Of course at some point Miala would have to get back to work—Murgan hadn't been her only client, naturally, and while some matters had been put on hold while she was gone, they would start to clamor for her attention as soon as word got out that she was back on Nova Angeles. But she also knew there was no way she could make it back in so soon. "I think I'm going to take a long weekend, if the schedule permits."

A long pause, during which Risa gave Miala a penetrating look. Obviously she wasn't buying the whole "space-lagged" argument. But after a moment she shrugged and said, "Well, since we weren't expecting you back until early next week anyway, I think I can hold it together—as long as that damn decorator stays out of my hair."

"Tell him if he changes his mind one more time, he's fired," Miala suggested, and Risa grinned.

"With pleasure. I'll keep you posted if anything else comes up."

"Thanks for everything—I couldn't do it without you," Miala said, and she meant it. Without Risa watching her back, she couldn't possibly attend to the current upheaval in her private life and hope to keep her business going.

"Just remember that the next time I ask for a raise," returned her assistant, her blue eyes laughing. Then she switched off the comm, and the screen went black.

Smiling a little, Miala returned to her duties in the kitchen. Trust Risa to always know the right thing to say. Even the unwelcome knowledge that Jerem had managed to perpetrate yet another assault on the sensibilities of the locals couldn't completely erase her smile. The exchange with her assistant had helped a bit to put things in perspective, and Miala made a mental note to arrange for a nice bonus for Risa on her next payday. Technically she wasn't due for a raise for at least another six standard months, but Miala figured it was the least she could do, considering what Risa had had to put up with while watching Jerem.

She had just finished placing the steaks under the flash-broiler when the door to the kitchen banged open and Jerem bounded in, followed by Eryk Thorn, who moved at a slightly more sedate pace. Her son was all glowing dark eyes. Obviously the news that Thorn was his father had been met with enthusiasm, and she allowed herself a small inward sigh of relief.

Jerem skidded to a stop by the refrigeration unit and opened it. After he had pulled out a pouch of carbonated fruit juice and taken a long drink, he fixed Miala with a slightly accusing stare. "You should have told me my dad was this cool."

"Would you have believed me?" she replied, thankful that her voice sounded light and casual.

Apparently thinking about it, Jerem finally gave a reluctant shrug. "Probably not."

Thorn himself paused by the high counter that separated the kitchen from the informal dining area where Miala and Jerem usually ate. The house of course had a proper dining room, but it only saw use once or twice a year. He watched her and her son with that same careful dark gaze she remembered so well, and again she wondered what he was thinking. His next words were ordinary enough, however. "That smells good," he said. "What's for dinner?"

Feeling right at home already, aren't you, Thorn? Miala thought, but she only replied, "Steaks and red-eye crab. I assume that's all right—or did you become a vegetarian over the past few years?"

He almost smiled. "Hardly."

And he stayed there, watching as she busied herself in the kitchen and had Jerem set the table for dinner. That was one of her son's usual chores. Although she had a housekeeper mech to make sure the house stayed clean, Miala had never been comfortable with owning an array of domestic mechanoids the way some of their neighbors did. Possibly it was simply because she had been raised to do for herself. Jerem occasionally complained about his chores, few as they might be, but she thought it better that he learn how to do these things himself instead of simply asking a mech to take care of them for him. Somehow she believed that Thorn would have approved.

It was impossible to ignore that watchful figure across the room. Jerem continued to pepper his father with questions as the boy went about his task, but Thorn somehow managed to remain noncommittal without actually seeming rude. And Jerem apparently didn't notice how little information the mercenary was revealing. He seemed happy enough just to be spending time in his father's company.

Not until they were all seated, and the first platefuls of food had been served, did Miala finally turn to Jerem and say, "Risa called this afternoon."

Her son paused mid-bite, staring back at her with wide brown eyes.

Miala tried to keep a smile from pulling at her mouth. Jerem of course knew what she was about to say—they had been through this countless times before—but his face was pleading with her not to reveal anything in front of Eryk Thorn. However, she had already decided that she would not keep this from the mercenary.

"She told me an interesting story about that prank you pulled, Jerem," Miala went on. "You really topped yourself this time, didn't you?"

Thorn looked from Miala to Jerem, a forkful of crab halfway to his mouth. "What prank?"

"Why don't you tell him, Jerem?"

Her son's eyes—Thorn's eyes—narrowed. "It was no big deal," Jerem muttered.

"That's not what Risa—or Dr. Chand—thought," said Miala, before she took a sip of her wine.

"Dr. Chand?" Thorn inquired.

"The principal at Jerem's school."

"Who has no sense of humor," Jerem complained. But then he glanced over at Eryk Thorn, who kept watching his son steadily, no expression on his dark face. It was fairly obvious he wouldn't get any support there. With a sigh, Jerem said, "We reprogrammed the holo-sign at school to say something different. No big."

"What did you program it to say?" asked the mercenary. His tone was even, betraying no curiosity.

Jerem dug his fork into a piece of steak and smeared the morsel around on his plate, staring down as if the pattern of juices it left behind fascinated him. "Well…"

Thorn said nothing, apparently content to wait however long it took for Jerem to reply.

With a sigh, the boy muttered, "It said, 'Free Nova Angeles.'"

Miala thought she saw the faintest quiver of the muscle in Thorn's cheek, as if he had just repressed the urge to smile. But she doubted that Jerem would have noticed the twitch—she'd been looking for it, whereas her son had immediately cast his eyes back down toward his plate after he'd made his confession.

A short pause. Then Thorn asked simply, "Why?"

"'Why' what?" Jerem said.

"What was the point?"

The boy scowled and then met Thorn's bland stare. "We just thought it would be funny," he said, his voice taking on the sulky tone Miala recognized from countless other confrontations.

"Ah." The mercenary lifted his own neglected glass of wine and took a sip, then set it back down. Then he said, "Your ancestors weren't the original settlers here."

"Well, duh."

"Jerem," said Miala, her tone a warning, and the boy seemed to deflate a little.

"They teach you about the Angel's Flight expedition in school?" Thorn asked.

"Yeah," Jerem said, his tone wary, as if he suspected a trap but wasn't sure from which direction it would be sprung.

Eryk Thorn speared a piece of steak on the point of his knife. "So did they teach you about how the original colony here was set up to be independent of the Consortium, only to have Gaia decide Nova Angeles was too rich a prize to let go that easily? They teach you about the property seizures and the internments?"

Jerem bit his lip. Suddenly he looked even younger than his eight standard years. "Ye—es," he faltered.

The mercenary lifted the piece of steak to his mouth

and chewed it deliberately before continuing. "So why would you think it was funny?"

Miala couldn't help but feel for her son as he sat there, staring back at Eryk Thorn and looking suddenly stricken. It was quite obvious that Jerem hadn't even paused to consider all the ramifications of his prank.

To his credit, though, he lifted his chin a little and met his father's watchful gaze. "I don't know," Jerem said finally.

For a second father and son faced off, identical eyes staring back at one another in a face different only in the years it had lived. Then Miala saw just the slightest softening in Thorn's features, even as he said, "Well, you'll learn," and stabbed at another piece of steak.

Jerem seemed to sag in his chair; it was no easy thing to be faced down by Eryk Thorn, even if he did happen to be your father. "I'm sorry," he said at last, in a very small voice.

"I'm not the one you should be apologizing to," Eryk Thorn replied, and Jerem squirmed slightly in his seat. "Maybe the people whose ancestors were disenfranchised or downright murdered, or to your mother—or maybe this Risa, since she had to clean up your messes while Miala was off-planet."

"Sorry," Jerem said, and even though he uttered the word in barely above a whisper, he did sound as if he meant it.

"Accepted." Miala spoke immediately before Thorn could say anything else. Jerem might be occasionally thoughtless, but he wasn't cruel—she could tell that Eryk Thorn's words had had an impact.

The years had taught her not to dwell on Jerem's mistakes—once he realized what he had done wrong, he never repeated the offense. True, he usually came up with new and inventive ways to get into trouble, but as aggravated as she got at times, Miala always recognized his mishaps as being born from a soul that simply needed to test its limits. There had never been anything malicious in his actions.

She sent a beseeching look in Thorn's direction, and the mercenary nodded slightly. He raised the wine glass to his mouth once more and drank, then said, "I got into trouble often as not, myself. Let me tell you about this one time I had a tangle with a crime lord called Gared Tomas—"

And he launched into a tale she would have thought highly unlikely if anyone else had told it. Knowing Thorn, however, it was probably no more than the simple truth.

The rest of the evening passed quietly enough. Jerem still had homework, although he protested mightily having to do it at all, considering Thorn's presence in the house. But after the mercenary reminded Jerem that he had promised to stay for as long as he could and would most likely be here far longer than just this one night, Jerem had taken himself off to his room, looking very put upon.

His absence left Miala staring awkwardly at Thorn and wondering what on earth they would do next. The table had been cleared and the kitchen tidied. She had no other necessary tasks to distract her. On a normal evening she would have retired to her office if Jerem had his own schoolwork to occupy him, or, lacking that, they would have sat down and watched a vid together. But none of those homely pursuits seemed at all appropriate for Eryk Thorn.

He spoke first. "He's a good kid."

How had Thorn known exactly the right thing to say? Miala smiled. "I think so."

"But a handful," he added.

"Were you any different?" she countered, and a corner of the mercenary's mouth lifted.

An odd expression crossed Thorn's dark eyes. "Worse. Much worse."

"Care to elaborate?" Despite her diffidence, Miala moved closer to the mercenary. His expression—as much of it as there was, at least—seemed to be an odd mixture of bitterness and wry humor.

Thorn shook his head. "That's a story for another night. Past is done, anyhow." Then he looked over at her, and again she saw that quirk at the corner of his mouth. "What's the kid's bedtime?"

Puzzled, Miala slowly replied, "Usually around 21:00. Sometimes half-past, if he has a lot of homework."

Thorn's gaze slid past her to the chrono on the kitchen wall. "So about two standard."

She nodded, and then her brain caught up to what he was driving at. No doubt the harsh overhead lighting in the kitchen illuminated her sudden blush perfectly.

"I didn't rescue you from Murgan to worry about some kid playing chaperone," Thorn said, and the sudden swift look he gave her made the blood flame even further in her cheeks. "I need to check on a few things. I'll be back in a few hours."

"Check on what?" she asked, but she knew he probably wouldn't give her a straight answer.

But he surprised her. "My ship, for one. The rest isn't important."

"Of course not."

Thorn pulled her to him then, and kissed her hard on the mouth. She didn't have time to react before he released her and began to move toward the front door.

"Don't you need the code?" she asked desperately.

"Sixteen two aught five, right?"

It was pointless asking how he had gotten the key code to her home security system. He'd only give her another one of those infuriating smirks. Instead, Miala watched him slip away into the night, feeling still the pressure of his mouth against hers, and forced herself to wait.

Hours passed. Jerem was finally put to bed at almost 22:00, protesting that he wanted to see his father before he went to sleep. It was only after Miala showed her son that truly the two of them were the only ones in the house that he settled down and at least pretended to go to sleep, although his sulky expression boded ill for Thorn. Her explanation that the mercenary had business to take care of had not sat very well with the boy, but it was the only excuse she could give Jerem. Truth be told, she wasn't altogether thrilled with the situation herself. So the high and mighty mercenary couldn't bear to spend a few quiet hours in the house with her? Too dull, perhaps? At least she wasn't so boring that he didn't want to spend the night with her!

Fuming, she returned to her own bedroom suite and prepared herself for bed. She was tired, and if Thorn thought she was going to stay up until all hours waiting for him to return, well, then, he was in for a little surprise. Her anger didn't prevent her from donning an expensive nightgown of black synth-silk and Castopol lace, but she told herself it was just in case. After all, she'd been waiting for this night for more than eight years, and she wasn't about to look like a frump just because Thorn had abandoned her for a few hours.

Sleep took its time in coming, but the feel of her comfortable, familiar bed soon lulled Miala away into oblivion. She therefore had no idea how much time had passed before she sensed movement in the room and sat up, blinking in the soft semidarkness. Ever since Jerem had been a baby she'd kept a small lamp on its lowest setting in one corner of the chamber in case she had to get up in the middle of the night and look in on him. It wasn't difficult for her to make out Thorn's form at the foot of the bed, where he seemed to have paused, looking uncertain.

This is a hell of a time for him to develop a sense of propriety, she thought, and pushed back at the quilted bedcover. "I'm right here, Thorn," she snapped, wondering what in the galaxy he was waiting for.

He turned toward her. "Miala…" His voice sounded hoarser than usual, and she reached immediately for the button to turn on the bedside lamp.

As the light flooded the room, she looked back over at Thorn and gasped as he began to sag toward the floor. Heart beating a mad staccato in her breast, she hurled herself out of bed in a vain attempt to catch him before he collapsed completely. She caught him, but his weight was too much for her, and she fell to the floor with him, even as she realized the entire left side of his jumpsuit was stained with dark blood.

XIX

Shock didn't prevent Miala from exclaiming, "What the hell—" as she began to pull at the fastenings on Thorn's jumpsuit.

"S'all right," he muttered. "Other guys look worse than me."

Miala didn't have a hard time believing that—it was Eryk Thorn she held in her arms, after all—but she didn't waste time with replies. Instead, her fingers wrestled with the pressure tabs and snaps, slipping once or twice from the blood that soaked his garments. Once she had the jumpsuit removed, she could see the gaping wound that slashed from below the ribcage on the left and upward to the right. If they had come in at him from even a slightly different angle, he'd probably be dead. As it was, she didn't know exactly what to do, but reached up and yanked one of the pillows off the bed, then hurriedly removed its case and pressed the wad of fabric against the wound in the mercenary's chest.

"Damn molecular blades," Thorn said, his eyes narrow slits in the half-darkness. "Bad?"

"You've probably had worse," she replied. "But I need to get you to a hospital. You're losing a lot of blood."

"No," he said immediately, clutching her arm with a grip that seemed unnaturally strong, given his current condition. "No hospitals."

"So I just let you bleed to death in my bedroom? This isn't exactly a scraped knee that I can just put a bandage on, Thorn!" Fear had sharpened her tone, and Miala lowered her voice before she went on, "One of my neighbors is a physician. Can I at least call him?"

The mercenary shut his eyes for a moment, and at first Miala worried he might have fainted. She should have known he was made of tougher stuff than that. After a few seconds he nodded, and said, "If you can trust him."

I hope so, she thought. But although she knew Quin Lassiter slightly—his son Alic was one of Jerem's best friends—it was one thing to let your son sleep over at someone's house or share a backyard grill fest on Founder's Day and quite another to go to that same person's house in the middle of the night to patch up a wounded mercenary. Still, she knew she had no choice.

"He's a friend," she answered, after a short pause. "I'll think up some story to tell him. But first we need to get you off the floor."

She saw his mouth tighten slightly, but he didn't protest. Keeping her right arm firmly placed around his upper body, Miala slowly staggered to her feet, pulling Thorn upward as she went. He was trying to help, she could tell, and luckily he still had some strength left in his legs—just enough to maneuver himself onto the bed, where he collapsed in a heap on top of the covers. She guided his left hand to keep pressure on the makeshift bandage she'd fashioned out of the pillowcase, then wrestled with the bedding until she had him covered as well as she could. Her knowledge of first aid was far from complete, but she knew he had to keep warm or risk going into shock.

"I'll go downstairs to make the call," she said. "I'll be back as soon as I can," she said. "Whatever you do—don't move. I'm locking the door behind me."

"Gun," he replied, with a weak gesture toward the jumpsuit.

At first Miala wasn't sure what he meant, then realized there must have been a holdout weapon hidden somewhere in the garment. She went immediately to the discarded heap of fabric on the floor and searched it quickly, feeling the distinctive shape of a small sidearm in a pocket concealed by a seam. Fumbling with the awkward configuration, she drew it out after a moment and handed it to Thorn.

"Just a precaution," he murmured. "Didn't see anyone following."

Miala uttered a silent prayer of thanks once she heard that, for she had already begun to worry that whoever had attacked Thorn had friends who might be along at any moment to finish the job. At least the mercenary had entered the house quietly, and her son had a tendency to sleep like someone pumped full of high-octane tranquilizers, so she thought she could slip downstairs without him noticing.

Quickly she leaned down and gave Thorn a swift kiss of reassurance, then hurried to her wardrobe and pulled out a loose long-sleeved tunic and baggy pair of pants, an outfit usually reserved for the rare days when she planned to stay at home. Not wanting to waste time with a proper pair of shoes, she slid her feet into a pair of sandals and then went out, making sure the door was locked behind her.

The house was dark and still, and Miala slipped downstairs quickly, her feet quiet on the carpeted steps. Then she went into her office, shut the door, and flicked on the lights.

Of course she already had the Lassiters' number keyed into her comm, since Jerem spent a good deal of time at their home, but even as the readout displayed their comm code Miala hesitated, her finger hovering over the "send" button. She had to decide what would be the best approach. Obviously the complete truth was out of the question. On the other hand, she couldn't hide the fact that Thorn had been sliced open by a molecular blade, the sort of weapon one didn't usually encounter on Nova Angeles. Actually, crime of any sort was rare on this civilized and well-regulated world. The risks were too high, the payoff too low. The few lurid stories Miala had seen on Nova Angeles' news channels usually involved crimes of passion, not underworld activity. It was better to engage in that sort of business on a world that didn't possess such a well-trained, highly motivated police force. Not enough profit in it here.

Still, muggings did occur every once in a great while, and usually near the spaceport, which was where Thorn had been attacked. She thought it best to leave it at that, and give Quin Lassiter the mercenary's false name of Galen Marr. He would be an old friend from Iradia, come to visit her, and some unknown thugs had jumped him as he left his ship in the dark hours of the night…

Gathering her breath, she pushed down on the button

and waited as she heard it buzz once, twice, three times. *They won't answer*, she thought. *It's the middle of the night…they'll think it's a mistake…* Never mind that the calls which came at such times were usually those that couldn't be ignored, those which told of accidents, of trauma, of unexpected death…

But then the call went through, and Miala found herself staring at Quin Lassiter's half-puzzled, half-annoyed features. He was a man some ten standard years older than she, with his son's fair hair and sharp features. The annoyance in his eyes turned to worry as he recognized her. "Miala?" he asked. "Is something wrong with Jerem?"

"No," she said swiftly. "Jerem's fine. But I do have sort of a situation here—"

"What is it?"

"A—a friend," she faltered. "He's been hurt. I was wondering—I was hoping maybe you could come over and help me."

"Hurt?" he repeated, with a frown. "Why didn't you call a medical transport?"

Damn. She'd been afraid he would ask something like that. "It's a little complicated, Quin." She took a breath and continued, "Please. I don't dare leave him too long—it's bad—" And then she stopped, knowing if she went on any longer the lump in her throat would turn into outright sobs, and she wouldn't be of any use to anyone.

A slight hesitation, and then Lassiter nodded. "All right. I'll get over there quick as I can. Could you at least tell me what the problem is?"

Well, he would know soon enough. "A chest wound. From a molecular blade."

Her neighbor's eyebrows lifted, but he seemed to restrain

himself from any further comment. "Got it. I'm leaving now."

And the screen went blank. Miala stepped away from the comm and went to the front door to await Lassiter's arrival. She wondered if she should go back up and check on Thorn, but she didn't dare leave the front door unlocked, and she didn't want to be upstairs when the doctor arrived. All she could do was stand there, consumed by worry, and hope that Lassiter would be as fast as he had said he would.

His assurances turned out to be real. More quickly than she had thought possible, a small knock sounded at the front door. Obviously he was being careful and had avoided using the much louder door chime.

She hit the button for the door, and Lassiter stepped in, wearing a loose shirt over what looked like the bottom half of his sleeping garments and holding a hard-sided case, no doubt filled with medical supplies. He wasted no time on preliminaries, asking only, "Where is he?"

"Upstairs."

And she led the way back to her room, where she unlocked the door and went immediately to the bed. "I've brought Doctor Lassiter," she said.

Thorn nodded, although he didn't open his eyes. As he had during those tense hours immediately following his ordeal at the Malverdine Cliffs, he seemed focused on himself, directing his energies inward.

Lassiter set his case down on the table next to the bed, carelessly pushing a lamp and her chronometer to one side. With swift, deft hands he lifted the makeshift bandage Miala had placed against the wound. She thought she saw the doctor's lips thin a bit as he took in the extent of the damage, but he said nothing as he lifted out a spray hypo and shot something into Thorn's arm.

Miala raised her eyebrows in question, and Lassiter said, "Simple anti-infection agent. Wound looks clean, but I don't know about that pillowcase."

At once she opened her mouth to defend the cleanliness of her bedding, then thought better of it. The man must know what he was doing, after all. Although medical mechanoids taken over many of the basic health-care tasks in the galaxy, Miala had found here on Nova Angeles the prevailing thought was that anything a mech could do, a living sentient being could do better. Having one's health-care needs taken care of by a mechanoid instead of a live doctor smacked of the lower class, or the sort of thing practiced out on the frontier but not here on a civilized world. Quin Lassiter had a very successful practice catering to the upper levels of Rilsport society, although Miala herself went to a different doctor, simply because she would have felt odd seeing someone socially who knew all the intimate details of her or her son's medical history.

She wondered suddenly whether he'd ever had to patch up a molecular-blade wound before…

Whether or not he had didn't seem to be a problem, however. After applying a topical anesthetic, Lassiter worked swiftly, cleansing the deep slice through Thorn's chest muscles, then running a micro laser-cauterizer over the gash to draw the torn muscles back together again. After that he brought out some antiseptic patches and applied them to the wound.

Throughout these ministrations the mercenary remained silent, his face showing no hint of the pain he was most likely suffering. It was only when Lassiter brought out a second hypo-spray that he spoke. "No tranqs."

Lassiter lifted an eyebrow. "You need to rest. This is only a mild soporific—it'll wear off in a few hours."

"No."

The doctor looked across at Miala, obviously expecting her to be the voice of reason here. But she knew there was no arguing with Thorn. Instead she shook her head slowly, and Lassiter lifted his shoulders, as if to say, *Your funeral.*

When he spoke, though, his tone was mild enough. "Then make sure you stay flat on your back, and don't move." Lassiter's gaze shifted to Miala. "If I might speak to you for a moment?"

Unwillingly, she nodded. Then she glanced over at Thorn. He looked pale under the usual dusky olive of his skin, but at least he didn't have those frightening black circles under his eyes, the ones she remembered all too well from the time after his ordeal in the Iradian desert. It would probably be safe to leave him for a while.

So she followed Lassiter out into the hallway and shut the door behind them. The doctor paused on the landing, and glanced down the corridor. Jerem's door was closed all the way, however, and Lassiter nodded, as if he were satisfied that they would be able to have a discussion in confidence.

Without preamble, the doctor asked, "He's Jerem's father, isn't he?"

Shocked, Miala stared back at her neighbor. How could he possibly have known? But even as she asked herself the question, she realized that a man far less perceptive than Quin Lassiter probably could have recognized the extraordinary resemblance between father and son. And the Lassiters had known Jerem almost all his life.

Mutely, she nodded.

Lassiter was too much of a professional to allow any satisfaction to show on his face. Instead, he inquired, "Does Jerem know?"

"Yes," she replied immediately. At least she would not have to lie about that.

"And I don't suppose there's any point in asking what's really going on here?"

For a long moment Miala was silent, staring back at the doctor. Quin Lassiter had always been far more understanding of Jerem's pranks than Alic's mother, Kya—possibly because he might have remembered being a boy and getting into a few scrapes himself. Miala had known the doctor for more than seven standard years, and they had always been on friendly terms. But she knew she couldn't tell him the truth—at least, not all of it.

"I don't know what happened exactly," she said, hoping her pause hadn't been too telling. "Galen—Captain Marr—wasn't in much shape to give me the particulars when he came here."

"Any reason why someone would have targeted him for such at attack?"

Only a few million. Thorn had enemies all over the galaxy, but what any of them would have been doing here on Nova Angeles, she couldn't guess. The mercenary was always so careful to cover his tracks, and besides, there were better places for an ambush than a spaceport on a well-policed planet. She didn't dare voice her growing worry that this had been personal, that somehow a tendril of Murgan's organization had reached all the way out to Nova Angeles for its revenge. And if that were the case, was her home soon to be under siege?

"People have gotten attacked at the spaceport before," she offered.

"True," Lassiter said. "But they call the local security force and go to the hospital to get patched up. And if you don't mind my saying so, your 'friend' in there looks as if he usually can take care of himself."

You have no idea, Miala thought, but she did not bother to argue with the doctor. After all, he was correct—if they truly had nothing to hide, then they would have gone to the hospital and submitted a report from there. "He doesn't like to deal with local security if he can avoid it. He's had a few...bad experiences in the past."

Up went the eyebrow again, but Lassiter said only, "Well, I don't see any reason why he shouldn't make a full recovery. He's in remarkable physical condition, and the wound looked worse than it really was. But he still needs to rest for a few days, to recover from the blood loss."

Miala knew that was easier said than done, but she nodded. She would fight that battle with Thorn when necessary. Knowing the simple words were not enough, she said, "Thank you, Quin."

"I'm glad I could help." A thoughtful look crossed his clear gray eyes. "And I'm glad Jerem got to know his father—even under these circumstances."

On that much they were certainly in agreement. "So am I," Miala replied. Then, feeling she needed to offer some explanation, she went on, "I didn't know whether I would ever see Captain Marr again. I thought perhaps it would be better if Jerem thought his father was dead, rather than spending his childhood hoping to see a man who might never have a part in his life."

"You don't have to explain yourself to me, Mia," Lassiter said. "I'd say this is all between you and Jerem and Captain Marr." His expression grew more sober. "But I would seriously consider contacting the local security force if you have even the slightest worry that this isn't an isolated attack. For your safety, and your son's, if nothing else."

She knew he was probably right, but she also knew that she could never expose Thorn to the probing questions of RilSec's detectives. That way was fraught with danger. Besides, having Thorn around—even in his current condition—was probably safer than surrounding the house with a detachment of local officers. His adversaries might have gotten the drop on him once, but she was sure that wouldn't happen again.

"I'll take that into consideration," Miala said, which was the standard line she always used in consultation when she didn't want to offend a client but knew she would go probably go ahead and do it her own way in the end.

Sharp as he was, Lassiter caught her meaning. He shook his head slightly, then lifted his shoulders in a gesture recognized across the galaxy as one that would absolve him of all future responsibility. "I'll just get my things and check on him one last time."

Miala unlocked the door, and the doctor went in to reclaim his medical case, but not before listening to Thorn's pulse and checking him for any fever. Apparently Lassiter was satisfied with what he found, for he returned the last of his implements to his case and locked it up.

Thorn opened his eyes and fastened the doctor with his level dark stare. "Thanks."

"You're welcome," Quin replied. "Now show how thankful you are by staying in bed and getting some rest."

"Sure," was all the mercenary said, but Miala knew that his agreement would last only as long as the current peace did. If his adversaries showed themselves within a mile of the property, she was sure Thorn would be off to take them down in a flash.

Shaking his head slightly, Quin moved past Miala, out into the upstairs corridor. She followed him down the stairs and on to the front entry, thanked him again, then closed and locked the door behind him, triple-checking the security system as she did so. Every way into or out of the house was wired with motion detectors and hidden micro-cameras; the place was as secure as a bank vault. But still she felt uneasy, as if unseen eyes watched her every movement.

Troubled, Miala ascended the stairs once more, only to find Jerem's pajama-clad form standing in the upstairs hallway.

"What's going on?" he asked.

"Nothing," she said sharply. "Go back to bed."

"I thought I heard voices. It sounded sort of like Dr. Lassiter."

Damn it, she was just too tired for this. Of course at some point Jerem would have to be told what happened, but Eryk Thorn wasn't in any immediate danger, and explanations could wait until morning. Right now she just wanted to crawl

back into bed—slowly and carefully, so as not to jar the mercenary—and let black sleep blot out the evening's worries.

"Everything's fine," she lied. "We can talk in the
morning."

Jerem threw her a dubious look, but Miala fastened her
sternest "don't you dare question me" parental stare on her
son, and after a few seconds he heaved an exaggerated sigh
and went back into his room. She thought she heard him
mutter, "Why do I have to miss out on all the fun?" before
the door shut behind him, and she shook her head.

Oh, this is just a barrel of fun, kid, she thought. *Don't
worry, Jerem—I'm sure the party is just getting started.* But
since Jerem had not directed his words at her specifically,
she felt safe enough in ignoring him and going on back into
her own room.

Even in the soft semidarkness Miala could see Thorn
startle as she entered, the barrel of the gun pointing in her
direction, but he relaxed as he saw it was only she and not
some hostile intruder. Going to the wardrobe, she pulled off
the clothes she had donned to meet Lassiter and, with a sigh,
drew out a sleeveless nightshirt and matching pair of loose
pants. No need for lacy nightgowns tonight, that was for sure.

"Sorry," came Thorn's voice from the bed, and she
turned, feeling slightly guilty. Surely he couldn't have
known what she was thinking.

"For what?" she asked, approaching the bed and then
sliding gingerly under the covers. Her pillow now had no
case, but she was too tired to get back up and go to the linen
closet to retrieve a new one. With care she turned onto her
right side so she could face the mercenary, and then gave

him a quizzical look. An apology was the last thing she had expected from Eryk Thorn.

His face was impassive as always, but she thought she could detect a gleam of anger far back in those dark eyes. "For being sloppy. I should have been more on my guard."

"Well, downtown Rilsport isn't exactly known for its criminal activity," Miala pointed out.

"Just because a place looks safe doesn't mean it is safe."

She couldn't argue with him on that. Instead, she asked, "Did you have any idea that we might have been followed?"

"We weren't. I know that much."

"So?"

"So the bastards must've still had agents here on Rilsport. Someone at Murgan's compound survived, probably. We didn't exactly hang around to check for sure—just blasted away as soon as we could." Thorn's jaw line tightened slightly. "That was sloppy, too. I was just thinking about getting you out of there."

"And I appreciate that, believe me."

His head moved just the tiniest fraction on the pillow, but he made no comment. After a few seconds, he said, "So whoever was left on Iradia sent a subspace transmission on ahead to their buddies here, just to let them know that things had gone sour at Murgan's place. And they were waiting for me."

"Who were they?"

A small lift of the shoulders. "Typical goons for hire. Locals, looked like. Doesn't matter—they're not breathing anymore."

No doubt. Thorn's casual attitude toward death—even deaths he had caused—still could give her pause, but in this case it had been simple self-defense. All she could do was be thankful that three to one was still easy odds for the mercenary. "What—what did you do with them?" she asked, after a small pause.

"Rolled 'em into an alley, and dumped some old packing crates on top of them. Someone'll find them by the stink eventually."

Miala absorbed that, then said, "And what now? Will there be more?"

"Probably."

Nothing like a little sugar-coating to make the bad news go down better, she thought, and swallowed. "So shouldn't we be doing something?"

A gleam of white teeth in the half-dark. "Don't you trust me?"

It was in her to make a sarcastic retort, but instead Miala only said quietly, "Yes."

A lesser man would probably have made a teasing remark at that point. But Thorn simply continued, "We're as secure here as probably anyplace else in Rilsport. You've got a good system in this house. I doubt they'd try anything else tonight—and right now I don't even know how many more of them there are. Besides," he went on, with another half-grin pulling at his mouth, "I'm under doctor's orders to get some rest. And so should you."

Miala wondered how she could sleep with unknown assailants possibly surveiling the house as they spoke, but she also knew Thorn would not say it was safe to rest if in fact it weren't.

Suddenly he reached out and smoothed the hair back

from her face, and she wanted to weep from the rush of desire she felt for him, desire that must be denied yet again.

"There'll be other nights," he said quietly.

Somehow his simple words calmed her. They hinted at a future together, proved that he still wanted her. This was a momentary delay, nothing else. She nodded, and shifted her weight as carefully as she could so she lay flat on her back. Closing her eyes, she told herself that it would be better in the morning. She could feel the calm slowly overtaking her, brought on no doubt by the reassuring sound of Thorn's deep, steady breaths. At least she could lie here beside him. Sleep began to creep over her slowly, slowly…

Only to be startled upright by the sound of the door chime breaking the late-night stillness. Blinking, Miala immediately pushed back the bed covers, even as Thorn sat up as well. She stared over at him, wondering what in the world she should do.

"I doubt Murgan's thugs'd ring the door chime," he said.

The monitor mounted on the wall across from the bed had a direct feed into her home's security system. Miala grasped the remote and turned on the monitor, then tapped in a command to bring up the view of the front courtyard. No, they were most certainly not more of Murgan's hired killers. The two men who stood on her front step were clean-cut and starched, wearing the dark green uniforms of RilSec, the local police force.

Miala glanced over at Thorn, who merely cocked an eyebrow as he looked at the flat video feed. Damn him—why couldn't he ever look as worried as she felt? Then she transferred her gaze back to the monitor and thought, *This can't be good…*

FOR THE SECOND TIME THAT NIGHT Miala hurried down the stairs to open the door, but this time she did not bother to change out of her nightclothes, thinking that showing up fully dressed might look too suspicious. Instead she quickly drew on a warm quilted dressing gown and went to meet the officers with what she hoped was an appropriately puzzled expression.

"Can I help you?" she asked, after tapping in the code that would allow the door to open.

The older of the two police officers replied. "Sorry to disturb you, Ms.—" and he paused for a second to look down at the tablet he held— "Felaris. I'm Officer Korr, and this is Officer Rhyse. We need to ask you a few questions."

"Questions?" Miala echoed. At least she didn't have to feign the note of worry in her voice.

"It will only take a few minutes," the other officer, the younger one, said. He flashed her a quick smile. His blue eyes seemed to radiate reassurance.

"All right," she said, after a slight pause. After all, what else could she do? If she refused them entry, it would only make them more suspicious. She could only hope that Thorn would continue to make himself scarce. And they hadn't said anything about wanting to search the place, so if she could just keep the two of them downstairs, everything should be all right.

She led them to the larger of the two salons on the ground floor, a formal room where she and Jerem spent very little time but which she hoped might intimidate them, with its sleek *marrit*-hide couches and expensive canvases on the walls. At the very least the room seemed to breathe out respectability through its pores.

"Coffee?" Miala asked. Part of her motivation was simple courtesy, but she also thought if she were allowed to hide in the kitchen for a few moments to prepare the beverage, she could take the time to school her thoughts, to think up plausible lies for whatever questions they might ask. Had they somehow divined Thorn's presence within her home? But how would they even know who he was? And—

"No, thanks," Officer Korr replied, and Rhyse shook his head as well. "If you'd take a seat, please?"

Fighting a sensation of overwhelming futility, Miala sat herself down on the smaller of the two leather divans and threaded her fingers through one another, forcing them not to clench.

The lights had come on automatically as they entered the room, and so she was better able to get a good look at the two men. Even on closer inspection they appeared to be no more than who they said they were, two officers from Rilsport's security force. Somehow Miala doubted that any crony of Murgan's would part his hair so ruthlessly, or have such clean fingernails.

"Now, then," Korr went on, pulling a stylus out of his breast pocket. "Just a few things, for the record. You are Mia Felaris, currently of 98 Starcrest Court?"

She nodded. That was harmless enough, anyway.

"And your place of business is Felaris Security Systems, 22 Sherrol Tower?"

Again she nodded.

Korr made a few notations on his datapad. "Our records show that you recently went off-world, Ms. Felaris. The purpose of your trip?"

Miala paused, wondering what it was they really were after. An admission of Thorn's presence? A connection to the bodies the mercenary had so off-handedly dumped in a back alley? Her thoughts seemed to chase around one another, like dogs running after their own tails. How in the world could she concoct a plausible lie if she didn't even know which piece of information it was that they sought?

"Business," she replied at last.

"For whom?" asked Rhyse, the younger officer. For a few seconds his blue eyes didn't look friendly at all, but then he gave her a fairly reassuring smile.

A cold fingernail of doubt began to draw its way up her spine. "I'm afraid that's confidential," Miala said immediately, but she tried to temper the words with a smile of her own. "My business is security, after all. It would be a breach of contract for me to reveal my clients' identities."

Officer Korr's lips tightened for a second, but he said only, "This is police business, Ms. Felaris."

"I know that, officer," Miala replied. "But I also know that unless you have a warrant or something of that order compelling me to turn over client files, I am under no obligation to reveal that information to you. Besides," she added, wondering a little at her own audacity even as she did so, "you haven't even told me why you're here. Am I under investigation for something?"

This time there was no mistaking the hostile glance the officers traded before they turned their attention to her once more. Obviously they had been expecting her to be a bit more tractable.

I've faced down worse than you, boys, she thought. *It takes more than just a fancy uniform to frighten me.*

"No," said Officer Korr slowly, before he added with a nasty smile, "not yet."

"Do you know this man?" Rhyse asked, holding his own tablet computer out to her. The image on it showed a somewhat grainy three-quarter shot of Thorn in his non-descript dark jumpsuit. Probably the still had been taken from a security camera somewhere.

"He doesn't look familiar," she hedged. After all, it was a fairly bad image, Thorn's features only recognizable because she had known immediately that the shot could be of no one else.

"Really?" asked Korr, that unpleasant smile still pulling at the corners of his mouth. "Several eyewitnesses place a man of that description entering your property only an hour or so ago."

Miala raised her eyebrows. "Really? They must be mistaken." *And if I ever find out who was watching my front entry instead of minding their own business...*

"I'm afraid not, Ms. Felaris. Additionally, another man was seen entering your home a short time later, then leaving after about twenty standard minutes." Officer Korr made a show of looking back down at his tablet. "A Dr. Lassiter, it seems? Neighbor of yours?"

"Yes," she admitted unwillingly.

"You want to tell us what your neighbor was doing over here in the middle of the night, Ms. Felaris?" put in Officer Rhyse, with an expression dangerously close to a leer.

For one wild second Miala considered admitting to an affair with Quin Lassiter. Perhaps that would put these two hell hounds off the scent. But she had already dragged poor Quin into this deep enough—it wouldn't be fair to him or to his family to concoct stories that would only cause him more trouble.

"He's a doctor," she said smoothly, hoping they hadn't noticed her pause. "My son was having stomach cramps. Since Dr. Lassiter is a friend of the family, I called him to see if he could come help."

Again Officer Korr's mouth tightened. Then he asked, "So what was wrong with your son?"

"Quin said it looked as if he's starting to develop an allergy to shellfish," Miala replied, inwardly marveling as the lies seem to leap unbidden to her lips. She only hoped that the inner bullshit generator could keep going like this indefinitely. "The red-eye shells are still in the compactor—do you want to take a look?"

"I don't think that's necessary, Ms. Felaris," said Officer Rhyse hastily. It was fairly obvious that the last thing he wanted to do was start rooting through the contents of her trash compactor.

"That still doesn't answer our question about this man," put in Korr, who tapped his tablet with a significant gesture.

"And I told you that I don't know who he is." Miala narrowed her eyes at them in what she hoped was an expression of annoyance mixed with curiosity. "So who is he, anyway?"

"A dangerous off-world criminal," Officer Korr said, watching her carefully as if to gauge her reaction.

Miala allowed her eyes to open wide. "Really? I haven't seen him—but if someone else spotted him lurking around, maybe he's still here…out in the backyard, maybe?" Anything to get them out of the house. All she could do was trust that they were buying her big-eyed, frightened act.

The two men looked at one another for a second. Then Korr sighed, as if Miala had forced him to some action he really didn't want to take. He fixed her with an almost respectful gleam in his dark eyes. "You're good," he said. "For an amateur."

"Excuse me?" The fingernail of doubt turned into a whole set of icy fingers that seemed to settle around her throat.

"But we're not amateurs," Korr went on, and with a smooth, easy movement he drew his gun out of its holster, training the muzzle directly on her heart.

Oh, hell, she thought. But she remained silent, holding

herself very still as Korr continued to watch her with that half-regretful stare.

"This could have been so much easier if you'd just handed over the money in the first place," said Officer Rhyse.

Miala glanced over at him and wondered how she could have ever thought his blue eyes were friendly. Right now they looked about as cold as the ice caps that topped Nova Angeles' poles. She opened her mouth, not really knowing what she should say even as she did so—*I don't know what you're talking about...you've got the wrong person...possibly even I'll get it for you, just don't hurt me or my son*—but she never had the chance to speak.

Instead, a blast of blue pulse fire flashed past her cheek, missing her by inches just before it caught Rhyse squarely in the chest. His eyes widened for a second—eyes that Miala distantly noted were almost the same color as the pulse that had killed him—and then he slumped over against the arm of the couch.

"Get down, Miala," came Thorn's voice, and she slid off the couch and onto the cold tile floor even as Korr did almost the same thing, dropping to the ground as the mercenary advanced into the room. Miala's and Korr's eyes met as they stared at each other from under the coffee table, and then she quickly backed away before the officer—if that's what he really was—could reorient the blaster in her direction. Scuttling crab-like, she moved around the corner of the divan just as Korr up-ended the table, putting a makeshift barrier between Thorn and himself.

Reddish-orange fire erupted from the end of Korr's gun.

Miala couldn't see where it went, but she heard it hit the far wall of the salon, followed by the acrid smell of burning paint and canvas.

Fifty thousand units down the tube, she thought, even as she kept moving away from the firefight. She felt her foot bump into something and realized it was the side table that stood against the wall nearest to the divan. That seemed as good a place to hide as any, and she knelt there, arms wrapped around her knees, before cautiously lifting her head to see what was happening.

Thorn had dropped to a half-crouch, using the bulk of the divan where she had just been sitting as some protection from Korr's blaster fire. As she watched, the officer shifted his position slightly and lifted his gun to shoot at Thorn once more, but the shot passed harmlessly over the mercenary's head, this time catching in the heavy curtains that framed the floor-to-ceiling window on the wall behind him. Red and orange flames began to feed hungrily on the glossy silk.

All Miala could do was watch. She didn't dare move from her hiding place, even though every instinct in her cried out to run to the comm, to call fire control before the flames spread even further. She thought of Jerem, lying upstairs in his bed, and prayed that he would have the sense to stay put and not come down to investigate the noise. Every ounce of her wanted to go to him, to hold him until this was all over, but she forced herself to stay still, to watch as Thorn traded gunfire with Korr, as new flames caught in other corners of the room, and smoke began to fill the chamber and catch at her throat and lungs.

The mercenary's expression never changed. He looked as calm as a man choosing which shirt to wear, even as Korr's blasts ripped past his head. From her vantage point Miala couldn't see the officer, but even if one of Thorn's pulses had hit him, it was obvious he was still in good enough shape to continue returning fire.

Then, suddenly, the red pulses from Korr's blaster ceased.

Thorn didn't move. Instead, he asked, "Had enough?"

A long silence, filled only with the soft, hungry sound of the flames feeding off the drapes and the expensive artwork on the walls. Miala could only be thankful that she'd decided to keep the tile floors in this salon clean and bare, or no doubt any carpets she might have placed here surely would be on fire as well.

Then Korr finally spoke. His voice sounded hoarse, but whether that was because of some unseen wound or merely the smoke-filled air of the salon, Miala couldn't be certain. "Time enough." He coughed. "You've lost, Thorn."

"I'm not the one bleeding on the floor."

So Thorn had wounded him. Good.

Korr coughed again. "Nice hit, mercenary. But that doesn't matter."

"Why not?"

"Because I'm not the one you should be worried about. Checked on the boy lately?"

At those words Miala felt as if someone had thrown a bucket of ice water over her head, although the room had grown suffocatingly hot over the past few minutes. Jerem— he had to be talking about Jerem.

Enough of hiding. She pushed herself out from under the table and bolted toward the door, even as Thorn called after her, "Wait—you don't know who's up there!"

That didn't matter. None of it mattered. If someone were there, trying to harm her son, she'd rip them apart with her bare hands.

The stairs seemed twice as high as they usually did. Miala pounded up the steps, terror giving her speed, the breath choking in her throat as smoke drifted out the open door of the salon and rose up the staircase, seeming to follow her like a malevolent spirit.

The door to Jerem's room stood open. She plunged inside, crying his name, but only silence greeted her. Her son's bed was mussed, the sheets half-pulled down on to the floor. But he was nowhere to be found—not under the bed, not hiding in the closet. Nowhere.

A movement at the window seemed to mock her. For a long moment Miala stood and watched the blinds shift as a salt-smelling breeze blew through the open casement. The photoreceptive material of the blinds was torn at one end, as if clutching hands had grasped it in a desperate attempt to keep from being pulled out through the window. At least he had not gone without a fight, this son of hers.

She didn't know how long she stood there, fighting the tears as the scent of smoke swirled around her.

Then Thorn's voice. "Gone." It was not a question.

"They took him through the window." Her voice sounded strangely flat, without emotion.

The mercenary came to stand next to her, then looked

over at the broken blinds and the mussed bed. "We have to get out of here. The fire's spreading."

His words didn't seem to register. She could only stay rooted in place, looking at her son's empty bed even as her mind screamed at her, *He's gone! They took him! All that time you were hiding, worried about your own miserable skin—*

"You can't help him if you're dead of smoke inhalation."

As if to give weight to Thorn's words, a huge wave of smoke filled the corridor, followed by a sudden rush of skin-crackling heat. From far away, outside the open windows, the night was broken by the sound of approaching sirens.

"Out the window," Thorn commanded. "Now." And he grasped her by the arm and pulled her toward the open casement, using as an escape route the same path the kidnappers must have taken. The branches of the tree outside reached almost to the windowsill, and Miala roused herself enough from her misery to focus on crawling out there, inching her way along until she reached the trunk, then began to slowly step from branch to branch until she reached the ground. Thorn followed along behind her, his wound seeming to give him no trouble even during these contortions.

From ground level the true scope of the blaze that had engulfed the house could finally be seen. Orange glowed from almost all of the first-level windows, and smoke billowed out of the window they had just used as an egress.

Miala stood there and watched the destruction of her world. How unfair that the grass underneath her feet should feel so soft, the cool night air so gentle against her cheek, while her house burned and her son was gone.

"Let's go," said Thorn, and she let him pull her along, away from the house, away from the curious clump of people who had begun to gather on the walkway that bordered the cul-de-sac where she lived. He kept to the shadows at the edge of the property, and no one seemed to note their passage. Perhaps the men who had stolen Jerem and those who had employed them hadn't bothered to stay around. After all, they'd gotten what they came for.

Just putting one foot in front of the other required most of her concentration. A few moments—or possibly just a few seconds—later, a fire-control vehicle roared past them, followed by another, and then the squarish blue airtruck of the local medical services branch. After they passed, Miala stopped, and turned to face Eryk Thorn.

"Shouldn't I have stayed to meet them?" she asked. "Shouldn't I be calling the police—the real police?"

Thorn lifted an eyebrow. "With two dead bodies dressed in the uniforms of RilSec officers in your living room?"

At least Thorn had taken that small vengeance for their son. But her despair wouldn't allow her to feel any joy at the thought of the two men's deaths. Instead she inquired, "But shouldn't we report Jerem's kidnapping?"

"Not if you want to see your son alive."

His words took a moment to penetrate. Then she said, "He's your son, too."

In a darkness only partially broken by the streetlight a few yards away, Thorn's expression was even more unreadable than usual. He met her gaze squarely, and replied,

"Right now he's an asset that needs to be reacquired."

For a few seconds Miala could only stare back at him, shocked by his coldness. Then she seemed to hear his voice in her mind, the phrase he had uttered only that afternoon. Had it really been just a few hours ago? It felt as if centuries had passed since then. But he had looked at her much as he did now, and said, *Connections kill.* He couldn't allow himself to become emotionally involved now. If he did, he risked losing the very edge that was necessary to bring Jerem back to her.

The horrified words that had risen to her lips seemed to evaporate. She had to think he did care at some level, but that concern was the last thing he could indulge right now.

"So what do we do?" Miala asked at length. Suddenly she realized that they were standing on the street in their nightclothes, and barefoot as well. Enough of her neighbors had gone out to watch the fire similarly garbed that perhaps she and Thorn had escaped notice for now, but they couldn't wander around like this for much longer.

"Get off the street," he said immediately. "I'd say go back to my ship, but I know it's being watched. A hotel somewhere, probably."

Miala wanted to retort that no decent place would take them in looking as they did, but in Rilsport just as everywhere else in the galaxy, money talked. Much of her life had just been swallowed up in flames, but she still had her bank accounts. On Nova Angeles, most smaller transactions were handled through simple thumbprint I.D.—they should be able to walk into any hotel in the city and get a room that way, at least. Most public transport was paid for in a similar fashion.

"Keep heading east," she said, and began walking. "About five blocks from here is a main street. We should be able to get a taxi there."

He nodded and kept pace with her. As they moved farther away from her home, Miala could feel the cold beginning to seep up through her bare feet, slowly overtaking her entire body. Perhaps it should have bothered her. Instead, she almost welcomed the numbing sensation. At least when she was numb she didn't have to feel anything. She didn't have to think about her son in the hands of kidnappers. She didn't have to think about the ruin of her home. She didn't have to think about anything except making sure that her feet kept moving, taking her away from the life she had built over the past eight years.

Thorn said nothing throughout their journey. Only when they reached the main street did he say, "Wait here," and seat her down on a bench outside a restaurant now shuttered for the night. Then he moved to the curb, watched the traffic move past, and finally raised his hand when a mech-driven jitney approached.

The aircar whooshed to a stop, and Thorn leaned down to ask something of the driver—probably the direction to the closest reputable hotel. Then he straightened and gestured for Miala to join him.

She stood and walked with mechanical steps to the taxi, and settled herself in the back seat. The vehicle smelled of stale breath mints and perspiration, but it was also warm. Thorn climbed in beside her, and the taxi took off.

Only once they were in motion did the mercenary finally turn to give her an appraising look. "You all right?"

She said, "I'll manage."

Outside the car's window the streets of Rilsport streamed past, well-lit, clean, and orderly. It seemed another world from the one that had stolen her son and destroyed her home. Perhaps this was only a nightmare, one from which she would awake to find Jerem still in his room and her home safe around her, with Thorn unwounded and lying next to her in bed. But as much as she'd like to believe that, she knew it was a lie. This was the truth—she was alone, and the home where she had raised her son, seen his first steps, fought with him over sticky counters and spotted beans, was gone forever.

The tears came then finally, flooding down her cheeks as she leaned her head against the battered synth-leather upholstery. It was the only thing she could think to do to ease the enormous aching void within her.

Then she felt him reach out, wrap his arms around her, draw her close to his chest. The rhythm of his heart seemed to offer its own strange comfort, and she let him hold her, even as her tears soaked the loose soot-stained shirt he wore. He said nothing, only reassuring her with his touch, letting her know that, whatever she might think, she wasn't alone after all.

MIALA HAD TO REPRESS THE URGE to mutter, *Locked myself out,* when the desk clerk at the Rilsport Plaza Towers gave a goggle-eyed look at her stained dressing robe and bare feet.

But, as she had thought, her request for one of the top-floor suites was granted once she had placed her thumb against the hotel's biometric registry and paid for two nights in advance. Eccentricity was obviously allowed when accompanied by a fat credit balance.

"Any baggage?" the desk clerk asked.

"Just him," she said, with a jerk of her chin toward Thorn, who was watching the exchange with imperturbable dark eyes.

The clerk goggled again, but he handed her the access card to her suite without further comment. She took it and headed toward the bank of elevators at the far end of the lobby, which at this hour was mostly unoccupied except for a sweeper mech off to one side and a bleary-looking man who obviously had spent the better part of the evening in the hotel lounge and who now had propped himself against one of the rock-crystal pillars that held up the brightly painted roof. Possibly he was considering whether it would be better to call a cab or just sleep it off on one of the lobby couches.

Although Miala had never stayed in the Rilsport Plaza, she had attended several conferences here over the years and knew the layout well enough. The suite she had just rented was located in the same tower as the main lobby, so it hadn't been necessary to cross the courtyard to access the second set of elevators. She stepped in, slid her access card through the slot so the elevator would go all the way to the penthouse level, then gave Thorn a worried look as the doors shut behind them.

"Maybe that wasn't so smart," she said, giving voice to the doubt that had plagued her ever since she signed off on the hotel room. "I mean, what if the people who took Jerem and attacked us can figure out where we are from my credit information?"

"I'm counting on it."

"Excuse me?" Miala stared at Thorn, who, with his stained sleeping garments and soot-smeared face, looked somewhat out of place in the travertine and chrome interior of the plush lift. "You mean you want them to find us?"

The elevator doors chose that inopportune moment to open. Even though the small foyer that fronted the entrances to the two penthouse suites was empty, Thorn remained silent until the door of their room slid shut behind them.

"They're after money," he said, as he went to the bank of windows that comprised one wall of the suite and activated the sunshield that rendered the glass opaque. "Now we just have to wait and find out how much."

"I thought paying ransoms never worked," Miala objected, her throat tight with worry and unshed tears. "At least, that's what the news reports and vid-flicks always seem to say."

"Sometimes it does…sometimes it doesn't." Thorn moved past her to the bathroom and turned on the hot water. Seemingly unfazed by her glare, he stripped off the stained sleep shirt and baggy pants he wore and stepped into the stream, closing his eyes briefly as the water sluiced off his hair and ran down his shoulders and chest. The waterproof bandage Quin Lassiter had applied looked shockingly white against his dark skin.

"And what's that supposed to mean?" Miala refused to let herself get distracted by the sight of his naked body. Except for a few more scars, he looked much the same as he had eight years ago.

"Every situation is different." Thorn opened his eyes and looked at her through the clouds of steam the hot water was generating. "Want to join me? Plenty of room in here."

"Thank you, no," Miala said icily. How could he possibly think she would be interested in sex at a time like this?

"You could use one," he replied.

"Later," she gritted.

He shrugged, poured some liquid soap into the palm of his hands, and began working it into his hair. "This is all about Mast's money. You and I both know that. They failed with you on Iradia, so now they're trying a different angle. That's all."

That's all? she wanted to scream, but losing control right now wasn't going to do anyone any good, least of all Jerem. It still infuriated her to think that Murgan and whatever cronies he had left thought they had some divine right to the treasure that had once lain in Mast's vaults, but so be it. They could have it all. What was money, compared to her son?

While these unpleasant thoughts occupied her mind, Thorn finished his quick, efficient shower and stepped out under the molecular dryer. Within seconds the moisture had been wicked away from his body, and he reached up for the clean white robe that hung from a hook next to the shower unit.

"We'll need clothes and other supplies," he said.

"I can order those up in the morning," Miala replied, her voice dull. Logically she knew that those commonplaces would have to be dealt with at some point, but for now all she could think of was Jerem in the hands of kidnappers, men so desperate they were willing to endanger the life of an innocent boy just to achieve their own mercenary ends.

Thorn gave her a keen look. Then he disappeared into the main room of the suite. After a few seconds he called, "I need your thumb."

"What?" The bizarre request shook her momentarily out of her stupor, and she followed after him, wondering what the hell it was that he wanted. As soon as she took a few steps, she thought she understood. He had paused in front of the bar unit with which the suite had been supplied, but it had a biometric lock keyed to the person who had rented the rooms.

"You looked like you could use a drink."

Well, she couldn't argue with that. Miala crossed to the bar, applied her thumb to the sensor-lock, and then stood there for a moment, staring at the gleaming little bottles and wondering how many it would take to make her forget that her son had been stolen.

"Here," said Thorn. He reached past her, grasped a bottle filled with some deep reddish-orange liquor that reminded her of the color of an Iradian sunset, and poured a few centimeters of the liquid into a square glass he found conveniently placed on top of the bar unit.

The sharp smell of it hit her nostrils even as he handed her the glass. Lately she hadn't drunk much at all save a glass of wine with dinner once or twice a week. She didn't know what Thorn had poured for her—not that it really mattered. Shutting her eyes, Miala tossed back approximately half the drink, feeling the fire of it as it hit the back of her throat and began to burn its way down her esophagus. She wanted to cough but refused to allow Thorn to see her inexperience with this sort of thing, so she settled for a slight throat clearing before she set the glass down on top of the bar.

"Smooth," she managed.

A corner of his mouth lifted as his dark eyes gave her the lie, but he said nothing.

Still, Miala had to admit the sensation of heat that traveled down to her midsection and then on to all her limbs was fascinating. The blurred gray dullness of a few minutes ago had been wiped away by the potent liquor. Now she felt charged, energized. If Murgan's henchmen had shown themselves in the suite at that moment, she would have taken them all on with her bare hands.

"Think I'll have that shower now," she said, after a brief pause.

"Good idea."

Although she hated to keep having to acknowledge that Thorn was right, the shower felt sublime. She cranked the heat to the very edge of tolerance and let the massaging waves of water knead away some of the despair and terror that had stained her psyche just as surely as the soot had smudged her clothing. The alcohol coursing through her veins probably helped, too. Things were bad, no doubt about that, but at least she was still alive, and she had Thorn at her side to make sure Jerem was returned to her safely.

Miala stepped out of the shower and let herself be dried off before reaching for the second, smaller robe with which the bathroom had been supplied. When she went back out into the main room, she noticed Thorn had tuned the large vidscreen on the wall opposite the bed to a local news channel.

"Looking for something in particular?"

"Your house."

"Excuse me?"

He waved the remote at the screen in a gesture of contempt. "Local channels love house fires...especially big, expensive house fires. But I can't find any mention of yours."

"So?"

"Obviously someone doesn't want it publicized."

Miala stood there for a moment, watching as Thorn flipped through the channels. At this hour of the night, the fare wasn't particularly appetizing—vid epics most people had seen a hundred times before, hacks peddling improbable inventions guaranteed to make your life better, rebroadcasts of serials for those whose schedules kept them away from the vid during the daylight hours. But there were also three channels locally that broadcast the news twenty-five hours a day, and certainly an item such as her house fire would have caught the attention of one of the crews that trolled the city all day and night in search of those sorts of tasty items.

"What do you think it means?" she asked, the warm glow of the liquor abruptly turning into a heavy weight in the pit of her stomach.

He frowned. "Nothing good."

"Thanks."

Ignoring her brittle sarcasm, he turned the remote over in his hands and then abruptly switched off the vscreen. "Those police officers…"

"What about them?" Right now all she cared about was the fact that Thorn had managed to kill them before they killed either him or her. Or both of them at once.

"They didn't seem like criminals masquerading as cops. They talked like cops, looked like cops, shot like cops." Thorn ran a thoughtful finger down his chin, as if feeling the stubble there might aid in his logic processes. "I'm starting to think they really were cops."

"But if they were real cops—if they weren't just faking it—" Miala trailed off, watching Thorn's impassive dark face.

"Then I think we have to consider the possibility that the local security force is somehow involved in this," the mercenary said.

The bottom seemed to fall out of her world. Oh, she'd grown up on Iradia, and she knew how crooked a place the universe could be, but once she'd found refuge here on Nova Angeles and settled her life in line with its orderly, long-civilized routines, she'd thought she was safe. But men were infinitely corruptible, it seemed.

She stood very still for a long moment. Then she looked directly at Thorn and said, "I think I'll take the second half of that drink now."

Jerem had never seen a Stacian in person before. Sure, one of his favorite vid heroes was Lem sen Korsadda, a Stacian whose fictional war injuries led to his riding around in a hover-chair everywhere—a hover-chair that had been specially modified with guns and grappling hooks and everything else a chair-bound crime fighter might need. It had been a gamble, casting one of the aliens in the lead when the Stacians and the Gaians maintained at best an armed neutrality. But the show had been a hit, and Jerem loved it because the hero wasn't some square-chinned Gaian. However, what the vid series never really got across was how big a Stacian in the flesh really was.

Of course, this Stacian wasn't confined to a hover-chair. He loomed, all fiercely knotted hair and glaring copper eyes, over the boy as the two kidnappers—a pair of scruffy-looking humans—who had stolen Jerem from his room stood slightly behind him. One of them held him by the shoulder. For some reason, he felt almost glad of their spurious protection.

Jerem wasn't really sure how he had gotten here—wher-ever "here" was. They stood in a smallish room with blank concrete walls. Off to one side was a narrow cot with some meager bedding, and a few feet away from that was a small round table flanked by a pair of no-nonsense metal chairs. There were no windows; unshielded glow tubes glared down from the ceiling.

How it had all happened, he didn't quite know. Jerem had heard the door chime sound, but he'd figured it must be Dr. Lassiter coming back for some reason. But he'd still slid his bedroom door open a crack, just in time to see his mother pulling on a robe and heading purposefully down the stairs. Jerem had been able to hear some muffled voices, but he couldn't really understand what they were saying. He'd stood there for a minute, wondering whether he could get away with going over to the landing to hear things better, but suddenly Eryk Thorn had been standing in front of Jerem's partially open door.

"Not a good idea," said the mercenary.

Jerem had noticed that his father was dressed for bed, but the baggy sleep shirt he wore couldn't completely conceal the gun he held down below hip level.

"What's going on?" Jerem asked.

"That's what I'm about to find out," Thorn replied. "But you're going to stay in your room, and lock the door. Don't let anyone in except me or your mother."

Somewhat mystified, Jerem nodded and shut the door. His mind had sprouted with questions, but Thorn could put on an even more no-nonsense glare than his mother, and the boy knew it would be useless to try and get any more information. Instead, he shut the door and locked it, then went back to his bed and waited. All remained quiet for a few more minutes, but then Jerem thought he heard a sound he immediately recognized from his favorite shows—guns going off. Guns! In his house! And all he could do was sit there on the bed like an idiot and miss out on all the excitement.

Of course, that thought had barely crossed his mind before the window next to his bed abruptly swung open, and two dark-clothed figures wriggled through. Jerem let out a little yelp of fright, but he didn't even stop to think— he dove for the floor, knowing these intruders couldn't mean any good.

It might have worked, except that his feet got tangled in the stupid bedclothes, and instead of bouncing back immediately to his feet and making a run for the door, as he had intended, he tripped. That gave the intruders enough time to regain their bearings and close on him. The last thing he remembered was the hiss of a hypo-spray against his neck. After that, it was just darkness, until he had come to even as he was being carried into this room.

Jerem thought about it for a minute, decided he probably was supposed to be afraid, then realized he wasn't, not really. This was, after all, the height of coolness—to be kidnapped from your room in the middle of the night like the hero of some vid adventure story! Besides, he had to think that pretty soon Eryk Thorn would be hot on these guys' trail anyway, and that was certain to be a lot of fun once the mercenary caught up with them.

The taunt—*Just wait until my dad shows up and kicks your butt*—rose to Jerem's lips, but then he thought maybe that wasn't such a good idea. After all, Thorn had made

Jerem promise not to say anything about him being his father, and Jerem certainly didn't want to let Eryk Thorn down. There was no way of knowing whether these goons had any idea that Thorn was Jerem's father, and if they were unaware of the fact, it would be even more satisfying when the mercenary showed up out of the blue and started doing some serious damage.

So he remained silent, staring up at the Stacian with some curiosity. The alien definitely looked irritated about something, but maybe that was just his usual expression.

After a moment the golden-skinned kidnapper snapped, "What the hell are you looking at, kid?"

"You," Jerem replied truthfully. "See, there's this show, *Moon of Syrinara*, with this guy who—"

"Yeah, I've seen it," interrupted the Stacian. "It stinks."

Jerem opened his mouth to protest, caught the glare out of the alien's hard copper eyes, and thought better of it. Obviously this guy had no taste in vid series.

"Better," the alien said. "You—go sit over there. And keep your mouth shut." He gestured with a huge fist in the direction of the cot, and Jerem scowled but went. After all, it was no use arguing with someone three times your size and armed to the teeth with at least two guns that Jerem could see, as well as a molecular blade in a sheath at his sizable hip.

So Jerem sat down on the cot, which was hard and lumpy and boded ill for any kind of decent sleep if they ended up keeping him here for any length of time. He wrapped his arms around his knees and balled himself up into the section of the cot that was shoved into the corner. From this position he hoped they would think he was defeated and afraid, but instead he shut his eyes and listened furiously.

He'd discovered some time ago that grown-ups tended to ignore a child's presence if said child wasn't doing anything to attract their attention. It was in this manner that he'd managed to overhear the complete details of Risa's sister's unplanned pregnancy and the lengthy "vacation" on New Chicago that had ensued. Not that Jerem really cared whether or not Magri had gotten herself "in the family way," as Risa had put it, but you never knew when information might come in handy. And it wasn't until he'd sneezed unexpectedly during this discourse that his mother discovered he'd been curled up behind the back of the sofa the whole time. She'd gotten that funny expression on her face, the one she got whenever she was trying to be stern but instead wanted to just start laughing instead. Somehow managing to clamp down on the smile, she'd ordered him from the room. He hadn't gotten punished for that, but he'd also noticed she was a lot more careful in the future to make sure he wasn't around whenever she was having a sensitive conversation.

The Stacian was asking the older of the two men who had kidnapped Jerem whether there had been any further "trouble." The guy looked nervous and shifted his weight, but admitted that Eryk Thorn had intervened and shot the two RilSec officers dead.

Yeah, Dad! Jerem thought, but made no outward response.

"What the hell is the connection between those two?" the Stacian demanded, and the two humans looked at each other and shrugged.

"Don't know for sure," said the other man, who had a slight singsong accent Jerem didn't recognize. "I mean, she's a good-looking bit, that's for sure, but who ever heard of Thorn giving a damn about that sort of thing?"

"No one," replied the Stacian grimly. "Something to do with Iradia, I don't doubt, but my brother didn't have time to figure it out, and right now I don't care. If he's working for her, then he'll do as she says. And if we make it very clear that if Thorn shows up, the kid dies, then there shouldn't be a problem."

Those words, spoken so carelessly, made Jerem swallow. Maybe this wasn't such an adventure after all…

"Anyway, Chaddick just told me she's checked into the Rilsport Plaza, so now we have a contact point. We'll wait until morning—let's give the woman her beauty sleep, shall we?"

Jerem felt rather than saw the leer that accompanied that statement, but he knew better than to move or look up. But why would his mother have gone to a hotel? You'd think she would have stayed at home and waited to find out what had happened to him. But wait—Jerem supposed maybe it wouldn't be such a good idea to hang around a house that had a couple of dead police officers in the main salon.

"And then?" the first man who had spoken asked.

"Then we find out how much this kid really is worth."

XXII

In her dreams Eryk Thorn reached out for her, drawing her close, bringing his mouth against hers. His hands moved down her body, touching her once more, in a way she had only been able to imagine during the last empty years of her life. Miala sighed and relaxed into his encircling arms, reveling in the sensations even if they were only the phantom embraces of a dream…

Suddenly she realized she wasn't dreaming. Those really were Thorn's hands on her, his mouth moving against the sensitive places on her body. For a second she froze, wondering if she should make some protest, but then she realized she didn't want him to stop. For eight long years she'd thought of Eryk Thorn, ached for him, and now she desired nothing else but to become one with him once more. Was it really so wrong to want to leave behind the worry and doubt and fear, if only for a while? This was no betrayal of Jerem. Rather, it was an affirmation that hers and Thorn's lives had become inextricably entwined.

She clung to the mercenary, feeling the heat of his body in the darkness, and when she finally cried out, Thorn held her until the last wracking shudders had worked their way through her frame. Then he continued to hold her until she fell into a deep, dreamless sleep…

The chime of the comm woke her. Miala sat up in bed, blinking, at first uncertain of where she was. Then the unfamiliar surroundings of the hotel room fell into place around her, and memory came rushing back. Jerem kidnapped. Her home destroyed.

And across the room from her, Eryk Thorn sitting calmly in a chair, sipping at a cup of coffee. His dark eyes met hers for a second, and then he nodded toward the comm unit. "It's them."

Panic gripped her stomach. "How do you know?"

"Who else would have this number?"

"Who else?" indeed. No one could possibly know Miala was here in this hotel. She would have to contact Risa soon, because Miala had the feeling that Risa was probably climbing the walls with worry at this point—Risa was listed as Miala's emergency contact, and someone had to have called her about the fire. But first things first.

With shaky fingers she pushed her hair back behind her ears, then gathered up her discarded nightshirt. She hated the thought of answering the comm in such disarray, but at least her appearance would make it fairly obvious to the kidnappers that she had gone straight from the destruction of her home to the hotel. Then she slid out of bed and went to the comm unit, jabbing the button to accept the incoming call.

The screen stayed dark; obviously they had blocked the visual stream. Miala wished she'd had the presence of mind to do the same, but it was too late for that now. Whether by happy accident or design, the chair Thorn occupied was well out of camera range.

"Who is it?" she asked. At least she thought she sounded reasonably calm.

"That's not important," the caller replied.

Male, of course, but not noticeably alien. Not that that meant anything. Murgan hadn't had much of an accent, either, as Miala recalled.

"What do you want?" She wished that she and Thorn had had the time to discuss how best to handle this conversation before the kidnappers called, but after their hurried lovemaking she had passed into the heavy sleep of exhaustion, and probably he had decided it was more important for her to rest and regain her strength than to spend the time speculating on the kidnapper's demands.

A pause. "I like a woman who knows how to get to the point," said the kidnapper. "It's very simple, really. You give us fifteen million units, and you get your boy back."

Miala tried to school her face into impassivity, but she knew she'd felt her eyes widen for a second before she could catch herself. Fifteen million. If she liquidated everything she had, including her business, and somehow managed to get the insurance to pay up quickly on the house, then she might have enough. Barely. Not that it mattered. She'd give up more if it meant getting her son back.

"I want to talk to him," she said. "How do I know you even have him?"

A pause. Then, "Speak up, kid."

"Mom—"

It was Jerem's voice, and, wonder of wonders, he didn't sound all that scared. Relief washed over her, cool as the waters down in Rilsport Harbor. "Jerem, are you all right? Where—"

"No questions," the kidnapper broke in. "He's alive. That's all you need to know. Give us the fifteen million, and he stays that way."

"That's going to take me some time," she said, thankful that somehow she'd managed to adopt the cool, precise tones she always employed when nailing down a deal with a prospective client. It would be useless to ask to speak to Jerem again; she could tell the kidnapper wasn't about to let her son say anything else. "My assets aren't that liquid."

"You have two standard days," came the immediate reply. "Fifteen million in Gaian units. We'll contact you at this number for further instructions."

"Fine," she said. "But I'll need to speak to my son again before any money changes hands."

"Agreed." A pause, and then the caller added, "If you care about your son, you won't bring the mercenary into this."

The red light on the comm went out, indicating that the kidnapper had hung up.

Miala turned and looked at Thorn, who gave her the same impassive stare he always did. *Don't bring Thorn into this*, she thought. *That's like telling the sun not to rise in the morning.*

Then Eryk Thorn asked, "Do you really have it?"

"Yes. Maybe. I think so."

He raised an eyebrow.

Crossing her arms, she snapped, "It's not that simple, Thorn. Some is tied up in investments. I can get it out, but I'll have to pay penalties for early withdrawal. I haven't had my business appraised lately, but I know it's worth a good four to five million. I doubt I'd be able to sell it in that amount of time, though—I'll have to try and take out some sort of loan against it. And I'll have to contact the insurance company about the house—"

"There's my money."

The comment was so unexpected that Miala stopped abruptly, staring at the mercenary in surprise. "What?"

"The funds on New Chicago. My half."

She had completely forgotten about that. For so long she'd had only her own resources to depend upon that it had never occurred to her Thorn might be willing to pitch in to meet the ransom. "You'd do that?"

"He's my son, too."

The simple declaration almost brought tears to her eyes. But she blinked them away. She couldn't dissolve into a mess now.

Eryk Thorn watched her carefully, and she thought she saw a flicker of approval cross his features.

"Thank you," she said, after a moment.

"No problem," he replied. "We'd better get moving. We need to get outfitted, and we need to get over to New Chicago."

Since the two planets shared the same system, that wasn't much of a problem. She and Thorn could travel to

Nova Angeles' sister world and back within the space of the same day. But there were still a lot of details to attend to—not the least of which would be contacting Risa and letting her know that Miala had survived the fire which claimed her home.

"I'll find some way to make this up to you," Miala ventured, and Thorn gave her one of his quick downturned grins.

"I know you will," he said. "Besides, just because I'm giving the kidnappers this ransom doesn't mean I'm going to let them keep it."

I should have expected that, Miala thought. *I should have known Thorn wouldn't go along with this so easily.* Still, the thought of the mercenary bringing his considerable skills to bear on the men who had taken his son brought a smile to her own lips. They were expecting payment, and what they were going to get instead was payback.

"Is that a promise?" she asked.

"Oh, yes," Thorn replied. There was something in the cool voice that made a shiver run down her spine. "And you know I always keep my promises."

They were somewhere near the ocean. Jerem was almost sure of it. The men who had kidnapped him made him stay in this boring little room, but he'd grown up within sight and smell of the sea, and the air that blew in whenever they opened the door was moist and cool, smelling of salt and jagos, the giant seaweed that grew off the coast of Rilsport. He'd tried to peer past them to see what was outside, but they'd been quick enough that all he'd been able to catch of glimpse of was a flash of white sunlight and the edge of another building—one that looked to be an improbable combination of orange and blue.

Even that one brief look had set something tickling at the back of his mind, as if he should somehow know where he was. But try as he could, Jerem couldn't figure it out. And it wasn't as if he didn't have plenty of time to sit and think about it. Truth was, sitting and thinking were about all he could do. You'd think these guys would at least have given him a handheld game console or a tablet or something to while away the hours. But no. They seemed to think he shouldn't do anything except sit on his bed and wait for his mother to pay up.

The worst punishment his mother could give Jerem consisted of forcing him to sit in his room and do nothing while he thought about what he did wrong. This was even worse, except that he was pretty sure he really hadn't done anything wrong. Maybe there had been one moment back in his room where he could have thrown a chair at his assailants or something, but Jerem had the idea that there wasn't much he really could have done to prevent them from taking him. Sure, he'd turned out to be Eryk Thorn's son, but he was still just eight standard years old, after all.

Cameras mounted in two of the corners of the room kept watch on him at all times. After he'd woken up this morning, he'd spent about fifteen minutes making faces into one, just to irritate his captors, but they'd made no response, and the game got dull after a while. It was one thing to twist your face into inventive grimaces to get a rise out of your friends or to upset your mother so she'd snap, "Do you want your face to freeze like that?" It was an entirely different proposition to do it for an uncaring audience.

He'd slept badly the previous night; the cot had proved to be just as lumpy as it looked. Breakfast actually wasn't too bad—they'd fed him the sort of over-sweetened packaged meal he'd always bugged his mother to buy for him but which she'd always claimed was unhealthy and full of sucrose. Now he felt the sort of edgy energy that always followed an over-consumption of sweet things—the precise reason why his mother avoided feeding him that kind of stuff in the first place.

Since he had this big empty room with nothing much in it except that lumpy cot and a pair of equally uncomfortable chairs, Jerem decided this was a good place to practice walking on his hands. He'd seen a Bathshevan dancer do it once on the vid and had been fascinated by the move ever since. In the past he hadn't been able to stay up on his hands for more than two paces in a row, but he'd vowed he'd master the skill eventually. The only good thing about it was that Mikhal and Alic were even more hopeless than he was.

It had to be all in the balance. His hands and wrists were strong enough from years of climbing trees, walls, and anything else he could think of, but it was tricky getting your mass to redistribute itself so you didn't over-balance and allow the weight of your legs to topple you over.

Jerem tried a simple handstand, and that worked well enough. Then he reached out with one hand and inched forward. That seemed all right, too, so he shifted his weight to the alternate hand and lurched a few more centimeters ahead. He could feel his legs begin to wobble, so he stayed in that position for a moment until it seemed as if he'd regained equilibrium. Then once more with his right hand—

"What the hell are you doing?"

The sound of his captor's voice caused Jerem to jerk his head sideways so he could see who was speaking, and that was the end of the experiment. He collapsed in a messy heap but bounced back up to his feet almost immediately. After all, he'd taken worse falls than that every day of his life.

Jerem brushed at the dirty knees of his pajama bottoms and said cheerfully, "Walking on my hands. Do you know how to do it?"

The man scowled at him. He had a sort of rat-like face anyway, with his pointed nose and close-set eyes, and the frown didn't exactly improve his features. "I've got better things to do with my time, kid."

"Well, maybe I would, too," Jerem retorted, "if you guys actually gave me something to do in here. This place is boring."

"Oh, excuse me," the man scoffed. "Sorry if we're not set up for a full-service baby-sitting business."

Jerem wanted to snap, *I am not a baby!* but thought better of it. Arguing with adults was pointless, anyway. Even if you were right they always came up with something to prove how wrong you were. "So since you won't even give me a console or anything, I'm walking on my hands."

The man looked nonplussed, as if he wasn't quite sure what leap of logic Jerem had taken to go from playing electronic games to walking on his hands. But since he was an adult, and therefore obviously felt he had to issue some kind of order, he said, "Well, don't break anything."

"What's there to break?" Jerem asked. "One of those chairs? The bed?" Actually, he might be able to break the bed, if he jumped on it hard enough. Then again, if he broke the bed he wouldn't have anyplace to sleep. Not that the floor would be much of a downgrade.

"Listen, kid," the man said. His tone had turned sneering, as if he'd watched too many vids in which a criminal had to deal with a bratty kid and was taking his cue from them. "You sit in here, you stay quiet, you don't get in trouble. Otherwise, we're going to give you back to your mama in a box." And with that pronouncement he turned and left, giving Jerem another tantalizing glimpse of the world outside before the door slid shut once again.

Orange and blue, Jerem thought. *Orange and blue.* To be honest, it was an ugly color combination. You'd think its outstanding hideosity would have jogged his memory, but nothing. Well, either it would come to him, or it wouldn't. You couldn't force these sorts of things—you had to just let them come to you in a drift of inspiration. Sometimes he'd bounce awake right in the middle of a dream and would write it down so he wouldn't forget. His mother always kept a tablet by the side of her bed, too, in case she woke up in the night and had an idea that she wanted to jot down. Jerem thought that was a pretty good idea and had started doing the same thing himself. The only problem was that he didn't have his tablet here, so even if he did have a stroke of inspiration at some point, he didn't have any way to save it. Oh, well. If he did think of something, probably it would be important enough that he wouldn't forget it, anyway.

Jerem sighed and looked at the closed door, wondering what lay beyond it. Then he stuck his tongue out at one of the watching cameras, pushed himself back up on his hands, and resumed his practice. What else was there to do, anyway?

Rafe Creel of RilSec Internal Investigations stood in the smoking rubble of what had once been Mia Felaris' home, a frown creasing his forehead. The airvan carrying the bodies of Officers Korr and Rhyse had just driven away, but he remained on-site, secure behind the glowing green barrier that blocked the crime scene from any curious onlookers. There had been a sizable crowd earlier, but finally they'd drifted off. Probably the sight of him standing there making notations on a tablet wasn't quite enough to hold their interest. Anyway, it was moving on to the middle hours of the morning, and most of them no doubt had to be off to work or school.

Normally, Internal Investigations wouldn't have anything to do with a simple house fire, but the discovery of the two officers' bodies had put an entirely different slant on things. Creel had had his eye on those two for some time now; he didn't have any concrete evidence yet, but he was fairly certain they were on the take from someone. Who, he didn't know, but the fact that they had both just turned up dead couldn't be a coincidence. But why here?

There hadn't been a whole lot left of them, but what little physical evidence remained seemed to indicate they had both been in uniform when they arrived at the Felaris residence. Odd, since the roster had them going off-duty at 18:00, hours earlier than the time of the fire. RilSec had strict rules about off-duty officers going around in uniform. Ignoring the regs just once was enough to get you written up, and repeated offenses would result in expulsion from the force. So whatever they had been doing, obviously it was worth the risk to them to be wandering around Rilsport in uniform while off-duty.

He squinted into the bright morning sunlight, surveying the ruin of what had once been a well-appointed, extremely expensive home. This neighborhood was the best in town; RilSec didn't usually make too many calls out here, since the people who owned these homes could afford security systems that put whatever protection the police might offer them to shame.

In fact, security was Mia Felaris' business. The information on her he'd downloaded to his tablet showed that she had a highly successful security firm in downtown Rilsport, and he didn't doubt that her home had been a high-tech fortress. But obviously the uniforms Rhyse and Korr had worn allowed them entry past whatever safeguards she might have had in place.

Interestingly, there was no trace of Ms. Felaris in the home, nor of her young son. It seemed fairly obvious that they had escaped the fire somehow, but if they had survived, why was there no further sign of either one of them? One would think that she'd have made contact with the authorities at some point. But she hadn't—and she hadn't been in touch with Risa Terrano, her assistant, either. That young woman had apparently called the police as soon as she had gotten word of the fire, but she had no idea where Mia Felaris or her son Jerem had gone. The Fire Control investigators who had already come and left had informed him that the fire, though fierce, certainly hadn't been hot enough to consume human remains that completely.

Creel stared at a charred metal picture frame and chewed his caffeinated gum thoughtfully. Nasty habit, but coffee had started to get to his stomach, and he just couldn't function without caffeine.

None of this was adding up. If one followed the assumption that Korr and Rhyse were dirty, then it was likely they had been here to put pressure on Ms. Felaris for some reason. Korr had been more circumspect, but it was Rhyse's sudden acquisition of a Zephyr 3000 aircar—a car way out of Rhyse's pay grade—and a few other anomalies that had raised Creel's suspicions in the first place. Careful digging revealed a plump new bank account on New Chicago and a hefty order placed at Rilsport's top electronics supplier for a variety of expensive consumer goods. Maybe he'd inherited a chunk of change or just got lucky playing the commodities market, but Creel didn't think so, since further investigation hadn't uncovered any recently dead relatives or payouts from a brokerage firm. Korr's sudden influx of new wealth had been more difficult to trace, but eventually Creel uncovered a bank account back on Gaia's moon, an account with a much higher balance than anyone with Korr's income would have been able to save in fifty standard years, let alone the fifteen-plus Korr had spent with RilSec. And it wasn't as if he had a rich wife, either...the man had never married. No steady girlfriends, either, which wasn't atypical for a career cop.

But there hadn't been any concrete evidence, so Creel had continued with his digging. Luckily his track record at Internal Investigations was good enough that his superiors usually allowed him to follow his instincts and go about his activities in his own way. He'd been certain at some point Korr and Rhyse would make the mistake that would finally allow him to bring them down. He just hadn't thought that it would be such a fatal error.

Why Mia Felaris, though? Her own record was clean as an operating room, as far as he could tell. She'd emigrated to Nova Angeles approximately eight standard years ago and hadn't made a spot of trouble the entire time she'd been here. In fact, she was just the sort of high-class immigrant the planet wanted.

Maybe Rhyse and Korr had put pressure on her to do security work for whatever criminal was paying them, and she'd refused. Even if that were the case, it didn't explain who had gotten the drop on the two officers. The Fire Control investigators had informed him that it looked as if the fire had started on the ground floor, possibly in the draperies in one of the rooms there. But so far they hadn't been able to determine why the curtains would have caught fire in the first place.

Creel had the feeling he was missing an important piece of the puzzle. Mia Felaris seemed about the last person who would be able to take out two highly trained officers, but as he well knew, appearances could be deceiving. Records indicated that she had never owned a gun, but again, that didn't mean much. Even on a civilized world such as Nova Angeles there was a thriving black market for unregistered weapons.

Technically, his investigation was almost over. Once the officers under suspicion were dead, there wasn't much point in Internal Investigations continuing its inquiry, although Creel figured he could argue for a few more days with this one. Now it would be Homicide's turn to try to figure out who had killed Rhyse and Korr—and why.

Creel didn't like it. Something else was going on here, and he didn't much relish the idea of turning the investigation over to someone in Homicide. But maybe he could get work it so Jessa Kodd would be assigned this case. She'd been helpful in assisting him with the Thaxton investigation, so maybe she wouldn't mind him riding along on this one, so to speak.

With that thought to cheer him, he pocketed his tablet and strolled away from the crime scene, deactivating the barrier tape momentarily with the remote device all RilSec officers carried with them. Whatever else might be uncovered here, it would be the work of the evidence mechs who even now were crawling over the still smoking remains of Mia Felaris' home. They'd catalogue everything down to a square centimeter of rubble and pass their findings along to the officer in charge. If anything turned up, he'd hear about it. He could only hope that whatever might have happened to Mia Felaris and her son, she had a good reason for maintaining her silence…and that her silence wouldn't prove deadly.

XXIII

THEY TOOK A STANDARD SHUTTLE to New Chicago—just two ordinary travelers in the nondescript street clothes Thorn had recommended Miala purchase. He sat next to her now, dark face impassive as he regarded the working-day crush around them. Certainly none of the other passengers on the shuttle could have had any idea how dangerous the dark-haired man of no particular height actually was. Somehow Thorn had the gift of blending in when he wasn't wearing the wrappings that hid his face from everyone around him. Perhaps he had allowed that swath of dark fabric to take on all the mystique of being Eryk Thorn, thus giving him the ability to become completely anonymous when out of it.

For herself, Miala wasn't sure what the other passengers might see. She'd made sure that her own suit was a bland shade of brown, a color that didn't do much for her copper-colored hair or fair skin but one which would certainly help her blend with the crowd. Every personal item she'd owned had been destroyed in the fire, and Thorn hadn't seemed too thrilled with her notion of trying to replace some of her more important cosmetics, so she'd had to content herself with buying a tube of tinted lip balm at the kiosk down in the hotel lobby before they caught a taxi to the spaceport. At the kiosk she'd also bought a pair of photo-reactive eyewear.

At least the glasses will hide the shadows under my eyes, she thought ruefully. *I never realized how much I relied on all that stuff until I didn't have it anymore.*

But, her appearance aside, she felt some measure of relief as the shuttle lifted off from Nova Angeles. No one seemed to have noted their departure from the hotel, and Miala had been able to purchase their fare to New Chicago without incident. She'd been starting at shadows, certain that either RilSec officers or agents of whoever had hired the kidnappers were going to swarm around her and Thorn at any second. No doubt the mercenary could have handled the situation with ease, but the whole point was not to attract attention, after all. He had a small holdout gun tucked into the inside pocket of his own suit jacket. One of these days she was going to have to ask him precisely what he had done to gimmick it so it would pass spaceport security.

Technically speaking, Miala could have withdrawn the money from the New Chicago accounts here on Nova Angeles. But if she had done that, it would have sat in escrow for seventy-five standard hours until the funds cleared. Ridiculous, of course, but that was bureaucracy for you. And those were seventy-five hours Jerem didn't have. This way, she could take out the funds directly with no waiting period. She and Thorn would be back in Rilsport by sunset.

Taking a breath, she leaned her head back against the padded rest and tried to calm herself as best she could. Just thinking about Jerem in the hands of kidnappers was enough to send her heart pounding and the adrenaline racing along her veins. But continually worrying over the situation wouldn't change it. She was doing everything she could—and so was Eryk Thorn.

As if his name in her thoughts were some sort of signal, he casually reached across the armrest and took her hand in his. His own fingers were callused and very strong, and she found their touch to be intensely comforting. Miala let her fingers entwine with his and shut her eyes, allowing herself to take this small space of time to shore up her strength. And although she didn't know whether she would ever admit it to Thorn, their lovemaking of the night before had done much to restore her equilibrium.

Good thing, too, considering that Miala's first task of the morning had been to call Risa and let her know that she and Jerem had survived the fire.

"But where are you?" Risa had demanded. "All hell is breaking loose around here—I've been dodging insurance agents all morning—RilSec was here asking questions—"

"I'd better not say right now," Miala had hedged. "I know it's really awkward, but just stonewall them the best you can. You really don't know anything, so they can't say you're hiding something."

Risa had raised an eyebrow at that. "Sounds like circular logic to me. How am I supposed to be your assistant if you won't let me assist you, for God's sake?"

"You are helping, Risa," Miala said. "You're my first line

of defense. But I really can't tell you where I am. Just know that I'm safe."

Her assistant frowned. "Are you in some kind of trouble, Miala? Quin Lassiter said something about some strange man being at your house—"

Miala had to stifle a groan. And here she had thought Quin could be trusted to keep his mouth shut— "What did Quin say, Risa?" she asked, in tones that didn't bode well for the good doctor if she happened to see him any time soon.

"I'm the only person he said anything to," Risa said quickly. "He knew you had had him over in confidence, but he figured it would be safe enough if he told me. Come on, Mia—your house burned down!"

"I'm aware of that," Miala snapped. "And this person Quin mentioned had nothing to do with it." *Well, mostly*, she thought. After all, she wasn't completely certain whose pulse bolt had caught the curtains on fire in the first place.

"If you say so," Risa replied, but her dubious tone indicated that she didn't believe a word Miala was saying.

Which was fine, as long as Risa continued to play human shield and kept the bureaucrats and police away from Miala long enough for her to recover Jerem. After that, she would try to deal with all the inevitable legal messes that the destruction of her house had initiated.

"Look, I know this must be awful for you," Miala said. "And I'll try to get in to handle it as soon as I can. But until then, I'm going to have to stay out of contact. Just do the best you can, and I'll come into the office whenever it's feasible."

Risa remained silent for the space of a few seconds, watching Miala out of narrowed blue eyes. Her pretty face was uncharacteristically grim. Then she sighed and said, "I'll do what I can, Mia. But I have a feeling this is going to get ugly."

Oh, it's gone well past ugly, Miala thought. *But unfortunately there's not much I can do about it right now.* All she said, however, was, "Dodge as much as you can, and if it gets too bad, call Lenner." Jakim Lenner was Miala's personal attorney, and as far as she could tell, he ate insurance representatives and RilSec personnel for breakfast.

Her assistant had brightened a bit at that suggestion. "Of course. Thanks, Mia—and take care."

Miala made a noncommittal sound and switched off the comm. Not much had been resolved, but at least she had given Risa the one vital piece of information she needed—that Miala and Jerem were alive.

For now, she thought, and tightened her fingers around the mercenary's for a second.

He gave her a quick sideways glance, although his expression never changed. But in response she'd felt the pressure of his hand on hers increase ever so slightly. And that was enough.

Whatever happened next, at least she'd go through it with Eryk Thorn at her side.

Most of the male personnel in RilSec would admit, if pressed, that sometimes it was damn hard to concentrate on a case when Jessa Kodd was assigned to it. Tall, blonde, and icily beautiful, she was the type of woman who immediately called attention to herself just by her mere presence. She was also, in Rafe Creel's estimation, the best detective Homicide possessed.

She sat at her battered charcoal-colored steel desk and leaned forward now, elbows resting on a thick pile of pale blue paper. Despite the fact that all their files and records were stored in electronic format, somehow most of RilSec's officers seemed to take an obscure pleasure in printing out those files and keeping them in random stacks of blue flimsies. Maybe they thought a desk that was clean of all paperwork gave the appearance of a desk of someone who wasn't working very hard. Whatever the reason, Jessa Kodd's workspace didn't look much different from that of any of the other Homicide officers, even if the person occupying the battered synth-hide chair behind it sure did.

A frown creasing her elegant brows, she gave Creel a dubious look. "This is a little irregular—" she began.

That was the understatement of the millennium. "I know," he said. "But the deaths of Rhyse and Korr did start out in my jurisdiction. I'd just like to be able to follow this through to the end."

"I don't know—" Then she broke off and gave a small laugh. "You're just going to keep after me on this until I say yes, aren't you?"

"Something like that," Creel admitted.

She tapped the stylus of her tablet against the desk. Her nails were unpolished, cut short. Creel liked that. "All right," she said at length. "We'll go after this one together. Besides, if I tell Lonegar that you're working on it with me, I won't get saddled with Janson." Jessa threw a significant look past Creel's shoulder in the direction of one of the other Homicide officers' desks.

He grinned. Janson did all right, but he could see why

Jessa wouldn't want to get stuck with him on a case—the man seemed to have serious difficulty in focusing his attention on something other than Inspector Kodd's chest. Creel had to admit that certain portions of her anatomy were somewhat distracting, but he had more self-control than Janson.

At least, he hoped he did.

"So," he said, forcing his mind off Jessa Kodd's more spectacular assets, "what have we got so far?"

The "we" elicited an amused glance in his direction. "The coroner's report seems to indicate that both officers were killed by pulse bolts to the upper torso, and not smoke inhalation or other fire-induced trauma." Jessa shuffled through the stacks of paper on her desk, then drew out a multi-page document that had been perma-sealed together along the top edges. She flipped past the top two pages and then looked down at the document for a few seconds, frowning slightly. "The evidence mechs haven't been able to turn up much beyond what we already knew. The fire was started in the larger of the two downstairs salons, and spectrographic analysis seems to bear out the theory that it was started by a stray pulse bolt. Obviously Rhyse and Korr got into something they hadn't quite expected. But as to who was shooting at them, and why—?" A lift of her shoulders under the plain synth-silk shirt. "I haven't a clue. Care to contribute anything to my useless theorizing?"

"I've got a little more." Creel drew out his tablet and scrolled to the file he'd been compiling on the case. "I just got authorization to tap into both Rhyse's and Korr's computers. The guys in C.S. were able to crack their access codes for me."

"Nice."

Occasionally the Computing Services people could be helpful. On the other hand, if you needed a password reset or your files shifted to a new server, you could be left cooling your heels for days. Ah, bureaucracy. He went on, "According to some files I found on Korr's tablet, he's had Mia Felaris' residence under surveillance for a little more than a standard month. And it was about the same time that he set up the bank account I found on Gaia's moon. He opened it with 75,000 units, then added another seventy-five about two standard weeks later."

Jessa Kodd's full lips pursed as she gave a small whistle. "Not bad for someone who has to work almost a full year to earn even half that."

"Exactly."

"Any indication as to where the funds came from?"

Creel shook his head. "Not yet. The deposits were made in Gaian units—hard cash, untraceable. Same with Rhyse—although he was stupid enough to open his account just over on New Chicago, and he couldn't resist buying some fancy toys with it."

She settled back in her chair, frowning slightly. "So someone was throwing money at them to at least surveil Mia Felaris, and probably more. Why her?"

Why her, precisely, Creel thought. He had a feeling that Mia Felaris formed the crux of the whole matter, even if he didn't yet know the reason. "Hard to say. I've been doing some digging. Had to sweet-talk the records clerk at the University, but eventually she let slip that Mia Felaris had come here from Iradia—and that her birth name was actually Miala Fels."

"Iradia, huh?" Jessa tapped her fingers on the battered synth-hide arm of her chair. "Not exactly a garden spot, right?"

"Hardly." Oh, sure, Iradia was famous for producing the moth silk used the galaxy over for all sorts of luxury goods, but that didn't prevent it from being one of the more spectacular armpits in the Consortium, a hangout for crime lords, slavers, smugglers, and a whole bunch of other types you probably wouldn't want to invite to a cocktail party. "You can see why she'd want to keep that part of her background quiet. Not that anyone should discriminate against her because of where she came from," he added quickly.

"Of course not," Jessa replied, the wryness of her tone indicating she didn't buy that for one second.

Neither did he. Oh, he was sure Mia Felaris was an upstanding citizen, but Nova Angeles had been populated too long and was too hidebound not to turn up its collective nose at refugees from scrubby worlds such as Iradia. Quite possibly that was the only reason Ms. Fels/Felaris had changed her name and her identity. Or had she been running from something...or someone?

Apparently Jessa had made the same leap of logic. "Do you think it could be someone from Iradia who's after her, who hired Rhyse and Korr?"

"Possibly." Creel rubbed his forefinger against his chin, considering. "Makes more sense than anyone here wanting to do her harm. She's got no record, no civil actions filed against her—and for someone running her own security firm, that says a lot right there. Usually someone who's been in business as long as she has would have gotten sued at least once by now."

"Such faith in our judicial system," Jessa mocked, and he flashed her a quick grin.

"Are you calling me jaded?" he asked.

"You?" The laughing gleam in her eyes faded. "So… Iradia. Any suspects?"

"Are you kidding? They barely keep records over there—I was able to find one notation that showed a Miala Fels had attended some sort of secondary school for a few years, but that's about it. No birth record. No known residence." The frustration at dealing with such a backward planet resurfaced easily; he'd been fighting with balky information relays and incomplete databases all morning. "The place really went to hell for a few years following an insurrection about eight years ago. I'm guessing a lot of data was deliberately destroyed to piss off what they saw as their Gaian overlords. Never mind that almost all their ancestors had come from Gaia in the first place. Anyway, there isn't much left to find."

"Dead end, then?"

"You think I'd let them beat me that easily?"

Jessa looked at him for a long moment, giving him a cool, appraising stare out of those lush green eyes. Then she smiled. "No," she said. "They're not going to know what hit them."

One thing about standing on your hands—it gives you an entirely different perspective on the world. After the meager lunch the rat-faced kidnapper brought him, Jerem had resumed his practice, partly because it seemed to irritate his captor far beyond what it actually should, and also because he couldn't think of anything better to do.

He'd had to wait a bit after he ate; he tried right after lunch, but it felt as if the heavy noodle soup was sliding right back up his esophagus, so Jerem sat down for a while until he thought he'd probably digested enough so he could turn his stomach upside-down without risking any unpleasant side effects. Maybe it was like swimming. His mother was always harping on the fact that he wasn't supposed to go in the water until at least a half-hour after he'd eaten.

But now he felt as if he could get back on his hands without barfing up his lunch, so he sprang into action once more. And it was while he staggered around upside-down next to the bed that he spotted something interesting, something the dragging bedclothes couldn't quite hide.

There was some sort of opening in the wall behind the bed.

Oh, it wasn't much—just a hairline crack in the smooth mud-board walls. The bed had been pushed up against it, and it ended a little more than half a meter above the floor, so if Jerem hadn't been looking at it upside-down, there was a very good chance he wouldn't have seen it at all. And as soon as he noticed the opening, he realized he had to act as if he hadn't seen it. After all, those stupid cameras were still in place. If he displayed too much curiosity, the kidnappers would notice and come to investigate.

So he turned and made a few staggering hand-steps back into the center of the room before vaulting onto his feet and standing upright. His head pounded a little, and his hands felt tingly, but Jerem didn't know if that was because of the extended time he'd just spent upside-down, or because he might have just found a way to escape.

The hole wasn't very big. He'd have to find some way to pry the mud-board loose, and even then he'd have to wriggle flat on his stomach to get inside. There was no way of knowing where it went, or if he'd even be able to get out of the building through the opening. Maybe it went nowhere. But maybe— just maybe—it was a blocked ventilation chute or something that linked up to an air circulation system or something like that. He remembered an episode of Moon of Syrinara where the hoverchair hero's sidekick had to do much the same thing in order to defuse a bomb before it went off. And Jerem was a lot smaller than the sidekick. He should fit in the shaft or vent or whatever it was a lot more easily than an adult ever could. The trick would be getting in there before anyone else noticed.

Frowning, Jerem walked over to the bed as casually as he could and sat down, leaning up against the wall and pretending to shut his eyes as if he had tired himself out with all the hand-walking. In reality, he was pushing against it with his upper back to see whether he'd be able to move the bed away from the wall without anyone noticing. He felt it shift an inch, but it also made a horrible scraping noise against the faded linoleum floor, so he stopped immediately, heart racing as he tried to decide whether the sound had been loud enough for the cameras' microphones to pick up.

No one burst into the room, demanding to know what he had been doing. Jerem still remained that way for a few minutes, though, eyes shut as his mind worked furiously. What would his father have done in such a situation? *Not gotten himself kidnapped in the first place*, Jerem thought in disgust. *He would have shot their butts off the second they came in the bedroom window.*

But he'd already beaten himself up enough about what he should or shouldn't have done. All that accomplished was to waste more time. Instead, he clenched his hands, feeling the rough blanket and thin sheets ball up between his fingers. Then he opened his eyes and looked down at the bedclothes as if seeing them for the very first time. He thought for a moment, then glanced casually at the cameras. Once was mounted in the corner right above his bed, and the other one sat perched in the far corner, over by the door. He couldn't tell by looking at them whether they were just regular video devices or whether they shot other spectrums like infrared. His mother knew all about that stuff, because of her business, and Jerem had picked up some of it, but he had to admit he wasn't a huge expert on surveillance cameras. Too bad, because if they weren't infrared-equipped, then there might be a chance to render both of them useless by tossing a sheet or blanket over them. The kidnappers would notice, of course, but all Jerem really needed was about a minute or so.

Of course, that would only work if he were able to get the sheets to stay on the cameras. He'd have to weight them down somehow, probably. And then of course there was the problem of even prying the mud-board out of the wall without their noticing…

Every problem has a solution, his mother always told him. *You just have to give it time.*

Well, time was something he had plenty of. Closing his eyes once more, Jerem leaned his head up against the wall and began to plot.

XXIV

MIALA WALKED OUT OF THE MAIN BRANCH OFFICE of New Chicago Central Trust, a plain synth-hide satchel clutched in her right hand. She had the feeling she should have a sign blinking on and off over her head that screamed, *Rob me—I'm carrying ten million units!*

But even if she'd had such a sign floating above her, and even if someone had been foolhardy enough to attack her, the robber would have had to go through Eryk Thorn first. Miala knew the plainly dressed man striding beside her offered better security than anything her firm could have provided. He walked with an air of casual unconcern, but she could see the way his gaze drifted through the crowds, pausing occasionally on those who might present a threat, and then moving on after any anomaly had been noted and filed for future reference.

Not that there seemed to be anyone or anything remotely threatening here on New Chicago. A sister planet to Nova Angeles, it had long been civilized, its urban areas dedicated to centers of higher learning and commerce. The crowds around them were a mirror to the people Miala saw on her way in to work every day in Rilsport—neatly dressed, preoccupied. Probably she would have had to turn cartwheels naked down the street while throwing units into the air for anyone to take any particular notice of her.

A cab whooshed to a stop at the curb in answer to Thorn's hail, and Miala slid into the back seat, followed by the mercenary. Not until the door shut behind the two of them did she realize how on edge she had been. She forced herself to exhale, but she still retained her death grip on the satchel she carried.

Once they were back on Nova Angeles, she would have to pull five million out of her own accounts to supply the fifteen the kidnappers had demanded, but that would be a slightly simpler process. Miala had used cash in several large transactions previously, most notably the purchase of her home. The managers at her bank had given her sideways glances over that particular deal, muttering things about "irregularities" and "escrow," but in the end the previous owners of the house had told the bank officials to get stuffed, because not even a native of Nova Angeles would turn up his nose at a few million in shiny hard Gaian currency. So while the withdrawal of such a large amount from her personal accounts might raise a few eyebrows, at least it wasn't without precedent.

Eryk Thorn was watching her with an oddly speculative expression on his face.

She asked, "What's the matter?"

"Nothing," he replied. "That went smoothly enough. But I've been thinking—"

Here we go, she thought. *He's suddenly decided he doesn't*

want to chip in quite that much cash. Or maybe none at all.
"What?" God, that sounded accusatory even to her.

"About what we're going to do afterward."

"Afterward?"

The dark eyes narrowed slightly. "After Jerem is safe.
After we're all together again."

Relief coursed through her. When was she going to
stop expecting the worst of people? Oh, her early life had
certainly done nothing to engender a trust in others, and
this latest incident with Murgan and now the kidnappers
had brought her estimation of sentient life to an all-time
low, but if she couldn't trust Eryk Thorn, who in the galaxy
could she trust? Not sure she could speak without letting
slip a revealing tremor in her voice, she settled for nodding.

Thorn spoke slowly, as if gathering together thoughts
he'd been turning over in his mind for some time. "You've
made a good place for Jerem on Nova Angeles. But it's not
really his home world, is it?"

"Well, he was born there," Miala pointed out. "But
you're right—it's just sort of the place I ended up. It's not
as if his roots go back very far."

"Then let me take him—take you—home."

"'Home'?" Miala echoed. "Sorry, Thorn, but you seem
about the most rootless person I've ever met—not that
there's anything wrong with that."

He didn't appear to take offense. For a few seconds
he watched her with that familiar unreadable expression,
then said, "Until now I had no reason to go there, to have
anything to do with my heritage. But my son should know
where his people come from."

"And where is that?"

"A place on Gaia called New Zealand."

She tried not to let her shock reveal itself in her eyes. That a man who had spent his life on the edges of the galaxy would want to go to Gaia, the center of the Consortium, seemed strange enough. That anyone would want to repatriate to a world that had almost slipped into ecological oblivion was even stranger. It didn't sound particularly inviting, especially compared to the comfortable life she had built up for herself and her son on Nova Angeles.

Still, Thorn was offering far more than she had expected. He would not be mentioning Gaia to her if he didn't visualize some long-term future with her and Jerem. Wasn't that what she had always dreamed of and thought she would never have—a chance for them to be a real family? Miala realized suddenly she would go to the wildest frontier planet if it meant that Eryk Thorn would stay in hers and Jerem's lives, and whatever its current shortcomings, Gaia was hardly the frontier. Besides, she'd grown up on Iradia and certainly knew how to fend for herself in a rough environment. She might have spent the last eight years living soft on Nova Angeles, but once a person has been toughened in a crucible such as her home world, the lessons learned there were indelibly etched in the psyche.

"What sort of a place is New Zealand?" Miala asked, hoping her tone was neutral enough, even though she thought, *Please, God, not more desert...*

When he replied, Eryk Thorn sounded almost amused, as if he had known exactly what was preying on her mind. "It's a temperate country—it has forests and open land.

And it's an island. Lots of water. No desert. It escaped a lot of the damage Gaia suffered during the environmental breakdowns of the twenty-first century."

"And that's where your mother is from?"

He nodded. "Both my parents, actually. I think that's why she kept me. There are far too few of us left in this day and age. Guess she wanted the bloodline to continue."

There was so much Miala wanted to ask, but she also knew that Thorn had already revealed far more to her than he probably had to any other living being. She pushed most of the other questions aside, but felt compelled to inquire, "Have you ever been to New Zealand?"

"Once." At first it seemed as if he would offer no more than that, but after a brief pause he added, "It can be a harsh place, but I think you will find parts of it beautiful."

Then let's hope that we end up in one of the beautiful parts, she thought. But she only said, "I'm looking forward to it."

Thorn's lifted eyebrow handed her the lie, but he said nothing, instead reaching over and laying his hand on top of hers where it rested on the handle of the bag she carried. He didn't bother to offer her any soothing words. She somehow doubted he had any, but the fact that he was already planning for their future together reassured her far more than any facile words about how he was sure Jerem was fine and that this would all go off without a hitch. Whatever else he might be or do, Eryk Thorn looked at the galaxy through a set of keen, unsentimental eyes. If he thought they would come out on the other side of this relatively unscathed, well, then, that was good enough for her.

Still, she couldn't help wishing the rough parts were well past them. Too bad that life didn't come with a selective remote control, one that would allow you to skip over the frightening or dangerous sections. If only that were the case, then she'd push the button that would put her, Jerem, and Thorn safely on the *Fury* and flying off to Gaia, with the kidnappers vanquished and all the loose ends on Nova Angeles neatly tied up. But life didn't work that way, unfortunately, and she knew they would all have to live through whatever lay ahead to get to that particular happy ending.

Miala glanced over at Eryk Thorn's imperturbable features and wondered if he ever experienced such moments of doubt. It would be nice, she thought, to be that sure of one's self, to never seem to experience a moment of indecision or fear.

She tightened her fingers around his, hoping to feel some of his strength bolstering her own sagging will. Let me be strong enough, she prayed silently.

Let me be strong enough to save my son.

"Well, dip me in shit," breathed Creel, who had to read the terse automated message several times to make sure he'd gotten it right.

Jessa Kodd paused at the edge of his desk, green eyes widening slightly. "Excuse me?"

He looked up. "Sorry. But I think I've got something here."

She set down the case file she was holding and walked around the corner of the desk, then leaned over his shoulder so she could get a closer look at his computer screen. A spicy scent wafted from her loose hair as she bent toward him, and Creel had to swallow and attempt to recall what had grabbed his attention in the first place.

"I tagged Mia Felaris' bank accounts so I'd be notified in case of any unusual activity," he said, hoping she wouldn't notice his increased respiration. "Two standard hours ago she withdrew ten million in cash from a holding account she had on New Chicago."

"Ten million?" Jessa's tone was carefully neutral, but he thought he could hear the incredulity behind it.

"Just about emptied the account. There's a couple hundred thousand left, but that's it."

"Think she's getting ready to blow the system?"

He shook his head. Although Mia Felaris' actions seemed to be those of someone preparing to pull up stakes and move on, somehow Creel didn't think that was the case here. There seemed to be something else going on, some other motivating factor.

He just wished he could figure out what it was.

"I'm pulling in the security feed from New Chicago Central Trust now," he said, watching as the flat video images scrolled past. They showed a normal weekday morning of patrons moving in and out, some tapping away on their tablets as they stood in the queue, higher-level customers getting one-on-one service from the bank's various functionaries.

Creel let the feed continue on its loop, his eyes only half-focused on the flood of data. He'd done this enough times that he knew he'd catch the anomaly when it popped up.

And there it was.

Mia Felaris strolled in, accompanied by a nondescript-looking man in a plain dark suit. He stood off to one side while she went to speak with an older woman who obviously was a mid-level bank officer. After a few seconds, they disappeared into a private office. But the strange man continued to wait in the main lobby, his stance relaxed, his gaze appearing to continually move over the other patrons as they went about their business.

"Who's that?" Jessa asked.

Creel shook his head but didn't lift his gaze from the monitor. "Don't know. Let me do a capture and see what the databanks have on him." He paused the image, typed in the commands to have the image-matching software take a snap of the stranger's face, and then waited as the computer began the process of trying to line up the pixels with the billions of records on file in the Consortium's databases. The process could take a while, Creel knew, but it was an invaluable tool in a galaxy-spanning civilization that all too often had galaxy-spanning criminals as well. Of course, anyone who'd had a photo identification taken at some point in their lives was also stored in the database, but usually it was the shady types who tended to have more official "portraits" on file.

He turned away from the computer to see Jessa Kodd watching him with speculation in her cool green eyes.

"Think he's coercing her?"

That had been Creel's first thought, but somehow he didn't believe it was the case. "I don't think so," he replied with a frown. Leaning forward, he tapped in the command to have the image back up a few frames, then watched carefully as the pair entered the bank. "You'd think she'd look more nervous around him. Look at the way he touched her elbow there—" He paused the image. It was the briefest of gestures, but somehow it looked as if the stranger were trying to give a reassuring pat to Mia's arm before she went off with the bank officer. "If he'd been threatening her, she would have reacted negatively, even if she were trying to look cool. But instead she got that little smile on her face. I don't think he's forcing her to withdraw that money."

"Boyfriend?"

"Maybe. All my research so far has shown she leads a pretty solitary life, though. Just her and the kid." The kid, whom no one had seen since the house fire. The boy hadn't been injured, as far as Creel could tell. He'd checked with all the local hospitals and clinics, and no one answering to Jerem Felaris' description had been admitted to any of them. Maybe Mia Felaris had just stashed her son at a friend's house. He wasn't at the suite she'd booked in the Rilsport Plaza, either. Creel had already searched the rooms after she'd left and found nothing. For someone leading a quiet civilian life, Ms. Felaris seemed to know an awful lot about not leaving any clues behind.

The computer beeped, indicating that it had completed its search, and Creel swiveled back around to check out the results.

"Captain Galen Marr," he read. "Shows he's got a light cargo ship registered on Monteverde…looks as if he landed here on Nova Angeles two days ago. The vessel is right here at the Rilsport spaceport. Landing pad eighteen-twenty. Paid for a week of docking privileges in advance."

"So they didn't take his ship to New Chicago?"

"Doesn't look like it. Must have traveled by regular shuttle."

Jessa frowned. "Why would they do that if they had a private ship at their disposal?"

"Maybe it needed repairs or something."

At that comment she shot him an unbelieving look, and Creel lifted his shoulders.

"All right, that doesn't seem likely."

"To put it mildly." She glanced at the computer screen, as if trying to commit Captain Marr's hard features to memory. Then she gave Creel a slow smile, a smile most men in the department would have lined up to be on the receiving end of. "Guess we'd better get going, then."

"Going?"

In answer she reached forward and typed in the command that put his computer into locked-down sleep mode. "Landing pad eighteen-twenty. I figure this Captain Marr's got to come back to his ship some time…"

After hours of careful scrutiny—well, what felt like it, anyway—Jerem was convinced that the cameras watching his quarters were simple video units, no infrared or anything fancy like that. Of course he couldn't just walk up to the cameras and inspect them without the kidnappers guessing he was up to something, but he'd gone back to the hand-walking, cartwheels, and anything else he could think of that would look as if he were simply an active kid who was going out of his mind with boredom. Who would ever notice that the cartwheels and somersaults usually brought him close to one of the cameras, or that the time he spent lying on his back, staring blankly at the ceiling, he was actually trying to focus on the compact pieces of photographic equipment, attempting to remember what his mother had told him about cameras and video surveillance.

Jerem knew that his grandfather—who had died before Jerem was even born—taught his mother everything he'd known about hacking into computers and writing security programs. When she'd started her own company on Nova Angeles, she'd taken that one step further, enhancing the practically hacker-proof programs she wrote with sophisticated surveillance equipment for those customers who needed it. She always had catalogues for the latest stuff lying around, and since Jerem had seemed interested in it (because although he would never have admitted it to her, he thought what she did was actually kind of cool), she'd explained some of the basics to him.

So he knew to look for the telltale film on the lens of a camera that had infrared capabilities, and how to tell if it could see into other spectrums—ultraviolet, for instance. Not that they'd need something that sophisticated to keep watch on a regular human boy. It wasn't as if he could just turn invisible like one of those Specter creatures he'd seen featured on a particularly exciting episode of *Moon of Syrinara*. Too bad, because right now invisibility would have come in pretty handy.

But the second best thing to turning invisible was just disappearing, and now that he was almost certain the cameras wouldn't be able to register his body heat, Jerem figured he could probably sneak out without anyone noticing. Or at least he hoped. He just had to wait for night to fall.

The same pointy-faced kidnapper came in around dinnertime—not that Jerem knew the hour, of course, but the hollow feeling in his stomach told him it had been at least four or five hours since lunch—and brought him a tray of some gluey-looking noodles with a heavy sauce. It looked pretty gross, but Jerem knew if he was going to make a break for it, he'd need to have eaten something. So he picked up the fork and plowed in, trying to ignore the nasty aftertaste the food left in his mouth and making a mental note to ask his mother for a big, juicy burger the second he got out of this hellhole.

The kidnapper apparently was ready to find fault in anything Jerem did. After a few minutes of watching him eat in silence, he demanded, "What's up with you, kid? You seem awfully quiet."

Jerem forced another glutinous mass of food down his throat and replied, "That's because this food is so rank that I have to concentrate on not throwing up."

"You're lucky you're getting anything," the skinny man said, but he looked satisfied. Obviously Jerem's rudeness had convinced him it was business as usual in the prison quarters.

"Yeah, tell my stomach that," Jerem muttered, but he finished the food in grim silence, drank the glass of water that had come with it, and then pushed the tray away...but not before slipping the fork up the sleeve of his sleep shirt just as the man watching him glanced down at the chrono on his wrist.

The kidnapper picked up the tray, gave Jerem one last squinty-eyed glare, and then paused at the doorway. "Just behave yourself. Stay out of trouble, and if everything goes according to plan, you just might see your mama tomorrow."

Even though he knew the kidnapper was probably just messing with him, Jerem couldn't help feeling a stab of hope at those words. At least it sounded as if his mother had been in contact with them—probably to pay off the ransom. He wondered how much they were asking for, and whether his mother would be able to come up with it. Sure, they lived well, and there always seemed to be enough money for trips over the summer holidays and the latest toys and electronic gizmos for the house, but he got the feeling these guys probably were asking for a lot more than a couple thousand units. Otherwise, what would be the point of hiding him off someplace like this and feeding him and all the other stuff they'd probably spent money on?

The kidnapper was looking at him with suspicion in his close-set dark eyes, so Jerem said, "Okay," and settled himself back on the bed, crossing his arms and trying to make it look as if he was so tired he couldn't keep his eyelids propped open any longer. He wasn't sure how convincing the act was, but after a "Hmpf" and a final once-over of the room, the kidnapper went out, letting in a brief glimpse of a dusky purple sky before the door shut behind him. Probably it wouldn't be time to go to sleep for a few more hours, unfortunately, and he would have to wait until they dimmed the lights before he could move on to the next step of his plan.

Of course the kidnappers hadn't turned out the lights completely the night before—they weren't that stupid—but they had dimmed the illumination in the room to the point where you could at least go to sleep. Jerem knew he couldn't do anything too obvious, but since his bed was in a corner, and the blankets were dark, he figured he could do a good bit of wriggling underneath them without anyone noticing.

Jerem shut his eyes, but he wasn't about to fall asleep. For one thing, it was way too early, and sleep was about the last thing on his mind anyway. Instead, he lay there as quietly as he could, mind running over his plan and finding about a million holes—but, as his mother sometimes said, sometimes you just had to bite the power-pack casing and go for it. For a while he worried that his escape attempt might bung up the whole thing. After all, the kidnappers had made it sound as if his mother was cooperating, but of course they wouldn't tell Jerem if something was going wrong anyway. Obviously they'd want him to sit quiet and not cause any trouble, no matter whether they were getting the ransom or not.

Best he could figure, if he were out of this room at least he would have options. Stuck in here, he couldn't do much except sit and wait for them to free him or come in and kill him. And there was always a chance they'd kill him anyway even if they got the ransom, because Jerem had seen a few shows like that on the vid when his mother wasn't paying attention. Not even vid shows always had happy endings, after all.

But if he got out, even though he had no idea where he was, he'd be doing a lot better than he was now, stuck in this stupid room like a rat in a cage. Besides, he'd bet money that his dad wouldn't sit around doing nothing, waiting for a bunch of simps like these kidnappers to come in and do away with him.

That decided it. Jerem opened one eye and saw that the lights in the room had already been dimmed. It was time to show them they should have known better than to mess with Eryk Thorn's son.

He made a show of pulling back the covers and wriggling under them. All he could do was hope that the kidnappers hadn't noticed he'd kept his shoes on; he'd contemplated taking them off, but decided against it. After all, he didn't know what lay behind that wall, and he'd seen too many shows where the hero had to run on broken glass or burning rock or whatever unpleasant item the writers could come up with for Jerem to think that going barefoot was a very good idea.

Once he was under the covers, he began inching toward the back wall. After he felt it touch his back, he began pushing the bed slightly outward. Slowly, of course—he'd found that it didn't make so much of a scraping noise if it got pushed just a fraction of a centimeter at a time. It seemed excruciating, but somehow Jerem didn't think about how long it was taking. Instead he just concentrated on making as little noise as possible.

Finally the gap between the wall and the bed felt big enough for him to slip down into. He grasped the pillow, wadded it up as best he could, and pushed it into the center of the bed, hoping it would make a reasonably boy-sized lump for the surveillance cameras to pick up.

Jerem slid down into the gap, feeling the cool roughness of the mud board scrape against his cheek. Once he had touched the floor, he reached out and felt around on the wall, trying to locate the edges of the rectangle he had spotted the previous day. His fingers found the crack, and he traced back along the outline of the opening, stopping finally at the bottom. Then he slid the fork out of his sleeve and pushed it into the crack, trying to lift up and outward at the same time.

At first it didn't seem as if it wanted to budge. The fork made a horrible scraping noise, and Jerem froze, waiting for the inevitable angry hand to reach over the side of the bed and haul him out of his hiding place. But no one came, and he continued to work at it until he finally felt the edge of the thin mud board slip just a bit. With shaking fingers he reached under it and lifted it out, flattening himself against the ground as he did so in order to give the board enough clearance.

A black hole now gaped in the wall, a square of darkness that revealed nothing of what lay beyond. Taking a breath, Jerem squeezed in, noting how his shoulders touched the edges of the opening. At least he knew that none of the kidnappers would ever be able to fit in here.

He pushed himself along the metal-lined tunnel, and hoped he'd be far away before his captors realized that he'd disappeared right out from under their noses. With any luck, he could be long gone by the time day returned and revealed that their precious prize had evaporated with the night.

XXV

A WAVE OF COOL, DAMP AIR greeted Miala and Thorn as they disembarked from the shuttle at Rilsport's main spaceport terminal. The last traces of sunset smoldered off to the west, leaving a bloody trail across the thin strip of ocean barely visible beyond the peninsula where the 'port was situated. They'd been gone barely eight standard hours, although still she was conscious of time ticking inexorably away. The kidnappers had given her two standard days, but she'd just used up one of them. Tomorrow, they would be expecting payment.

She continued to clutch the satchel that held the ten million units; Thorn had offered to hold it for her, but she'd declined. Somehow it seemed important to keep it close to her, as if its proximity would somehow increase their chances of success. He'd taken one look at her face and hadn't argued.

From the spaceport they went to the outskirts of Rilsport, to a smaller branch of her bank where she wasn't as well-known. From what Risa had said, it sounded as if the authorities were still looking for her, and Miala and Thorn had agreed that it would be better to handle the remaining withdrawal in a location that was less likely to be watched.

The bank manager gave her a sour look when she made her request to withdraw five million units. "We don't keep that much on hand here," he said, his light eyes narrow with disapproval. "We'll have to send out to another branch."

Miala shot a questioning glance at Thorn. The mercenary nodded slowly. "That's fine," she replied. "We can wait."

So they stepped off to one side and watched as the manager got on the comm and began making the necessary arrangements, all with that same pinched, disapproving expression on his face. Miala supposed she really couldn't blame him— it wasn't as if she looked forward to saying goodbye to those units, either.

Of course, if Eryk Thorn were to be believed, the units were just going to be a short-term loan at best for the kidnappers. Despite the worry that knotted her stomach, she couldn't help smiling at the thought of what sort of interest Thorn might charge for such a loan.

She looked over at him. He seemed unperturbed, and had reached into one of his suit pockets and pulled out what looked like a tiny video monitor.

"What's that?" she asked.

"Babysitting device."

Miala raised an eyebrow and waited.

"It monitors my ship. Just want to make sure she's ready and waiting for whenever we might need her." For a second the lines around Thorn's eyes seemed to deepen.

It wasn't much of an alteration of his expression, but she liked to think she'd gotten better at reading him from those small tells. "What is it?"

"Looks like the *Fury*'s got company."

"What?" Miala shifted a little closer to him and peered down at the tiny screen. It showed a flat video image of the Fury, still resting securely in its docking bay at the space-port. But even as she watched the video feed she saw two small figures—apparently a man and a woman, though it was difficult to make out much detail at that resolution—approaching the ship. They stopped a few meters away and appeared to enter some sort of discussion.

"More of the kidnappers' goons?" she asked.

Thorn shook his head. "No, I don't think so." He watched for a few more seconds, face impassive. "I'd say it was the cops."

"The police?" The last syllable came out in a sort of undignified squeak.

The right corner of Thorn's mouth lifted ever so slightly. "That's right."

Miala scowled down the tiny image. "How can you tell?"

"The way they stand, the way they're talking to each other."

"But you can't even hear what they're saying!"

"Don't need to," he replied.

Sometimes he was impossible. Actually, most of the time he was impossible. Miala crossed her arms and stared at him, waiting.

"With cops, it's all about the procedure," he said, appearing to relent after gauging exactly how much she was willing to put up with at that moment. "They're standing back, comparing notes. Observing. That means they probably don't have a warrant. They're just gathering information."

"And you got all that from watching a couple of tiny images a centimeter high?"

"Yeah."

Still dubious, Miala glanced back down at the minuscule video screen. As Thorn had said, the two...whoever they were...didn't seem to be doing much besides standing there and looking at the ship. The man had pulled out a tablet and was apparently entering something into it, while the woman walked a few paces away and stopped to stare up at the closed hatchway to the ship. She had very pale blonde hair that caught a sudden gleam of light from the harsh artificial lighting overhead. True, she didn't much look like a member of Rilsport's underworld—if the planet even had one—but then again, she didn't look much like a cop, either.

What happened next, Miala would never know, because of course at that inopportune moment the bank manager decided to materialize at her shoulder.

"Ms. Felaris."

She jumped, then shot him an accusing stare, even though he really was just carrying out his duties. In her peripheral vision she caught a glimpse of Thorn flipping shut the video unit and sliding it into his pocket once more. The movement was so quick and unobtrusive that she doubted the bank manager even noticed.

"What?" she snapped.

"We're ready to complete the transaction," he replied, somehow managing to look even more pained. "If you'll step this way—"

So she followed him over to his private office, where she signed forms and submitted her thumbprint and retinal scan, knowing as she did so that she was probably setting off alarms all over Rilsport. Oh, well. With any luck, this would all be handled by the time anyone figured out what she was really up to.

After the minutiae were taken care of, the bank manager slid a heavy plastene folder of units toward her.

"Thank you for choosing Rilsport Mutual," he said, although his tone indicated that he wanted nothing more than to rip the folder of money out of her hands and take it back to the vault where it belonged.

"You're welcome," she replied sweetly, gathering up the folder and sliding it into the satchel of units she already carried. The damn thing was getting heavy, and she wondered whether she should entrust it to Thorn after all.

She did notice that he stood even closer to her as they exited the bank and went out to the street to hail a taxi. Now it would be back to the Rilsport Plaza, she supposed, as the kidnappers expected to be able to contact her at the comm number she had registered there.

A mech jitney stopped soon enough to gather them up. Once they were safely inside, Miala felt just the slightest easing of the tension that had knotted her shoulder and neck muscles. At least they had gotten the cash together. One step at a time.

Thorn gave the mechanoid driver a destination—one of Rilsport's large shopping and entertainment centers. She shot the mercenary a puzzled look, and he replied, after he'd closed the scratched plastic privacy barrier separating them from the driver, "That's not really where we're going. I just wanted him to head someplace that would take some time."

"Time? For what?"

In answer he pulled the video surveillance device out of his pocket and opened it. Now the ship sat on its landing pad quite alone, with no evidence of the two RilSec officers—if that was really who they were—having ever been there.

"They're gone," she said.

"I thought they might be."

"But if the police have left, maybe we should head straight there and get the ship out while we can."

He shook his head. "No. I'm sure the kidnappers are still watching the landing pad. In fact, I'm counting on it."

Miala crossed her arms and glared at the mercenary. "So are you going to let a poor naïve Iradian girl in on your little master plan?"

Her plaintive question elicited a faint chuckle. "I don't think you've been naïve for a long time…if you ever were. Anyhow, I'm pretty sure our friends from RilSec haven't gone far. They're probably checking their leads, and will come back with a warrant. I'm also fairly certain that the kidnappers are planning to get the drop on them the second they try to gain entry to the ship."

Although Miala knew logically that she and Thorn should stay as far away from any such a confrontation as possible, something in her felt distinctly uneasy about allowing the two officers to walk right into a trap. "Shouldn't we do something? Warn them?"

"Guess I was wrong. You really are naïve."

An angry retort rose to her lips, but then she stopped when she saw the wicked gleam in Thorn's dark eyes. So she settled for making an exasperated "hmph!" and waited for him to explain himself.

"If we try to warn them, we risk giving our position away. Right now the one thing keeping us safe is that the kidnappers don't know where we are. Sure, they probably know you headed out to New Chicago today, but we wanted them to know that. They need to think that you're going along with their plan, that you're cooperating. Right now whoever is surveilling the Rilsport Plaza is probably waiting for you to return...which you'll do eventually. In the meantime, though, our main problem is that we don't know who they are, or where their base of operations is." He paused, all hint of amusement gone from his face. "The best way to find Jerem is to use our friends there as bait. They draw the kidnappers out, I grab one of them, and we're set."

"Set for what?" Miala asked, although she had an uneasy feeling she wouldn't much like the reply.

For a few seconds he didn't answer. Then he gave her a ferocious smile and said, "For me to extract a little information."

And even though Miala would have said she didn't much care what happened to any of the kidnappers as long as she got Jerem back, she couldn't help feeling a sort of uneasy sympathy toward whoever ended up as Thorn's victim. A bit of the impenetrable façade had dropped there, and she got the distinct impression that the mercenary was truly looking forward to the interrogation.

She wished she could say the same for herself.

It wasn't the enclosed spaces so much, Jerem reflected, pausing at the intersection of two ducts. It was what might be enclosed in there *with* you.

He could handle the dust and the odd smell, even the overwhelming, unrelieved blackness, which was so absolute that it felt almost like a weight on his eyeballs. Even though he knew he wouldn't be able to see anything, he still found himself staring into the dark, as if he tried hard enough he could make out some sort of detail.

Worse than that, though, were the noises, like the skittering of small feet. Probably the place was infested with *tarns*, small rodent-like creatures that liked dark, confined spaces. His mother always said they didn't really hurt anything, but even she'd called the exterminator when a nest of them had been discovered in the basement of their house. Then there were the webs left behind by some of Nova Angeles' more ambitious arachnids. Again, all the poisonous species had been eradicated ages ago, but it still was no fun to get those sticky webs caught in your hair. He'd broken through one that stretched across the width of the duct and had blundered through it in a panic, wiping at his face and hair with terrified fingers. After he'd gotten the worst of it off, he'd lain flat on the floor of the durasteel tube, breathing heavily. It was only after a few minutes had passed that he was able to calm down enough to chide himself for acting like a baby. It was just a few webs, after all. It wasn't as if a *fer*-snake had come crashing through and tried to eat his head or something.

He really couldn't tell how long he'd been stumbling through the blind dark. Jerem supposed he should just be glad that the kidnappers hadn't heard his blundering around and started poking holes in the ventilation system at random intervals to track him down.

But for some reason they hadn't, and even though he didn't really believe in such things, maybe God or something else was guiding him in the right direction. Maybe there was a power in the universe that looked out for little boys who had gotten in way over their heads.

He hesitated, reaching out with shaking fingers to feel each of the ducts. Down the left-hand one the air felt stuffy and warm, and it smelled funny. But the right-hand passage seemed a little more promising. Jerem thought he felt a slight draft in that one, and he almost fancied he could smell a faint tang of salt, as if the air were coming in from off the ocean.

Well, that settled it. Jerem turned down the rightmost shaft, still inching his way forward. The feel of the air against his face cheered him a little. Maybe it meant he wasn't too far away from a vent that opened to the outside. If he managed to make it that far unnoticed, then maybe he would have a good chance of getting away entirely. Unless, of course, they had the perimeter staked out with force fields and infrared scanners and all the other nasty stuff his mother used to trot out for the really high-paying clients. Then again, these guys seemed pretty cheap, at least based on what they'd fed him and the room they'd given him to sleep in.

The sound of people speaking stopped him dead, and Jerem pressed himself flat against the floor of the air duct. A few inches from his noise was another smaller duct that left a gap about a half-meter wide. If he hadn't halted so suddenly, he might have pitched right down into it.

A man's voice that sounded vaguely familiar said, "So she made it back from New Chicago all right."

"Looks that way. She disembarked at approximately nineteen-thirty local time."

"What about this man you spotted with her, Chaddick?" Jerem thought he heard something that sounded suspiciously like a growl, and he realized it was probably the Stacian who was speaking. "I thought we told her to leave the mercenary out of it."

The other man gave a derisive laugh. "That guy's no mercenary. Probably her accountant or lawyer or something. I mean, who ever heard of Eryk Thorn wearing a suit?"

A silence. "Maybe...maybe not. Any trace of them?"

"Took a cab, but we're not sure where they went after that. It's mealtime—maybe they went to get something to eat. She knows she's not going to be contacted until tomorrow anyway."

"But you're sure she got the money."

"Oh, yeah. I tell you, Korvan, she's so scared we're going to send her precious ickle boy back to her in a box that she's not going to do anything to risk his skin."

Korvan—the Stacian, Jerem decided—laughed unpleasantly. "I'd like to see the look on her face after she gives us the cash and then finds out the kid's already dead."

The other man chuckled as well, and Jerem felt the gluey meal he'd consumed earlier turn over in his stomach. Well, at least his instincts had been right. He'd done the right thing by getting out of that holding room when he could.

Barely daring to breathe, he reached out across the duct opening and scrabbled for purchase on the other side. It was a stretch for his short arms, but he'd heard enough. He knew he had to keep going and not look back.

A quick question, the words sharp with suspicion. "Did you hear that?"

Jerem immediately froze, fingers clutching the slick metal of the duct surface, the toes of his shoes threatening to slip off the edge of the far side of the gap.

"Just more of those fragging *tarns*. Told you we should've fumigated this place before we moved in."

The Stacian made another one of those low rumbling noises, and Jerem took advantage of its cover to kick off with his rear feet, propelling himself across the gap and then scrabbling down the tunnel as quickly as he could, his heart an overwhelming drumbeat in his chest, body slick with nervous sweat even though it was relatively cool in the air duct.

He wondered how many more close calls like that he could have before his luck finally ran out.

Warrant safely stored in his tablet, Creel still forced himself to read the corroborating information several times, just in case his overactive imagination had somehow gotten the better of him. Sure, the ship had set off alarm bells in his mind the second he'd laid eyes on it, but he'd never expected to hit pay dirt quite this spectacular. Jessa hadn't argued with him when he said he wanted to call in for a warrant, but her pointed silence had told him she thought he was grasping at straws. Now, however, he thought he had the data he needed to convince her he hadn't completely lost his mind.

"Take a look at this," he called out to Jessa, who had walked a few paces away from him and was staring up at the strange spacecraft with a speculative expression on her face. He gestured at the tablet.

Frowning slightly, she stepped back toward him and looked down at its screen. Then her finely arched eyebrows lifted. "Is this for real?"

"I think so."

Jessa glanced back up at the ship. "What in the seven hells would he be doing here?"

Well, that was a good question, wasn't it? Of course the ship had no identifying markers anywhere, but only one Quasar-class vessel of that particular vintage still existed… if the rumors were true. And that unique starship belonged to someone equally unique.

"Yeah, Nova Angeles isn't exactly Eryk Thorn's usual stomping grounds," Creel replied. "But I've got a theory."

Crossing her arms, Jessa gave him a questioning yet skeptical look, the sort which plainly said that although she might be willing to listen to his argument, she wasn't quite sure she was ready to believe him.

He didn't know if he believed it himself. The connections were tenuous at best, but at the same time the mercenary's presence began to explain some of the niggling loose ends in the Felaris case. "Hear me out," he said.

The cool green eyes met his. "All right."

"So we have one missing woman, Mia Felaris, who hails from Iradia originally. At the same time we have a ship owned by the galaxy's most notorious mercenary showing up in our spaceport. Coincidence? Maybe at first glance." He slid the tablet into his breast pocket, trying to ignore how piercingly green Jessa's eyes were, like the purest chromium beryl. They seemed to glow in the hard, blue-white lighting of the light strips overhead. Clearing his throat, he continued, "However, let's look at the facts. Thorn's movements are almost impossible to track, but it's fairly common knowledge that he was seen on Iradia a little over eight years ago, right around the time the insurrection took hold."

Jessa didn't blink. "And?"

"It's also a fact that Mia Felaris, an Iradian native, relocated to Nova Angeles years ago. She has a son whose father she claims is dead, killed in the siege of Arlinais." Still Jessa's expression didn't change, and he began to feel a little impatient. After all, it had begun to seem glaringly obvious to him. "But what if Jerem Felaris' father isn't really dead? What if he's actually Eryk Thorn?"

At that Jessa gave an unbelieving little laugh. "That's a bit of a stretch, don't you think?"

"Is it?" Whenever he got nervous or excited about something, Creel had a tendency to run his hands through his hair. He'd lifted a hand halfway there before realizing that he probably didn't want to look quite so distracted in front of the apparently imperturbable Jessa Kodd. He settled for fishing inside his pocket for his pack of caffeinated chewing gum, then popped a piece inside his mouth. "Gum?" he asked politely.

"No, thanks." Her full lips curved slightly in amusement.

"Anyhow," he said, realizing that while he probably could use the caffeine, chewing the gum also had the unfortunate side affect of making him look like a ruminating cow, "as far as I can tell, both Thorn and Mia Felaris—or Miala Fels, if you want to use her real name—were on Iradia at about the same time. He was working for Mast when the crime lord was killed. And Ms. Felaris comes from the closest settlement to Mast's compound. I couldn't get much from her records, but one thing I was able to discover was that she was dirt poor. I doubt she could have come up with enough cash to book passage off-world, let alone set herself up in style the way she did here. But our records show that she bought the house only a few standard months after she emigrated here, long before she set up her security business. So where did the money come from?"

"I have no idea," Jessa replied, but a wicked glint in her eyes seemed to indicate she had begun to pick up on his train of thought.

"Mast had a lot of money lying around, or so the stories go. But I wasn't able to get any information on what happened to it after he departed this mortal coil. Far as I can tell, no one knows what happened to his treasure—which leads me to believe that someone must have made off with it."

"That someone being Mia Felaris, I presume."

"Exactly. And who better to assist her in such an enterprise than Thorn—who was known to be in the vicinity at the time?"

"I can't imagine," said Jessa. Then she shook her head. "From what I know, Thorn's a pretty mercenary customer. I can't really imagine him splitting a treasure with someone, no matter how attractive she might be. That's not really his style."

"True," Creel admitted. "I think there's something I'm still missing here. But it does explain the identity of the mystery man who accompanied her to the bank, and since Ms. Felaris' own company records show that she just returned from a business trip to Iradia, it doesn't exactly take a genius to put two and two together."

At that moment Jessa opened her mouth to reply. She didn't get the chance to do much more than that, however, since a green pulse bolt whizzed past her left ear, only to bounce harmlessly off the hull of the mercenary's ship.

Although both of them had been manning desks for several years, the reactions drummed into them during their cadet days immediately took over. They dropped to the ground, Creel scrabbling to pull the gun out of his shoulder holster, Jessa no doubt doing the same.

The shot had come from behind them, and so Creel immediately pointed his pistol in that direction and fired, even though he really couldn't see who he was shooting at. Still, it never hurt to let your opponent know you were armed.

There were a couple of packing crates less than a meter away from where they had stood, and on instinct he and Jessa had both rolled in that direction. He wasn't sure how much protection the crates would offer if the firing got really intense, but anything was better than lying out there on the open ground of the docking bay.

"You all right?" he asked her.

"Fine," she said. "A few centimeters to the right, and I would have had a new haircut, but I'm okay."

She sounded ferociously cheerful, which didn't bode too well for whoever their attackers might be. Creel risked a quick glance over the top of the packing crates but couldn't see much of anything. The attackers hadn't returned his fire; maybe they hadn't expected to come up against armed opponents.

Even as he did so, he heard the sound of another gun going off, this time from the opposite side of the docking bay. The bolts echoed off the concrete walls and made his ears ring.

"I'm calling for backup," Jessa said, pulling the handheld out of her jacket pocket.

"Good idea," Creel replied, then ducked down behind the crate once more. "Sounds like we've got two sets of interested parties out there."

"Well, you know how I love a party." The handheld made a chirping sound, and she said, in brisk, businesslike tones, "Dispatch, this is Detective Kodd. I'm at Rilsport spaceport, landing pad eighteen-twenty, with Detective Creel. We are pinned down under hostile fire. Requesting backup units."

"Right away," came the reply, from a kid who sounded so young they must have just decanted him from the academy the week before. "ETA is five minutes."

"Oh, don't rush on my account," Jessa snapped, then turned off the handheld. Giving Creel a direct look, she asked, "Can we hold them off that long?"

"Probably," he said.

She raised an unbelieving eyebrow.

He shot her a wicked grin of his own. "They're not shooting at us," he went on, and jerked a thumb in the direction of their unknown assailants. Pulse bolts in varying hues were being traded in a dazzling display of rainbow-colored death. Even as Jessa looked on, unbelieving, he began to laugh. "They're shooting at each other."

XXVI

I REALLY WISH THORN HAD WARNED ME that we were walking into a firefight, Miala thought, huddling behind a pillar as the mercenary traded potshots with their unidentified assailants. *I would have stopped to put on some flats.*

She risked a quick glance past Thorn's shoulder but could see nothing except three shadowy figures, two human-sized, the other a good deal larger. In a direction roughly forty-five degrees off from where she and Thorn stood, a second set of combatants traded fire with the attackers as well. Miala couldn't be sure, but she thought they might be the police she had seen on Thorn's video surveillance unit. She spotted a quick glint of pale blonde hair before the smaller of the two people—who had only the dubious protection of a couple of packing crates to stave off the pulse fire—ducked out of view once more.

"So what's the plan?" she asked, taking advantage of the fact that the three men or aliens had paused to return fire with the two police officers.

"I need to take one of them alive," Thorn replied. "The cops complicate things a bit, though."

"Do tell," Miala said, and felt a sudden absurd impulse to laugh. Jerem had been kidnapped, the dregs of the galaxy were shooting at them, and her house had been burned to the ground, but somehow she hadn't felt so alive in years. Maybe it was just standing here shoulder to shoulder with Thorn, feeling the muscles of his back shift as he returned their attackers' fire. On the way over to the spaceport he'd discarded the proper suit jacket and now wore a close-fitting, short-sleeved black knit shirt that did marvelous things for his biceps. *That's a hell of a thing to be thinking about at a time like this*, she reflected, but she grinned anyway. It was hard not to feel invincible when Eryk Thorn had your back.

Then the mercenary lifted his gun once again, and Miala saw the largest of their three attackers slump to the concrete floor of the landing pad. Two to go. Of course, she still had no idea what Thorn was going to do about the cops, but she supposed that, as always, he had some sort of plan up his sleeve.

The kidnappers' goons began to fire even more wildly, with great enthusiasm if not much accuracy. Thorn stoically waited out the volley in the shelter of the pillar, then got off another deadly shot as the two attackers who were left met with a fresh assault from the two police officers. This time the man caught the pulse bolt square in the neck, and he pitched forward over the prone form of his fallen companion. A few more erratic shots from the one assailant remaining flew in their direction, but he'd obviously decided that he didn't have much going for him, outflanked and outnumbered as he was. A quavering plea emerged from the shadows where he'd been hiding.

"Don't shoot—I give up!"

"Step out here," Thorn ordered. "Hands where I can see them."

A nondescript-looking human male, probably around thirty standard, emerged from the corridor where he'd been lurking. He held his hands up at shoulder height, his gaze darting nervously from Thorn, who walked out from behind the pillar with his pistol still leveled at the man's chest, to the hiding place of the two RilSec officers.

"Stop right there," came a crisp, business-like voice, and Miala turned to see the police, a man and a woman, come out from behind their packing crate. It was the man who had spoken.

Only the slightest movement of Thorn's dark eyes showed that he acknowledged their presence. Miala remained silent. She was certainly out of her league here, and she figured the best thing to do would be to wait and see what, if anything, the mercenary needed from her.

He continued to hold his gun on the man who had surrendered. "Who are you working for?"

The man went a sickly yellowish color. "I—I can't tell you that."

"Sir, I'll have to ask you to lower your weapon," the RilSec officer said. He wore civilian clothing, but the gleaming badge affixed to his collar was enough to identify him. Not a regular beat cop, obviously.

His partner, a strikingly beautiful woman probably a year or so older than Miala, came up behind him. "I'm sorry, but this is our jurisdiction. We can get this hashed out when you all come in to make your statements."

"Sorry," said Thorn, "but the only statement I'm concerned with is the one I'm going to get from him." He jerked a thumb in the direction of their captive, who looked positively miserable.

Miala almost felt sorry for him. Almost.

The male police officer didn't seem particularly concerned. Lanky and tall, with a face Miala would have called pleasant rather than handsome, he smiled and said, "Around these parts, we take a dim view of those who take the law into their own hands, Captain Marr…or should I say Eryk Thorn?"

Miala couldn't help letting out a little gasp of shock at the officer's words, even though Thorn didn't blink. "'Captain Marr' is fine," he replied. "This man has information I need. I don't think you'll be able to get it out of him in time."

"Time for what?" asked the female cop, her green eyes narrowing slightly. Even with her plain synth-silk shirt smudged with dirt and her hair starting to slip out of the clasp that held it away from her face, she had the sort of looks that would stop most men in their tracks.

Thorn, however, wasn't most men. Barely giving her a glance, he said only, "This doesn't concern you."

"Oh, yes, it does," said the male officer. "Engaging in a firefight on Rilsport public property? Piloting a ship here under a false I.D.? And we haven't yet begun to discuss what happened to Ms. Fels' house."

For a second Miala wondered how the hell the cop could have figured out who she was. But she realized if he had guessed at Thorn's true identity, then he must have been investigating the case thoroughly enough that he'd begun to make some disturbing connections.

"You forgot one," Thorn answered. His expression never changed, but Miala caught the sudden glint in his dark eyes and thought, *Uh-oh...*

"What's that?" the cop asked.

"Assaulting a police officer," the mercenary replied. From a clip on his belt, he suddenly grasped a small device only a few centimeters square. Before Miala could even blink, a thin, self-propelled line shot out and wrapped itself around both the RilSec officer and his partner, pulling them against each other and continuing to wrap itself around them until they were securely bound, their guns caught uselessly at their sides. Thorn stepped up to them, retrieved the weapons, and gave them a quick shove. Unable to balance, they toppled over, with the female cop pinned beneath her bulkier partner.

Miala heard the woman gasp, and the other RilSec officer grunted and uttered a breathless curse—he'd probably had the wind knocked out of him.

"You kids have fun," Thorn said. "I've got work to do." And with that he pointed his pistol at the surviving attacker. "You. You got a vehicle?"

"Out—out back," the man faltered, staring down at the trussed-up forms of the police officers. He looked as if he would have dearly preferred for them to come out ahead in this particular confrontation.

"Let's go," the mercenary commanded, and the man led them down the corridor, away from the two fallen RilSec cops. All Miala could do was glance over her shoulder and mouth "I'm sorry" before hurrying after Thorn. Neither one of them looked particularly thrilled with her…not that she could blame them.

Whatever happens, she thought, as she trotted after Eryk Thorn and his captive, *I have a funny feeling I'm not going to be welcome on Nova Angeles for much longer…*

"If you ever tell one person at the station about this, I'm going to give you hell for the rest of your natural life," Jessa gritted, after struggling against the slender but impossibly strong line that bound the two of them together.

The movement of her body against his was distracting, to say the least. Creel forced himself to take a breath, then another. About the last thing he needed right now was for certain parts of his anatomy to signal her that he might be enjoying this far more than she was. Once he thought he had things more or less in order, Creel replied, "You think I want to brag about how I got outmaneuvered by Eryk Thorn?"

"I don't know," she shot back. "This kind of story could keep you in free drinks for quite a while, couldn't it?"

Well, he had to admit that could be true, but he wasn't about to tell Jessa that. Besides, what really mattered right now was getting free somehow so they could try to catch up with their elusive quarry. "I won't say a thing," Creel told her. "Let's just try to see if we can get out of this thing. Maybe if I slip out of the top loop—"

And he attempted to slide downward, hoping that maybe his bonds would hold tight around her as he shifted his body weight. Unfortunately, all he accomplished was to come dangerously close to dislocating his shoulder. He stopped before it popped completely out of joint, but he knew that particular ploy wasn't going to work.

"Let me try," Jessa offered. "I'm smaller than you are." She wriggled again, struggling first to free her shoulders and then her legs, but nothing seemed to work. After a minute she stopped and made a disgusted sound. "Well, this is getting ridiculous."

"We'll have to cut it," Creel said.

"With what?" Jessa asked, managing to sound both worried and scornful. "I'm afraid I'm fresh out of molecular blades and laser cutters."

"There's got to be something sharp around here we can use," he said, eyes scanning the deserted hangar. Then his gaze rested on the two dead men at the entrance to the hallway. "Maybe one of them's got something."

A good four or five meters separated them, and since they couldn't walk, he and Jessa were forced to hitch themselves along the grimy concrete until they finally reached the inert forms of the two dead men.

Jessa made a sound of muffled disgust.

"What?" Creel asked, fighting a sudden stab of alarm.

"Nothing," she replied. "Except that I'm sitting in a pool of blood. Lovely."

"I'm sure the department will reimburse you for those pants," he said. "Can you reach into any of their pockets?"

"Maybe. I think I've got a little more movement below my elbow than you do. Hang on." Creel could feel his bonds cut more closely into his skin as Jessa strained to get her fingers moving freely enough to reach into the closer of the dead men's pockets. He winced but made no sound—no point in distracting her.

"I think I have something," she said, after a few agonizing seconds. "Can you shift this way just a little more?"

In reply he hitched himself a few centimeters closer to the body of the dead alien. Again the thin, unyielding line cut into his flesh. Creel knew if he hadn't been wearing long sleeves, the mercenary's evil rope probably would have broken his skin.

Another agonizing second, and Jessa said, "Got it. Nice little pocket m-blade. Hang on." Then came the low-level hum of a molecular blade, and suddenly one coil of the line that bound them was cut, then another. Creel flexed his fingers as the blood began to return to his hands. Within a moment they were free.

He stood, but didn't offer to help Jessa up—he got the feeling any such gesture would have been rebuffed. After shutting off the m-blade, she rose as well, brushing at her hopelessly begrimed pants.

"Now what?" she asked.

Well, that was a good question. For a few seconds Creel looked past Jessa to the arrowhead shape of the mercenary's vessel. Although he itched to get inside it, he knew that Thorn must have safeguards in place to keep unwanted intruders away from his precious ship.

"Let's take a look outside," he answered, even though by now Thorn, his captive, and Mia Felaris were probably kilometers away.

Sure enough, after they had emerged from the short corridor that led out of the landing pad, all that met their eyes was the stretch of tarmac which backed up to the bay. No vehicle, no sign of the mercenary and his companions. A cool breeze, smelling of salt and night air, ruffled at his hair.

"You didn't think it would be that easy, did you?" Jessa inquired. Although only a few dim sconces illuminated the exit from the docking bay, Creel didn't have any trouble recognizing the wry look she gave him.

"Of course not," he replied. "Let's take a closer look at our dead friends, shall we?"

It turned out that they carried no identification—typical. What was the point of being a hired goon if you made yourself easy to track down? They both were packing hold-out guns, along with an assortment of m-blades and old-fashioned plain composite cutlery, but neither he nor Jessa could find anything that gave the slightest clue as to who they were or where they had come from.

Creel wanted to swear, but decided that wouldn't do him any good. Besides, he didn't want Jessa to know how stymied he currently felt, how outmaneuvered and outmatched. True, he'd been bested by Eryk Thorn, which wasn't exactly the same as having some local street punk outsmart you, but—

"Hey, what's this?" Jessa asked suddenly.

"What's what?" Creel responded, forcing himself to snap out of the unexpected bout of self-pity.

"Probably nothing, but this guy's got a bunch of sand and what looks like some broken shells caught in the soles of his boots. Maybe the lab could get something out of it."

Frowning, Creel crouched down next to Jessa and looked where she was pointing. Sure enough, the heavy grid pattern of the man's boot tread was caked with pale sand and larger specks of iridescent reddish material that definitely appeared to be bits of shell. Well, it was a start, anyway.

At that moment, the sound of approaching sirens assaulted his ears. Their backup had arrived—far too late, naturally.

"Tell you what," Jessa said, giving him a tired grin, "you get to do all the explaining on this one."

Thanks a lot, Creel thought, but he managed to smile back at her. It seemed a small price to pay, considering that they'd gone up against the fearsome Eryk Thorn and lived to tell the tale.

Somehow he doubted the man Thorn had captured would enjoy the same fate.

"I swear I don't know anything!" the man gasped, his pale, bloodshot eyes almost round with fear.

After Thorn had commandeered the hired goons' vehicle, the three of them had blown out of the spaceport with just enough haste to put a good distance between them and the two police officers they'd left behind, but not so fast that they'd be likely to attract any undue attention. The car was a large, six-seat enclosed model, new enough to be unobtrusive but certainly not flashy in any way.

Thorn piloted it to an area largely dominated by warehouses about two kilometers from the 'port, at which time he'd hauled his hapless captive outside and into the cozy intimacy afforded by a locker unit guarded by a simple code that Miala was able to hack in only a few minutes. *Just great*, she thought, after Thorn instructed her to circumvent the lock. *Now we can add breaking and entering to the list of charges we're racking up...*

She hadn't bothered to argue, though. The pasty-faced man they'd taken hostage was their only link to finding Jerem, and it wasn't as if the owner of the warehouse was using it at this particular time, anyway. Actually, it didn't look as if it had been used in a long time. All the packing cases around them had a liberal coating of fine gray dust.

Their captive sat on one of those cases now, literally shaking in his boots, his hands bound behind him with more thin cable. He looked as if he were about to expire of fright. Whoever had taken Jerem, Miala didn't think much of the caliber of people he'd hired to do it.

"Come on, now," Thorn said, crossing his arms and lifting an eyebrow. "You mean to tell me you don't know anything about where they're holding the boy?"

The boy. No mention of her son's name. She recalled the conversation she'd had with Thorn about how he had to stay focused, how he could only think of Jerem as an asset to be reacquired. If he allowed himself to get emotionally involved, Eryk Thorn might lose the edge that made him what he was.

Still, that recollection didn't make it any easier for her to listen to the mercenary discussing their son in such a dispassionate way.

"No!" the captive said. "I never heard anything—Korvan just hired me from the street here, said it would be easy money, that I just had to go with those other two to take out someone at the spaceport—"

"Korvan, eh?" Thorn replied. "So he's your employer? He from Nova Angeles?"

The man licked his lips and shot a beseeching stare in Miala's direction. Just thinking of her son in the hands of men such as these made it easy enough for her to harden her mouth and give him a narrow look in return. He gulped and immediately glanced away.

"No," the man said. "He's a Stacian."

"Ah," said Thorn, and glanced over at Miala.

Well, that made sense. This whole thing had felt a little too personal, and if the late, unlamented Murgan had been related to the kidnapper, then she supposed it made sense that he had struck out at her by taking the thing she valued the most. In this instance, however, that desire for a more intimate revenge could end up biting this Korvan in his big yellow ass, because by taking Jerem he'd unwittingly pulled Eryk Thorn into the plot.

As she stared at Thorn, he smiled suddenly. A sudden hum caught her attention, and she watched with some trepidation as he pulled a small but very efficient-looking molecular blade from his pants pocket.

Even from where she sat, Miala could see the lump in their captive's throat give a convulsive movement as he stared back at the mercenary.

"You know, it's too bad you didn't hear anything worthwhile," Thorn said, his tone so casual that Miala knew something very, very bad was about to happen. "If you don't actually use those ears of yours, then maybe I should just get rid of them for you." And he brought the blade up against the man's right ear, near the top where it connected to the skull. A few drops of blood, almost black in the dimly lit warehouse, began to well up as the blade touched flesh.

"I swear I don't know!" the man shrieked. "I swear I don't! Nobody told me—" And then he broke off into a sort of inarticulate gargling screech as Thorn continued to press down.

Bile rising in her throat, Miala looked away. She knew they didn't have time for anything more humane, but that didn't mean she could coolly sit there and watch as Eryk Thorn tortured another living being.

"I don't believe you," Thorn said, still in that off-hand tone. "Right now you've just got a big cut here. Not much of anything, really. But I could make it worse—" The m-blade begin to make a high-pitched whining noise, as if it had suddenly met more resistance than mere skin and flesh. Probably it had begun to cut into cartilage.

The screams intensified. Miala wanted to put her hands up to her own ears to block out the horrible sounds, but she knew she shouldn't betray any weakness in front of their captive. So she sat very still, reminding herself that this man had been in league with the people who had stolen her son, and that he was most likely the only chance she and Thorn had of recovering Jerem.

Suddenly she heard a terrible little thud, and risked a quick glance over at their captive. Blood streamed down the side of his head and neck. He stared down in horror at the fleshy lump in his lap, a lump which up until that moment had been attached to his skull.

You will not get sick, she told herself, *you will not...*

"So," Thorn said casually, "any thoughts pop into your mind now? If you get to a hospital in the next half hour or so, they'll probably be able to attach that ear. Of course, I can't let you go unless you tell me something."

The man was crying, Miala realized, his face streaked with a dreadful mixture of tears and blood and snot. But he remained silent, and Thorn sighed and lifted the m-blade once more.

"I can keep doing this, you know," he remarked. "There's your other ear, and all your fingers—and other portions of your anatomy you'll probably miss even more."

"All right, all right!" the man screamed.

Thorn lowered the molecular blade the merest fraction of a centimeter and waited.

"I—I never been there," their captive gasped. "But I overheard Rogin say something about meeting up later at Stony Point Park. That's all I heard. I swear."

The mercenary looked over at Miala. "You ever heard of a place called that?"

"Yes," she replied, thanking God or whatever power governed the universe that she actually had. "It was an amusement park out on Rendarlin Point. I think I took Jerem there when he was three or four. It's been closed for the past few years, though—they kept saying they were going to give the place a major overhaul, but I think the deal fell through. Last I heard, some developers were trying to buy up the place for a high-priced housing development."

"But it's empty now," Thorn said.

"I think so. That is, the place has had a security perimeter up for at least the past two standard years, and it sure looks abandoned."

"Great place to carry on a clandestine operation," the mercenary said. "No prying eyes, no one to see what you're up to. Isn't that right?" he added, fixing his captive with a flat, black-eyed stare.

The man gulped. "Uh, yeah, guess so. Like I said—"

"—you've never been there. Yeah, I got that part." Thorn glanced over at Miala. "Looks like we'd better get going."

Immediately she stood, taking care to keep from looking at the blood-smeared face of the man Thorn had tortured. Even though she supposed that the torture had proved useful, she didn't feel any better about it.

"What about me?" the man asked. "I told you what you wanted to know. Aren't you going to let me go?"

"No," Thorn replied, pulling out his gun. As Miala looked on, horrified, he shot their captive directly in the head. At once the man slumped over, and slid off the packing crate and onto the dusty ground.

Although she didn't remember doing so, Miala realized she must have made some sound of protest. Thorn glanced over at her, his face expressionless.

"But—why?" she managed at last.

"I don't leave messy loose ends. He could have I.D.'d us." Moving purposefully, he grasped her by the arm and pulled her away from the dead man, back out through the entrance to the warehouse. Then he re-entered the security code to lock the door. Afterward, he pulled a piece of silky gray cloth out of his pocket, wiped down the keypad, and gestured for Miala to get into the commandeered car.

It was only after they'd left the warehouse complex that he spoke again. "I'd rather you didn't have to see that. But these things are necessary."

Yes, she supposed in his mind they would be. Everything else had to be subordinated to acquiring the target. If that meant torturing a petty criminal who was clearly in over his head, or killing him in cold blood when he was no longer useful, then so be it. It certainly wasn't the first time she'd seen Eryk Thorn kill someone—and she suspected it probably wouldn't be the last—but she still felt shaken by what she had witnessed.

For a long moment she said nothing, and merely watched as Thorn piloted the aircar through Rilsport's streets. He didn't seem to have any apparent destination, but she knew better. No doubt he was simply making sure that they weren't being followed.

Finally she cleared her throat and said, "Just get our son back."

He gave her a long, searching look, no doubt seeing in her face the inner struggle she felt over having to accept what he had done as an ugly necessity. When he spoke, he sounded supremely confident. "You know I will."

Miala wondered how high the body count would be by the time Thorn accomplished his goal. At what point did one say the cost was too great?

Never, she realized. *Not when it's the only way to save our son.*

And with that grim resolution to steady her, Miala reached out and placed her hand on top of Thorn's, where it rested lightly over the gear shift. He said nothing, but she could feel his fingers wrap around hers and squeeze gently. Taking strength from his touch, she let him drive them forward into the night, as they headed toward a confrontation she couldn't begin to imagine.

XXVII

Some days, Rafe Creel thought, *I'd really like to tell my bosses what they can do with their "police procedures."* But frustrating as the routine might be, he knew there was a reason for all the painstaking care that had to be taken at a crime scene like this, all the slavish following of departmental policy. Still, right now he just wanted to tell them where to stuff it.

He watched glumly as Jessa Kodd stood a few paces away, apparently having a polite but heated debate with Dax Trandis, a fellow Homicide detective. As Creel was technically a member of Internal Affairs, he had no official connection to the investigation of the two dead men Thorn had left behind in the docking bay's corridor. After the initial questioning was complete, he had shuffled off to the side while Jessa dealt with the less pleasant fallout of their involvement in the firefight. Although she seemed to be keeping her cool, he could tell she wanted nothing more than to reach out and give Trandis a good smack across the jaw.

It would be worth seeing, Creel thought, but he knew Jessa would never blow a gasket like that.

So he shifted his gaze from the two bickering officers to Thorn's battered-looking ship. If it even had been Eryk Thorn after all—the man hadn't batted an eye when Creel called him by his real name, but that didn't mean much. Of course Thorn would have to be a pretty cool customer. But you'd think the galaxy's greatest mercenary would have been a little more…impressive. Oh, sure, the guy had gotten the drop on Creel and Jessa without much trouble, but up until that point he hadn't seemed particularly fearsome. Just average height, swarthy, features somewhat coarse— this Captain Marr, or whoever he was, didn't seem the type to attract someone as beautiful, talented, and rich as Mia Felaris. So what was the deal?

Still, the ship did match the description of the mercenary's fabled Fury, even with the serial numbers scraped off the hull and a number of other heretofore uncatalogued custom touches in place. Several officers had tried to get near it, and immediately a series of internally mounted pulse cannons had bristled forth, obviously ready to take out any intruders. Since the ship hadn't been directly involved in the firefight, the investigating personnel had decided to leave it alone for the time being. Creel wondered if they'd ever be able to get inside.

Of more pressing importance, however, was getting the dead man's boots taken to the lab and analyzed as quickly as possible. At the rate the crime scene team was handling the investigation, that wasn't going to happen before Mia Felaris and her mysterious companion were long gone, but Creel refused to give up hope that the shell samples might yield some sort of valuable evidence.

At last, though, Jessa stepped away from Trandis and headed over to where Creel leaned against the rough concrete of the corridor's wall. "Hope we're not boring you," she remarked.

"Not at all," he replied, standing up straight and giving her a quick grin. "I was about to start taking bets on how long it would take before you ripped out Dax's jugular."

"I wish," she said, and then gave a disgusted shake of her head. "Talking to him is like trying to explain Marland's third law of thermodynamics to a service mech."

Creel almost laughed, took a closer look at her tired face, and decided against it. Instead, he dug in his pocket for the little plastic case of gum and handed it to her. "It really does help."

She didn't bother to protest, but instead shook one of the pale blue oval tablets into her hand and popped it in her mouth. "At least I finally managed to convince him that we could take one of the boots over to the lab, so as soon as they're done tagging it, we can get out of here."

"Great," Creel said, but with a lack of enthusiasm that was obvious even to him.

To his surprise, she gave him a quick pat on the arm before saying, "I know it's not much, but we do what we can, right?"

He had to remind himself of that during the excruciating minutes that followed, right up until the time the precious boot was finally released to them, and Jessa was able to beg a ride for herself and Creel back to the station. The evidence labs were located on the fifteenth floor of RilSec's headquarters, and luckily they were staffed around the clock.

As he and Jessa entered the the main lobby, Creel gave a quick glance at the chronometer that hung on the wall above the reception desk and tried not to shudder. By now it was almost 0100, and he guessed the night was going to drag on for a lot longer than that. His work didn't usually require him to run around at all hours of the night, but he was going to see this through to the end, even if it meant being up for fifty standard hours or more.

They showed their badges to the woman at the reception desk and went on into the maze of hallways that connected the offices and workrooms of RilSec's crime labs. Jessa seemed to know where she was heading, so Creel followed her lead. Her job required dealing with physical evidence, whereas his work of late had mainly involved conducting interviews and sifting through innumerable computer records.

After going around several corners and down one long corridor, Jessa stopped in front of a set of double doors. She pressed the button on the intercom and said, "Howard? It's Jessa. I've got something I need you to look at."

The right-hand door beeped, then swung inward to admit them. Creel raised an eyebrow at Jessa. "Howard?"

"Howard Dael," she replied, and paused. "My ex-husband."

He felt his mouth drop open slightly, then said, "Oh." After that he gave a small mental groan: Real suave, Creel! How the hell had she managed to keep such an important piece of information hidden from everyone in her department? He worked in a different division, true, but if something like that had been common knowledge, Creel would have eventually found out.

Jessa's own mouth curved slightly in one of her patented "I've got a secret" smiles. All she said, though, was, "Let's go."

Still feeling a bit off-kilter, he followed her down a narrow hallway that had a faint chemical smell he couldn't quite identify. From there they entered a large room lined with all sorts of complicated equipment and a number of computer displays, both flat-screen and holographic.

From seemingly nowhere appeared a rumpled-looking man only a few inches taller than Jessa. He blinked at her, then at Creel, and said, "The evidence?"

For a second Creel could only gape at the man, who had to have at least ten standard years on Jessa and who probably would have been the last person Creel would have picked out of a lineup as her ex-husband. Then he recovered himself enough to hand over the boot, which had been vacuum-sealed in non-permeable polymer at the crime scene.

Dael took it and immediately set off for an elaborate piece of equipment that Creel thought he recognized as some sort of high-powered microscope. He raised an eyebrow at Jessa, who shot him an amused glance but said nothing, and instead turned to watch as her ex dipped his hands in the self-skinning nano-polymer material that would prevent any contaminants from touching the evidence.

Well, she sure didn't love him for his people skills, Creel reflected. *Or his looks...maybe that means I have a chance.*

That pleasant line of thought, however, was interrupted by Dael saying, "Definitely local."

"What's definitely local, Howard?" Jessa asked, in tones more patient than Creel would have expected of her. Then again, she'd probably had plenty of time to get used to her ex-husband's quirks.

"The shell fragments," he replied, not bothering to look

up from the eyepiece of the microscope. "Let's take another pass…" He made a minute adjustment to a dial, then said, "That's got it."

"Got what?" Creel demanded, but Dael just pushed past him to the flat computer screen immediately to his rear.

"That's what I thought."

"So what is it, Howard?" Jessa inquired. She appeared to take in Creel's scowl, and a tiny flicker of a smile ghosted around the corner of her mouth.

"*Arthreni rilsportianus*," Dael replied, with a note of triumph in his voice.

"Arth…what?" Creel demanded.

The lab tech blinked, then said, "A rare breed of mollusk, one that's found in only one location."

"And where would that be?" Creel asked. Damn, he'd had hostile witnesses who'd given up information more freely than this guy.

"Rendarlin Point," Jessa said. Creel gave her an incredulous look, and she went on, "I minored in marine biology at the university."

She's just full of surprises, isn't she? Creel thought. "So you're saying our bad guys are hanging out somewhere on Rendarlin Point?"

"It looks that way, doesn't it?"

It snapped into place then, as he tried to figure out what could possibly attract a bunch of thugs to Rendarlin Point. The old Stony Point amusement park. It had been closed for several years, but the structures were still intact, and it offered rare isolation while still being in close proximity to Rilsport proper. Maybe he still hadn't quite gotten the why of all this, but at least he'd narrowed down the where.

"Let's go," he told Jessa, who looked a little surprised.

"Shouldn't we be calling in a strike team?" she asked.

Creel shook his head. "Not until I know who—and what—we're up against." He nodded at Dael. "Thanks for the intel."

The man blinked. "It was an interesting specimen."

There being no real way to reply to that, Creel just nodded again and then headed out to the corridor, with Jessa following him, a slightly puzzled look on her face. Maybe she'd been expecting some sort of sarcastic comment about her ex, but Creel knew better than to go here. Instead, he stopped in the main lobby, and grinned down at her.

"You ready for some good old-fashioned recon?"

She grinned back. "Of course. I'm glad you know how to show a girl a good time." And with that she sauntered off to the elevators.

Typical, he thought. *Always has to get in the last word.*

Somehow, though, he found he didn't mind too much.

Finally Thorn brought her to a small café on the outskirts of town. Miala ordered a tall mug of coffee and hoped it would be enough to see her through the night.

"Isn't this a waste of time?" she asked. Now more than ever, she had the sense of time flying past her, every precious second increasing the possibility that something terrible could have happened to Jerem.

The mercenary hadn't bothered with artificial stimulants. He drank some of the local mineral water he'd ordered, and took a bite of the steak he'd gotten to go along with it. Miala knew she should have gotten herself something as well, but between a few horrendous flashbacks to what had happened in that dingy little warehouse and her ever-growing worry over Jerem, she knew her stomach wouldn't tolerate anything heavier than the coffee.

Thorn shook his head. "The kidnappers are expecting to meet with you in the morning. After this you're going to take a cab to the Rilsport Plaza and try to get some sleep."

"Sleep?" Miala repeated, with open incredulity. "How the hell do you expect me to sleep at a time like this?"

"Because you need your rest," he replied. "I can go seventy-two standard without sleep. Can you?"

Much as she hated to admit it, Miala knew she couldn't. Even now, despite the spurious energy brought on by the coffee surging through her veins, she knew her current wide-eyed state wouldn't last. Sooner or later she'd have to get some sleep.

Thorn appeared to take her silence as tacit agreement, for he continued, "I'll ditch the car someplace in the city. Then I need to get back and retrieve the *Fury*."

"And how do you propose to do that?" she asked. "You know RilSec's going to have people watching the landing pad."

A lift of one straight dark eyebrow. "Not a problem."

From anyone else, such a comment would have sounded like false bravado. Coming from Thorn, however, it was probably no more than the simple truth. Something had been bothering her ever since they left the two RilSec officers trussed up on the floor of the docking bay, however. "You know, Thorn, you say you don't like loose ends, but you didn't kill those two cops. Why?"

His mouth quirked a bit. "It's one thing to waste a two-bit hood that nobody's going to miss. It's quite another to be a cop-killer. I thought about it, but I decided that having all of RilSec's resources focused on finding me probably wasn't that great an idea. Besides, the one officer might have guessed at who I am, but he still doesn't know for sure... and who's gonna believe him? Anyway, he doesn't know where we went, or where to find us. This city's big enough that I don't think he'll be able to track us down by the time you rendezvous with the kidnappers."

"And then what?" Miala asked, not sure she wanted to hear the answer.

Thorn's expression didn't change. "Leave that to me."

She'd been afraid he'd say something like that, but maybe it was better she didn't know much about his plans. If something went terribly wrong and she fell into the kidnappers' hands, at least she couldn't reveal any important information to them.

"So I go back to the Rilsport Plaza—won't the police be able to find me there?"

"Calculated risk," said Thorn. "I'm pretty sure the cops have already come and gone. They might have the place under surveillance, but we can sneak you in disguised. You have to be there, since that's where the kidnappers will be calling."

Of course. She'd almost forgotten about that. The only way they had of contacting her was through the hotel comm, since of course she had none of her own with her. Had the conversation she'd held with the head kidnapper only taken place thirty-six standard hours earlier? Somehow it felt like a lifetime.

She took an oversized swallow of coffee and managed a weary smile. "I can't wait to see what sort of disguise you have planned for me…"

It turned out to be simple enough, just the enveloping cloaks and full-face mask of a Zhore. Thorn procured the items from a secondhand shop near the spaceport that dealt in such off-world oddities and which stayed open around the clock in order to serve its exotic clientele. Miala waited in the car while he handled the transaction, and then had to climb into the garments as best she could from her place in the front seat of the vehicle. Once that was done—and she could have sworn she saw Thorn's mouth twitch, as if he were trying to repress a smile at her awkwardness—he dropped her off at a transit station where she could get a cab to take her back to the hotel. At that point the panic almost overtook her, as she realized she would have to do the next part of this alone, but the mercenary gave her hand a reassuring squeeze as she alighted from the vehicle, at the same time pressing a tiny handheld into her palm. That steadied her a bit; at least she knew she could reach him in an emergency.

Still, it took all her strength for her to remain there on the curb, to stand quietly and watch him drive away. No one approached her. Even in this civilized part of the galaxy, the mysterious Zhore were regarded with some suspicion, as they did not often mingle with other races. She was able to hail a mech-driven taxi with no problem—mechs didn't share the same prejudices as the living—and ride without incident back to the Rilsport Plaza. Once there, she hurried through the lobby, her head down, and slipped into the lift farthest from the front desk. At that hour the ride up to her suite was uninterrupted, and she almost ran the few steps that separated the elevator door and the entrance to her suite. After she had locked the door behind her and checked it twice just to be certain that it really was secure, she pulled the stifling mask from her face and flung it on the bed, followed by the heavy, awkward robes.

A glance at the chrono on the side table next to the bed told her it was a little past 0200. The room seemed preternaturally still after the events of the past few hours. Miala had to quell an urge to turn on the vid-screen that took up the wall opposite the bed and fill the silence with some mindless programming. But no amount of 25-hour news channels or replays of vid dramas she'd seen several times before would change the fact that her son was still being held by kidnappers, or that she'd allowed Thorn to go chasing off on his own in order to secure the *Fury*. At the moment she felt very superfluous, and very, very tired.

She stood in the center of the room for a long moment, not sure what she should do. Then she sighed and went off to the bathroom. If nothing else, maybe a hot shower would relax her to the point where she could catch a few hours of the sleep Thorn had instructed her to get. Then this useless time would be past, and she could move on to reclaim her son.

He'd fallen asleep at some point. Jerem couldn't be sure exactly when, since he hadn't been wearing a chrono when he was taken, and the ventilation tunnel around him was darker than a black hole. After that near-miss with the kidnappers, he'd scuttled on in search of the source of the sea breeze he'd felt coming down the right-hand shaft. It had sloped upward for a while and then leveled out…and then had come to a dead end where the tunnel met a piece of mesh screen that was bolted down so securely Jerem was pretty sure he wouldn't have been able to get it off even if he'd had the correct tools, which he didn't. Feeling exhausted and very near to tears—but he wouldn't cry, no way, not when his father could show up at any moment to rescue him—he'd curled up in a ball, thinking he'd rest for just a bit. But the next thing he knew, the draft across his face had intensified to almost a breeze, and the sky beyond the grating had turned from black to gray.

His mouth tasted gummy, and the back of his neck had developed a crick from sleeping half-propped up against the wall of the ventilation shaft, but at least Jerem felt a little less tired. And obviously the kidnappers hadn't yet discovered that he'd broken out of the room where they'd been holding him. But Jerem knew he probably didn't have much time. The sun was rising, and when they came in to bring him his morning meal, they'd know right away that he was gone.

Moving as quietly as he could, he went back down the ventilation shaft. He remembered passing another junction point, one about ten meters beyond the spot where he'd overheard the kidnappers discussing how they were going to kill him. At the time he'd ignored it, thinking the fresh air and sea salt he'd smelled were the ticket to freedom, but now all he could do was hope that the tunnel he'd overlooked the night before would prove to be the right one. It sloped upward and to the left. He had to press his spine flat against one side and inch his way up through it using his leg muscles to propel him. Good thing he'd spent almost every waking moment running and climbing and tumbling, or he would never have been able to manage it.

Still, it was a hard slog, and Jerem could feel his thigh muscles starting to tremble in protest by the time he got to the top. His parched mouth begged for water, but he couldn't do anything about that. He could only dry-swallow and hope that he might be able to find something to drink if he ever did manage to get out of this place.

The last meter or so the ventilation shaft went directly upward, and for a few seconds he wasn't sure he was going to make it—his feet lost their purchase on the slick surface, and he began to slip backward. But he shoved himself against the wall of the shaft, legs shaking with the effort. Overhead he could see a circle of pale grayish-blue sky, and that welcome sight gave him the strength for the last push. At last he half-fell, half-slid out of the shaft and onto a flat roof of gray concrete.

For a few minutes all Jerem could do was lie there, taking in deep gulping breaths of the cool sea air. The light seemed dazzlingly bright, even though he realized after a few minutes that the familiar dawn-clouds hugged the coast, and the morning was actually quite cool and dim. He rose, his legs shaking under him, and tried to take stock of his surroundings.

The building on which he stood appeared to be several stories high. On either side he saw more structures, oddly shaped and garishly painted, but familiar somehow. He frowned, trying to remember where he'd seen them before. But then he spotted the looming shape of the gravity wheel ahead of him—the ride his mother had refused to take him on—and realized that he was right smack in the middle of the abandoned Stony Point amusement park. A good place to hide someone, he supposed, considering the place had been locked up for a couple of years. At least now he knew where he was—and, more importantly, he knew how to get out of there. The park occupied most of the promontory known as Rendarlin Point, but there was a road that led out of the park and back into downtown Rilsport. All he had to do was get to that road without being spotted and make a run for it.

He'd just begun to trot over to the far edge of the rooftop, where he thought he spotted the curved railings of an access ladder—similar to the one he'd climbed back when he'd sabotaged his school's holo-sign—when he heard the sound of someone shouting. Immediately he dropped to his hands and knees, then scuttled over to the edge and looked down.

The big Stacian—Korvan, Jerem remembered—had just emerged from the building and was yelling at a dark-haired human who had to have been fairly tall himself, since his head met Korvan's chin. In response the man shouted something back, although Jerem couldn't make out what he was saying. Then the rat-faced captor Jerem remembered all too well came running outside, and all three of them engaged in a shouting match for a few minutes. Obviously his escape had just been discovered, and as far as Jerem could tell, everyone was trying to blame everyone else for it.

Good. If they were distracted, maybe they wouldn't be paying attention to the rooftop. He continued to inch along the edge of the roof, trying to keep the kidnappers in view as he headed toward the ladder he had just spotted. Then the Stacian stopped yelling and appeared to be issuing a series of orders. The two humans went off in opposite directions, no doubt to start searching the property for their lost captive.

Well, it was now or never. Jerem swung his legs over the edge of the roof and felt his feet meet the topmost rungs of the ladder. Then he skidded all the way down, not really climbing, but letting himself down in a sort of controlled fall as he gripped the handrails and prayed he could make it to the bottom before any of the kidnappers came around this corner of the building.

He landed with a thud in an overgrown *maranita* bush. There wasn't time to worry about the scratches he'd collected—he rolled over and got back on his feet, then hurried over to the corner of the building and risked a quick glance around. He didn't see anyone, but what he did see, he didn't like much—there was no cover between him and the next building, a low shed that had once housed the holographic freak show (yet another attraction his mother wouldn't let him near). Once there had been a low-walled planter filled with exotic off-world bushes, but they had mostly all died from neglect, and the bare earth left behind didn't offer much in the way of protection.

Still, if he loitered here much longer, he was going to get caught. He had to run now, while the kidnappers were off someplace else. Even though his heart pounded and he was almost sick with dread, he forced himself to take off toward the freak-show building. Fear lent him a speed he didn't think he was still capable of, and he covered the distance in far less time than he thought he would. No rough shouts stopped him; no guns fired in his direction. He flattened himself against the wall and moved along a few centimeters at a time, trying to breathe through his nose so his panting wouldn't give his position away.

Then the sound of a pulse pistol cracked through the air, and Jerem fell to his hands and knees once more. It was only after he had lain there for a few minutes, shoulders hunched against the pain of the bolt he was sure he would feel at any second, that he realized no one was shooting at him. Puzzled, he crawled along the ground, using the shelter of some more scrubby bushes to hide him, until he was able to peer around the corner of the building to see what was going on.

The Stacian was nowhere in sight, but Jerem could see the rat-faced kidnapper and the tall dark-haired man trading pot shots with a pair of intruders who had apparently taken shelter inside one of the abandoned ticket kiosks. At first he thought it might be his mom and dad, but then he caught a glint of pale blonde hair from one of the unknown shooters and realized it had to be someone else. Well, if it wasn't Thorn and his mother, then it didn't really matter who it was—what mattered was that they had the kidnappers busy, giving him the perfect chance to slip away.

Jerem stood and turned. Then he stopped dead at the sight of Korvan pointing an ugly-looking pistol right at his head.

"Going somewhere, kid?" the Stacian inquired.

XXVIII

THE CHIME OF THE COMM woke her. Miala sat up in bed, feeling groggy and disoriented. It had taken her a long while to fall asleep. She didn't dare take anything that might have helped her, since the last thing she wanted was to feel drugged and slow whenever the kidnappers did end up calling.

She glanced over at the chrono next to her bed. About half-past 0600, which meant she'd probably been asleep for only three hours or so. It could be Thorn, but somehow she doubted it. Pushing the covers aside, she stumbled out of bed and pushed the button on the comm unit to take the incoming call.

The screen remained dark. She heard a rough voice ask, "You've got the money?"

"Yes," she said. Her brain seemed to start firing, adrenaline coursing through her veins and giving her the energy she so desperately needed. "I want to speak to my son."

"No," said the kidnapper. "You can talk to him when you've brought us the money."

Miala had been halfway expecting something like that. Trying to remain calm, she replied, "Then how do I know he's even still alive?"

Without pausing, the kidnapper said, "You want him back? Bring the money to the Stony Point amusement park. Be there in fifteen standard. If we see the merc, the kid dies." The flat buzz of a disconnected line followed, signaling that the kidnapper had hung up.

Damn, she thought. *Damn, damn, damn*. But she knew there wasn't anything she could do at this point except follow the kidnapper's instructions. Thorn had left her a small signaling device the night before; all she had to do was press the button, and he would know that she was on her way to rendezvous with the kidnappers. He didn't want her using a comm, in case outgoing transmissions from her hotel room were being monitored, but he'd told her the signal from the tiny unit he'd given her was nearly undetectable. Exactly what he was going to do after he received the signal, he hadn't told her. She supposed that, once again, he'd kept her in the dark for safety's sake. If she didn't know anything, she couldn't give it away.

Right before she had gone to bed, Miala had laid out her clothes in preparation for the meeting with the kidnappers, and she threw them on now, fastening the tunic with shaking fingers and sliding her feet into the low-heeled, comfortable boots she'd gotten the day before. After that she pulled her hair back into a clip, then knelt and retrieved the satchel which contained the ransom from its hiding place under the bed.

It was early, but she should still be able to catch a mech jitney without too much trouble, as they tended to congregate outside the larger hotels. Clutching the satchel in one hand, she took a breath, then pushed the button on the signaling device Thorn had given her. He already knew where to go, of course—now she just had to get there as well.

She left the hotel room and didn't look back.

"So how's your power pack doing?" Jessa inquired, sounding as cool as if they were parked in an unmarked car performing routine surveillance instead of trading potshots with a couple of thugs who apparently had an unlimited supply of charges for their guns.

"Not good," Creel replied, risking a quick glance at the glowing readout on the butt of his pistol. He had three, maybe four shots left. "How about you?"

"The same," she said, and squeezed off another blast before ducking down behind the countertop once more. At least this time her shot elicited a gasp and an outraged curse. Apparently she'd connected this time. "Any bright ideas?"

"Not really," he admitted. Things had gone from bad to worse in such a short period of time that he hadn't had much of a chance to stop and analyze what had gone wrong. It had seemed like a simple enough plan—head over to Rendarlin Point, do a quick survey of the perimeter of the property, try to get a read on how many perps might be involved. He'd even performed a quick scan with the equipment in their patrol car to see if the place had any security systems online.

Unfortunately, whoever these guys were, they seemed to be well-backed and -supplied. Their equipment had obviously been designed to fool standard-issue detection devices, and snoop sensors had gone off almost the second he and Jessa had alighted from their vehicle. They'd been forced to run for the dubious cover of the ticketing kiosk in which they now hid, since it was the only unlocked structure they could find. While Creel hadn't been able to determine exactly how many attackers they faced, it had to be at least two and possibly as many as three or four. He thought he'd wounded one of them in the first volley they traded, and now it sounded as if Jessa had done the same, but with their power packs about to die on them, he knew they probably wouldn't be lucky enough to take out all of their attackers with the few shots the two of them had left.

"Maybe they don't know we're cops," Jessa said. She was wedged under the counter that fronted ticket window, her face looking pale in the shadowy half-light of the coming dawn.

"You think they'll let us go if we tell them that?" Creel inquired, not bothering to keep the derisive edge from his voice.

"I wish." Taking advantage of a small lull in the firefight, she popped up from her hiding place, got off two more shots, then slipped back into position under the ticket counter. "But there might be a greater chance of them taking us captive instead of just shooting us outright. Anyone who knows anything about RilSec knows that we take cop-killers very seriously."

That much was true. Of course, crime was far from nonexistent on Nova Angeles—or he and Jessa would have been out of a job—but much of it involved high-stakes industrial espionage, embezzlement, or just good old-fashioned theft. The last time a RilSec officer had lost his life in the line of duty, a gang of off-world smugglers had turned out to be the culprits. They'd been tracked across ten systems by a task force specially assigned to that purpose, and brought back to Nova Angeles for justice. All parties involved had been found guilty and executed. Capital punishment still existed on the books here, but as far as Creel could recall, those cop-killers had been the only ones he could remember facing such final justice. No, anyone with two brain cells to rub together would probably think of a good reason for trying to avoid taking down one RilSec officer, let alone two.

He hated the idea of just giving up, but they didn't have a lot of options. Of course the vehicle they'd left behind at the entrance to the amusement park had its normal transponder signal activated, and probably after a while someone at HQ might notice they hadn't checked in and send out a team to investigate, but Creel doubted that would happen quickly enough to save their asses. Stupid of him not to have signed out more guns, but taking anything more than their usual sidearms would have sent up a lot of red flags. He'd thought they could do this quickly and quietly, then send out for backup if the situation warranted it. After all, there had been a distinct possibility that he and Jessa wouldn't find anything here at all.

Oh, we found something all right, he thought grimly. *A whole big bag of something. Not exactly the sort of maneuver that's going to earn me a commendation. But right now the*

*most important thing is survival. We can deal with the con-
sequences later.*

"Do you want me to do it?" Jessa asked. Her voice
sounded almost too calm. "Maybe they'll be less likely to
shoot if they see a woman first."

Creel didn't like that idea at all, but he knew she had a
point. You could preach all the equality of sex and species
you wanted, but when it came right down to it, humans at
least were still hard-wired to view females as less threatening. "All right," he said. "But only because I can't think of a
better idea."

"Tell you what," she replied, giving him a smile that,
despite their situation, somehow made his knees feel a little
weak. "If we get out of this, you can buy me dinner."

"Deal," he said immediately.

"At Angel's Flight," she added with a grin.

Only the most expensive restaurant in Rilsport. A dinner there would probably cost the equivalent of a week's
salary. Still, considering the circumstances, it was a bar-
gain. "No problem."

The slightest flicker of a dimple showed in Jessa's cheek.
"I should've let you get me into a compromising position
long before this, Creel," she said. As his brain tried to wrap
itself around that statement, she rose, hands held at shoulder height, and called out, "Don't shoot—we're with RilSec.
Surrendering our weapons now." And she tossed her spent
sidearm out through the kiosk's window.

For one heart-stopping moment Creel was sure the
thugs outside would shoot her anyway as she stood there,
exposed and unarmed. Then he heard a voice say, in an

unfamiliar accent, "What about the other one?"

Silently he handed his dead pistol up to Jessa. Once again she threw it out onto the ground. Creel heard it clatter against the concrete walkway.

"Both of you, out," the thug said. "Now."

Feeling a little stiff, Creel climbed to his feet and stood next to Jessa. Without speaking, she reached out to open the kiosk's door. It was an old-fashioned, unpowered entry and so swung slowly outward. Then she stepped outside, and he followed close behind her.

Their attackers turned out to be three in number, all human, though with a scruffy, wary mien that suggested they were off-worlders. The tallest of the three limped forward and said, "Keep your hands up." His lower right leg showed a scorch mark from a glancing pulse blast. Too bad it hadn't been a few centimeters to the right. Then he gestured toward his two companions. "Check 'em."

In spite of the dire circumstances, Creel had to force a grin from his lips as he watched the men head in Jessa's direction, only to see the bigger of the two elbow his compatriot in the ribs and push him off toward Creel. No doubt the man had been hoping he'd get a chance to pat down Jessa, who certainly didn't look like your standard RilSec officer.

She kept her head up, barely seeming to notice as the man searched her for any additional weapons with more enthusiasm than was strictly necessary. His partner, who favored a wounded left arm, did the same to Creel in a much more perfunctory way. Then they stepped back.

"Clean," said the man who had checked Creel.

"Same here," the other one chimed in.

Keep smiling, little man, Creel thought, after shooting a quick glance in Jessa's direction. She had remained expressionless, but he could see the muscles knot in her throat as she swallowed. *I get the feeling that in this case payback is going to be a real bitch.*

"RilSec, huh?" said the apparent leader, staring down at Jessa. "So what brings you out this way?"

Still looking straight ahead, she replied, "Jessa Kodd, RilSec Homicide, badge number 328879-A."

The man did not look amused. "Fargging cops." His dark gaze shifted to Creel. "What about you?"

"Rafius Creel, RilSec Internal Affairs, badge number 274392-D," Creel said. Maybe he'd survive this, and maybe he wouldn't, but in the meantime it gave him a great deal of pleasure to complicate this thug's life in any way he could.

"Cute." Still, the man seemed to realize that he wasn't going to get much more out of them at the moment, because he plucked the handheld off his belt and said, "Korvan, we've got a situation here…"

Jerem stood there, frozen in place, looking down the snout of the Stacian's gun. He hadn't realized how scary those things were up close. His whole body screamed at him to run, but he knew better than that. One move, and he'd probably get fried on the spot. Then again, these guys had been planning to kill him anyway. What was stopping Korvan from shooting him now and getting it over with?

Right then the Stacian's belt-mounted handheld squawked, and, apparently caught off-guard, he looked down at it.

It wasn't much of a chance, but Jerem knew it might be the only one he got. He also knew there was no way he could turn and run back the way he came. He had to get past Korvan, off into the main section of the park, where he could (hopefully) lose himself among the maze of derelict attractions there.

So he did the last thing anyone would expect—he ran toward Korvan, dropping to his knees at the last second and scuttling between the Stacian's legs like a red-eye crab flushed from its hiding place in the rocks.

Korvan let out a bellow and dropped his handheld, reaching down to grasp Jerem before he could make his escape. But although the Stacian's bulk was impressive, it also seemed to slow him down, and Jerem had sheer terror and agility on his side. Before he could quite register what had happened, he found himself behind Korvan, running toward the heart of the amusement park, feet pounding against the pavement as if a pack of Bathshevan devil-dogs were after him. He couldn't stop to think. Instinct had taken over, and the only thing that filled his thoughts was finding someplace to go to ground, someplace where the kidnappers couldn't possibly catch him.

From behind him he heard a confused jumble of shouts, some random pulse fire, and then more shouting, not all of it from Korvan. At some point he must have retrieved his dropped handheld and called in the rest of the goons. Jerem still didn't know how many of them were out there, and he didn't know what kind of scanning equipment they had. All he did know was that he had to put as much distance between him and them as possible. The shooting had stopped, so he guessed that whoever the strangers involved in the firefight were, they'd either been killed or captured, which meant he couldn't look for help from them, either.

You don't need them, he thought. *You're Eryk Thorn's son. What would he do?*

Well, failing his father's enormous arsenal, about the only thing Jerem figured he could do was make himself as unfindable as possible. Stall for time. Surely sometime soon his father would be able to track him down and rescue him. Wasn't he the greatest mercenary in the galaxy? After all the bad guys he'd defeated and bounties he'd claimed, locating his own son shouldn't be that difficult.

His headlong dash had brought Jerem into the center of the park, where the coated steel forms of abandoned rides surrounded him. They couldn't rust, of course, but their paint had started to look faded and blotchy, exposed to the sun and wind and salt air. They rose up around him like an odd metal forest, sheltering him, although Jerem knew he couldn't let himself get too comfortable.

They'll figure out where I am pretty soon, he thought. *So I need to get someplace where they won't think to look. But where?*

The creaking of a broken gate caught his attention. Most of the rides had been closed off pretty effectively, all their gates chained shut and guarded with electronic barriers, but somehow the entrance to the one nearest him had been compromised. The barred metal gate shifted slightly in the rising dawn wind, and Jerem stared at it for a second, then past it to the looming shape of the ride it had shielded. *Sky Tower*, the sign read, in faded Anglic characters. It was one of those impossibly tall attractions where you got taken way, way up in a little car and then dropped from the top, free-falling before the repulsor jets kicked in. His mother had avoided things like that, citing a problem with heights, but Jerem knew he sure didn't have any fear of high places. Good thing, too, since this one was really, really tall.

The car that had taken people to the top was long gone, but the access ladder built into the ride's infrastructure was still there. Jerem pushed his way past the gate, wrapped his fingers around the ladder's rails, and began to climb.

The ride to Stony Point seemed excruciatingly long, although Miala knew that they were actually making quite good time. At this time of the morning, the streets weren't nearly as crowded as they would be in an hour or so. She had instructed the mech driver to stop about a hundred meters from the entrance to the park. It just seemed safer that way.

Mouth dry, she paid off the driver and alighted from the cab, then began making her way toward the large gateway that sealed off the park. The air felt cool and damp, a breeze rising off the ocean. The day was still mainly overcast, but Miala could sense rather than see the sun as it came up to her left.

As she drew closer, the gate swung inward, although there did not seem to be anyone around. The skin along the back of her neck prickled. Even though Thorn had been alerted that she would be here, and even though she knew he somehow had to have this place under surveillance, she still felt horribly vulnerable and exposed as she walked through the gate and on down the road that stretched out past it. In happier times it had led to the parking lots where visiting families could leave their cars, but now she followed it through those empty concrete spaces, on to the area where the main ticket windows had once stood.

They were still there, although shuttered and dark. On one of them she saw evidence of a recent firefight; scorch marks showed dark on the faded paint of its sides. She frowned, wondering if somehow Thorn had already met up with the kidnappers and engaged them.

That hope was immediately destroyed, however, as the immense figure of a Stacian moved out from behind the ticket kiosk, followed by the slighter form of a tall human male, one who appeared to be limping from a grazing pulse blast to the leg. The man held a pistol trained on her, but the Stacian appeared to be unarmed.

"Miala Fels?" he asked.

He used the name she had been born with, the name she thought she'd left behind on Iradia. Obviously he knew all about her past. Just because he was Stacian didn't mean he was necessarily one of Murgan's relatives, but Miala had had the feeling for quite some time that this matter was personal. Stacian clannishness was known the galaxy over. It stood to reason that Murgan and Korvan must be related somehow.

There was no point in prevaricating. "Yes," she said.

The alien's copper eyes narrowed slightly. She recalled that Murgan's had been a darker shade, almost dark red rather than true copper, but the two did seem to share a certain similar cast of features—the same high-bridged nose, the same humorless, thin lips. "You have the ransom?"

In answer she lifted the satchel she held in her right hand. "I want to see my son, Korvan."

He scowled at her use of his name, but said only, "I'm afraid you're in a position to demand nothing. Chaddick, take the money."

Still holding his gun pointed at her, the Stacian's partner stepped toward Miala and plucked the satchel from her fingers with his free hand. Then he backed away and handed it to Korvan.

He opened the satchel and looked inside, then gave a small, approving nod at the sight of the neatly bundled stacks of shining Gaian currency it held. "I'm glad you decided to be smart about this, Ms. Fels."

Even though she knew Thorn had promised her that the kidnappers wouldn't be holding on to their ransom for very long, Miala couldn't help experiencing a pang at seeing Korvan take the money. Of course it was nothing compared to getting Jerem back safely, but she and Thorn had paid for that money with blood and sweat and toil, and it hurt to see it in that foul Stacian's hands.

"My son?" she asked.

At her question, Korvan and his compatriot exchanged a half-annoyed, half-amused glance. "Wait here," Korvan said.

Something felt very, very wrong. Quelling the panic that had begun to rise in her stomach, Miala said, "Look, I've done everything you told me to. But do you really expect me to just sit here and wait while you walk away with my money without giving me any indication that my son is even alive?"

A look of anger flashed across the Stacian's face before his features stilled themselves once more. "As I just said, you're in a position to demand nothing. But if you insist—" He made a slight gesture with his free hand, and immediately his partner reached out and grasped Miala by the arm. "We can all take a look together."

Trying to guess what exactly Korvan had meant by that, she stumbled along behind the Stacian as his partner dragged her toward the center of the park. She didn't bother to make an attempt at freeing herself. The man's grip was like cold-poured steel.

Once they had reached an open area that served as a courtyard in the center of several abandoned rides, Korvan stopped. Almost immediately two more men came out from behind a small structure that Miala guessed used to be a power substation. Places like this required enormous amounts of energy, and probably the little shack had contained back-up generators in case the main feed from Rilsport's city center failed.

"How are our guests doing?" Korvan inquired.

The smaller of the two newcomers grinned, showing yellowing teeth that only enhanced his rodent-like appearance. "Just fine, boss, although they probably find the accommodations a little cramped."

"No matter," said the Stacian. "In a little while they'll discover their quarters are the least of their problems."

Miala briefly wondered who his "guests" might be, and why their problems were apparently going to increase in the near future. Of more pressing concern, however, was Jerem. She cleared her throat. "My son?"

An ugly smile distorting his thin lips, Korvan replied, "Ah, yes, your son. The ever-resourceful and agile Jerem. Apparently he had issues with his accommodations as well, and escaped."

"Escaped?" she repeated, incredulous. "You mean you don't even have him?"

"Not exactly," Korvan said. His head tilted upward, as if he were focusing on one of the rides that loomed overhead. "We have managed to track him down. Unfortunately, he's not being very cooperative."

Unease sweeping over her, Miala looked up as well, trying to follow the Stacian's gaze. To her horror, she saw a small figure inching its way along the gantry that had once suspended small cars for a free-fall thrill ride. A few meters away, a second, larger figure crept steadily closer toward the first one, which could only be that of her son.

She didn't even realize she had begun to move forward until the wounded kidnapper dug his fingers even more tightly into her upper arm.

"There's not much you can do," Korvan said. "At this point, I suppose it doesn't really matter. If he falls, he falls. We already have the ransom." And he stared down into her horrified face and began to laugh.

An anger deeper than any she had ever known boiled up from somewhere deep inside, white-hot as a plasma drive. Without thinking, she kicked back at the man who held her, feeling a sense of visceral satisfaction as the heel of her boot connected with his groin and he let out a muffled groan. Immediately he released her arm, and she lunged forward.

Her moment of freedom was short-lived, however. Even as she gathered her breath so she could bolt off in the direction of the ride where Jerem hung suspended a hundred meters off the ground, Miala felt a heavy hand descend on her shoulder and yank her backward. She collided with Korvan's massive bulk, and then his arm settled around her throat with crushing force.

"Going somewhere?" he asked, his breath hot against her ear. "Let me applaud your maternal instincts, Ms. Fels. But there's no way you could get to your son in time to rescue him, and since I have your money, I couldn't care less whether he falls from that tower and ends up flatter than an Eridani saucer-fish." The pressure against her throat decreased slightly as he added, "But you—you could be worth a great deal in certain sectors of the galaxy. A little something extra for my trouble, as they say."

A wave of revulsion swept over her, and Miala raised her hands to claw at the arm that held her in a choke hold. Better to go out fighting than to let him take her prisoner, this monster who had kidnapped her son and was now willing to let him die, who threatened to turn her into a slave.

But even as she prepared to dig her nails into the Stacian's enormous golden-skinned forearm, a shadow seemed to pass over the rising sun. And out of that shadow shot a bolt of acid-green fire, one which connected with the kidnapper who had stood before her. The acrid smell of charred flesh hit Miala's nostrils even as the man fell to the ground, his corpse smoking from the intense heat.

About time, Thorn, she thought. Korvan's grip on her had loosened slightly with shock, and she took advantage of that fact to drop to the pavement, feeling it scrape her palms as she flattened herself to get out of the line of fire. Two more bolts followed, and she heard Korvan's accomplices cry out in agony.

The Stacian could not move as quickly as she. He began to reach for her, but another bolt of shocking green fire burst forth, hitting him directly in the chest. Miala heard him scream, a curiously high-pitched sound for someone so huge, and then she felt him crumple, landing on her outstretched legs. The impact was so painful and unexpected that for a few seconds she could only lie there, wondering if he had managed to break both her limbs in his fall. Then she gave a cautious little wiggle of her right leg. It hurt, but not enough to have been broken. Probably she'd be covered in bruises tomorrow—if she ever managed to get him off her.

Somewhere off to the right she heard the distinctive whine of turbos, followed by a wave of hot air hitting her cheek. Metallic footsteps clattered against the pavement, and then the appalling pressure of Korvan's dead body on her lower half suddenly eased.

A gloved hand appeared in front of her face. "You all right?"

She reached out and wrapped her fingers around Thorn's, letting him haul her upright. The *Fury* sat a few meters off to the right, looking completely out of place in the amusement park setting. It was only his voice that told her who he was, because somehow he'd gotten his hands on a suit of GDF power armor, and it covered him from head to toe.

No time to ask him where the hell he'd gotten it, or whether he'd had it stashed in the *Fury* all along, so she said only, "As usual, your timing is impeccable, Thorn." Once she was standing—and to her surprise, Miala found she could stand upright, even though her knees shook and every muscle from her hips downward told her that they didn't much care for the way they'd been treated—she gasped, "Jerem's up there. One of them is still after him." And she pointed up toward the gantry, where, thank all the gods ever dreamed of by sentient species, their son still clung to the heavy steel framework.

His helmeted head swiveled upward. "Got it." And Eryk Thorn took off at a run, moving more swiftly than she would have thought possible, until her addled brain suddenly realized that he was airborne, a jet pack on the back of his armor lifting him up and away from her, up to rescue his son.

Maybe this wasn't such a good idea after all, Jerem thought. *'Cause now they've found me, there's no place to go.*

He clung grimly to the weathered gantry, legs dangling a good hundred meters above the pavement. Sure, he could say he wasn't afraid of heights, but it felt a lot different when there wasn't much separating you from a particularly nasty death. He wondered if he slipped and fell whether he'd die on the way down, or whether he'd have to wait until he hit the bottom to meet his end. Either way, it didn't promise to be too much fun.

How they'd managed to find him so quickly, Jerem couldn't be sure, although maybe they had some sort of scanning device that would track a living being among all the steel structures. Not that it really mattered at this point, he supposed. What really mattered was how he was going to get out of this.

He didn't recognize the man who crawled along the gantry toward him—it wasn't the rat-faced kidnapper who had brought him his meals, or the tall dark-haired one who was scary in a quiet way. And of course Korvan couldn't have hauled his big Stacian butt all the way up here. Still, it didn't really matter—Jerem could tell from the look of angry determination on the man's face that he wasn't exactly thrilled with having to scramble up here to chase after a kid, especially one who was supposed to sit in his cell like a good little boy and wait to be killed.

About a meter separated Jerem from his current perch and the absolute endpoint of the gantry. He inched backward a bit, not because he thought it would do any good, but just because he felt like he ought to be doing something.

"Where do you think you're going, kid?" the man called out, sounding breathless and annoyed. "Gonna dive off the end into the bay?"

That would have been a spectacular stunt, but even if he could have survived such a fall, the waters off Rendarlin Point were too far away to offer even a hint of escape. No, the only way Jerem was getting off this thing was either the way he came, or by going ker-splat on the pavement below.

"Maybe," he said, wishing his voice didn't sound so weak and trembly. "What about you?"

The man muttered something. Jerem couldn't be exactly sure, but it almost sounded like he said, "I'm not getting paid enough for this…"

Jerem didn't have time to think about that, though, because all of a sudden a bolt of green pulse fire shot past him, right toward the kidnapper. The man cursed, and reached for the holster at his hip—not an easy maneuver when clinging to a gantry some hundred meters off the ground. And while the man scrabbled for his sidearm, another bolt whizzed past Jerem's other ear, this time hitting the kidnapper square in the chest and knocking him backward. He screamed, fingers scrabbling for purchase on the steel structure, before his body went limp, and he slipped, tumbling away into the cool sea-scented air. It seemed as if an awful lot of seconds went by before Jerem heard the man's body finally hit the pavement with a sickening thud.

And then he looked up, to see Eryk Thorn—his father—hovering in the air a meter away from him, jet pack holding the mercenary up in defiance of Nova Angeles' gravity, just like the shock troops Jerem had read about in his graphic novels. It was only the coolest thing ever.

"Ready to get down from there?" his father asked.

Trying to look nonchalant, Jerem said, "Yeah."

Of course the helmet hid Eryk Thorn's expression, but Jerem got the impression his father smiled behind the helmet's smoked-plastic visor. "Okay. Wait there."

He sailed closer, then extended a hand. Jerem reached out to take it. There was one heart-stopping second where it seemed as if he were free-falling, just like the ride advertised, but then he felt his father's strong arms close around him, holding him tightly as they swept downward toward the ground. Even with all the times Jerem had tried to think what flying might feel like, he had never imagined it could be this much fun.

They settled on the ground in an open area between all the high-rise attractions. Jerem saw his mother waiting for him there, her face white with worry. At her feet lay the bodies of Korvan, the dark-haired kidnapper, and two other men. He guessed that his father must have gotten to them first and then come after him. Maybe it should have scared him a little to see dead bodies like that, but Jerem could only feel a rush of satisfaction that Eryk Thorn had killed them all.

His father released him once they stood on solid ground again. Jerem sort of wished they could have kept flying around, but he supposed his mother might not have been exactly thrilled with them for leaving her behind while she waited on the ground. Still, he couldn't help exclaiming, "That was fun! I want to do it again!"

For a second his mother just stared at him. Then she gave a sort of hiccuping laugh, and rushed forward and pulled him into her arms. Her body shook, and Jerem realized she was laughing and crying at the same time.

Grown-ups, he thought, with a mental shrug. He didn't see what the big deal was.

After all, he'd always known his father would come rescue him.

THE SUPPLY ROOM WHERE THE THUGS had unceremoniously shoved Creel and Jessa was dark and smelled of mildew and stale lubricants. From the sounds of gunfire that he could barely make out through the door, a major pile of crap must have hit the air circulator. Almost immediately after the one man had contacted his boss on his handheld, a commotion erupted from the other side of the park, and Creel had found himself getting pushed in here without the goons even bothering to tie him and Jessa up.

Not that having his hands free helped much. The door had been locked from the outside, and since the cramped little compartment didn't have any windows, there was no way he could tell exactly what was going on. Jessa, ever resourceful, had gone to the lock mechanism and had begun the tedious work of prying off the faceplate using the edge of her belt buckle as a crude lever. It wasn't much and would probably take her forever, but a quick survey of the supply room had shown that it was swept bare of everything except a few discarded containers, which appeared to be the source of the stale lubricant smell.

"What do you think's going on out there?" he asked, after sidling closer to watch Jessa struggle with the lock. He knew better than to offer to help.

"Don't know," she gritted. The belt buckle slipped, and she swore under her breath. "But it was pretty obvious that our guys weren't happy about it."

True, Creel thought, smiling a little to himself. It was maddening not to know what might be going down in the park outside, but anything that brought a little grief into those goons' lives had to be a positive.

Metal scraped against metal, and he gave an involuntary wince. Still, at least it seemed this time as if Jessa had gotten a better angle to shove the buckle under the edge of the faceplate. Maybe it would actually work. If they got out, maybe they could sneak up on the perps, take them from behind...

With no weapons, and outnumbered two to one, Creel told himself, shaking his head. *I think you read too many comic books growing up...*

Suddenly the door slid into the jamb with a whine of miniature servos. Creel opened his mouth to say, "Good work, Jessa," then realized she hadn't even begun to lift the faceplate from the lock mechanism. The door had to have been opened from the outside.

Outlined against the gray-white early morning light stood a stocky figure in armor, the distinctive shape of the GDF shock-troop helmet he wore clear even in silhouette.

Behind him Creel could see the slighter frame of Mia Felaris, who had her arm around a boy of eight or nine standard years. The kid's eyes were shining, and he looked as if he were trying to maintain a serious expression, but a little smile kept lifting at the corners of his mouth. Creel got the impression that the boy was having a great time but was under strict orders to behave himself.

For a second Creel just stood there and stared at the odd trio, ignoring the shocked intake of breath that came from Jessa's direction. *So I was right*, he thought. Still, he knew he'd have to play this very, very carefully.

"Good morning…Captain Marr," he said.

The helmet tilted the smallest fraction of a centimeter. "Morning, detective. Thought you might want to get out of there."

"That's for sure," Creel replied.

Eryk Thorn stepped back out of the doorway, allowing Creel and Jessa to exit. Her lifted eyebrow indicated that she had all sorts of things she would like to say but wouldn't… at least not until later.

Creel glanced over at Mia Felaris, at the boy she held so close. The kid was swarthy and dark, and didn't look much like her. He did seem oddly familiar, though, as if Creel had seen his face somewhere before.

Even though he had had his suspicions, this sudden confirmation of his theory hit him with as much force as a blow to the gut. He glanced back at Eryk Thorn, who reached up to remove his helmet. Creel supposed the mercenary had nothing to hide at this point—after all, both he and Jessa had seen Thorn's face back at the docking bay, when the man had been dressed in simple civilian clothing. But it was still a little shocking to watch him lift off the helmet and then tuck it under his left arm.

Looking from the mercenary to the boy who stood next to Mia Felaris was like watching one of those time-lapse vids where you see a flower sprout from a bud to full bloom in the space of a second. So it was true. Eryk Thorn really was Jerem Felaris' father.

"You see, then," Thorn said, and Creel nodded.

"They took him," Mia Felaris put in. For the first time Creel noticed she held a battered-looking synth-hide satchel in her free hand. "We had to get him back."

And her simple words allowed the last of the puzzle pieces to fall into place. The criminals who had taken over the Stony Point amusement park had kidnapped Jerem, hoping to hold him for a fat ransom. Creel wondered briefly how much cash Mia Felaris and Thorn had taken away from Iradia all those years ago and then decided it didn't really matter at this point. Obviously the kidnappers had thought it was a great deal.

But now they must all be dead. Creel knew too much about Thorn's reputation to think that he would have allowed any of them to live. Either they hadn't known of Mia Felaris' connection to the mercenary, or they'd thought they could match him.

Well, there's your first mistake, kids, he thought, and couldn't help smiling a little.

"So what now?" Jessa asked. She had abandoned her work on the locking mechanism's faceplate and had come to stand next to Creel.

"You let us go," Thorn said simply.

That would be a violation of about fifty line items in Nova Angeles' penal code, but Creel knew protests were useless. "And then what?" he asked.

Thorn and Mia Felaris exchanged a glance, and then the mercenary's gaze moved to the boy who stood at his mother's side. Something about the hard lines of Thorn's mouth softened almost imperceptibly. "We leave," he said. "You won't need to worry about us mucking up your nice, tidy little world anymore. And you get to take all the credit for eliminating a band of dangerous criminals."

He couldn't ask for much more than that, Creel knew. Any attempt to stop Thorn from simply walking out of here would at best end up with him and Jessa locked back in the supply room.

"All right," Creel said. Beside him Jessa shifted, as if she wanted to make some further protest but realized that wouldn't be very smart.

Thorn's dark eyes looked almost amused. Then he turned to Mia Felaris and his son. "Let's get out of here."

And, simple as that, it was over. Creel stood in the entrance to the supply shed and watched the three of them walk away, off toward a sort of courtyard area where he could see the arrowhead-shaped outline of Thorn's ship waiting. The hatch opened at an unseen signal, and then the mercenary's unexpected family disappeared from view. A moment later, Creel heard the engines warming up, and finally the ship lifted into the air and sped away to the east until it at last disappeared in the sun.

For a few seconds he could only remain where he was, gazing off into the hazy morning sky. Then he became aware of Jessa staring up at him, a half-amused expression on her face.

"You look like a kid who just found out his birthday present was a new school uniform," she remarked.

Creel shook his head and forced himself to smile. "That bad, huh?"

"Only to someone who knows you." Then she laughed. "Cheer up, Rafe. It's not that bad."

"It isn't?" he asked. God only knew what sort of mess the mercenary had left behind, and what kind of lies Creel and Jessa would be forced to invent to cover it up.

"No," she said, and again he saw that trace of a dimple in her cheek. "Remember, you owe me a dinner date." And she actually reached out and gave his hand a quick squeeze before she stepped away, striding purposefully toward the open area Thorn's ship had just vacated.

It's a mess, all right, Creel thought, as he followed along after her and then paused to catch his first glimpse of the carnage the mercenary had left behind. Then he saw Jessa turn and shoot a wicked smile in his direction, a smile that brought a sudden flush of heat to his face.

Suddenly, the aftermath didn't seem all that important. They'd get it ironed out eventually. In fact, he welcomed this particular mess, if it had somehow brought him and Jessa closer together.

Besides, he thought cheerfully, *I could probably make a pretty good case for all this being self-defense, considering the kidnappers instigated the whole thing by taking the boy.*

"So," he said to Jessa, who stood a few paces away and surveyed the bloody aftermath of Thorn's own particular form of justice with a look of bemused respect on her face, "you ready to test the outer limits of plausible deniability?"

They didn't bother to stop for anything, because there was nothing left to take. All of Miala's and Jerem's belongings had burned with the house, and of course Thorn had everything he needed right here in the *Fury*. The ship's cockpit would only accommodate two; Miala had given up the copilot's seat so her son could take his place there next to his father. She found she didn't mind too much— after all, the two of them had eight years of catching up to do. However, the only other chamber in the ship that could house a living being during the acceleration of take-off was Thorn's holding cell. Miala had lain down on the cot there, trying not to think of all the hapless souls who might once have been kept in the cramped compartment, and attempting to ignore the restraints that had probably been used on its previous residents—save for the one chest strap that would hold her in place while the ship was breaking free of Nova Angeles' gravity well. Of course, Thorn hadn't locked the cell, and once they were in space she could get up and move about the ship, but it still was unsettling to lie there and wonder if anyone had died on that cot, and if so, whether their uneasy spirit hovered about the place.

The second the ship leveled off, she undid the strap and pushed herself off the cot, then headed forward to the cockpit. She could hear Jerem inquiring in enthusiastic tones as to which button did what and how many guns the ship had, but he subsided once he heard his mother approach.

"Do you think they'll come after us?" Miala asked.

Jerem shot her a scornful look, but Thorn appeared to carefully consider her question. "No," he said. "After all, we did them a favor, getting rid of that scum."

Well, that was true, but she had lived on Nova Angeles long enough to know how much its inhabitants loved order and the rule of an intricate legal system. It had taken some getting used to, accustomed as she was to Iradia's rough frontier justice. She found it difficult to believe that RilSec wouldn't mount some sort of pursuit.

Then again, that one officer had agreed to let them go. For some reason she found she trusted him—he had a pleasant face, if not exactly handsome, but there was something steady and level in his eyes that seemed to inspire trust. He'd given his word. She had to take his promise at face value and hope he had meant it.

"How far?" she asked, changing the subject. Maybe later she could discuss her doubts and worries with Thorn, but she didn't want to do it now in front of Jerem, who was clearly still riding the euphoria of his rescue and who perhaps didn't realize how close a call the whole thing had been.

"Approximately nineteen standard hours," Thorn replied. His hands moved easily across the console. "We're just about to drop into subspace." He reached for the handle that activated the subspace drive and pulled it down.

Miala gripped the back of Thorn's seat as the *Fury* jumped forward. She probably should have just stayed strapped down in the holding cell until they had dropped out of normal space, but she couldn't have stood another minute in the confined space of the dim little chamber.

Besides, this wasn't really so bad. It wasn't much worse than standing up in one of Rilsport's public transports while the driver accelerated to merge with traffic.

"Cool," Jerem breathed, watching the chaotic play of light and dark outside the ship's forward viewports. Miala had taken him into space before, but only to New Chicago and back, and therefore he had never seen subspace in all its unsettling glory. He looked over at his father. "So how does it work?"

Thorn gave his son an amused glance. "How does what work?"

"The subspace drive."

At that question the mercenary actually chuckled. "Can't tell you for sure, Jerem. All that concerns me is that it does work, not how. I can perform some repairs if I have to, but if you're looking for the theory…" He shrugged. "I can't help you there."

Jerem appeared to consider Thorn's reply for a moment. "Well, I guess that makes sense." Then he turned back to look outside, chin on his hands as he continued to study the churning heavens. Suddenly his eyelids drooped a little, and he gave what sounded like a jaw-cracking yawn.

At once Miala asked, "Jerem, did you get any sleep last night?"

He managed to look both guilty and proud at the same time. "Sure. I think I must have gotten at least two hours. I couldn't tell for sure, since I was in the ventilation shafts after I escaped, and there wasn't a chrono, obviously."

"Obviously," she repeated, trying to give him a stern glance and knowing she had failed miserably. How many eight-year-olds could have broken themselves out of whatever place the kidnappers had been keeping him and gotten away through the ventilation system?

Not many, she thought. *Just Eryk Thorn's son...and yours.*

"Well," she went on, "I think you should really get some sleep."

"Mom!" Jerem groaned. "I don't need to sleep. I'm fine—"

"Your mother's right," Thorn remarked. "It's nineteen standard hours to Gaia. Plenty of time for you to sleep and still be awake when we make planetfall."

Jerem still looked sulky, but after glancing from his father's face to Miala's, he appeared to realize he was outnumbered. He heaved an exaggerated sigh. "Fine. I'll go lie down. But I won't sleep."

"Of course not," Miala replied, trying not to smile. After everything he'd been through, Jerem would probably be asleep about five standard seconds after his head hit the lumpy pillow on Eryk Thorn's cot. Then she asked, "Do you want me to come with you and tuck you in?"

"*Mo-om!*" Jerem protested, sounding more put out than ever. "I'm not a baby."

After that Miala maintained a tactful silence, and waited behind Thorn's seat while Jerem undid his restraints and then slid out of the copilot's chair. Still with an aggrieved air that announced to everyone present he thought he was being woefully misused, Jerem stalked out of the cockpit and down the short corridor that led to the one passenger cabin on board.

After the door had shut behind him, Miala climbed into the seat he had just abandoned. For a few moments neither she nor Thorn said anything.

Then the mercenary commented, "He sounds fine."

She turned and looked at him, this man who had taken her away from Iradia and who had helped her to conceive a son in a night of passion. He had rescued her once again on her home world and then come to her adoptive one, only to find a child whose existence he had never suspected— a son who could have been taken from him before they even came to know one another. *If Jerem's father had been anyone but Eryk Thorn, he probably would be dead now*, she thought, and shivered a little.

"He *is* fine," Miala replied. "He's your son. To him this was probably all one big adventure."

Thorn watched her for a moment, dark eyes opaque, unreadable. "And what was it for you?"

Good question, that. Moments of unspeakable terror, mixed with moments of impossible joy, the horror of Jerem's kidnapping somehow made almost bearable by knowing that she didn't have to face it alone, that Eryk Thorn was there to prop her up through all the doubt and worry and strain. She couldn't even say she wished it had never happened, since it had brought Thorn back to her.

She said at last, "It was a chance for us to be a family."

For a few seconds the mercenary said nothing. Then he reached out and laid his hand on top of hers, letting her feel the warmth and strength of his fingers. Somehow she still had difficulty believing he was really here, that he was taking her and Jerem to the homeland of his people. Such actions signaled a shift, she knew—Eryk Thorn had never allowed any associations, any connections other than the spurious ones that might come into being during his brief stints in the pay of one crime lord or another. He, the eternally rootless, appeared ready at last to reclaim his heritage.

Of this New Zealand she knew little, except that it had survived a good deal of Gaia's ecological devastation because of its isolation. It sounded wild and desolate, although at least not as outwardly inhospitable as Iradia. Life there would not be one of comfort and luxury, unlike the one she had known on Nova Angeles. *But we can start fresh*, she thought, remembering the satchel she had brought on board and the riches it contained. *Fifteen million units is plenty to begin a new life.*

She had hoped and dreamed through many long, lonely years that one day Thorn would return to her. It had never seemed possible that those dreams might actually come true. And now that they had, what else could she possibly want?

A sudden thought occurred to her, and her mouth curved in a smile.

"What are you plotting now?" Thorn inquired, eyebrow lifting.

"Nothing much," she answered, and gave his hand a squeeze. "I was only thinking how much I'd like for Jerem to have a sister…"

THE END